Erin Kaye was born in Co. Antrim in 1966 to a Polish-American father and an Anglo-Irish mother. One of five siblings, she was raised a Catholic yet educated at a Protestant grammar school. In the decade following university she pursued a successful career in finance before re-inventing herself as a writer. She now lives with her husband and their two young children on the east coast of Scotland.

MOTHERS AND DAUGHTERS

Catherine Meehan was born into a respectable working-class Roman Catholic family in
Ballyfergus on the coast of Antrim. She is
determined to flee the poverty, bigotry and
antagonism that shaped her early years
. . . Jayne Alexander is infused with the
privileges that go with being part of a
well-to-do Protestant family. Despite her
self-assurance, she has a need for love and
yearns for approval . . . From 1959 to 1984,
the lives of the Meehan and Alexander
families become inextricably linked, in
moments of great passion and hatred, as
deeply held loyalties are threatened.

ERIN KAYE

MOTHERS AND DAUGHTERS

Complete and Unabridged

CHARNWOOD
Leicester

First published in Ireland in 2003

First Charnwood Edition
published 2005

The moral right of the author has been asserted

British Library CIP Data

Kaye, Erin, *1966* –
    Mothers and daughters.—Large print ed.—
    Charnwood library series
    1. Domestic fiction
    2. Large type books
    I. Title
    823.9′2 [F]

    ISBN 1–84395–649–7

Published by
F. A. Thorpe (Publishing)
Anstey, Leicestershire

Set by Words & Graphics Ltd.
Anstey, Leicestershire
Printed and bound in Great Britain by
T. J. International Ltd., Padstow, Cornwall

To Dorothy and Mervyn

1

At the age of five-and-a-bit Catherine Meehan realised she wanted more. It was 25th December, 1971, with her first and lasting recollection of Christmas, when she opened her meagre pile of parcels to discover they contained cheerful, but cheap, presents.

A shriek from her brother caught Catherine's attention and made her look up.

'Look what I got! Look what I got!' he cried, running barefoot round the sparsely furnished room, rattling a box of Meccano above his head. In his excitement Michael seemed oblivious to the sharp pine needles underfoot that had fallen from the tree.

She heard Geraldine gasp, 'Oh, he's lovely!' and turned to find her sitting, cross-legged on the floor. In front of her a newly-lit fire spat and crackled in the grate, steam rising from the wet lumps of earthy coal. In her arms Geraldine nursed a fluffy white lamb.

'Lambsie,' she cooed softly as she stared, besotted, into his little black face.

Some gifts were surprises. Most, especially for the older children, were long-awaited necessities disguised as presents. But the children were happy all the same, glad to have new jumpers and shoes and underwear at long last.

Catherine, alone, sat in a corner unwrapping her neat parcels with grave and serious intent.

Every now and then her small frame shuddered involuntarily as her emotions fluctuated between heart-stopping excitement one moment and gut-wrenching anxiety the next. It took her longer than the others to complete the task, largely because she spent most of her time with an eye on everyone else, fearful lest they got more or better presents than she.

'Hurry up, slow coach,' said Sean, the eldest, coming over to observe the proceedings. 'Everyone else has finished and you've hardly started.'

'I have to save this, Sean,' explained Catherine as she painstakingly smoothed out and folded up a sheet of thin Christmas paper. 'Mammy says we've to recycle it. So it can be used again next year.'

And with each parcel she opened her dismay intensified. A quilted pink nylon dressing gown, pyjamas, a pair of pink slippers, underwear and things for school; pencils and rubbers and notebooks. When she was done, Catherine looked at the carefully folded garments piled neatly on the scrubbed-clean floorboards and felt insanely jealous. Of whom she had no idea. But she knew deep within her that someone, somewhere, was having it better on Christmas morning. And more than anything she wanted to trade places. She crossed her arms and settled them petulantly across her chest, the sleeves of her outgrown dressing-gown riding up to her elbows.

'Don't you like your presents, Pet?' asked Mammy, reaching down and giving Catherine a squeeze across the shoulders.

'No,' she said slowly. 'How come Sean got Monopoly and Geraldine got . . . got Lambsie and I . . . ' Here she started to break down, 'and I . . . I only got a dressing-gown and slippers and things?'

She set her lips tight in an expression of resentful disappointment and Mammy knelt down beside her.

'But look at this lovely petticoat and these colouring books,' she cajoled, holding up the items for Catherine to admire.

'And look,' she said, caressing a shiny red plastic pencil-case in her dry, slender hand, 'won't this be great for putting your pencils and things in for school?'

'No, it won't,' thought Catherine as she turned her head away and shrank, deliberately, from her mother's touch. She would not cry. She would not let her see how terrible her agony was; how she would have to lie at school about the toys she got for Christmas — the Cindy doll, the glittery Cinderella 'glass' slippers and the till with prices that popped up in a clear plastic window when you pressed the buttons. And inside pretend money that you could play shop with. Her heart ached for all these wonderful things. If only she'd got just one of them, she would have been happy.

Getting no response from Catherine, Mammy let out a long sigh, rolled backwards onto her heels and stood up.

'I don't know what to do with you, Catherine Meehan. You're the most ungrateful child God put on this earth.'

3

She was cross now.

'What's wrong with my little angel?' Daddy said, laughing, and moved to swing Catherine up into his arms. She was already anticipating the roughness of his chin against her cheek and the painful pleasure of his firm grip under her armpits when she heard Mammy's stern voice from the other side of the room.

'No, Frank,' she commanded. 'Leave her be. She'll have to learn that sulking doesn't get rewarded in this house.'

Catherine looked up woefully at Daddy. He hesitated and, for a heart-stopping moment, Catherine thought he was going to defy Mammy.

'I said. Leave her be,' repeated Mammy, her voice tight and thin.

Daddy shrugged his shoulders, gave Catherine an apologetic smile, and retreated to the other side of the room.

Catherine turned her face to the wall and leant miserably against it. Out of the corner of her eye she could see the Christmas tree in the window recess, the branches dense at the bottom, sparse at the top. It was not at all like the ones Catherine had seen on Christmas cards that were always tall and straight and perfectly conical. The children had made the silver decorations from milk-bottle tops and they hung lifelessly from the branches by white cotton thread. Catherine yearned for the shiny coloured baubles and thick gold tinsel she'd seen in Woolworths.

After a while, when she thought no-one was looking, she peeked over her shoulder. Woodchip paper, freshly-painted in Magnolia, warmed the otherwise bare walls. The only picture in the room, a gilt-framed Sacred Heart, had pride of place above the mantlepiece. With one hand Jesus held back his blue robe to reveal a plummy gold-crowned heart beating luminously in his breast. His other hand was outstretched in a gesture of pleading serenity, a faint smile playing round the smooth red lips. The image seemed somehow pathetic to Catherine yet it filled her with unexplained feelings of guilt. Mostly, she avoided looking at it, but she was always conscious of those vacant blue eyes watching her every move. Like now. Chastising her with that gentle, piercing stare.

Mammy stood by the tree staring out the window, her long brown hair pulled back from her face. She seemed to be looking at something far beyond the row of newly built council houses opposite and the lush green hills beyond. Her work-worn hands rested on the back of a brown velour chair, her expression wistful and longing, like she was remembering something that happened a long time ago.

Catherine hated it when Mammy went like this. She reminded her of the women she saw in St Malachy's on Saturday when the family trooped to confession. Not Catherine of course — it would be two more years, an eternity Catherine thought, before she would be seven and old enough to experience the thrill of the confessional for herself. The women 'doing the Stations of the Cross' stood transfixed with grief in front of each gruesome crucifix, mumbling prayers under their breath and staring dreamlike into the space in front of them. Then they would shuffle silently to the next 'station', twelve of them in all, spread out along the walls of the chapel, each depiction of Christ's suffering more heart-wrenching than the one before.

But today, it was Catherine who was making Mammy sad. It was her fault. Mammy and Daddy did their best — Catherine had always known there was no Santa — and she should be grateful. She knew it wasn't their fault — they didn't have much money. But if they weren't to blame, who was?

No, somewhere along the way Mammy and Daddy had got it wrong and Catherine was determined not to fall into the same trap. She was quite certain that money was the secret to a happy life. She'd heard her parents arguing about it late at night, when she sat listening, half-way down the stairs, in her nightie.

'If only we had the money,' Mammy would say, or, 'When we have the money we'll do this and we'll do that . . . ' But the money never seemed to come their way and things never got any better. And so Catherine decided that money, or rather the lack of it, was at the root of all their problems. 'When I grow up,' she promised herself, 'I will be very rich and then everything will be all right.' And so she resolved to have lots of money at any cost.

Michael came up quietly and enquired softly with his gentle brown eyes.

'Do you want to play with my Meccano?' he said. 'You can have first go.'

6

She looked at him imploringly, but said nothing. The pain of her despair had begun to lessen and Catherine was getting bored. Her legs ached from standing in the corner. But she was still angry and determined that Mammy should be left in no doubt as to the extent of her misery. She didn't want her to see that she was dying to join in; she wanted to be coaxed and encouraged. So that she wouldn't lose face.

Michael understood all this without a word passing between them.

'Come on then,' he said simply and, taking Catherine by the hand, dragged her over to his little bundle of presents. Within minutes Catherine was absorbed in building a windmill, the morning's wretchedness almost forgotten.

⋆ ⋆ ⋆

It was much later the same day and Theresa sat in her low Parker Knoll armchair by the fire with her darning. She narrowed her eyes into a frown as she examined the elbow of a jumper worn thin by sharp, growing bones and rough play. The wooden-cased clock on the mantelpiece, a hand-me-down from Frank's mother, said eleven-thirty. Frank sat opposite, staring thoughtfully into space, a cigarette dangling from his right hand.

'Do you think we did the right thing telling the children there wasn't any Santa?' he ventured.

Theresa wet a strand of grey wool with spittle and threaded it expertly through the eye of a darning needle.

'Why?' she said, without looking up.

'Ach, it's just seems a shame, especially for the little ones, to have the magic taken away from them, that's all.'

'Frank, it was done for the best. You know we can't afford to buy them much in the way of presents and it's even worse to let them think they're getting punished for not being good.'

She was right, of course. Santa had no place in a home full of children and tight purse strings. It seemed cruel to deprive them of the dream that their good behaviour and earnest prayers would be rewarded with presents from Santa. But it was even harder letting them believe and then, on Christmas morning, having to endure the bewilderment of good boys and girls who could not understand what they had done wrong, for Santa had not brought them the toy they longed for. So, yes, it was best they knew the truth.

Frank sighed and looked across at Theresa, the faint red glow from the hot embers reflecting off her dark hair. It was nearly eight years since their wedding and Theresa hadn't changed much at all. She had borne four children and so, naturally, she was a little thicker round the waist but, all things considered, she had kept her looks and her figure.

'Besides,' continued Theresa, 'it's best for Catherine that she knows.'

Frank lent forward and frustrated a renegade coal that was about to escape onto the hearth.

'Why's that then?'

'She's so jealous of other kids — envy would just eat her up. It's best she knows the truth and learns to live with it,' said Theresa, stopping to examine her handiwork.

'She worries me that one,' she continued, the needle weaving like a sand-eel between thin threads of wool. 'I've never seen a little girl so tied up inside herself with . . . well, I don't know what, but she's awful resentful about things, about everything, don't you think? It's like she thinks the whole world's against her.'

'Well in Ballyfergus it is, Theresa, and maybe it's time she started getting used to it,' declared Frank, ironically, sinking back into the chair.

He thought for a moment and then added, 'She's a fiery little cracker though I'll grant you that.'

'And one that'll blow up in our faces one day, if we're not careful.'

'You're getting yourself all worked up about nothing, Theresa. She's just a determined wee girl and I'll tell you something, I wish those boys had as much spirit as she has.'

Theresa looked at Frank across her darning, the needle suspended momentarily in mid-flight.

'But don't you worry about her? Don't you think she's a bit odd?'

'Maybe, but I've got a feeling about her, you know, like one day she's going to make something of herself. Get out of this god-forsaken country for a start like we should have done years ago.'

'Now there's no mileage going over that old ground again, Frank. We made a decision to stay in Northern Ireland and we have to make the best of it. I'm sure the situation will improve with the New Year. The British government's going to have to do something — they can't let things drift on like this forever.'

'Oh face up to it, Theresa. Stormont will never change and things are getting worse not better. And I don't care what anyone says, it's just as well the British sent troops in when they did or who knows where things would have ended up. But they're not prepared to do any more. The Unionists won't give an inch. You only have to listen to them on the TV to work that out for yourself.'

'You're beginning to sound like Brendan Mulholland,' said Theresa, looking at him from underneath raised eyebrows.

Ignoring her he went on. 'And there's the state of the economy as well. I read in the paper the other day that unemployment's at an all time high. I just don't know,' he said, shaking his head thoughtfully, 'what kind of a future's ahead of the wee uns.'

Theresa intervened, more briskly this time: 'Well, as I said, we made a decision and that's that. Anyway, Frank, you couldn't have left your mother when she was ill, now could you? And then it would have been very difficult to move with the two boys so young and you just starting up the business. Sure we'd have lost everything.'

'I still don't know if the business was a good idea, Theresa. We're only just washing our face at the minute.'

'I know, Frank, but it's bound to be difficult at first. It's only five years since you left the Power

10

Station and it takes time to get established. People decorate once every two or three years, at the most, so you've only started to benefit from repeat business in the last couple of years. And you're getting more and more work from word of mouth which means we'll be able to save on advertising this year.'

'Hmm,' agreed Frank reluctantly.

'When you think about it, we've done well Frank, really. Considering we started out with nothing.'

It was true. When he was laid off at the Power Station Theresa encouraged him to start the painting and decorating. He began with nothing more than a set of ladders and a few tools, confining himself to jobs within walking distance. When they'd scraped together a few pounds from this endeavour he bought an eight-year-old Austin van. With Theresa's help he began to advise on colour schemes and did a profitable line in supplying wallpaper and paint, taking a small percentage for his trouble.

Frank was a hard worker, not like his father, and he'd managed to make a go of it, although it was still a struggle. Yes, times were hard, but they were hard for everybody. And he was proud of the fact that, apart from a few months in the early days following redundancy, his family had never relied on Social Security or 'the burew' as it was commonly known. Not like his poor mother, God rest her soul, with that useless git of a husband.

'You should go and see your father more often in the New Year, Frank.'

11

It was almost as though Theresa could read his mind.

'For your mother's sake,' she added. 'You know she would've liked you two to bury the hatchet. He's an old man now, Frank.'

'Well, we never did have much to say to each other. Anyway, Mary and Rose take good care of him. He doesn't need me.'

'All the same, it would be nice to go up and see him now and again.'

Frank didn't reply but stole a subversive glance at Theresa who was still darning industriously, oblivious to his scrutiny. In many ways he owed her a great deal; she was a good wife and mother, practical and full of common sense. In that respect his mother had been right. He just wished he could love her more, the way a husband should. She was always telling him what to do and, though he admired her strength, he resented the extent of her control.

Like this morning and that incident with Catherine. He thought she was awful hard on the wee soul, but Theresa always knew best as far as the children were concerned.

In fact, when he thought about it, she always knew best about everything. But it was his own fault for not standing up to her from the outset.

'I'll do what I damn well please,' he said, irritable now.

Theresa looked up sharply.

'I was only saying.'

'You're always 'only saying',' he repeated, bitterly.

'What's wrong with you?'

12

'Nothing.'

'You know, Frank,' snapped Theresa, 'I've it just as hard as you. What do you think it's like for me scraping to make ends meet, day in and day out?'

'I know, I know,' he interrupted, 'because I'm not providing for you properly. That's right, blame it all on me.'

Theresa went to speak then appeared to think better of it. Instead she picked up the sleeve of the jumper and returned, tight-lipped, to her darning. A long silence followed.

'Mark my words, that girl is setting herself up for a big disappointment in life,' she said, suddenly returning to the subject of Catherine. 'Yes, she's setting herself up for a fall, that's for sure.'

But Frank was not listening.

'I'm going to bed,' he announced, getting up and walking to the door. 'And a Happy Christmas to you too,' he heard Theresa say sourly as he closed the door behind him.

★ ★ ★

Even though it was Christmas morning, the church service seemed to drag on forever. Every time Jayne Alexander shifted in her seat her father yanked her sharply by the arm and applied even pressure until she sat up, straight and attentive, in the pew. He expected both his children to behave themselves in church, even though Jayne was only five-and-a-half years old.

Jayne stole a glance at her brother Eddie,

13

sitting on the other side of Dad. He was engrossed in picking chewing gum off the sole of his shoe until his father's hand swooped down and captured the offending fingers. Eddie looked over at Jayne and rolled his eyes in exasperation.

The suspense was killing them. Despite their loud protests that morning they hadn't been allowed to open their presents, even the ones from Santa, until, Dad said, 'praise had been given to the Lord for their wealth and good fortune'.

Eddie crossed his eyes, then rolled them up under his eyelids until all Jayne could see was the whites and the red rim of his lower lids. He tried to touch the end of his nose with the tip of his tongue and Jayne fought hard to stifle giggles. She must have made some sort of noise for the next thing she knew Dad was whispering in her ear.

'Jayne. If you don't stop that this minute, you'll go straight to your room when we get home. Christmas morning or not.'

Dad didn't make idle threats and Jayne immediately composed herself, folding her hands primly in her lap and forcing her back to follow the unnatural angle of the wooden pew. She tried to concentrate on what the minister was saying, something about the true meaning of Christmas, whatever that meant. Instead she found herself remembering what she'd put in her letter to Santa. Had she been good enough, she wondered, to get everything? Probably not, she thought, and tried even harder to listen. This was her last chance to show Santa that she could be a good girl.

Then the sermon was over and the minister was standing in front of the pulpit wishing everyone a 'Happy and a Peaceful Christmas'. The congregation stood up suddenly and sang the final hymn, 'Oh, Little Town of Bethlehem'. Jayne joined in enthusiastically, mumbling most of the time because she didn't know the words. At the end of every verse she paused, expecting it to be over, but the hymn seemed to go on forever and Jayne had to stop herself from pushing past Mum and running out of the church.

Finally, the organist ground to a halt, the last few notes long and mournful. And then a low murmur of voices filled the church as everyone shuffled out of the pews and down the aisle.

Getting out of church was only half the battle. Outside everyone hung around and Mum and Dad shook hands with people and wished them a 'Happy Christmas' as though they had all the time in the world. It was made worse by the fact that it was dry. Jayne looked up at the sky hopefully; if only it would rain everyone would scurry home.

Then, to her horror, she saw a fat woman from the congregation waddling towards her. Her legs appeared bowed down by the strain of carrying all that weight and the bag clutched against her chest was doll-size in her pudgy slabs of hands.

'How's my pretty girl today then? Isn't she gorgeous?' she puffed, turning to a wizened old woman, all edges and angles, who'd come up alongside her.

The thin one nodded in agreement then said

in a high voice, 'With those blonde curls and blue eyes she looks just like a little angel.'

'And isn't that outfit beautiful?' she added, bending down to stroke the arm of Jayne's new coat made from white rabbit fur. The skin on the back of her hand was dry and brown like Tommy the tortoise's neck. Jayne recoiled from her touch.

The matching fur hat made Jayne's head itch and the muff made her hands too warm. But for appearances sake she had to put up with it.

'Stop fidgeting,' whispered Mum, coming up alongside Jayne as she gave her head a particularly vigorous scratch.

'We were just saying, Helen, what a lovely outfit that is,' said the thin woman, nodding at Jayne.

'Nana Alexander gave it to Jayne specially for Christmas morning,' said Mum, smiling down at her.

The origin of the clothes seemed to excite even greater admiration.

'You're a very lucky girl.'

Jayne was relieved when Mum said, 'Lovely service this morning,' so deflecting the attention away from her.

'Oh yes, Helen, wasn't it just?' said the thin woman. Then she added quickly, ingratiating herself, 'Mind you I always preferred Reverend Alexander myself. God rest his soul. How's Mrs Alexander keeping then?'

Jayne hated the way the two women poked and prodded and talked about her as though she wasn't there. So she was glad when the conversation moved on to discuss Nana. She soon stopped listening and sought out Dad from amongst the crowd. He was, slowly, moving towards the car parked just outside the church. If Jayne could just get Mum to move, now was her chance to escape. She began to tug at her arm.

'Mum, we have to go,' she said.

'In a minute, darling.'

Jayne kept tugging until, at last, Mum made as if to move.

'Well, goodbye, ladies,' she said, her voice full of forced cheerfulness. 'And a Merry Christmas to you both.'

And then they were moving. Jayne held her breath. A few more 'Happy Christmases' shouted across the courtyard and at last they were in the car.

Jayne pressed her face up against the cold glass of the car window and waited impatiently for Dad to drive off. After two false starts the engine fired up and they were away. They passed the blue-painted railings of the deserted Town Park, built by the Victorians, then pulled away from the coast and through the town centre.

They drove past rows of small red-brick terraces built to house linen mill workers at the turn of the century although the mills were long since gone.

'They're a terrible eyesore,' said Mum, referring to three towering blocks of flats under construction on the edge of town.

'I know,' said Dad, 'but now the mill houses are coming down they've got to put the people somewhere.'

17

'They're demolishing them?' asked Mum, surprised.

'Yes,' replied Dad. 'Mill Lane was the first to go and they plan to level the rest next year.'

'Oh,' said Mum abruptly and she sat back in the passenger seat and stared out the window.

'I don't suppose you were ever in them, Helen,' said Dad, continuing on without waiting for a reply. 'I used to go sometimes with my father on his rounds. They were terrible so they were. No inside toilet and full of damp. I remember families of twelve, fourteen even, brought up in two bedrooms. Shocking that people had to live like that.'

Then they climbed up the steep incline of the Grammar Brae, the houses and gardens becoming larger as they ascended. Jayne felt her heart quicken as the familiar lead-coloured facade of a large imposing house came into view. Variegated ivy clung over the front of the building and, across the top, small ramparts made the house look like a miniature castle. The excitement was almost unbearable.

'Look, Eddie, look! We're nearly home.'

Eddie jumped up and down in the back seat.

'Can we open our presents when we get in? Can we, Mum? Can we?'

'Yes, darling, of course you can. Now quieten down children. We're nearly there.'

The polished tyres of Dad's big grey car crunched up the gravel drive and almost before it had come to a stop the children clambered out. Jayne couldn't budge the stiff door handle so she had to follow Eddie out his side of the car.

18

Then they had to wait for Mum to open the front door. Once in the house, coats and hats were abandoned on the hall floor and they tore into the living room where mounds of presents waited for them under the tree.

Jayne threw herself down on the soft carpet and dived into her bundle. There were lots of presents from aunts, uncles, neighbours and friends of Mum and Dad, but she quickly sought out the presents from Santa. These would be the really good ones.

'Mum, Dad, look! I got a Cindy,' she squealed, waving the golden-haired doll, radiant in her shimmering evening dress, above her head.

Cindy was soon temporarily forgotten as Jayne's attention was captured by the next enticing present. This time it was a pair of roller skates and then, a plastic till with prices that popped up when you hit the coloured buttons and a real drawer for putting the money in.

'You can play bankers with that, Jayne, just like me,' said Dad smiling down at her and Jayne liked the sound of that very much indeed.

Once she had finished opening the big presents, the ones from Santa, Jayne sat back. She couldn't believe her luck. She must have been a good girl after all — much better than she'd thought.

Mum said, 'Jayne, what's that over there in the corner? Let's have a look,' and she went over to the back of the room followed by Dad.

Jayne noticed that they were laughing and smiling at each other, something they didn't normally do. Her heart surged with joy. Two large objects covered in white sheets were against the wall. Jayne's heart began to pound. She got up very slowly, opened mouthed, and stood unable to move in the middle of the floor.

'There's a label on this one. It says to Jayne from Santa,' said Dad, sounding very surprised, and then he read the label attached to the other white sheet.

'To Eddie from Santa!'

Jayne was astounded. Where had they come from? Had Santa been again when they were at church?

Eddie was already there, on the other side of the room, and he wasted no time in pulling the white sheet off his present. Jayne put her hands to her mouth. Before them stood a bright blue, shiny new bike. Eddie clambered onto the black leather seat and Dad held the bike upright as he pretended to cycle.

'Oh, Dad, it's magic. Look, Mum. Look, Jayne. LOOK,' shouted Eddie.

'I see you, son,' laughed Mum and then, turning to Jayne who was still rooted speechless to the spot, said, 'Jayne, aren't you going to open your present?'

Jayne nodded silently. She couldn't begin to imagine what lay beneath the white sheet but she was certain it was something wonderful. Mum took her hand and led her over to it.

'Go on then, love. Pull!' Jayne took hold of the corner of the sheet and, glancing uncertainly at Mum, pulled hard. The sheet fell to the floor and Jayne gasped out loud as her eyes fell on the most beautiful rocking horse she had ever seen.

He was made of varnished wood, different shades of glossy brown all over. Around his mouth was a bridle made of thin leather straps and, on his back, a padded brown leather saddle. Pulling the sheet off had set him rocking gently, back and forth, his glassy black eye twinkling playfully at Jayne.

'He's lovely,' said Jayne, her face breaking into a huge smile. She put her arms tenderly around his neck and, nuzzling her face into his, kissed him on the cheek. The new leather gave off a faint animal odour mixed with soapy newness, the way Jayne imagined a real horse would smell.

'I love you, Horsey,' she said, stroking his mane of coarse blonde hair.

After a little while, when Jayne could bear to pull herself away from Horsey, she went over to the fireplace where Mum and Dad were opening presents and sat down on the floor beside Dad.

'Oh, darling, thank you very much,' said Dad, getting up from his chair. He went over to Mum and planted a kiss on her cheek.

'It's super, Helen, really super.'

Jayne strained to see what he held in his hand.

'Let me see,' she wailed and Dad held out a red leather case. Inside was a pen, very uninteresting.

'Come here and let's see what Dad bought me for Christmas,' said Mum and Jayne shuffled over on her knees.

'Mind that new dress, now,' warned Mum, but she spoke gently and her deep blue eyes were soft and kind.

She opened the black square-shaped velvet

box that sat on her lap.

'Ahh . . . look at that. A gold chain. You can hold it if you like,' she said, dropping a rope of dark gold into Jayne's upturned palms.

'Thank you darling,' said Mum, but there was no kiss for Dad and her voice sounded as cold and heavy as the chain felt.

'You do like it?' asked Dad, apprehensively. 'I went all the way to Belfast for it. To get one just right.'

'Yes, it's lovely,' said Mum, but she seemed disinterested.

A sense of unease suddenly took hold of Jayne and she searched anxiously in her parents' faces for signs of their earlier affection for each other. But the moment had passed and instead she found the usual distance between them. A feeling of dread began to settle on her. Jayne handed the chain back quickly and thought for a few seconds. If she changed the subject, distracted Mum, maybe things would be all right again.

'Mum,' she began, 'when did Santa leave me Horsey?'

'I don't know, darling.'

' 'Cos he wasn't here when we went out to church. Did Santa come back when we were out?'

'We'll never know,' said Mum, her soft voice back to normal as she smiled dreamily at Jayne. 'You see that's the magic of Christmas, my love.'

★　★　★

22

Dinner was fun to start with. They pulled red and gold crackers and Jayne shrieked with delight at each loud POP! The jokes were read out and they all laughed and everyone, even Nana Alexander, put on paper hats. Then there was the food; broth made to Nana's recipe first followed by turkey from Uncle Robert's farm and all the trimmings. Mum brought the whole bird out to the table on a huge silver platter, the skin crisp and golden, and Dad carved it, standing up.

When the plates were all served, Dad stood at the head of the table and said grace. Then he raised his glass and said solemnly, 'God save the Queen!'

'And God save Ulster!' cried Uncle Robert and they all raised their glasses in a toast.

When the dinner plates were cleared away and Jayne had examined the contents of all the crackers, she wanted to leave the table. She was fed up with the grown-ups talking — talk, talk, talk. That was all they seemed to do and it was so boring. Most of the time she had no idea what they were talking about and she wasn't interested. Especially today, when all she wanted to do was ride Horsey.

'Can I leave the table please?' Jayne asked for the third time.

No-one heard her plea, or if they did, they ignored her because everyone was listening to Uncle Robert. He was very excited, his round face as red as the tiny hat perched on top of his head, his fleshy belly straining the buttons of his white shirt. And he was shouting.

'No, I'm with Paisley. We need decisive action; no good pussyfooting around. The country's out of control and Faulkner spends half his time pandering to London. The IRA and the Catholics don't want reforms,' he said, scornfully. 'They've had reforms and are they one bit interested? No. It's just a cover for what this is really all about — a Dublin inspired plot to force Ulster into a United Ireland. Look at the way Lynch keeps interfering in our affairs. And I for one am not going to stand for the Republic meddling in Ulster.'

He thumped his closed fist on the table and the crystal glasses quivered.

Jayne, sandwiched between Uncle Robert and Nana Alexander, cowered in her chair. She could hear clattering noises from the kitchen and wished Mum would come back to the table. Jayne didn't like it when Uncle Robert was angry although she wasn't sure exactly who he was cross with. She reckoned it had something to do with Catholics, whoever they were. Dad and Aunt Irene nodded slowly all the time Uncle Robert was speaking and Eddie, wide-eyed, was both alarmed and captivated at the same time.

'It's the fault of those journalists and TV people, you know,' said Nana. She made a snorting noise through her nose and went on. 'Foreigners coming here, not knowing a thing about it and trying to tell us how to run the country. They twist everything to make out like the Catholics have been hard done by. You don't hear anything about how people like us made

24

this country what it is today. And if Catholics are worse off, it's their own fault. If they don't like it, they can go and live in the Free State with their own kind. They're all traitors anyway.'

'I agree with you, Ma. Everyone's so busy worrying about the rights of the poor Catholics,' said Uncle Robert, injecting a sarcastic tone into the last two words, 'that no-one's stopping to ask the right questions.'

He paused for dramatic effect and looked round the faces at the table.

'Who's protecting the interests of the Protestants?' he said, 'that's what I want to know. We're the minority on this island and if anyone's in danger of being persecuted it's us, not the Fenians. Ulster hasn't been under greater threat since 1690.'

'We fought and won then and we'll do so again if we have to,' said Nana matter-of-factly, through thin lips and clenched jaw.

Jayne tapped the leg of the table with her foot. She wanted to jump up from the table and run away from the stifling atmosphere of the dinner table and the angry talk.

Uncle Robert took a deep breath and went to speak again, but this time he was interrupted by Dad.

'Now, now, Robert,' he said soothingly, observing Jayne's solemn face. 'It's Christmas, and we don't want to be spoiling the day getting all wound up. We all know where we stand on that subject. Let's save the debate for another day, shall we? Relax and enjoy yourself. Here, have another drink,' and he topped up Uncle

25

Robert's glass with juice from the crystal decanter.

Jayne never heard Dad talk like Uncle Robert although he never actually disagreed with him either. Dad always said that Catholics weren't bad people, you could pass the time of day with them all right, but they just weren't loyal to Ulster and the Crown and you couldn't trust them.

Uncle Robert's eye followed his brother's and came to rest on the worried face of his niece.

'You're quite right, John. We'll not let them spoil our day, will we pet?' and he gave Jayne's shoulders a rough squeeze.

'Time for Christmas pudding,' announced Mum, coming into the room. Turning to Jayne with a big smile, she said, 'Yes, Jayne, you can leave the table. But before you go don't you think Horsey might be hungry?'

'Oh, yes, he must be!' gasped Jayne, suddenly ashamed that she had been so busy filling her own tummy, she'd forgotten all about poor Horsey.

'Here, he'll like this,' said Mum. She handed Jayne a red apple and she scurried away from the table as fast as she could.

2

Catherine was ushered into the assembly hall along with the other Primary Seven pupils from St Mary's. Tables and chairs were laid out in neat rows and, on top of each wobbly desk, lay a thin sheaf of folded white paper, turned upside down. Catherine carefully laid out her pencils, rubber and ruler on a table, sat down, and waited calmly for the instruction to start.

A faint smell of Jeyes Fluid and sick rose from the floor, reminding Catherine of the indignity of having to eat her packed lunch in here every day on a smelly plastic sheet. Immediately after lunch the plastic was rolled up, still wet in places where it had been mopped, and locked in a store-cupboard beside the stage. Next day it was unrolled again and the process repeated so that, over time, it gave off such an odour that no matter what you had in your lunch-box it smelt of sick. Catherine would not miss lunch-times at St Mary's. In fact, she thought, there wasn't much she would miss of primary school at all.

The assembly hall was nearly full now and she watched the last children take their seats. Of course she knew this was the Eleven-Plus exam which would determine which secondary school she went to, but she felt strangely removed from it all. Some of the girls in her class were very excited about the whole thing. Fran Gallagher had worked herself up into a complete tizz and was now sitting two seats away from Catherine, glancing round anxiously like a rabbit caught in a trap. Catherine told Mammy about the way some of the girls were going on and she said it was because their parents were putting pressure on them to do well. She felt no such pressure, not from her parents anyway. Apart from when Catherine raised the subject, Mammy had only mentioned it the once.

'Just do your best, Catherine. There's no point worrying about it; you've either got it or you haven't.'

And Catherine took her at her word for she knew very well that she 'had it'. At a parent's night the Headmaster had told Mammy and Daddy that she was one of the most promising girls in the school. In the top three he said.

The stubborn determination to do well came from inside Catherine herself. She had a tremendous urge to beat everyone. To be first. And part of the thrill was in pretending that she didn't care when, in fact, she cared far more than anyone else.

Catherine realised that academic success was the only way out of the life she detested and it amazed her that none of her classmates, some of whom came from worse homes than she did, seemed to have worked that out. It was her passport to the wealth she could only dream of now; a brand new bicycle, a colour TV, a beautiful bedroom all to herself, holidays and

28

money for anything she wanted. It was really very simple. All she had to do was get good O-levels and A-levels and then she would get a good job and earn lots of money.

All of these thoughts Catherine kept to herself, firstly because she didn't want people laughing at her for getting ideas above herself and, secondly, she suspected that eleven-year-olds weren't supposed to be so obsessed with money and what it could buy.

Afterwards, Catherine couldn't remember much about the actual exam paper, the first one she had ever sat. She recalled the Headmaster telling them to start but after that it was all a blur.

She just remembered being totally absorbed and enjoying herself very much. And it was so easy. On the way out of the hall Moira Campbell grabbed her arm.

'What did you think, Catherine? Wasn't it awful hard?'

'Yes,' said Catherine, not wanting to make Moira's distress any worse by appearing too smug.

'Did you get it finished?' asked Moira anxiously.

'No,' lied Catherine and Moira visibly relaxed.

'Maybe I've done all right then.'

'Yes, I'm sure you have,' said Catherine, moving away, because she felt like a fraud.

She knew very well she had gotten most, if not all, of the answers right. And Moira was one of her few friends at school. She could trust her not to go blabbing about the fact that they'd no carpets at home or colour TV. Mostly, Catherine stuck to the company of her brothers and sisters, especially Michael. With him there was no need for silly white lies to protect herself from ridicule.

★ ★ ★

The Eleven-Plus results were due out and they were told that their parents would, that morning, receive an envelope telling them whether or not they'd passed. The day seemed to last forever and on the long walk home, up the embankment, over the playing fields, down the lane, up The Brae and finally into the housing estate, Catherine began to get anxious.

'Hurry up, Geraldine, we haven't got all day.'

Geraldine was two years younger than Catherine and inclined to dawdle.

'Thought you didn't care about the Eleven-Plus results,' said Geraldine, switching the long grass that grew at the side of the lane with a stick.

'I don't. I just want to get home, that's all.'

The lane was bordered on one side by an unfenced green field and, on the other, by a high wild hedge. It was early spring and bunches of pale yellow primroses peeked out from the undergrowth around the foot of the hedgerow.

'Oh, look,' said Geraldine, stopping to pick some.

'Geraldine, do you have to do that?' wailed Catherine. They would never get home at this rate.

30

'I'm going to pick some for Mammy. I think she'll like them.'

'Yes, I suppose she will,' said Catherine with a sigh and, dumping her satchel in the middle of the track, she began to gather primroses as fast as she could.

'There, now, I think that should be enough,' she said after a few minutes and she held out a fistful of delicate flowers to Geraldine, who had collected hardly any.

'Here, Geraldine, you take these in your hand. Like this. I'll take your schoolbag so you don't crush them. Happy now?'

'Oh, yes, Catherine. They're lovely,' said Geraldine, her little elfin face lighting up with joy.

Then she slipped her free hand into Catherine's who, smiling back, staggered down the lane under the weight of two satchels strapped across her shoulders.

They were a couple of hundred yards from the bottom of the lane when Catherine saw two girls turn the corner and walk towards them. When she saw their uniforms she felt afraid — they were Protestants from Greenfield Secondary School. Greenfield got out twenty minutes after St Mary's and they should have missed them. If only Geraldine hadn't been so slow. She gripped Geraldine's hand tighter and hissed, 'Just keep walking.'

Geraldine looked up, bewildered, but said nothing. Catherine stared straight ahead and willed them to walk on by. Their heads touched briefly as one whispered something to the other

31

and then they were heading towards them.

Instinctively, she gave Geraldine an almighty push and shouted, 'Run!'

Geraldine stumbled forward a few feet and then, confused, came to a standstill.

'Run!' screamed Catherine. This time Geraldine belted to the bottom of the lane as fast as her legs could carry her and disappeared from sight.

Weighed down by two heavy schoolbags, the big girls were soon upon Catherine. One of them pushed her in the chest and she staggered backwards onto the grass at the side of the lane. The other one pulled her to the ground by the hair and, grabbing the neck of her blouse, demanded, 'What school do you go to?'

Catherine knew the answer they were looking for. Adjacent to St Mary's Primary School was a Protestant Primary School. If Catherine could just remember the name of it chances are they would let her go. It began with an R. She knew it. Why couldn't she remember it?

Panic swept through her, paralysing her brain. It refused to deliver up the password. She lay on the grass, armpits damp with fear, her mouth dry. She was aware of her jaws working, trying to form the word that would protect her. But no sound came out. She waited for the girl on top to punch her in the face. Instead, the one who had first pushed her to the ground, tipped her and Geraldine's schoolbags upside down, and all their books and jotters fell out onto the grass.

'There's nothing here,' she said, her voice full

of disgust. 'You Taigs are all the same. Bloody useless.'

'Haven't you any money?'

The girl who was still holding Catherine down spat the words into her face.

Catherine shook her head and felt the hand release from around her neck.

She heard one of them say, 'Stupid little bitch,' and then, miraculously, they were gone.

Catherine remained where she was, on her back. An aeroplane left a white trail across the sky like the precise stroke of a gigantic paintbrush. She watched it dissolve into the pale blueness around it. She lay still and listened keenly, but there were no sounds save for the creak and rustle of the minute insect world in which she lay.

Catherine raised herself onto her elbows and looked around. They were definitely gone. She felt for a moment like she was going to be sick, but the feeling soon passed to be replaced with anger. A burning white anger that she had been so humiliated. The insult was all the more mortifying because they had done it for one reason and one reason only; because she was a Catholic. As well as anger, her face sizzled with the red heat of shame. Shame because she hadn't fought back and because she'd stupidly forgotten the name of the school. It was Redwood, of course, as she'd known all along. How could she have been so thick?

Suddenly she remembered Geraldine. She looked down to the bottom of the lane, but there was no sign of her. Quickly, Catherine collected the books and put them back in the satchels. She tidied her clothes and told herself that she was, apart from a shaky feeling in her legs, fine. She hurried down the lane and round the corner, but there was no sign of Geraldine up The Brae either.

Catherine walked as quickly as she could. If anything happened to Geraldine, she thought, but daren't entertain the idea any further. Passing by a flight of steps that led up to one of the big ivy-covered houses on The Brae she heard sniffling and stopped. Geraldine was sitting on the bottom step clutching her little bunch of primroses, red-eyed and sobbing.

'It's all right, Geraldine. I'm here now. There's no need to cry. Look! I'm fine,' said Catherine forcing a broad smile.

'I . . . I . . . thought they were going to hurt you, Catherine. I was so scared.'

'Well, they didn't.'

'Why did you get me to run then?'

'Well . . . I thought they were going to hurt us but I was wrong. They didn't even speak to me. Just walked past.'

'Honestly?'

'Honestly. Cross my heart and hope to die,' said Catherine.

'Why's your face red, then?'

'Because I've been running after you silly!'

'And what took you so long?'

'I had to tie my shoe lace.'

Geraldine looked up at her doubtfully but the crying had stopped.

'Here, let's get you cleaned up,' said Catherine

34

and, failing to find a tissue, offered Geraldine the corner of her white shirt. Geraldine blew her nose on it, one-handed, and wiped her eyes with the back of her hand.

By the time they reached home Geraldine had all but forgotten the incident and Catherine resolved never to tell anyone about it, not even Michael.

'We're home!' shouted Catherine cheerfully as soon as she was through the kitchen door, Geraldine trailing behind her. Catherine dropped the schoolbags at her feet and stood, gasping for breath. The climb up the hill took the wind out of you especially when, like today, you'd been hurrying.

Mammy came through from the hall tying her apron strings behind her back.

'Oh, good. I need you to go down to the shops for me, Catherine. We need a few things for the tea. Oh, aren't those lovely.'

Geraldine thrust the bunch of primroses at her mother, their stalks warm and starting to wilt from her sweaty grip.

'We'll just pop them in some water to revive them, shall we?' she continued, finding a glass, filling it with water and arranging the little posy on top.

Catherine was speechless. The most important day of her life and her mother had forgotten.

'What are you standing there for, Catherine? Put those schoolbags away would you and I'll get you some money. Now, you'll need a list.'

Mammy began to scribble on a notepad, stopping every now and then to chew on the end of the pencil and frown.

'Didn't you get a letter this morning?' asked Catherine sullenly.

'Yes, of course I did,' Mum replied, suddenly remembering, 'And you did very well, Catherine. You've passed! I have the letter here somewhere,' and she began to rummage around in the papers on the kitchen table.

'It's all right,' said Catherine, feigning disinterest, 'I can see it when I get back.'

'Well, if you're sure. We'll have a talk with Daddy tonight about which school you should go to. He'll be very pleased. You're a bright girl, Catherine.'

Catherine felt her chest swell with pride and set off, spirits restored, for the shops on the edge of the estate.

★   ★   ★

After tea, when everyone was sitting round the table, Daddy said, 'Well, Catherine, I hear you've done very well and passed your Eleven-Plus.'

Catherine smiled coyly, though secretly she was pleased as punch with herself.

'What school do you think she should go to then?' asked Mammy, sipping her tea.

'Well, it depends. What do you think, Theresa?' said Daddy.

Mammy put her cup of tea down on the table.

'The way I see it she has three choices. — St Patrick's, St Margaret's or the Grammar. Now I'm not keen on St Pat's for I think she could do

36

better elsewhere. They don't get very good results.'

'What's wrong with St Pat's?' piped up Sean. 'If it's good enough for me and Michael, it's good enough for Catherine.'

'Catherine passed her Eleven-Plus and you two didn't so that's the difference. If she's got any ability at all then it shouldn't be wasted.'

'What about St Margaret's then? It's got a very good reputation,' said Daddy.

St. Margaret's was an all-girl Catholic secondary school run by nuns. It was miles away; somewhere up the coast near Glenarm.

'Frank, it's too far to travel. She'd have to be up at the crack of dawn every day to catch a bus and we can't afford for her to board. So it's the Grammar.'

'Do you think that's a good idea, Theresa?'

'Why not? There's quite a few Catholics go there now; it's nice and handy and they get good results.'

So that was the matter settled and Catherine's Eleven-Plus wasn't mentioned again.

★ ★ ★

'To celebrate Jayne's achievement,' Dad said the day the results came out, 'we're all going out to the Marine Hotel for dinner tonight.'

The Marine was the smartest hotel in Ballyfergus. Jayne had never been out for dinner to a proper hotel before and it sounded awfully grand.

'What do you think, Mum?' she asked,

37

standing in the doorway of her parent's room.

She wore her best Sunday outfit; navy cord skirt and matching waistcoat with a white blouse and knee socks.

Mum was fastening a necklace at the nape of her neck. She looked up when she heard Jayne's voice.

'You look smashing, love. Why don't you come here and I'll do your hair,' she said, patting the back of a pink velvet chair.

Jayne sat down obediently in front of the kidney-shaped dressing table and watched her mother's reflection in the mirror. Between the soft contours of her bosoms a diamond pendant sparkled in the soft bedroom light. Mum smelt strongly of her favourite perfume, Chanel No. 5. A big bottle of it sat on the dressing table, a present, Jayne remembered, from Dad last Christmas.

Mum picked up a silver-backed hairbrush and expertly scraped Jayne's long hair off her face. Jayne winced.

'Nearly there, love,' said Mum.

Jayne looked at her own reflection. Her golden blonde hair was exactly the same colour as Mum's. They shared the same eyes and lips as well.

'Mum?'

'Yes, love.'

'How come I don't look like Dad?'

Mum was still for a moment and then continued, brushing more slowly than before. She did not look in the mirror to meet Jayne's questioning gaze.

38

'What makes you ask that?' she asked at length.

'Well, I don't do I? Not even the teeniest wee bit. Everybody's always saying how much I look like you.'

Mum was thoughtful for a moment.

'That's just the way it is. Sometimes people look like one parent or the other; sometimes neither. It's a bit of a lottery, really. There, all done!' she announced and stepped back to admire her handiwork. The ponytail was perfect and finished off with a navy ribbon to match Jayne's outfit.

'Thanks, Mum,' said Jayne.

Her tummy gave a little tumble and she laughed nervously.

'I'm so excited about tonight. I can't wait!'

'Neither can I,' said Mum. 'Now come on or we'll be late.'

★   ★   ★

'Look at the view,' said Dad when they got out of the car and they all stopped to take it in. The Marine Hotel overlooked the entrance to the lough and the hazy landmass beyond. Ballyfergus, on the coast of County Antrim, was known as the 'gateway to the North of Ireland' and the harbour, far below, was by far the main contributor to the local economy. Purely functional, it was dominated by an ugly grey terminal building that smelt of grease and diesel. The huge cargo and passenger ferries that criss-crossed the Irish Sea from Ballyfergus to

Scotland docked at great reinforced concrete quays. There was no ancient harbour wall or pier you could walk on or pretty fishing boats bobbing in the swell.

Inside the hotel the carpets were even deeper than the ones at home and the atmosphere was hushed and reverent. Mr Lyons, the owner, showed them into a sumptuous room off the main lounge with 'Private' on the door.

'So congratulations are in order then, young lady,' he said, grinning and rubbing his hands together like he was cold. 'I hear you've gone and passed your Eleven-Plus.'

'Thank you.'

Jayne was embarrassed and didn't know what else to say.

'Yes, tonight's a bit of a celebration, Mr Lyons,' said Mum, coming to the rescue.

'Well in that case the drinks are on me,' declared Mr Lyons.

'Oh, Mr Lyons, that's very kind,' said Mum. 'Thank you.'

'It's the least I can do, Mrs Alexander. Now, you enjoy your meal,' he said, backing out of the room, 'and if anything's not to your liking just you ask for me.'

'Thanks, Hugh, we will,' said Dad.

Jayne's drink came with ice and a slice of orange floating in it and a straw that made her nose tickle when she sucked through it. She took a sip, set the glass carefully on the paper coaster and sat back, hands crossed in her lap. She tried very hard to concentrate on everything around her; she wanted to remember every detail for the

40

rest of her life. The big black clock on the mantelpiece, two gold cherubs clinging to the sides, chimed seven o'clock and Jayne realised she was hungry.

Eddie finished his Coca-Cola in three gulps and wanted another.

'No, Eddie,' said Mum, 'you'll make yourself sick before your dinner. We'll be going through soon anyway.'

'Please Mum . . . ' began Eddie, but Dad interrupted him.

'Tell Nana what you got for passing your Eleven-Plus,' he said, looking up from the menu at Jayne.

Jayne perched excitedly on the edge of the burgundy leather sofa and listed all the money she had got from friends and relatives. She paused, counting on her fingers.

'That adds up to forty pounds! And as well as that, I got this watch from you, Nana, a box of Milk Tray from Eddie, and Mum and Dad are paying for this tonight,' she added, gesturing round the room.

'You have done well, haven't you, Jayne?' said Nana.

Jayne nodded happily, wondering what she should do with all the money. Dad would have it all worked out; how much she should save and what, if anything, she could spend.

'I think there's something missing from that list, Jayne,' said Dad, reaching in his pocket for a handkerchief.

Jayne frowned and counted silently on her fingers once again, before saying slowly, 'No,

41

Dad. I've counted everything; the money and the presents. There's nothing else.'

Then she realised that he was toying with her. She could tell by the way his eyes twinkled and the corners of his mouth turned up. Mum was smiling too, the way she did when something nice was about to happen.

Dad pulled the handkerchief from his pocket, but it wasn't a handkerchief, it was a small pale blue box. A jewellery box. Jayne felt light-headed. Another present for her?

Dad came over to Jayne, knelt down beside her and put the box in her open palm.

'This is from your Mum and me. For doing your best and because we both love you.'

He planted a kiss on her cheek and got up.

'Thank you,' Jayne managed to say, her eyes riveted on the blue box. She took the lid off and nestling inside, on a bed of crisp white tissue paper, was a silver locket on a chain. She lifted it out, the box fell to the floor and she held the locket up, triumphant, for everyone to see.

'It's beautiful,' she gushed. 'Thank you, Mum. Thank you, Dad,' and she dashed over and gave each of them a big hug and a kiss.

'Look at the locket again, Jayne. There's something written on it,' said Mum.

Jayne examined the locket closely. There was engraving on the front, swirly shapes like leaves. She turned it over and read out the words engraved on the back.

'To Jayne, on passing your Eleven-Plus. From Mum and Dad. April 1977.'

'Health to wear, pet,' said Nana. 'And you

deserve it, you clever girl.'

A surge of joy rushed through Jayne's veins and made her giddy. Then a pang of anxiety quickly followed. Could she do all her parents expected of her? She'd only just scraped through the Eleven-Plus — she was sure of it.

'Are you ready to order Mr Alexander?'

The waiter had come into the room unnoticed.

'Yes, I think so.'

Dad ordered for everyone. Prawn cocktail for starters, fish and chips and peas for Jayne and Eddie, steaks for Mum, Dad and Nana.

'What about pudding?' said Eddie anxiously, and everybody, including the waiter, laughed.

'You order that at the table. If you've any room left,' said Dad, and Jayne imagined all the treats they would have to choose from; chocolate cake, ice cream and apple pie and loads of other desserts she hadn't even heard of.

When the waiter had collected the empty glasses and left the room, Nana stated, rather than asked, 'So she'll be going to the Grammar then.'

'Why, yes, of course,' said Mum, 'Where else would she go?' Nana said nothing but nodded her warm approval.

'Yeah, it will be great, Jayne,' said Eddie, 'me and the boys will take care of you. You'll love it.'

Jayne beamed as she imagined all the pleasures the Grammar had in store for her; a new uniform, new friends, new teachers. It was too much excitement for one day.

By the time the waiter came back to take them

through to the dining room, Jayne's new locket was round her neck and she'd managed to calm herself a little. She wanted to enjoy every bite of her meal. Dad stood up and crooked his arm towards her.

'May I?' he said.

Jayne linked her arm in his and, her heart brimming with pride and happiness, they walked out together for all the world to see.

3

Spring 1959

Saturday night in the Meehan household was bath night and there was no way Frank could wait his turn or he would never make it to the dance. So he made do with a quick wash at the kitchen sink and he was, all things considered, pretty pleased with the result.

He stood now in his parent's bedroom in front of the oval mirror which was embedded in the door of a battered wardrobe, the only full length mirror in the house. He spat on his left palm, briskly rubbed his hands together, and smoothed back the lick of black hair which, no matter how much Brylcreem he applied, had a mind of it's own and never lay down flat and tame like it was supposed to. Then, turning slowly from side to side, he examined his profile in the mirror.

The tittering came from behind. 'Oh, you're just gorgeous, so you are.' Frank turned round to glare at his two teenage sisters, Mary and Rose, convulsed in giggles at the doorway. Unperturbed, they ignored the implied warning and plonked themselves on the bed.

Frank turned his attention once again to the reflection in the mirror and straightening his thin black tie said, 'Now off with you two and give me some peace or I'll have Ma up here in a minute.'

He tried to sound cross, but the comical sight of his sisters' hair in rag curlers like two Medusas amused him and he smiled in spite of himself. The girls weren't one bit afraid of him anyway.

'Ma'll kill you if she finds you in here,' Rose pointed out. 'You know we're not allowed.'

'You mean you're not allowed. Now me, ah well that's a different matter altogether. I'm the only wage earner in the house and I can do what I like. So there. Now get out the both of you — I have to go,' said Frank shooing them out of the room in front of him.

'Where are you going, Frankie?' Mary called after him as he descended the narrow stairs.

'Out.'

'Out where, Frankie? Is it a dance? Are you taking a girl, Frankie?'

'Yes, it's a dance and no, there's no girl. Now that's enough,' Frank laughed and then shouted up from the bottom of the stairs, 'I pity the man who gets you Mary Meehan — you'll nag him to death!'

Frank's smile faded on entering the back room for there was the large frame of his father slumped in his usual chair by the fire, fast asleep. A cloth cap covered his thinning hair and his big round face was bent forward, flushed. Little bits of spit played around the corners of his mouth in time with his breathing and every now and then he snorted.

Frank's mother sat opposite, her head bent over her sewing basket evidently attempting to repair some piece of female undergarment that, by the look of it, was long past it's best. As she sewed she threw grim, narrow glances in the direction of her husband and shook her head slowly as Frank came into the room.

'So what do you think of that, Frank? A man who says he's not fit to do a day's work and yet he's fit enough to spend all afternoon in the bookies and the pub. That'll be most of the burew down the drain,' she said, pointing at a brown paper bag on the floor. 'He makes me sick. Out there drinking good money when I have to scrape together every penny to put food on the table.'

Frank hated to hear his mother talk like this — you could almost taste the bitterness in her. Her hair was prematurely grey, her mouth more often than not turned down in a permanent scowl. He remembered a time when she was sweet and pretty and he hated his father with a passion for turning her into a worn-out, leached shadow of her former self.

'Look at him,' he said with disgust, taking in the muddy footprints on Ella's otherwise spotless floor. 'The filthy pig hasn't even bothered to take off his boots.'

The anger welled up inside him. Frank reminded himself that it was only respect for his mother that prevented him giving his father the good hiding he needed.

Ella sighed and shook her head in that slow resigned way of hers.

'If it wasn't for you, son, we'd have been out in the street long ago,' she said and smiled weakly up at him.

'I know Ma,' replied Frank, walking over to the fireplace and turning his back on his father so that he had his mother's undivided attention, 'but surely things are better now that Siobhan's married and out of the house? With the boys away working in England that only leaves me, the two girls and you and Da. And it won't be long before the girls are earning. Doesn't Bobbie send much?'

'Oh, he sends what he can I'm sure, but he's not like you, son. You're good to your aul Ma.'

Frank was a good son. As a boy and the eldest of six children he had always understood perfectly his role in, and responsibility to, the family. Just after his fourteenth birthday and still in short trousers, Frank left St Stephen's Primary School and started as a milk boy. The memory of bringing home that first precious wage packet to his mother still filled his chest with pride. Within a few years the opportunity to earn some real money came along when he was apprenticed at the new Power Station. And Frank was grateful as, at the age of twenty-four, he was the only one in the Meehan household with a job.

'That reminds me, Ma,' said Frank, reaching deep into his trouser pocket and pulling out a wad of folded money, 'I forgot to give you this.'

He peeled off most of the notes and returned the remaining few to his pocket. The rest he placed in a tea caddy that sat in a recess by the fire.

'Thanks, son,' said Ella.

'I'll always look after you Ma, don't you worry

48

about that,' said Frank, kneeling down beside her and patting her arm absentmindedly.

'I can't rely on that pathetic slob to take care of you and the girls,' he added glaring at his father, 'just so long as I have enough for my fags and a Saturday night out on the town.'

Ella brightened up and put a smile on her face. 'Well, son, you're looking grand tonight. Off out?'

'Yes, Ma. Brendan and me are going down to the dance at the Town Hall.'

'Oh, aye? I dare say there'll be plenty of wee girls chasing after you, me boy,' Ella teased and then, cupping Frank's handsome face in her gnarled hands, said seriously, 'just you be careful you don't get trapped by some flighty wee thing. Don't forget I need you here.'

Suddenly embarrassed, Frank pulled away.

'Don't you worry about me, Ma. Sure don't I know my place is here with you?'

Just then there was a knock at the back door.

'That'll be Theresa,' said Ella. 'Her Ma was to return those eggs I loaned her on Monday. Can you let her in on your way out?'

Frank opened the door to a pale face framed by rich dark hair which became animated on seeing it was him.

'Hello, Frank,' she said boldly with a big smile.

'Come on in then,' replied Frank as he moved back a few paces to allow her passage.

She stepped inside and squeezed past him, raising her face to his as she did so. Her dark eyes glinted moist in the dim light and he felt the soft mounds of her pert breasts rub against his

49

chest. Frank swallowed and pulled away.

'Right Ma, I'm off,' he shouted hoarsely and waited for her reply.

Theresa remained motionless on the other side of the room a teasing smile playing on her lips. Then Frank slipped out into the night.

Brendan Mulholland was waiting for him at the end of the street, the red tip of his cigarette glowing intermittently like a tiny lighthouse in the foggy night. As Frank approached, Brendan levered himself off the wall and stubbed out his cigarette. He was dressed almost identically to Frank — dark single-breasted suit with narrow collar, stiff white shirt, thin black tie and brogues. With the sole exception of Pat Gallagher, the town's only Teddy Boy, 'fashion' hadn't yet reached Ballyfergus and both men stepped out dressed much as their fathers would have done two decades before. Hands in trouser pockets to ward against the cold they fell in step as they walked down the road together.

'How about ya, Brendan?'

'As best as I can be without a bloody job.'

'I hear they're looking for a night watchman down at the docks. You should get down there tomorrow.'

'Ah, Frank, sure what's the use? You know as well as I do they have it all stitched up. They'll make sure the job goes to one of their own. I've as much chance there as I have getting a job with the Council.'

Frank said quietly, 'Well you don't know until you try.' But Brendan carried on talking as though he hadn't spoken.

50

'And do you know what pisses me off most of all? All those Proddie bastards sitting up there in Stormont making sure that we never get a chance. Sure they've the whole system rigged against us.' Brendan was off on his favourite theme.

'Ah, now, don't you think you're over-reacting Brendan? Look at me. I've a job and, if I keep my nose clean, good prospects for the future.'

Brendan snorted. 'You're a token Catholic, that's all. They just tolerate you so that the discrimination isn't completely barefaced. So they can defend themselves. Out of the hundreds of men employed at the Power Station you could count the Catholics on your fingers and toes. So what does that tell you?'

Frank shrugged his shoulders for he knew Brendan had a point. After the Civil War in 1922, Ireland was carved up because the Protestants in the North wouldn't go in with a United Ireland. They were afraid of popery and being a minority in the new Irish Free State. So they said 'No' and Britain just caved in and said, 'Oh, well, okay then you can have your own wee country with your own wee Parliament.' Then the Brits pretty much left the North to get on with it.

And the Protestants had been having a field day ever since. They controlled all the jobs in government and the civil service, controlled the allocation of council housing and pretty much owned or controlled everything else — land, police, banks, shops, businesses.

'I know you're right, Brendan, but things are

the way they are and we just have to make the best of it.'

'But, Frank, that's where you're wrong,' said Brendan his passion aroused. 'We don't have to put up with any of it. The system only works if us Catholics lie down and take it and we've been obliging them for years. It's pathetic. You only have to look around. Unemployment amongst Catholics is far higher than Protestants; we live in the worst houses. And the Protestants are determined not only to hold onto that power but to rub our noses in it. They're all scratching each other's backs and making sure Catholics don't get a look in. And we all know what the Orange Order's about — just another way of keeping us down and demonstrating their superiority. What else are the marches on the Twelfth about? They're nothing but an excuse to taunt and intimidate us. And they know we won't fight back because the RUC are all Protestants as well and they won't do anything to stop it.'

Brendan paused to spit viciously in the road and then continued. 'And the Brits couldn't care less so long as they don't have to be bothered with Irish problems.'

Frank felt his blood starting to warm, as it always did listening to Brendan.

'So what's to be done about it, Brendan? What are you suggesting?'

'I'm saying that it's time Catholics stood up and were counted. We've been grovelling in the gutter long enough. Now the Socialists have got some pretty interesting ideas. They reckon that all the workers, or the proletariat,' he said slowly to emphasise the exoticness of the word, 'both Protestant and Catholic, should rise up together against the middle-classes and take control. If we combined forces the pressure for change would be unstoppable.'

This time it was Frank's turn to snort.

'Brendan, you're soft in the head! Sure you can hardly find a Catholic and Protestant who'll drink side by side let alone take up arms together, so I don't much fancy your chances of seeing that one take off.'

'You can laugh, Frank,' said Brendan in a low and even voice, 'but I'm telling you, there's changes afoot in this country. You just wait and see.'

The two men walked the rest of the way up the Main Street to Rileys in silence. Four pints later Brendan was back to his usual jovial form, glued to the bar and entertaining the whole company with jokes. In between, he was earnestly chatting up the barmaid. Frank looked at the clock above the mirror that said 'Jamesons Irish Whiskey' and, finishing the remains of his pint in one gulp, he banged the straight-sided glass down on the worn bar.

'If we're going to this knees-up, we'll need to get our skates on,' he shouted over the din. Brendan responded by raising his near empty glass in a woozy salute. Content in the beery warmth of the smoky pub, he wasn't in any hurry to leave and he called out for a refill.

'Another pint here, love, when you've got a minute.'

'Come on, Brendan,' said Frank waving the

barmaid away, 'we can come back here if the dance isn't any good,' and he steered a reluctant Brendan out into the sobering chill night air.

Two minutes later they were at the Town Hall. Bright yellow electric light from within streamed out into the dark night transforming the grey, utilitarian building into a massive Chinese lantern. Frank and Brendan skulked outside enjoying the last drags on their cigarettes and pretending not to watch the groups of girls, starched petticoats swishing, skip up the steps and inside. A gang of grime-caked boys hung about the entrance to the hall scrounging half-smoked cigarettes and standing on each others' shoulders to see inside.

The band were coming to the end of a Jim Reeves number and the sugary sweet refrain drifted out into the night,

'Put your sweet lips a little closer to the
    phone
Let's pretend that we're together all alone.
I'll tell the man to turn the juke box way
    down low
And you can tell that girl there with you
    she'll have to go . . . '

The evening was evidently well under way for the slow dances had started already. Frank led the way up the steps, paid the two shilling entrance fee and stepped into the main hall where he stopped to survey the scene.

Foldaway wooden chairs lined both sides of the long hall, most of them occupied by girls of all shapes and sizes, resplendent in their finery. As the men wore a uniform of sorts — dark suits, shirts and ties — so too did the women. Theirs consisted of a brightly coloured dress nipped in at the waist, the full skirt stopping just below the knee, a string of pearls and high-heeled shoes with impossibly pointed toes. Some of the girls wore strapless dresses and the more modest ones draped their shoulders with knitted cardigans onto which they had painstakingly sewed shiny little beads and sequins.

The band was elevated on a stage at the far end of the hall. The words 'The Jim Crory Dance Band' were inscribed on the front of the rather grubby-looking drum which faced the audience side on. The music had stopped temporarily and the band members stood around drinking tea, no doubt fortified with something stronger, from white china cups.

The men huddled near the exit in a blue haze of cigarette smoke, hands in pockets, trying to look nonchalant. Occasionally two or three of them would make a foray up one side of the hall to chat to a particular group of girls and then retreat back to the safety of numbers. Girls would weave their way to the loos in small groups taking care to brush past the fellas they fancied and strike up a conversation. A low buzz filled the room, punctuated now and then by raucous laughter, a shrill giggle and the clippetty-clop of cruel stiletto heels on wooden floorboards.

'There's Pat,' shouted Brendan loudly, the way you do when you've had a few drinks. He waved vigorously at a group of men on the other side of the room.

'Well, you could hardly miss him,' said Frank. 'Look at the state of that.'

Pat stood out from the sea of drabness in a long pink jacket trimmed with black velvet at the collar, cuffs and pockets. From his slicked back hair, sideburns, tight black trousers, string tie and pointed shoes he was every inch the Teddy Boy. Possessing only the one suit, and his work clothes of course, style was pretty irrelevant to Frank and most of the other lads he knew.

'In the pink tonight then, Pat?'

Brendan seemed highly amused by Pat's attire and his greeting caused a ripple of laughter amongst the young men standing in the company.

'Oh, give over you shower of bastards,' Pat replied, entirely good-humouredly. As well as a term of abuse, 'bastard' was a term of endearment in these parts and much used by Pat.

'Sure youse have no sense of style whatsoever. Look at youse,' he said eyeing the cordon of dark suits that surrounded him with undisguised disdain. 'You're all like peas in a pod — boring to boot. Now this,' he said, caressing the soft velvet of his lapel between the finger and thumb of his right hand, 'is what you call a real jacket.'

'Where in the name of God did you get it, Pat?' someone asked.

'Belfast. Had to order it too.'

'Must have cost a bomb.'

'Well let's just say style like this doesn't come

cheap,' Pat replied, knowingly.

'Just as well he can afford it,' said Frank under his breath to Brendan.

'He's working for his Da now,' said Brendan, referring to the family plumbing business. 'And I hear he's never short of a bob or two.'

'Lucky beggar,' said Frank. 'I'd love to be my own boss. That's where the real money is for sure.'

Just then the band started up and, slowly, couples began to take to the floor, shuffling self-consciously in small circles. Young men, made bright-eyed and bold with drink, asked partners up and soon the floor was crowded.

Suddenly, Frank's attention was caught by a girl picking her way along the perimeter of the dance-floor, taking care to avoid collision with the more exuberant couples on the floor. As she moved towards him he could see her mouthing 'Excuse me' every few feet, a semi-smile on her face, her lips parted to reveal small even white teeth. She was closer now and soon, in a moment, she would brush right past Frank. He held his breath and felt the thrill of anticipation.

Then, just as she approached, the crowd on the floor surged away leaving her plenty of room to pass unhindered. But still she looked up at Frank, held his gaze purposefully for some seconds, and said, quite unnecessarily, 'Excuse me, please.' He noticed the irises of her eyes were an unusually deep, dark blue. Then she lowered her eyes and he watched her slight frame and golden hair glide away towards the powder room. He was not mistaken; she had definitely

57

stared at him the way girls do when they're interested in you and want you to chat them up. The come on.

He watched the door through which she had disappeared and, when she emerged again some minutes later, he turned to Brendan.

'Who's that girl over there in the blue dress? The one with the blonde hair?'

'Elsie Watson?'

'No, no. I know who Elsie Watson is,' said Frank, irritably. 'The other one.'

'I don't know, Frank. Never seen her before in my life. Why don't you go and ask her yourself?'

'All right I will, but I need you to ask up her friend.'

She must be a farmer's daughter down from the Glens of Antrim, thought Frank, or else she's a Protestant. He hoped it was the former.

'Jesus, do I have to Frankie? I was just away over to Riley's with Pat and the boys.'

'I'd do the same for you, mate. Now come on and look lively.'

'Oh, all right then,' said Brendan, sighing heavily. 'But just the one dance and I'm off.'

But Frank was already half-way across the dance-floor and Brendan had to hurry to catch up.

'Do you want do dance?' Frank asked the girl with the golden hair, simultaneously nodding in the direction of the dance-floor. She stood up and smiled at him.

'Love to,' she said and wove her way through the crowd.

Walking behind Frank could smell the

sweetness of her perfume and the stronger acrid smell of freshly applied hair lacquer. She came to a halt in the middle of the floor where there was just enough room for one more couple.

'This do?' she asked and Frank nodded dumbly.

And then she was in his arms. Her small hand fitted into his perfectly and he could feel the curve of her spine where his other hand rested lightly on her waist. Her red lips were parted in a smile and her teeth, moist with saliva, gleamed in the bright light. He could see traces of fine face powder on the soft down which covered her cheeks. Frank had to suppress a tremendous urge to kiss her, to press his mouth roughly against the soft fullness of her lips. He could feel the thin fabric of her dress damp now under the heat of his own sweaty palm. Conscious of the silence between them, Frank was deciding which chat up line to use, when she spoke.

'I'm Helen, Helen Simpson,' she said and then added, 'What's your name?'

In those few words Frank had all the information he needed to know — she was a Protestant. Immediately, subliminal disappointment registered and then he had to concentrate on Helen for she was speaking again.

'What's your name?' she repeated, looking a little puzzled.

'Oh, Frank Meehan.'

Frank thought he detected the faintest flicker of understanding in her eyes although she continued to regard him steadily.

'And what do you do for a living then?' she asked.

He told her that he worked at the Power Station, lived at home and was the eldest of six children. In return, she told him she was a teacher at Inver Primary School and an only child, so confirming his initial suspicions. By the time the dance came to an end Frank knew she was, most definitely and without a doubt, a Protestant.

The ancient ritual of establishing the religious persuasion of a new acquaintance was completed effortlessly, almost unconsciously, with the exchange of a few social pleasantries.

On the face of it, innocent questions and innocent answers, but all you needed to know was there, encoded in a name, the school you went to, where you lived.

The music finished abruptly: Helen stepped back from Frank and everyone clapped politely. They moved to the side of the dance floor as the band started up again. Frank noticed a long trestle table wedged in a corner at the back of the hall. Two plump women, penned in behind it, were dispensing tea, soft drinks and sandwiches.

'Would you like a drink, Helen?' he asked.

'Mmm, yes please. An orange. It's awful hot in here don't you think?'

Helen waved her hand in front of her face trying to shoo away her blushes. Frank thought this enormously attractive. He didn't like pushy girls.

'Something to eat?' he coaxed.

Helen deliberated for a few seconds and then said, 'Er, no thanks. Where's Betty?'

'Betty?'

'My friend, Betty. She was dancing with your friend.'

Frank had completely forgotten Brendan and, looking around, spotted him at the back of the hall gesturing furiously at Frank to join him.

'I'll go and get the drinks then, Helen. Would your friend like something too?' he asked, as Betty appeared, as if on cue, at her side.

'I'll have an orange and some sandwiches thank you very much.' Betty was heavy with coarse features.

Inexplicably, Helen blushed and said quickly, 'We'll just go to the powder room. Back in a minute.' And she dragged Betty across the dance-floor, arms firmly linked.

As Frank turned away he overheard Helen scolding Betty.

'Betty Smith! You don't even know him and you're taking sandwiches off him. You've got a brass neck.'

'Don't be so soft, Helen. If they're willing to pay, let them. That's what me Ma says.'

Brendan was not pleased.

'Right Frankie boy, I'm out of here. I've had quite enough for one night. I spent the whole dance trying to fight that one off. Her hands were all over me like a rash.'

He paused for Frank to titter but got no response, not even a smirk. Frank was not thinking about Betty. Brendan regarded him with narrowed eyes.

'What's up with you Frank? Don't tell me you're going soft on that girl? Come on, let's go over to Riley's now before last orders.'

'No, you go on. I'll stay on here for a bit.'

'Suit yerself. Don't forget you owe me one though after getting up with that heifer. Doesn't do my street cred any good you know. See you later.'

Helen and Betty joined the queue for the toilets which stretched out into the foyer. Helen's flushed face had nothing to do with the heat; nonetheless she was glad to be standing in the cool draft that wafted in through the opened doors. She breathed in deeply to steady her nerves.

'So, who's the boy then? Seems to have taken quite a shine to you,' said Betty sounding envious, and Helen wished some man would take an interest in her.

'His name's Frank Meehan. Says he works at the Power Station. He's great looking, isn't he?'

'He's handsome all right. Lovely brown eyes and a nice strong chin. I like that in a man,' said Betty with all the assurance of a connoisseur. 'Where does he live?'

'I never asked him.'

There was a brief pause as someone came out of the toilets and the queue shuffled forward a few feet.

'Sounds like a Taig to me.'

'So what if he is?' said Helen, surprised by the defensive tone in her voice. She wasn't normally given to defending complete strangers, Catholic or otherwise. But she knew already that Frank

Meehan was no ordinary stranger. He was going to be very important in her life.

'I'm not saying anything against him. I'm just stating a fact, that's all. Now come on,' said Betty, taking Helen's arm and brightening up. 'What did you think of his friend?'

Betty went home early with a headache. Normally, Helen would never have accepted a stranger's offer to walk her home but she felt so easy and comfortable with Frank that she didn't hesitate. The walk across the river to Victoria Park, a street of privately-owned mostly detached houses dating from the 1930's, should have taken fifteen minutes but took over an hour.

They walked slowly, Frank telling her all about how hard his mother worked, and how he supported the family. Helen admired him for that and she, in turn, found herself chatting away quite unselfconsciously about herself and her job at the primary school.

Halfway along the deserted street, Helen stopped in front of a pair of painted wooden gates.

'This is it,' she said glancing up the drive that led to a modest well-kept bungalow set back from the road in a leafy garden. She rested her hand on the latch of the gate.

'Well, good night then,' she said and waited.

Awkwardly, Frank put his hand over hers and said, 'When can I see you again?'

His touch thrilled her, his big hand hot and strong.

'Tomorrow if you like,' she replied quickly, remembering too late her mother's advice not to appear too available, that boys would take you for granted. Somehow that advice seemed totally irrelevant to her and Frank. They had already formed a bond beyond friendship. They were soul mates and she felt no need to play games.

'Frank, does it matter, to you I mean,' said Helen, 'that I'm not, well, that I'm a Protestant?'

They had skirted around the issue all night, but it was always uppermost in Helen's mind and, she had no doubt, Frank's as well. The question came out more abruptly than Helen had intended. It sounded so blunt put like that, but there was no other way to say it.

Frank cleared his throat.

'Hmm,' he said, after a pause. 'Why should it? Does it bother you? About me I mean?'

'Well, no. I don't think things like that should matter,' said Helen. 'After all we all believe in the same God.'

'That's true,' said Frank.

Helen glanced up the drive and noticed a light on at the back of the house. Dad must be waiting up.

'I'd better go,' she said, pulling her hand away.

'Just a minute,' said Frank and, leaning forward, he planted a soft kiss on the side of her face.

Grateful for the darkness which concealed her blushes, Helen skipped inside.

It was late, half past twelve, when Helen tip-toed in and shut the door quietly behind her. In the sitting room Dad was waiting up, or at least he'd tried to, for he'd fallen fast asleep in a chair. Helen watched him from the doorway, smiling to herself. His black glasses hung precariously on the end of his thin nose and his chest moved gently up and down, accompanied by the soft wheeze of his breathing, audible in the night silence. The electric light reflected off his silver hair reminding Helen that he was getting old.

'Poor Dad,' she said, bending down to pick up a book that had slipped off his lap.

He stirred and opened his eyes.

'Helen, there you are! Where have you been? We were worried.'

'Sorry, Dad, I didn't realise the time. I . . . Betty and me stayed to the end of the dance. It was such good fun and then by the time we'd said good-bye to everyone and all it must have been later than we thought. I'm sorry, Dad, I didn't mean to worry you. I never thought.'

'Well as long as you're home safe, love. I'm glad you had a good time. Put the lights out on your way up will you? Night pet,' said James Simpson, planting a big kiss on his daughter's head and going upstairs.

Helen sat back on the settee, kicked off her shoes, and thought about the evening which, she decided, was the most extraordinary of her whole life. She felt bad about telling tales to Dad, but for some reason she couldn't bring herself to tell him she had spent most of the evening with Frank Meehan. Not just because he would be cross with her for walking home with a total stranger but, instinctively, she knew he would be even more disturbed because Frank was a Catholic.

Helen had never heard her parents say bad things about Catholics and they liked to think of themselves as being open-minded. But without it ever being talked about she had come to understand that they assumed, no expected, that she would date, and ultimately marry, one of her own. She had to admit that the illicit nature of the relationship somehow made Frank dangerous and exciting. And yet it was more than that. Anyway, she reasoned, there wasn't anything to tell. Yet.

4

Frank woke early the next morning and lay in his narrow bed thinking of Helen. He listened for the soft pitter-patter of rain against the glass but there was no sound. And, although no rays of sun broke through the thin curtains, the air smelt fresh and dry.

Excited, Frank threw back the sheet and heavy blanket, jumped out of bed and pulled back the curtain. It was chilly enough in the unheated bedroom, but a perfect spring day for walking out. The clouds, blue-grey, hung low and motionless in the sky. However Frank could tell, from years of cloud-watching (the habitual hobby of everyone in Ireland), that no rain threatened. He couldn't get back to sleep now and he pulled on a fresh shirt, socks and trousers and went down into the back room.

His mother was already up, dressed, and tending to the fire in the old cream range. The wooden-cased clock over the fire struck half eight reminding Frank that first Sunday mass was in an hour. Ella turned round when she heard him and said, 'Morning, son.'

Frank walked over to the fireplace and pressed his lips to his mother's furrowed brow by way of greeting. After the beer last night he was dying for a drink of water, the roof of his mouth dry, his tongue shrivelled and parched. But no food or water was permitted to pass your lips after twelve midnight on Saturday until you'd received holy communion on Sunday. So, for reasons largely other than piety, it suited most of the Catholic population to attend the early mass. Frank wished he'd helped himself to a drink when he'd come in last night, but there was no chance of getting away with even a sip of water under Ella's watchful eye.

Ella knelt down on the floor so that she could see directly into the open door of the range. She lit the end of a tightly twisted piece of newspaper poking out from the coals and blew gently on it until she was satisfied that the kindling had caught. Then she heaved the door shut, the old hinges creaking under protest.

'You were in late last night,' she said straightening up with her back to Frank, and setting the big box of Cook's matches on the mantelpiece. 'Did you have a nice time?'

'I did, Ma.'

'And?' Funny how she always knew when there was more to tell.

'Well, I met a great girl last night, Ma. She was at the dance with her friend and we talked all night and then I walked her home. I think you'd like her, Ma. Not at all pushy.'

Frank waited for his mother's reply, keen for her approval. 'That's nice, son. Sit down at the table and you can help me peel the spuds for the dinner.'

She disappeared into the kitchen and returned with a hessian bag containing potatoes, several sheets of old newspaper and two small paring knives. She laid these down on the table in front of Frank and returned to the scullery. The old pipes creaked as she filled the big, black iron pot with cold water from the only tap over the Belfast sink.

Then, carefully, she carried it through to the back room, the fingers of her right hand wrapped firmly round the base of the charred wooden handle while her left gripped the small loop of a handle on the opposite side. She set the heavy pot down on the table where Frank had already laid out the sheets of newspaper to collect the peelings. Ella sat in the chair opposite Frank and they both began to peel the dirty tubers, dropping them, once peeled, one by one into the black pot.

'Now this girl,' said Ella, almost casually, 'what did you say her name was?'

She watched him carefully as he replied, 'Helen Simpson.'

There was a silence as Frank dug an eye out of a potato with the point of his knife and Ella considered the information.

'She'll be the daughter of James Simpson then, one of the teachers at the Grammar?'

'Yes that's right. I've never seen her before or at least I don't think I have. She's got blonde hair and blue eyes. We got on like a house on fire. And I asked her if she wanted to see me today and guess what? She said 'Yes.' So I thought we could go for a walk along the promenade. Maybe stop for a cup of tea in Bakers. Or would it be better to go to the Park? What do you think, Ma?'

Ella paused before answering.

'Either would be very nice for any girl and I'm pleased that you like her.'

She stopped peeling and considered Frank thoughtfully before continuing. 'There's plenty more fish in the sea you know, Frank, and you're awful young to be getting serious about any girl. Don't go setting your heart on this one too early. You've plenty of time before you want to be thinking of settling down. You only saw her last night. What do you need to be seeing her for again today?'

'For goodness sake, Ma,' said Frank suddenly annoyed, 'I never said I wanted to marry her. I'm only taking her for a blooming walk.'

Frank threw a peeled potato into the pot, splashing the newspaper, and glowered at his mother who returned his glare with a mildly surprised expression.

She turned her attention to the half-peeled potato in her hand and concentrated hard on wasting as little of the white as possible. Her disapproval hung in the air like the bad smell of boiled cabbage.

'No need to get all het up about it, Frank,' she said pleasantly. 'I'm only saying.'

Ella placed the last potato in the black pot, stood up, wrapped the peelings up by folding in the four corners of the newspaper and took the parcel into the scullery.

It was, of course, what she was not saying that bothered Frank. Naturally, she had sussed straight away that Helen was a Protestant and that reality hung heavy in the air, unspoken but palpable all the same.

70

Frank was crushed at his mother's response. Naively, he'd expected her to share his excitement and instead she was doubting his judgment. But he knew his mother had his best interests at heart. She was only trying to protect him from girls like Betty Smith; rude, pushy girls with no manners.

Suddenly he felt ashamed for losing his temper. It was a rare day indeed when he and his mother exchanged a cross word. He got up from the table and went into the scullery to find her. She was busy in the sink, scrubbing mud off carrots.

'Here, let me do that,' said Frank, gently elbowing her aside. He brushed vigorously with the hard bristle brush while Ella wiped her hands on the front of her apron.

'I'm sorry, Ma,' he continued after a time. 'I didn't mean to lose my temper like that. Do you forgive me?'

'Of course I do, son,' she replied softly, wiping something away from her eyes with her forearm. 'You know I love you.'

'I love you too, Ma.'

'Well, let's hear no more about it then,' said Ella brightly. 'Hand us those carrots over will you and I'll start scraping them?'

Armed with fresh newspaper, Ella went into the back room for the scullery was too small for a worktop or table for that matter. She laid out fresh sheets of newsprint, overlapping at the edges, and began to scrape the carrots downwards and slowly so that the juice and fine skin didn't spray everywhere. Soon she was joined by Frank and they fell into a companionable silence as they worked, Ella automatically taking over the job of chopping the carrots once Frank began to scrape.

Soon the girls appeared whining for something to eat until Ella threatened them with a wet dishcloth round their legs.

'So did you meet a girl last night, Frank?' Mary shouted from the parlour where she felt safe from Ella's threats.

'I might have.'

Mary's interest quickened and she bounced into the kitchen clapping her hands together.

'Oh tell me all about it. Who is she? Do I know her? When are you seeing her again?'

'Mary Meehan, you're far too nosy for your own good,' Frank laughed and, observing her pained expression, added mysteriously, 'I'm seeing her this afternoon.'

'You are not? Oh, my Lord,' and Mary jumped up and down on the lino.

'Mary Meehan, if I hear you take the Lord's name in vain one more time. Now make yourself useful and take those scraps out to the bin.'

Ella was cross and Mary didn't hang about for she sensed the threat of the dishcloth was, for some reason, very real this morning. Unprotesting, she picked up the neatly folded newspaper containing the potato peelings and disappeared out the back door.

'What do you mean you're seeing her this afternoon?' Ella's voice was crisp as she broke a cauliflower into florets over a saucepan.

'I told you. We're going for a walk.'

72

'I thought we had agreed to let it drop.'

'Ma, I understand that you're worried about me. It's only natural, but I know what I'm doing and I'm sure you'll feel differently when you meet Helen. Anyway the arrangements are already made. I can't very well stand her up now can I?'

Ella paused momentarily to add gravitas to what she said next.

'You're going against my wishes in seeing this girl Frank, so long as you realise that. And I have no intention of meeting Miss Simpson. Ever.'

★ ★ ★

Helen spent the whole service thinking about Frank Meehan and even though she should have, she didn't feel in the least bit guilty. She resolved to tell her parents she was going out with him. Helen wasn't afraid of them, but she didn't want to hurt them and she had a funny feeling she was about to do just that.

Sunday dinner in the Simpson household was a very predictable affair. The rich smell of roast beef, onions and roast potatoes greeted her nostrils on walking through the door. Helen's mother was a good housekeeper and a great cook.

A quiet, efficient woman, she talked little and left the decision-making to her husband. She seemed to produce meals from nowhere and never asked Helen to help in the kitchen. How the dinner was on the table for one o'clock sharp

73

was a mystery to Helen and she knew she was spoilt rotten.

'That was delicious, Mum. Thanks very much,' said Helen, resting her knife and fork neatly side by side on her plate.

She was trying to work out how to introduce casually the subject of Frank into the conversation when her father asked her what her plans were for the rest of the day.

'Actually, I'm going for a walk with someone I met last night. A boy.'

'You never said Helen,' said Dad, managing to sound both shocked and disappointed. 'Who is he? Do we know him?'

'I don't think so Dad. His name's Frank Meehan.'

'I see,' said James Simpson slowly. 'What else do you know about him, Helen? Where does he live?'

Helen didn't like her father's tone, struggling as he was to disguise mounting disapproval and rising anxiety.

She volunteered, 'He lives down Mill Lane.'

The mention of Mill Lane caused her father to throw a worried look across the table at his wife who remained silent.

'And what does this boy do? I presume he has a job.'

'Oh, yes. He works at the Power Station.'

'That's something at least.'

'What's that supposed to mean, Dad?'

'Nothing, pet,' her father replied, softening, 'it's just that your mother and I want to see you associating with the right sort of people. There's

74

no harm having them as your friends, but you just be careful, dear. We wouldn't want you getting too involved. We only want the best for our little princess.'

Helen knew exactly what her Dad meant by 'the right sort of people.' He and Mum were always trying to pair her off with the creepy son of some doctor or lawyer. They even tried once with John Alexander, the minister's son, inviting him and his parents round for dinner.

John was at least ten years older than Helen, but her mother thought he was wonderful because he had a job in the Bank and 'prospects' as she put it. John had seemed genuinely interested in Helen and she was mortified by his attentions. And, of course, they had all been Protestants.

'We'll get a look at him I dare say when he calls for you.'

'He's not calling for me. I said I would meet him at the bottom of Farmer's Loanan. To save him walking all the way up here,' she explained hastily.

In truth Helen had anticipated this reaction and wasn't keen to subject Frank to her father's scrutiny. Not yet anyway.

'That won't do, Helen. I can't stop you seeing him but he will call for you at the house, like a gentleman. Don't do that again. It's not proper.'

Sensing that the subject was closed, Mrs Simpson began to clear away the plates.

'You'll have some jelly and ice cream, dear, before you go out?'

On their second date Frank duly called at Helen's house armed with a bunch of daffodils. Mr and Mrs Simpson were polite and courteous but, despite the tea and biscuits, they didn't manage to make him feel at home. It was hard to keep the conversation going for they had no friends or acquaintances in common and resorted, at last, to small talk about the weather, the new picture house and the expansion plans for the harbour to cope with the increasing trade between Ballyfergus and Scotland. They studiously avoided politics and religion. They also asked lots of questions about his family and his prospects.

'Six children? My goodness! Your poor mother,' exclaimed Mrs Simpson with undisguised horror, catching at the base of her neck with a small white hand.

She made it sound as though a large family was something to be ashamed of.

'And what does your father do, Frank?' asked Mr Simpson, changing the subject.

'He used to work on the coal lorries for Hemmings, but he injured his back in 1949. I'm afraid he hasn't worked since.'

Frank saw Mr Simpson cast a knowing look across the room to his wife who remained perched nervously on the edge of the settee.

'On account of his back,' he added.

'Did you say one of your sisters is married, Frank?'

'Yes, Mrs Simpson. Siobhan.'

He could have sworn the Simpsons visibly flinched at the Irish name.

'She's two years younger than me. Married a fella from up the coast near Cushendun, oh, it must be two years ago now.'

'And does she have any children?'

'A boy, Fergal, and another one on the way.'

Mrs Simpson nodded her head slowly, her face fixed in a thin, unnatural smile.

'Helen tells me you have a job at the Power Station.'

'That's right, Mr Simpson — been there nearly eight years now.'

'And you like that?'

'Oh, yes. Great job,' lied Frank.

Frank got the feeling that far from putting their mind at rest, the more he told them the greater their apprehension. He was sure they were just as relieved as he was when Helen finally appeared and they escaped into the night.

At least Helen's parents had deigned to meet him.

Spring gave way to summer and Frank continued to see Helen regularly. His mother steadfastly refused to talk about Helen, let alone meet her. A coolness arose between them, but there were never any angry words and things at home continued on pretty much as before. He knew Helen was hurt by this but, at first, she said she understood. After all, it was pretty clear that her parents weren't exactly thrilled either.

★ ★ ★

They often went to the old limestone quarry, long since abandoned to the forces of nature and overgrown with grass and bracken, for some privacy. It was a late summer evening and the place was deserted except for Frank and Helen lying side by side on a promontory, the best place to catch the last rays of the setting sun.

Frank lay on his side, head resting comfortably in his crooked arm, teapot-style, with his back to the sun. He could hear the sound of crickets chirring busily in the long grass which had turned dry and brittle in preparation for the long winter ahead. Helen lay facing him in exactly the same pose, switching playfully at his face with a stem of yellow grass. Her tousled golden hair took on an auburn tinge in the soft red light and her face and arms were glowing with the after effects of a day in the sun. He thought she had never looked so beautiful and leaned over to kiss her once again, pushing her over on her back.

'Oh, Helen, I do love you. I adore you,' he whispered, bearing down and gnawing hungrily at her eager lips.

'I love you too, Frank.'

She ran her hands through his hair sending shivers down his spine. After a while he could feel the heat rising in him and, gingerly, he brought his hand up to rest on her firm breast.

He could feel her heart pounding as she strained under his touch. Feverishly he began to search for the hem of her skirt and slipped his hand up the outside of her bare thigh. Her skin was smooth and soft, and a heady smell of soap and perfume rose from her body. Moving round, his fingers began to search between her legs, all the while their lips glued in a seamless kiss, tongues probing.

Helen moaned again and then, turning her head away, cried out, 'Frank, stop. We mustn't.'

She pushed him off with both arms and sat up, legs clamped together, smoothing down her skirt with quick movements. Her chest rose and fell quickly as her breath came in shallow gasps. Frank rolled on his back and groaned, his right arm thrown across his brow.

'Helen, I'm sorry. It's just that I love you so much I get carried away sometimes.'

Calmer now, Helen replied, 'I love you too, Frank, but you know where this will lead if we're not careful.'

They were silent for several minutes until Frank, still lying in the same position, asked, 'Where is this leading us, Helen. Where do you think we're going?'

'What do you mean, Frank?'

Frank had rehearsed what he was about to say many times, but hadn't yet had the courage to say it, not because he doubted Helen's answer but because he couldn't see a way round 'the problem'. But he was sick of all the soul searching, going round in circles, coming back to the same inescapable conclusion, in his mother's own words, that 'oil and water don't mix'.

He revolted against it all when he said, 'I think we should get married Helen. I want you to be my wife. Will you marry me?'

He turned his head to look at her and she met his gaze with a dreamy smile. He knew

79

instinctively that the answer to his question was 'yes'.

Helen was flustered when she got home and went straight to her room. She sat on the pink nylon bedspread and tried to take it in. Her head was dizzy and she noticed that between her legs was still wet from where Frank had stroked her. She knew it was wrong but she yearned for his touch which gave her the most thrilling sensation she had ever experienced.

She loved Frank with all her heart and soul and she lay back on the bed, eyes shut, imagining what it would be like to make love. Helen's limited knowledge on the subject left the physical details a bit hazy. But she already knew what it was to be desired, utterly essential to someone else's existence and allowed herself to fantasise about being consumed with passion.

Then she tried to imagine the wedding, but for some reason she couldn't picture herself walking up the aisle, nor the flowers, nor the dress. Everything in this picture was foggy and confused.

Helen sat up and faced the issue she had tried to suppress. In their initial excitement, and both fearful of spoiling 'the moment', they hadn't discussed where they would get married and all the other implications that would flow from that crucial decision. Helen knew that the vexed question had no easy answers and rather than face it as she knew she must eventually, she choose to push it to the back of her mind. Thinking on it she remembered they hadn't actually talked about an engagement, a ring or even when they might get married. But their promise that night to each other as the evening shadows stole over them comforted Helen.

Frank had knelt before her and taken both her hands in his.

'Helen,' he said, 'I will never leave you. Promise me the same.'

His expression was anxious as his eyes sought reassurance in hers.

'I promise, Frank. I will never leave you. We will find a way to be together forever.'

And she meant it. Sooner or later, though, they would have to face up to the practicalities.

★ ★ ★

Soon after Helen told her parents that she was in love and wanted to get married, Mr Simpson cornered Frank. It was a Friday night and he was taking Helen to see *Vertigo* at the picture house.

'Hello Frank,' said Mr Simpson, amiably, as he opened the door. 'Come on in. Helen's still upstairs, but you can wait for her in here,' and he led the way into the living room. 'I wanted to have a quiet word with you anyway'.

Mrs Simpson was nowhere to be seen.

'The thing is, Frank,' he began, once settled in the easy chair and Frank was opposite him on the settee, 'Mrs Simpson and I are concerned about you and Helen. I know the two of you have feelings for each other but, as I'm sure you well know, it isn't what we'd planned for our daughter. It's not that we have anything against you, Frank,' he added hurriedly, 'but I'm sure you understand. Helen is a bright girl though I'm not sure she fully understands what a marriage like this would mean.

'People are funny about mixed marriages round here and it wouldn't be easy on either of you. I always say marriage is a partnership and there are certain things that bind a couple together, religion being one of them. In times of crisis — and, believe me, all marriages face crisis at some stage or another — it's sometimes the only thing you have to fall back on. How would you and Helen cope if you don't even share the same fundamental beliefs? How would you feel about your children not being brought up Catholics?'

His tone was gentle and persuasive making it hard to take offence. Frank said nothing and looked at the floor. Mr Simpson hit home with the last remark; that was one of Frank's main concerns.

Well, to be precise, one of his mother's main concerns. Since announcing his marriage plans Ella had taken a much keener interest in the relationship, taking every opportunity to point out the problems and pitfalls to Frank. Frank had to admit that what Mr Simpson said made a lot of sense.

'And you have to think of Helen as well Frank. A lot of her friends and family would find it hard to accept and she'd suffer because of it.

'She's grown up in the Church and with the best will in the world she'd lose a lot of her friends. Anyway, I'm sure your family would rather see you married to a nice Catholic girl.'

They both glanced at the door when they heard Helen's light footsteps on the stairs.

'I'm glad we had this chance to talk, Frank,' Mr Simpson said pleasantly. Rising from his chair and lowering his voice, he added, 'Just you have a think on what I've said, son.'

★ ★ ★

'The point is, Frank,' said Brendan, pausing for effect, 'she's a Protestant and you should know better. If it's a bit of skirt you're after there's plenty of our own sort running about.'

It was early evening and Rileys was relatively quiet, the Saturday afternoon drinkers gone home for their tea. In a couple of hours the bar would be packed for the night.

'Theresa Walsh for one,' continued Brendan, 'She's mad about you, you know. Always hanging round, trying to get your attention. I don't know why you don't take her out. She's a cracker. I wouldn't say no to her, I can tell you.'

Cathal, the barman, came over to their table, took their beer glasses away and brought them back minutes later, refilled.

'I'm not interested in Theresa Walsh,' hissed Frank, his speech slightly slurred. He welcomed the numbness that came with intoxication: that way he wouldn't have to think about things.

'What's it got to do with you anyway?' he said angrily.

'Take it easy,' said Brendan, glancing nervously around. 'All I'm saying, as a friend, is there's people don't like it. People who could make trouble for you.'

'Are you threatening me?'

'Now, now. Who said anything about threats?' said Brendan in a conciliatory tone. 'It's been taken note of, that's all I'm saying.' Frank was tired of the veiled threats and innuendoes conveyed by Brendan from his unnamed 'friends', too tired to even bother arguing about it any more. He wasn't so much afraid as irritated for he didn't take the threats seriously. Everyone knew the IRA was a real force only in the imaginations of old men.

Just then the door of the pub opened and Frank's father stumbled through it. A flash of anger took hold of him and Frank jumped up.

'What are you doing here?' he shouted. 'Can't you bloody well stay at home for even one night and look after her?'

'Don't you talk to me like that, you little shite,' retorted his father, squaring up for a fight.

Brendan intervened by placing himself between the two men.

'Now, now. Mr Meehan! Frank! Settle down the two of youse. Come on you,' he said, pushing Frank roughly out the door in front of him.

Outside Frank was still seething.

'There's me Ma lying in her sickbed all alone and he's out on the bevy, the aul bastard.'

'Where's your sisters?'

'Out at the pictures.'

'I see. Why don't you calm down, Frank? She'll be all right for one night. The girls won't be long.'

He regarded Frank for a moment and then

84

went on, 'Look, Pat Gallagher's got the loan of his Da's van the night. There's a crowd of us going to a ceilidh down in Cushendall. Why don't you come with us? It'll help take your mind off that wee Simpson girl. Who knows, you might even pick yourself up a wee Catholic bird!'

'No,' said Frank forcibly, although somewhat calmer. 'I'd better go home. I don't like to think of me Ma on her own. She might take a turn.'

'You'll be all right going up the road on your own?'

'Jesus, Brendan, I'm not a bairn!' said Frank and he made his way, somewhat unsteadily, along the road.

By the time he reached the house Frank felt very tipsy. He'd downed the last couple of pints quickly and they'd gone to his head.

The house was in silence, a dim lamp still lit in the back room. He heard footsteps on the stairs and waited.

'Oh,' he said when Theresa Walsh appeared in the doorway. 'I was expecting me Ma.'

'She's asleep now.'

'What are you doing here anyway?' he demanded tersely, wishing to be alone.

'Keeping an eye on your Ma. So Mary and Rose could get out. They deserve a break.'

Frank softened.

'I'm sorry, Theresa. For being short with you, I mean. It's good of you to help out. Thanks.'

He collapsed heavily on the brown settee and Theresa sat down beside him. The settee sagged in the middle crushing their thighs together.

'That's all right, Frank,' she said soothingly. 'I

know you worry about her. It's only natural.'

Frank turned to look at Theresa and it took him a few seconds to focus his eyes. Her face was very close to his, so close he could smell her sweet warm breath. She leaned slightly towards him her full lips parted.

'Kiss me, Frank,' she whispered and her flesh burned hot through the fabric of his trousers.

She pressed her breasts against his arm. Frank closed his eyes and felt her warm, moist lips against his. He felt both dizzy and enormously turned on. His penis became immediately erect and strained against the buttons of his trousers.

A rush of brutal desire seized Frank and he found himself on top of Theresa, tearing at her clothes. Her body yielded to him, straining to meet him as their bodies entwined in rhythmic thrusts.

Her skirt had ridden up and somehow the buttons of his fly were undone. He kissed her savagely on the mouth, his teeth closing on her bottom lip until he tasted the metallic sweetness of blood.

He grabbed her roughly by the buttocks, pulled her towards him and thrust his cock angrily inside her. Again and again and again. He was aware only of the exquisite pain and the release. Then he let out a muffled cry and collapsed, exhausted, on her chest.

They lay there quite still for some moments and then Frank got up awkwardly and pulled up his trousers. Theresa lay back on the settee and watched him. A trickle of blood ran out of the corner of her mouth.

Frank stumbled back and stared at her, aghast. What had he done? He felt very sober, the pleasurable numbness replaced by sickening horror.

'You'd better get yourself dressed,' he said, suddenly aware of her nakedness and looked away.

When she had straightened her clothing, Theresa came up behind him.

'Mary and Rose'll be in soon,' she said, 'so I'd better go.'

She kissed the back of his neck because he did not turn round and then moved to the door.

'I always knew we were meant for each other,' she said. 'And now we're engaged. It's funny how things work out in the end, isn't it?'

And then she was gone.

★   ★   ★

'You've had carnal knowledge of this girl?'

'Yes, Father.'

'Is she expecting a child?'

'No, Father.'

'And she's a Catholic?'

'Yes, Father.'

'Well, at least that's something. Now, are either of you otherwise promised?'

Frank paused and then said, 'I am, Father. Well, sort of.'

'What do you mean, 'sort of'? You either are or you aren't, son.'

'I am then. I asked her to marry me.'

'I see. Have you set a date for the wedding?'

87

'No. You see she . . . Helen . . . she's not a Catholic, Father.'

He heard the rustle of Father O'Brien's cassock as he shifted in his seat and considered the information.

'I would advise you,' he said at last, in a solemn voice, 'to forget this Helen. I can't emphasise enough the dangers of getting involved with someone outside the Faith. You have a moral obligation to marry the other girl. And she's a Catholic. You've committed one very serious sin already, don't make it any worse.'

It was no more than Frank expected. He stared at the metal grille in front of him where he knelt and then closed his eyes. A coldness seeped through his warm coat and settled on his heart.

'You don't need me to tell you that sexual intercourse outside marriage,' the priest went on, 'is a mortal sin. In this case I'd say you got off lightly. At least the girl's not pregnant and she's a Catholic. And don't be indulging again until she's your wife. Do you hear me? Now, is that all my son?'

'Yes, Father,' said Frank and he began to recite from memory, 'O my God, I am heartily sorry for having offended thee because thou art so good and perfect . . . '

An image of Helen came to mind and Frank pushed it away. In the musty privacy of the confessional, tears ran unbidden down his cheeks and his face contorted in silent agony.

' . . . and I swear I will not sin again.'

5

They sat opposite each other in Baker's, both cradling cups of lukewarm tea and watching the dismal scene outside through the rain-streaked window. The wind drove the rain up alleyways and down drains, chased people from shop to shop and polished the pavement till it gleamed.

This was their first meeting since they'd agreed to take a break from seeing each other. To get perspective on things, they'd said, to find a solution to the age-old problem. Helen had looked forward to the appointed date, counting down each minute of each day and now it was here she was nervous.

Frank seemed on edge.

'So how have you been?' she ventured wanting to touch him. But something about his demeanour told her not to.

'Fine,' he replied, avoiding eye contact. 'And you?'

'Oh, you know,' said Helen cheerfully, 'just the usual. I missed you though.'

No response. Anxious to fill the silence Helen spoke again. 'So has your mother said any more about meeting me?'

'No. I'm really sorry Helen, but she refuses even to talk about you. Sometimes she can be so stubborn. It makes me mad.'

Frank spat out the last words and clenched his fist until his knuckles whitened. His face was thin and despite the summer of sunshine, pale and drawn. He looked the way Helen felt — miserable.

'Don't be cross Frank. Mine might put on a front but they're no better really. They spend most of their time trying to talk me out of it. They think if we got married I would end up having loads of children and working all the time like your mother. That we'd be poor and never get on our feet. And they don't want that for me. It's very hard for them because I'm their only child and I know they mean well. They just never expected this to happen. It wasn't in their plans for me.'

'My mother doesn't regret having any of her children, Helen. And sure what's marriage for if it's not to have children? They're God's gift after all.'

Helen couldn't argue with that.

'But,' she said, 'you can see where Mum and Dad are coming from can't you?'

Frank didn't answer. He just stared out the window his eyes red-rimmed and bloodshot.

'Frank, are you listening to me?'

Once she was satisfied that she had his attention again she continued.

'Anyway what exactly does your mother say about me? Is it just because I'm a Protestant that she doesn't want to know.'

'Helen, we've been over this a hundred times. She says she would welcome you as a daughter-in-law, but we'd have to get married in a Catholic church and any children would have to be brought up Catholics.'

'You can't expect me to go along with that. It's tradition that a couple always get married in the girl's church. Reverend Williamson said we could get a priest to do a blessing. Wouldn't that do?'

'A blessing isn't the same as a marriage,' said Frank listlessly.

'So you're saying that a wedding in anything but a Catholic church isn't a proper wedding?'

'No, I'm not saying that. I'm just telling you what the priest said,' replied Frank, raising his voice and getting visibly agitated.

'Will you calm down? You'll be telling the whole town our business next,' hissed Helen, simultaneously smiling over at two pensioners who were eyeing them suspiciously from the other side of the near-deserted tearoom.

'And as far as children go, apart from anything else, how could I bring them up as Catholics when I don't know the first thing about it? Not that I'd want to anyway.'

'Mother would've helped with that side of things.'

Helen noticed Frank used the past tense and she fought to contain the panic rising within her.

'And then I wouldn't be a proper mother and she'd be interfering all the time.'

'You haven't even met her yet, Helen.'

Frank sounded weary.

'No and I'm not likely to the rate things are going.'

'You know she's not well. I don't want her upset.'

'And what about me Frank?' seethed Helen. 'Does it not matter that I'm upset?'

But Frank said nothing and a despondent silence followed, both of them lost in their own private turmoil. Helen watched the raindrops coursing down the window pane in little rivulets. A feeling of doom had settled on her which she couldn't shake off. Frank's mother had a tremendous hold over him and used every means of pressure she could to dissuade him from marrying her. The latest tack was her failing health which, coincidentally, started up round about the time Frank asked Helen to marry him. And Frank wouldn't hear a word said against her.

What peeved Helen the most was that she suspected the views Frank expressed weren't entirely his own. In fact she would go so far as to hazard that he really couldn't care less where they got married just so long as it won his mother's approval. And that galled her more than anything.

'If you loved me Frank, really truly loved me, you would do this for me,' said Helen.

Frank dragged his hands down the tired contours of his face and let out a long sigh. He'd tried to find a way out. He really had, but no matter which way he looked at it he was trapped. He'd done wrong and he must pay the price. And how could he possibly tell Helen that he'd slept with Theresa? She'd never forgive him. How could he expect her to understand? He didn't understand himself how or why it had happened. And in that one moment of madness his fate was sealed.

He looked up at Helen and her blue eyes were

full of pain. Her hair was damp and matted with the rain and she had smudges of mascara under her eyes. She looked so small and fragile and vulnerable. Frank had never loved her so much. He could never tell her the truth for it would break her heart. Even more than he was about to.

'It just isn't going to work Helen, can't you see that? We're too different and my Ma would never forgive me if her grandchildren weren't brought up Catholics. I couldn't live with that.'

Helen winced.

'I know things have been difficult for us recently,' she said, 'but you don't mean that Frank. There is a way for us to be together, there must be.'

'I think we should finish it, Helen.'

She reached out for his hand and held it fiercely in her own perfect one.

'We can't give up on each other now, Frank. Not after all we've been through. We promised we'd never leave each other, remember?'

She smiled, bravely holding back the tears that threatened to spill over and tumble down her cheeks.

Frank could not bear it. He pulled his hand away roughly. He could not look her in the face.

'I don't know what else to do,' he said hoarsely, choking back the tears.

'Please Frank, please. Don't do this to me.'

The words from the confessional rang inside Frank's head, 'I confess to almighty God and to you my brothers and sisters that I have sinned

93

through my own fault, in my thoughts and in my deeds . . . '

Frank shook his head and repeated, 'I don't know what else to do.'

For the first time in her life Helen felt a blinding flash of anger and she swallowed hard to keep the bile down in her stomach. She wanted to hit him hard in the face, to hurt him the way he had hurt her. Instead, she rose unsteadily to her feet and, gripping the checkered table for support, she lent forward slightly.

'Then go to hell, Frank. You're completely gutless. I hate you. Why don't you go and marry a nice Catholic girl just like your Ma wants you to? I never want to see you again,' she hissed.

Then, for the first time in her life, Helen swore.

'Fuck you and fuck your aul Ma,' she said.

And she left him there in the teashop, head in hands, as the two old ladies watched on, stunned.

* * *

It was New Year's Eve and Helen wasn't looking forward to the party her parents were throwing for a small group of friends. It was exactly four months, two weeks and three days since she and Frank had split up and it still hurt. Every single day.

'Can I give you a hand with those, Mum?' said Helen, watching her Mum expertly spear little cubes of yellow cheese and rubbery pink ham on

94

cocktail sticks. On the table were trays of triangular-shaped sandwiches with the crusts cut off and a home-made trifle.

'Thanks, love, but I'm just about finished. You look nice, dear. That red dress really suits you.'

'Thanks, Mum,' said Helen perking up a little and resolving to make an effort for her parents' sake.

The doorbell went.

'I'll get it,' said Helen cheerfully. At least it was better than sitting in alone on New Year's Eve.

It was Reverend and Mrs Alexander with their son, John. They were soon followed by Mr and Mrs Cahoon and the Irwins.

By eight o'clock they were all assembled and the evening began with hot punch (non-alcoholic of course). John came up to Helen in the hall with a glass of steaming red liquid in his hand.

'No disrespect, but this could do with something in it to liven it up a bit.'

'John Alexander!' exclaimed Helen in mock horror. 'And you a minister's son. I am surprised at you.'

They smiled conspiratorially at each other.

'I didn't expect you to be here,' said John. 'I thought you'd be out on the town.'

'What about you?' retorted Helen. 'Had you nothing better to do?'

'No, but now I'm here I'm glad I came,' he said regarding Helen thoughtfully.

'And with the average age through there over sixty,' he added, glancing over his shoulder to the front room where everyone was seated, 'I think you're in serious need of some company.'

Helen laughed and wondered if she'd been a bit premature in dismissing John altogether. Her parent's previous attempt at match-making had probably put her off. True, he was no James Dean, but he was good fun.

'Now,' said John, 'tell me all about those little terrors you teach. There's a couple of them in our BB company and they're always talking about the lovely Miss Simpson.'

Helen blushed and quickly moved the conversation on.

'I didn't know you were a Boys Brigade Officer,' she said.

'Oh, yes, have been for years. I love it, Helen', he said with passion. 'Some of those boys come from desperate homes and the BB is the only thing they have to give them some discipline and direction in their lives.'

'Hmm, I think I know the ones you mean,' said Helen thinking of some of the less privileged kids in her class, 'Do you think, though, that attending BB a couple of times a week is enough to counteract the effect of their backgrounds?'

'I don't know for sure, but I believe it can make a difference. You have to try don't you? Or else those boys are consigned to the scrapheap.'

'Yes, I feel that too when I'm teaching. I feel like I have a responsibility not just to educate them but to try and show them that they can better themselves.'

'When I was in Toronto at a conference last year there were ministers there from some really rough ghettos. It was amazing what they'd done in their communities, setting up youth groups and after school programmes. It was really inspiring.'

'You were in Canada?'

'Yes, I went with my Dad. Let's go into the sitting-room and I'll tell you all about it.'

* * *

'You and John seemed to be getting on very well,' said Mum after everyone had gone. She was scraping leftovers into the bin.

'He's a nice fella, Mum,' said Helen and after a bit added, 'but he's not very good-looking is he? A bit weedy.'

'Looks aren't everything, Helen. He's a secure job in the bank and great prospects. He would be a very good catch.'

'He's not a fish, Mum!' said Helen good-naturedly. 'I want to marry for love not for money.'

'And so you should. But there's different types of love, Helen, just remember that.'

Helen watched her mother cover the remains of the trifle with a plate and put it in the fridge. She'd never heard her talk like this before.

'Like you and Dad you mean?'

Mum paused with a squeezed-out dishcloth in her hand and thought for a moment.

'If you like,' she said, wiping down the kitchen table. 'Your father and I are very well matched. That's why our marriage works. Love on its own sometimes just isn't enough. John Alexander's a very nice fella, decent and kind. And he's very fond of you, Helen.'

Helen coloured and looked at the floor. She thought how nice it was to have someone fancy her. It made her feel attractive and desirable. Alive again.

When, a week later, John asked her to go out with him, she agreed and soon, to her parent's delight, they were seeing quite a bit of each other. And although nothing explicit was ever said, Helen knew they had high hopes for a match.

Summer 1962

Helen walked arm in arm up the long Main Street with her mother, a process that took some time for every few minutes they would stop and chat to a neighbour or an acquaintance from the church. Even though it had a population of over 30,000 souls, sometimes Ballyfergus seemed like a very small place.

But today Helen didn't mind the interruptions at all. They were on the sunny side of the street and she was happy to stand on the pavement, face to the sun, absorbing the warm rays and half-listening to the gossip.

The street was decorated in preparation for the marches on the 'Glorious Twelfth of July'.

'It's a grand sight, isn't it?' said Mrs Hoy, gesturing up at the string of small red, white and blue triangles that criss-crossed from one side of the street to the other like a very long shoelace.

The bunting went all the way down the Main Street, as far as Helen could see, the little flags

98

fluttering crisply in the morning breeze. The Union Jack or, more often, the Red Hand of Ulster was displayed on almost every building; people in Ballyfergus took their flag-flying very seriously.

'It is that,' agreed Helen's mother. 'The Council must have splashed out for the flags look new to me.'

'And they've freshened up the kerbstones by the look of it,' added Mrs Hoy and they all looked down. There were many junctions along Main Street and, at the corners, the kerbstones were striped red, white and blue, recently repainted and brilliant in the strong sunlight. That, combined with the flags, lifted the normally drab street into something altogether more heart-stirring.

'At least our taxes are being spent on something worthwhile,' said Mrs Hoy with a satisfied air.

'Will you be down here for the main parade?' enquired Helen's mother.

'I wouldn't miss it for the world!' replied Mrs Hoy with feeling.

Helen imagined the street lined with crowds all waving little cloth Union Jacks on wooden sticks. She never consciously thought of herself as a Unionist and considered some of the activities associated with the Twelfth, such as the burning of effigies of the Pope, a little vulgar. Even still she couldn't help but feel a surge of pride.

Then she wondered, as she often did, what Frank would make of it all. His feelings would, she was sure, be quite the opposite to hers. They hadn't spoken in nearly two years, not since the worst day of her life, but she thought of him every day.

For the first week she fully expected Frank to turn up at her door or to find him waiting for her outside school after the final bell. The weeks dragged into months until at last she realised that Frank was not going to come to her. Then, righteous anger gave way to a painful, deep-seated sadness that never truly left her even at her happiest moments. She'd been right about Frank after all. A weak mammy's boy without the will-power to defy his mother. She was just as well shot of him.

Helen heard her mother say, 'Well we must be getting along or we'll never get our shopping done. Come on Helen.' And she felt herself smiling sweetly at Mrs Hoy as she and her mother moved off again.

When things with Frank ended Helen's mother and father had been great. They hardly said anything against Frank, just that it was all for the best.

'We'll not have his name mentioned in this house again,' said Mr Simpson, barely disguising his sheer relief, and it never was.

'You seem a little distracted, dear. Anything wrong?'

Mrs Simpson, prim and neat in her flowered skirt, white blouse and navy cardigan, looked into Helen's face, eyebrows raised.

How could she tell her what was wrong? That she still ached for a love that had died two years ago. That she thought constantly of Frank Meehan. That he haunted her dreams and, after all this time, still made her wretched.

So she said, 'I'm fine Mum. Just a little hot. I think we maybe stood in the sun too long.'

'We'd better get you inside then. You wanted to go into Tweedie's for some dress material didn't you? We're nearly there now. I'll not come in with you though. I must get some lamb from Anderson's and I want to get to the Post Office before it shuts for lunch. Shall I come back for you?'

'No, it's all right, Mum, I don't know how long I'll be and you'll need to be getting back to put the dinner on. I'll see you at home,' said Helen cheerfully, leaning forward and giving her Mum a peck on the cheek. Suddenly she needed to get away from her well-meant concern.

'Well, if you're sure,' said Mum, scanning Helen's face closely. 'You're not going to faint or anything?'

'I'm fine, Mum, honest. Now off you go. I'll see you later. Bye,' and Helen disappeared through the door of Tweedie's Haberdashery Shop.

The tinkling bell above the door alerted Mrs MacDonald, the proprietress, as Helen came in and, looking up, she waved a greeting before returning to her customer in hand. The familiar smell of polished wood met Helen's nostrils and, in the sunlight streaming through the door, she could see fine dust particles drifting along on wafts of air. Immediately Helen began to relax and set about selecting a fabric from the rolls neatly stacked, ends up, on the deep shelves that reached to the ceiling on both sides of the shop.

'How's John keeping then, Helen?'

Mrs MacDonald's crinkled face emerged from behind rolls of coloured cotton, bright eyes twinkling mischievously. Helen jumped sharply.

'Oh! You nearly gave me heart failure Mrs MacDonald — I was a hundred miles away. John? Yes, he's grand, thank you.' She felt her cheeks start to burn and was at once annoyed with herself; almost twenty-five years old and still blushing like a schoolgirl.

The expectant pause continued and Mrs MacDonald's eyebrows remained raised as if to say, 'And?'

'We're going down to Bangor a week on Saturday,' Helen offered. She took an end of cotton between her forefinger and thumb and pretended to examine the pattern.

'His Uncle James has a boat down there and we thought we'd go out for a bit of a sail, make a day of it, you know. So that's what I need the cotton for — to make something nice and cool. Looks like someone has the same idea as me,' she said and laughed, gesturing at the rolls of cotton strewn across the deep wooden counter.

'Why am I rabbiting on like this?' thought Helen, 'Mrs MacDonald is such a gossip she'll only repeat all my business to the next person who walks in here!'

Seeing Helen wasn't going to divulge any more Mrs MacDonald bristled into action.

'Well, I think we've got just the thing for you here,' she said, holding up a roll of pale cream cotton covered with feminine sprigs of pink and blue flowers.

'I think John will like this one very much, don't you?' she added, suppressing a knowing smile. Just then, to Helen's great relief, the door to the shop opened and Mrs MacDonald was distracted.

'Morning, Mrs Walsh. Morning, Theresa,' she chirped, nodding twice and smiling broadly. 'And who's this pretty girl?' she asked moving round to the shop side of the counter.

Mrs MacDonald lowered her voice slightly. 'I'll leave you to have a wee look over these, Helen, if you don't mind. Back in a minute.'

'Of course, Mrs MacDonald. I'm not in any rush.'

'This is my youngest, Bernadette. Say hello to Mrs MacDonald,' directed Mrs Walsh, urging the child forward and, once a few pleasantries had been exchanged, adding, 'we're here to collect the dress.'

Tweedie's did a brisk trade in wedding dresses. They didn't carry any stock, but they had a glossy catalogue that you ordered out of. It was either that or you had to travel the twenty miles to Belfast which was more trouble than it was worth and, anyway, ordering your wedding dress from Tweedie's was a tradition.

'Not long now to the big day, Theresa, eh? I'll bring the dress down so you can see it better in the light. Back in a jiffy,' and Mrs MacDonald's large frame disappeared with surprising agility up the three shallow steps that led to the back of the shop.

103

Curiosity got the better of Helen and she turned towards the door as if to see more clearly the true colours of a particular printed cotton. Her gaze quickly came to rest on the bride-to-be who was plainly dressed in a simple grey skirt and sleeveless pink top which revealed skin of an alabaster hue, pale and transparent.

Her brown eyes were large and wide-set, well-defined cheekbones, but her brow was too narrow and her rosebud mouth, though pretty, slightly too small.

The overall effect was, however, not unattractive and any shortcomings were compensated for by her most striking feature — dark, straight hair that stretched all the way down her back to her waist.

Theresa Walsh glanced at her and, realising she was staring, Helen busied herself with her fabrics.

'Here we are, then,' said Mrs MacDonald returning, somewhat breathless, from her foray at the back of the shop.

She carried a full-length opaque plastic sheath, held out in front with both arms. She negotiated the steps carefully as the passage of feet over the years had worn a slippery indentation in each wooden step. She deposited the garment on the wooden counter and removed the dress from its cover.

'Now I've taken up the hem an inch-and-a-half and nipped in the sides where it was loose. You don't want the bodice too tight as you've to wear it all day and you want to be comfortable. And don't worry about the shoulders slipping

104

off; I've sewn in two bits of binding with press-studs. Look here, you put your bra straps through them like this and they'll stay put all day.'

The Walsh family surrounded Mrs Mac-Donald and all Helen could see was a sea of white. So she was pleased when Theresa said, 'Do you think I should try it on again? Just to be sure.'

'I'm sure it will be fine, love. But you'll want to make sure it's right won't you, in your own mind? Go on then and I'll give you a hand,' said Mrs MacDonald, warming to the idea. 'You don't mind do you, Helen?'

'Not at all, just you carry on,' she replied, thinking that Mrs MacDonald knew fine well she was dying to see the dress.

Mrs MacDonald and the girl disappeared up the back of the shop and returned a few minutes later. Theresa proceeded gingerly as she picked her way down the steps and across the shop into the natural daylight streaming through the glass door. They all turned to look at her.

The dress was a brilliant white, the bodice encrusted in lace, the cap sleeves and full length skirt made of satin. The hem was crumpled, but that was, Helen supposed, because she hadn't any heels on. The neat waist showed off Theresa's trim figure and, even without a scrap of make-up or head-dress, she had to admit the girl was stunning.

For some reason Helen detected a tiny pang of envy in her stomach. She suppressed it quickly. 'Just because you've had a disappointment in life

105

Helen,' she told herself, 'that's no reason to be jealous of other people's happiness.'

'Well, Ma, what do you think?'

Theresa looked down at her lace and satin encased body as though she couldn't believe it belonged to her.

'You look lovely dear, you really do. What do you think Mrs MacDonald?'

'The dress is a perfect fit and she's got such a neat figure too. Not many girls could get away with a dress like that, Theresa. It looks beautiful on you. Don't you agree, Helen?' added Mrs MacDonald.

Drawn unwillingly into the conversation, Helen summoned up a big smile and said, 'Yes, it's a beautiful dress. It looks lovely on you.'

The girl held her gaze uncertainly for a second and then said, 'Thank you.'

For a moment Helen thought Theresa was going to say more, but instead she lowered her eyes and stared at the bodice.

'Are you happy with the dress then?' asked Mrs MacDonald.

'Oh, yes, very,' said Theresa, looking up. 'You've done a great job with it, Mrs MacDonald. Very nice indeed.'

Mrs MacDonald beamed.

'I am pleased you like it. I like all my brides, for you know that's what I call you girls, to feel their best on their wedding day. It's the most important day of any girl's life. Now let me help you out of that, Theresa, and we'll get it all wrapped up.'

Left alone with Mrs Walsh and the youngest

daughter, who had not said a word throughout the whole proceedings, Helen felt obliged to make conversation.

'Still a lot to do then for the wedding?' she asked.

'Oh, my dear you wouldn't believe it. Hair appointments to make and she still hasn't seen the florist. And no matter how well you think you've planned it, everything always seems to need doing at once. You know how it is.'

Helen laughed and wished she did.

Theresa returned with a large brown box under her arm, and the Walshes set off for their next appointment at the hairdressers. Decisions had to be made about how Theresa was to wear her hair for 'the Big Day'.

Once they'd gone, Mrs MacDonald returned to her customary position behind the counter.

'How are you getting on, dear?' she said.

'I've decided on this one,' said Helen holding a swathe of pale blue checked cotton gingham up to her chin. It reminded her of Doris Day in *Calamity Jane*, after she'd been feminised that is.

'What do you think?'

'That'll look lovely on you,' approved Mrs MacDonald, pushing the unwanted fabrics aside and unrolling several yards of the chosen material.

'Bonnie girl that Theresa Walsh, isn't she?'

'Mmm . . . ,' agreed Helen wondering if she needed thread. She decided to risk making do with what she had at home.

'A Catholic mind, but a decent enough family all the same,' continued Mrs MacDonald,

107

searching for a pair of scissors. 'She's getting married a week on Saturday to a lad called Frank Meehan.'

Helen jerked as though she had been punched in the stomach.

'Ah, here we are, thought I'd lost them for good that time. He works in the Station with my boy Terence, not that he'll be getting an invitation to the wedding.'

Helen leaned both hands on the edge of the counter to steady herself as a wave of nausea swept over her.

'Apparently, there's five girls in her family. Can you imagine trying to find husbands for all that lot? What a nightmare! All pretty girls mind.'

Mrs MacDonald prattled on. 'What is it you're making Helen?'

'Why?' she managed to respond.

'Well how much fabric do you need, my dear? Is it a skirt, or a blouse or a dress?'

Helen couldn't think. 'I don't know,' she said, her voice trailing off.

Frank was getting married to that anaemic little bitch. No wonder she had looked at Helen strangely; she must know who she was. Had Frank told her about their past or had she seen them walking out together before the split? He'd chosen Theresa Walsh over Helen. She wasn't even good looking. How could he?

'Well, if you tell me what you're planning to make I can work out how much fabric you need.'

Mrs MacDonald waited for an answer, scissors poised in mid-air.

'Are you all right, dear? You look a little faint.'

'Yes. Yes, I'm fine. I just need a bit of fresh air.'
Helen needed to get out of the shop. Fast.

'A dress. I'm making a dress. Knee-length. This one,' she said grabbing a dress pattern from a revolving stand by the window with such force that she send it spinning round. On the front of the packet was an illustration of two smiling models in dresses, unnaturally tall and thin with impossibly tiny, belted waists and high heels with pointed toes.

Of course the reason was obvious. Theresa Walsh was a Catholic and, in the end, that mattered more to Frank than anything else.

Mrs MacDonald hesitated, put down the scissors, and went to speak. Helen cut her off. 'Really I'm fine, Mrs MacDonald. No need to worry. I'll just have a wee lie down when I get in.'

The effort required to appear normal was tremendous. Helen even managed to force a painful smile. Mrs MacDonald picked up her scissors again and, giving her head a little shake to indicate her concern, began to measure the fabric against the brass rule, worn shiny with use, that was screwed to her side of the counter.

Helen breathed out and tried to make the muscles in her face relax. Had he ever really loved her? Maybe it had all been lies on his part. A cruel joke? No, she couldn't believe that. What they had was real; he felt the same as her and she knew it. He just didn't have the strength to fight for their love. To stand up to his mother.

'Need anything else, dear?'

'No, nothing, thank you.'

Helen felt the hate rising in her. That old bitch must be happy now.

'That'll be five and six, please,' said Mrs MacDonald, wrapping up the purchase in a brown paper bag.

Helen handed the coins over and put her hand out for the change.

'You will be all right, Helen?' Mrs MacDonald asked, her normally cheerful face serious for a moment.

'Yes. Thank you,' she replied as calmly as she could and left the shop.

Outside the sun had disappeared behind low, black clouds, plunging the street into chilly darkness. Relief at getting out of the shop gave way to delayed shock. The feeling of anger slowly subsided and Helen became aware of a gnawing, raw sensation deep in her stomach.

'I'm going to be sick,' she said aloud and dived up the alleyway at the side of Tweedie's that led to the train station. The vomit spilled out immediately and she only managed to keep it off her clothes by bending almost double. She wiped her mouth with the back of her hand and stumbled into a doorway where there was less chance of being seen from the Main Street. Her mother was probably still out there somewhere. She rested the back of her head against the door.

With the immediate danger of detection over, Helen tried to make sense of it all. 'How could he do this to me?' she asked herself again. 'Didn't he love me after all? Was it all just some sort of sham? No, he said he loved me. I think he loves me still.'

And then Helen realised, too late, that she had never really believed it was over. Part of her had always been waiting for him to come back to claim her, to say he was sorry. To beg for her forgiveness. And now that would never happen.

'You silly, silly cow,' she cried out. 'If only you had gone to him. How things might have been different!'

She stood there sobbing like a child for a long time until, gradually, the sobs gave way to whimpers and at last she ceased, exhausted. Her nose had run all down her upper lip and she searched about in her bag for a tissue. Her eyes were dry and sore for no more tears would come and she stood staring blankly at the ground aware of nothing but the emptiness inside her.

Then a fleeting notion crossed her mind. She caught it and held it. She considered it cautiously, the idea growing large and bold in her imagination and, slowly, life came back into her deadened eyes.

'I'll show him,' she vowed. 'I'll show him that I can live without him.'

She smoothed her hair, straightened her skirt, checked for vomit stains and drawing herself up proudly to her full height she walked home.

6

Frank stood in front of the oval mirror in his parents' room, once again wearing a dark suit, white shirt and tie remembering a night almost three-and-a-half years ago when he had stood and preened himself in exactly the same spot. He had no idea then that he would meet Helen Simpson, nor that things would turn out the way they had. But, he kept telling himself, he was doing the right thing.

The face that looked back at him in the mirror was not as carefree as it had once been. Not that the years themselves had actually done much damage; he was still young and handsome. Only his eyes lacked some of the vitality they once had and his mouth had settled into a habitually straight line where before a hint of merriment had played round the upturned corners.

Mary appeared in the doorway.

'Brendan's here, Frank. Are you ready yet?'

She shared Frank's swarthy skin and dark colouring and at five foot nine inches she was tall for a girl, a fact she tried to disguise by wearing unfashionably flat shoes all the time. She had, almost overnight, turned into an attractive young woman, although the awkwardness with which she held the shiny square handbag showed she still had a bit more growing up to do. One minute she had it over her arm, the strap nestling in her crooked elbow, the next dangling at her side from her hand.

'I don't know what to do with this blooming handbag. Are you supposed to wear it over your arm or what? The strap's too short to go over my arm and too long to carry like this.'

She thrust her hand forward, her fist curled round the strap and demonstrated how the bag almost trailed the floor.

'And anyway I don't know what to put in it. Ma's insisting I wear it, though. What do you think, Frank?'

'Don't ask me, Mary. What do I know about handbags?' said Frank, amused. 'Now, don't be getting all annoyed at me. I think you look lovely and, if I was you, I'd do what Ma says. Why don't you go and ask her?'

'She's having a wee lie down to get her strength up for the day. I don't want to wake her up.'

Frank stopped examining his chin for five o'clock shadow and turned round sharply, his brow furrowed.

'Is she all right, Mary? Did you make sure she took her tablets last night? You know what she's like if she doesn't get a good night's sleep.'

'She's only resting, Frank. Nothing to worry about. She's going to be fine honestly,' said Mary, crossing the room and patting him reassuringly on the shoulder. 'And it's going to be a great day. You know how much Ma's been looking forward to it. I don't think anything could keep her away. Well, now, let me get a look at you. Is that you ready then? You do look handsome, Frank Meehan. Theresa Walsh is a lucky girl.'

'Enough of that nonsense. I'd better be getting down the stairs to Brendan.'

Brendan was in the front parlour, happily ensconced in an armchair and drinking from a small glass tumbler. The parlour, rarely used, had been specially aired for the occasion and smelt of polish, air freshener and a faint dusty smell that wasn't mustiness exactly, just the smell of disuse. In an effort to clear the air the windows were open, causing the cream lace curtains to billow gently in the warm summer breeze.

Being north-facing the parlour was always cool for which Frank was grateful on this warm day. Frank's father sat opposite Brendan, uncomfortable in his best Sunday suit, also drinking from a small glass. A bottle of Bushmills sat on the table between them. Normally Ella would not allow drinking in the house until after teatime, but today was a day for celebration.

'There you are, son. Come on in and have a drink,' cajoled Frank's father, nimbly rising to his feet and pouring Frank a rather large whisky.

He was obviously enjoying himself.

'Brendan here has just been telling me about socialism in Russia. Tell Frank what you were saying about it being no different from here,' he said, handing the drink to Frank and sitting down again without taking his eyes off Brendan.

'I was telling your Da here, Frank, that the real split in this country isn't between Protestants and Catholics, it's between the working classes

114

and the upper classes. Your Protestant Ascendancy have as much interest in keeping working-class Protestants down as they have Catholics. Look at Stormont — it's full of property owners and landowners, most of them related to each other one way or another. And all scratching each other's backs. The ordinary working man doesn't get a look in and that's the way the bastards want it.'

Brendan was getting excited now, his passion amplified by the amber nectar.

'The truth is that they don't want to share what they have with anyone, including their less fortunate brothers and sisters. They're very, very clever though. You see, what they've done is persuade your average Protestant that his enemy is the Catholic down the street when it's the upper and middle-class Protestants who are keeping everything for themselves and their own.'

Here Frank's father interjected.

'Ach, come on, Brendan, you're not saying that Protestants have it as bad as Catholics? You only have to look at unemployment and the housing situation to see who's looking after who.'

'No, no. I'm not saying that Protestants have been discriminated against the same way as Catholics. Nobody in their right mind would try to claim that,' Brendan reassured him. And, once he had visibly relaxed in his seat again, he continued: 'But the odd job here and there or pushing a name to the top of a housing list is the Ascendancy's way of keeping them under control. It's crumbs off the table, that's all. And letting them, not encouraging them, to run around on the Twelfth of July making mayhem is another way of making them feel that they're part of the establishment when the truth is they're just as disenfranchised as the rest of us.'

Brendan sat back in his chair, nodding his head sagely. He had a very persuasive way of talking, but Frank's father wasn't altogether convinced.

'I follow your logic all right, Brendan, and I know you'll not mind me saying I don't entirely agree with it. I think one lot's just as bad as the other. But, just out of curiosity, if what you say is true, what's to be done about it?'

'That's why we need a political movement that will appeal to all working-class people regardless of religion, make it non-denominational.'

'But, Brendan,' interrupted Frank, 'religion's all people in this country care about. They couldn't care less about socialism, the proletariat, or whatever you call it, and the rest of it. No Protestant is going to stand back and see Catholics getting equal treatment let alone help them. They're so afraid of losing what they have that they're terrified to concede anything. And anyway, since when have you been for Catholics and Protestants getting together?'

Ignoring the last remark, Brendan went on. 'I hear what you're saying, Frank, and, yes, maybe they are frightened. That's why we need to educate people, Protestants and Catholics alike. They won't be able to deny the facts once they understand what's been going on.'

No one heard Mary open the door.

116

'You're all very serious in here,' she scolded. 'Is that any way to be talking on my brother's wedding day?'

Suitably admonished, Brendan took the lead and proposed a toast. 'Here's to Frank and Theresa: health, happiness and lots of children.'

Frank's father joined in the drinking of the toast enthusiastically.

It didn't seem real to Frank. Everything felt as though it was happening to someone else and he was just an observer, looking on. Indifferent.

'I'm just going to get Ma up for the car will be here in half an hour,' said Mary, retreating from the room.

'No, I'll do it. Let me. You have a seat here and talk to Brendan,' said Frank.

Upstairs, he tapped gently on the door of his parents' bedroom and pushing it open, he entered. Ella lay on her side in the bed, her back to the door.

'Ma, it's me. Time to get up now. The car will be here soon.'

Frank shook Ella gently by the shoulder and sat down in the chair by the bed.

She rolled over, slowly, and smiled when she saw it was Frank.

'You'll need to get up, Ma. Have you much to do?'

'No, son. I was up and washed at eight. I only have to put on my dress and brush my hair. Mary's a good girl; she has it all ready for me,' she said, pointing to a dress with large blue and green flowers all over it, hanging on the outside of the wardrobe. On the chest of drawers was a peacock blue hat and matching handbag. A pair of freshly polished shoes sat on the floor.

'I just wanted a nap so that I was at my best for the day ahead.'

'Well, then, I'd best leave you to get on with it,' said Frank and rose as if to leave.

'No, wait a minute, Frank. I want to talk to you.'

Frank sat down again, obediently. Ella held her hand outstretched, palm upwards, until Frank placed his in hers. Then she closed her fingers tightly round his hand and closed her eyes. She sighed and smiled and opened her eyes.

'I love you very much, son, and I just want to say that I know Theresa is the right girl for you. I love her like she was my own daughter. She'll make you happy. I know she will.'

Frank looked down at the floor. The same way you knew Helen Simpson wasn't the right girl, he thought.

'I knew that one day you'd have to leave me,' his mother continued, 'to get married, I mean, and I'm glad it's Theresa you're going to. I won't have to worry about you.' She paused, then added significantly, ' — or your children.'

And Frank knew full well what she meant. He'd tried to come to terms with his children not being brought up Catholics and something inside him baulked. For his faith was integral to his identity and he could not countenance denying his children that privilege. Without the faith they would be strangers to him, their souls, like his, damned for eternity.

118

'I'm glad you like her, Ma. She's a good girl and I know she's fond of you.'

Ella gripped Frank's hand, hard.

'You are happy, son, aren't you?'

'Of course I am, Ma, just pre-wedding nerves, I think. I'll let you get on,' he replied and he kissed her softly on the forehead and went out quietly.

Frank crept back into his own room and sat on the edge of the bed trying to work out what was going on inside his head. He didn't feel nervous; in fact he wasn't sure he felt very much at all. It all seemed so surreal. He heard the springs of the bed creaking in the other room as his mother got up and, down below, the loud voices of his best man and father continuing their debate. What concerned him was that he had thought of Helen on this, of all days, for God's sake.

It hadn't been easy after they broke up. Frank's misery was alleviated only by the fact that his mother started to pick up soon after and, since then, had regained a lot of her strength. And he knew that her recovery was in some small way helped along by news of his engagement to Theresa. A relationship which won her full approval.

In a strange way the break-up with Helen had brought some peace of mind to Frank. For he could not overcome the fact that she was a Protestant. His mother merely gave voice to the reservations that festered within him; Frank's religious convictions were deep-rooted.

He took great solace in the weekly rituals of

mass, communion and confession. All of these, he reminded himself, would have been denied him if he'd married Helen, just as surely as if he'd been excommunicated. The Church would've turned its back on him. He'd seen it happen before to people who married outside the faith. No single act was more abhorrent to the Irish Catholic Church.

With Theresa there would be family rosaries, instruction in catechism for the children, First Holy Communions, First Confessions and Confirmations to celebrate. All the significant milestones that formed the bedrock of a Catholic home.

At first he resented Theresa, blaming her for what had happened between them. As time went on though his anger lessened and he admitted to himself that he was as much to blame as she was. And marriage offered them both the remedy for the mortal sin they had committed.

In the months that followed Frank grew fond of Theresa, although ironically, given their history, the attraction wasn't primarily physical. He enjoyed talking with her in much the same way as he did with his mother and, when she said she loved him he was, eventually, able to reply truthfully that he loved her too. A different sort of love than he had experienced before. A more restrained love built on companionship and respect and shared values. One that would last, his mother said.

No, he wouldn't think about Helen anymore, nor dwell on the past. What they had was special, he knew that, but, on reflection, it seemed more of an infatuation than the mature relationship he shared with Theresa. And they had so much in common: religion, traditions, memories of school, friends, even distant relations. Frank told himself he was looking forward to his new life with Theresa, especially since it carried his mother's blessing.

The squeals of children outside announced the arrival of the wedding limousine. Few people in the street had cars and the sight of a gleaming black Austin Princess Sheerline, stately and majestic, on Mill Lane was quite a spectacle. Frank thought it a bit extravagant as the chapel was only a ten-minute walk away, but Ella insisted that, on her eldest son's wedding day, they would all travel in style. Ella, his father and Mary were to go first and the car would come back for the groom and best man. Frank rose from the bed and, putting a spring in his step, went downstairs to see off the first car-load.

* * *

On their way home from a long day out in Bangor, Helen asked John to pull into a carpark along the Coast Road at Carrickfergus. At this time you could pretty much guarantee that it would be deserted, save for courting couples out in their father's car.

Tonight was no exception and, as John pulled in slowly, careful to avoid spraying gravel on the paintwork, only one other car was evident, discreetly parked at the far corner. John seemed to be driving towards it.

'No, not over there, John. Over here, away from that car. We can look out over the sea.'

The sky was completely clear leaving the moonbeams free to roam on the night air, skimming brilliantly over the water and caressing the contours of the car bonnet.

When he had applied the hand-brake and switched off the engine John turned to her, the right side of his long face bathed in blue light, the other shrouded in darkness.

'What do you want to stop here for, Helen? Shouldn't we be getting back?'

This was going to be harder than Helen thought. Sometimes she thought John was stupid. Did he want her to draw him a diagram? She inched over towards him, a manoeuvre made easier by the bench seat that stretched from one side of the car to the other.

'I just wanted to look at the sea in the moonlight,' she said, snuggling up beside him. 'Isn't it romantic?'

'Well, yes, I suppose so. Your Mum and Dad will be worried, Helen.'

'Not when I'm with you, John, they don't worry.'

That seemed to please him and she saw the side of his mouth turn up in a smile.

'I'm a bit cold, John.'

Her new summer dress, made specially for the occasion, had been cool and comfortable during the day, but now, with bare legs and nothing but a thin cardigan over her shoulders, she was genuinely feeling the cold.

'Do you want me to switch the engine back

on? It'll still be warm. Here, we can have the heater on in a jiffy,' he replied, thrusting the key in the ignition.

'No, don't,' Helen cried out quickly. Then, lowering her voice, 'Why don't you hold me instead?'

'If you like.'

He put his arm around her shoulder awkwardly and she nuzzled in under his arm. She could feel his heart pounding, the rhythm picking up as she rubbed her left hand lightly over his chest, making occasional forays down across his stomach, careful that her little finger extended far enough to brush the waistband of his trousers. Her right hand rested on John's back and she could feel his shirt dampening with sweat as his body temperature rose.

'Kiss me, John,' she whispered, turning her face up towards him.

He didn't need encouragement now and pressed his lips firmly on hers. After a few moments, Helen pushed the tip of her tongue between his resisting lips and found his. They jousted for a little while, she teasing, him chasing, until she deliberately retreated back into her mouth willing him to follow.

All of a sudden, his tongue burst through her lips and probed hungry and deep in her mouth, John moaning all the while. He knelt up on the seat and clasped her face in both his hands. Helen allowed her body to slide backwards and pulled him gently down on top of her. John was writhing on her now, pushing with his rigid penis against her belly through the thin fabric of her dress, hurting her.

Surprised, Helen found herself responding to his excitement. Between her legs began to throb exquisitely, almost painfully. Her pelvis rose and fell, matching John's thrusts, both of them now panting and gasping while he continued to explore her mouth, even more urgently than before.

This was it, then. The moment Helen had been waiting for. Earlier, when they'd stopped for their tea at a hotel in Bangor, she'd taken off her knickers in the ladies loo and stuffed them in her handbag. Fleetingly, she worried about staining her dress. Then, purposefully, she groped down and began to stroke the shaft of John's penis through his trousers. He was very hard and the moaning had become a painful groan. She found his zip and began to pull it down.

'No, Helen, we mustn't.'

John went to pull away but Helen wouldn't release his mouth, pushing her tongue round the inside of his lips, feeling his teeth.

'Let me take it out, John. I just want to touch it. Please, John.'

This time, when she tried his fly he didn't resist and his cock popped out almost unaided into her hand. The hot rigid flesh thrashed about like a fish out of water and Helen could feel, alternatively, dampness at the tip and wiry hair at the bottom as she ran her hand up and down. She reckoned she must be doing it right because John cried out 'Yes!' every now and again.

As John slid on top of her, her dress had

ridden up almost to the top of her thighs. While one hand continued to massage his dick, she yanked her skirt up to her waist. John seemed completely unaware of what she was doing. Helen had worried about this bit for, whilst she knew the mechanics of sex, she could never visualise exactly how it was accomplished. But she needn't have been concerned; instinctively, she knew what to do.

She pushed down on John's shoulders, firmly, so that his cock slid down her belly and she stopped pushing when the tip was just between her legs. She wondered if she would have to use her hand to guide him in, but she hadn't anticipated being so wet nor the eagerness of his cock. Suddenly the top of his penis, hard like rubber, was stroking her, wallowing in her juices and, then, pounding blindly against her.

Helen was no longer aware of John, only of this insistent beast thrilling her, making her whimper and cry out. The pit of her stomach was throbbing rhythmically in time with its thrusts and she was aware of a pulsating sensation on the outside of her vagina. She felt herself open up and take it, no suck it, in.

'There, it's done,' she thought, lying with the back of her head on the car seat.

The thrilling sensation had given way to numbness and she watched John dispassion-ately, pumping away, his face contorted as if in agony. He was leaning on his arms and he looked, not at her face, but down between her legs watching himself go in and out. Helen turned her face towards the glove box and wished he would hurry up.

She thought of Frank and his bride on this, their honeymoon night, in a seedy hotel somewhere in Ballycastle or maybe even as far afield as Donegal in the Free State. She saw them in an empty dining room, candles and wine on the table, and soon after, Frank leading Theresa up to their room. They were probably in bed now, the sheets thrown back, Frank's lithe body glistening with sweat as he fucked his new wife, lying there inert and anaemic beneath him. She could hear him whisper 'I love you, Theresa,' and bitter tears crept out of the corners of her eyes.

'Oh, darling, don't cry. Did I hurt you? Oh, Helen, I'm so sorry. I love you, darling, I love you. Please forgive me.'

John was finished and Helen hadn't even noticed. She felt something warm running out of her and her buttocks were sticky against the cool leather below.

'I'm not crying John,' she lied. 'I'm just so happy.'

'You're not sorry are you, Helen?' he asked hesitatingly, leaning over and searching her face anxiously.

'No, John, no. Not at all.'

That seemed to reassure him.

'Good, because neither am I, Helen. I know we should have waited until we were married but I love you so much I just couldn't help it. You're so beautiful. You don't feel as though I've taken advantage of you?'

'No, John.'

126

'Well, that's it then. We'll have to get married now.'

John was grinning at her, ecstatic. This was not the first time marriage had been talked about, though before she had avoided giving him a straight answer.

John continued as she knew he would.

'Helen,' he said, 'will you marry me?'

This time, she replied, 'Yes, John, I will.'

7

Summer 1977

It was the first week of the summer holidays; eight long weeks stretched ahead of Catherine before she started her first year at the Grammar School. She sat on the red brick wall in front of the house with Michael. The road between the straight rows of semi-detached council houses had been re-surfaced the day before. The black tarmac glistened wet and sticky in the hot sun making it impossible for the children to play their usual street games. Normally busy, the road was deserted. Catherine and Michael squinted in the bright sunlight and considered their options.

'What will we do?' asked Catherine.

'Do you want to go the beach?'

Catherine thought of the lovely golden sand at Ballygally, but that was four miles away and they had no money for the bus. Yesterday they'd made do with the grey shingle of Drains Bay and not an ice cream or chip shop in sight. Besides her arms were still sunburnt from the day before.

'I don't think so. My arms are sore,' she replied, looking down at the long sleeves of the white shirt Mammy had made her wear to protect her arms from further damage.

'I know,' said Michael, his eyes lighting up, 'let's go to the Quarry.'

The Quarry was right on the edge of

Ballyfergus before the open countryside began and the road that took you the twenty miles to Ballymena.

'Daddy said we weren't to go. He said it was dangerous.'

'But he's at work. We'll be there and back before he gets home.'

'He said the farmer doesn't like trespassers, that he'll hound us.'

'Oh, Catherine stop being such a scaredy cat! You don't always have to do what you're told you know.'

Slightly hurt, Catherine was silent for some moments then asked, 'What about Mammy?'

'That's easy; we'll just tell her we're going somewhere else. No-one will know where we've really gone. We can explore that old house and secret cave we found last time,' coaxed Michael.

Catherine hesitated but the attractions of the Quarry outweighed the drawbacks both of disobeying Daddy and lying to Mammy.

'All right then,' she said at last, giving in.

'I'll tell Mammy we're going to look at the farm,' said Michael springing to his feet.

He returned minutes later with something hidden under his jumper.

'Come on,' he urged Catherine and she ran down the road after him.

He disappeared through a hole in the hedge and was halfway across the field that lay behind their 1960's red-brick housing estate when Catherine caught up with him.

'What have you got under your jumper?' she asked, as they trudged across the springy grass.

129

Michael produced a brown paper bag.

'A secret,' he said. 'I'll show you when we get to the cave.'

They had the exit to the Quarry in sight when Catherine saw the cows. Two of them looked up, and started to amble slowly across the field towards them. Catherine froze in terror, heart pounding and mouth dry.

'What is it?' asked Michael, following Catherine's terrified gaze.

'Oh, the cows. Come on,' he said, taking her by the hand. 'They're not going to hurt you. They're just curious. Look!' he shouted and waved his free arm high above his head.

The cows stopped dead in their tracks.

'See, they're afraid of me!'

With Catherine in tow Michael marched confidently past the ugly beasts who ignored them completely, chewing glumly and flicking flies off their hindquarters with their tails.

Catherine felt safe under Michael's protection and clung tightly to his hand. She didn't let her breath out until they were safely on the other side of the fence. Then she laughed and ran off down the path.

After a couple of hundred yards Catherine stopped in front of a hole in a limestone outcrop, partially hidden by overhanging trees and brambles.

'Come on!' she shouted to Michael, as she dropped to her knees and disappeared inside.

They crawled along the narrow tunnel smelling of sweet, wet earth and Catherine felt the dampness seep through the knees of her

130

trousers. Mammy would kill her. After twenty feet or so the soil gave way to rock, cold and dry.

Catherine whispered to Michael, 'We're here. Turn the torch on.'

They surveyed the cave, wide enough for both children to sit cross-legged on the floor, but not high enough to stand. Stalactites hung from the roof of the cave and, in the middle of the floor, was the black remains of a fire.

'We're lucky there wasn't any rain last night,' said Michael, grateful that the cave was dry.

'What's the secret then?' asked Catherine.

'You'll see,' Michael replied mysteriously, tipping the contents of the paper bag onto the hard limestone floor. A large battery, wire, two boxes of matches, bits of newspaper and pellets from a toy gun.

'I'm going to make a bomb.'

'A bomb! What for?'

'Just to see if it works.'

Michael set about scraping the heads off the matches onto a piece of newspaper. Catherine joined him.

'Where did you find out how to do this?' she asked.

'Some of the boys at school. They said that's how the IRA started out. Making bombs at home.'

When they'd finished scraping off all the match heads Michael added the gunpowder from the pellets and scrunched the package up tight, two ends of wire sticking into it. He attached one wire to a terminal on the battery, and held the other one ready to do the same.

131

'This is it! Stand back in case it explodes!'

He touched the other terminal on the battery with the wire in his hand. There was a little puff, the package caught fire and then, after a few seconds, fizzled out.

'It worked! It worked!' said Michael, clapping his hands.

He then set about examining the charred remains of the experiment.

'Michael, don't do that again,' said Catherine gravely.

'Why not?'

'I don't like it, that's all. Promise me. Somebody could get hurt.'

Michael looked at her face.

'You are scared, aren't you. What is it?'

'It reminds me of those people in Belfast on TV. In bombs. With cuts on their faces and blood all over them.'

Catherine shuddered at the memory of the images. Sometimes they didn't show you pictures of the wounded and Mammy said that was because they were so badly burnt or injured. And sometimes there were no wounded at all, just pictures from a distance of dead people being carried away on stretchers covered in white sheets.

'Promise me you won't do it again. Please,' said Catherine as she grabbed Michael's arm.

'Okay, okay, I promise, if it makes you happy. Anyway it wasn't very good, was it?'

When hunger told them it must be teatime they emerged stiff-legged from the cave and set off for home. Michael was already over the fence between the Quarry and the field, and Catherine balanced on top of it, when they heard a shout some way behind them.

'I told you little buggers to stay off my land,' the voice yelled.

'Jump, Catherine, jump,' screamed Michael. 'He's got a gun!'

Before she had time to think Catherine leapt off the fence and ran as fast as she could. All fear of the cows was gone. She imagined a man chasing after them, his long sturdy legs gaining on them every second. Soon he would be upon them. Somehow, she found extra reserves of energy and put them into her stride. She ran so hard that her cheeks shook violently and her eyes rattled in her head, making them water and blur her vision. He was going to kill them. He would shoot them with his gun. Daddy was right. They should have listened to him.

'Stop!' she heard Michael shout after her. 'He's gone.'

Catherine slowed down slightly and, disbelieving, looked over her shoulder. There was no-one there, only Michael, hands on hips gasping for breath. She stumbled to a halt, collapsed on her knees and couldn't speak for some minutes. Terror still coursed through her veins.

'He was going to kill us,' she gasped as Michael came alongside and threw himself down on the grass beside her.

'He wouldn't have killed us, silly. He only had a pellet gun.'

'A pellet gun?'

'It doesn't fire real bullets. Just hard pellets

like dried peas. They sting like hell but they can't kill you.'

'Yes they can, Michael,' said Catherine, speaking rapidly. 'You hear about people getting killed all the time by rubber bullets. And they're not supposed to kill you either.'

Michael regarded her for a few moments and his expression changed from amusement to concern.

'It's all right, Catherine,' he said softly. 'We're safe now. Come on, let's go home.'

He stood up, held out his hand and pulled Catherine to her feet.

They trudged the rest of the way home in silence. Catherine's terror gradually subsided to be replaced with a vague sense of unease. Michael was different somehow. How did he know about bombs and pellet guns? There were things he was not telling her, things he was hearing at St Pat's. And though she couldn't have said exactly why, she worried for him.

*   *   *

'Time to get up,' said Mammy coming into the bedroom. But Catherine had been awake for a long time.

Mammy pulled back the curtains and looked at Catherine's brand new school uniform laid out neatly on the chair at the bottom of her bed.

'I just hope that sister of yours follows in your footsteps,' she said, frowning, 'so that she gets the good of these clothes. Otherwise it's a lot of expense wasted.'

134

'It's not wasted, not if I wear them,' said Catherine, annoyed that Mammy was finding fault. Taking the fun out of her first day at the Grammar.

'Your brothers never got new clothes for St Pat's. Sean had to make do with hand-me-downs from his cousins and that's what Michael wore as well when the time came.'

'I know that,' said Catherine, guilt threatening to eclipse her excitement.

'Still I suppose there's no point going on about it,' continued Mammy more cheerily. 'That's what comes of having a clever girl in the family.'

Geraldine sat up in the bed opposite and rubbed her eyes.

'You'll be okay walking to school on your own?' asked Catherine.

Geraldine nodded bravely and Catherine felt a pang of guilt for the second time that morning. At least she had Moira to accompany her to school.

Thinking of Moira made her leap out of bed. They'd arranged to meet at the bottom of the road and it wouldn't do to be late on the first day!

She was there first and minutes later Moira's mop of curly red hair came into view, bobbing up and down as she came running down the hill.

'Sorry I'm late. I couldn't get this jerkin-thingy on,' said Moira, pulling at a shapeless navy tunic underneath her blazer. 'And the tie took forever!'

'Me too,' said Catherine, who'd spent a full

135

fifteen minutes in front of the bathroom mirror refusing all offers of help, determined to do the navy and green striped tie all by herself.

'So, what do you think of the uniform?' said Moira, turning round slowly, her nose in the air.

Catherine laughed.

'I like it,' she said, running her eye approvingly over Moira and then down at herself. 'It makes me feel very . . . very grown up!'

'Oh, Catherine, aren't you excited?'

'Yeah, I am. I don't know, though. I feel a bit funny too.'

'What do you mean?'

'Well, there's hardly any Catholics go to the Grammar. Everyone else has gone on to St Pat's or St Margaret's. Sean says the Grammar's 95 per cent Protestant. You don't think anyone will pick on us?'

Moira laughed.

'I don't think so and anyway, they can say what they like.'

She burst into song. 'Sticks and stones can break my bones but words will never harm me,' she chanted and skipped off down the road.

She stopped a little further down and waited for Catherine, rolling her big blue eyes as if to say 'hurry up'.

'You take people too much to heart you know, Catherine. Half the time they say things to wind you up. Just ignore them. Anyway, I'm sure there'll be lots of nice people there. And that aside, the Grammar gets really good results. Everyone gets at least eight O-levels and they all do A-levels as well.'

'That's good,' replied Catherine, thinking that the Grammar sounded like the sort of place that would fit in very well with her plans. 'You know Moira, we could even go to university.'

'Yeah, right,' said Moira sarcastically.

'No, seriously. Apparently the government give you grants to go if you're not well off.'

'Don't you have to be dead brainy?'

'Well if we got into the Grammar we must be bright enough.'

'Look we're nearly there,' interrupted Moira as the lichen-covered slate roof of the school came into view and Catherine's tummy churned.

She hadn't expected to be so nervous. She thought back to the Open Day in June when all the new pupils, with their parents, went to the school to look round and talk to the teachers. She remembered she would be in Inver House, whatever that meant.

'What House are you in, Moira?'

'Drumbrae. You?'

'Inver.'

'Oh, I was hoping we would be in together.'

'So was I,' said Catherine. 'What exactly does it mean, anyway? Being in a 'House'.'

'It's just a way of splitting classes up for teams on sports day and that sort of thing. And each House sits together in assembly.'

'Does that mean we won't get to sit together?' said Catherine, dismayed. 'We're not even going to be in the same class.'

' 'Fraid not. But we can meet up at breaktime and lunchtime.'

'I'd like that.'

'Me too,' said Moira.

Soon they reached the school gates and, glancing apprehensively at each other, they approached the red brick building, green ivy almost completely covering the front wall. At the very top of the edifice, where the ivy hadn't quite reached, Catherine read '1897'. A girl wearing a badge that said 'Prefect' on it waved them over to a side entrance.

'You first years?'

Catherine and Moira looked at each other and nodded.

'Go up the stairs, turn left and someone will show you where to leave your coats and bags.'

The two girls set off and she called after them, cheerily, 'Welcome to the Grammar!'

Inside the assembly hall they were met by hundreds of navy blue blazers squirming in seats. Catherine suddenly felt very small and vulnerable. Someone directed them to the front of the hall, Moira to the seats on the right, Catherine to the left.

'See you later,' said Moira as she turned into an aisle and the only friendly face disappeared from Catherine's view.

★　★　★

Sitting in her allotted seat in assembly that first morning Jayne was a bit overwhelmed by the sheer number of boys and girls at the big school. But she recognised quite a few of them from church and she knew all of Eddie's friends as well. Amongst the first years, there were many familiar faces too from Jayne's primary school. And she knew the headmaster, Mr Wilson, for he'd been to their house with Mrs Wilson on several occasions.

So, although in one sense everything was new to Jayne, in another she felt very much at home. She'd no doubt this was the right and natural place for her to be, amongst people she knew, people like herself. And that was comforting; to be sure of who and what you were. Jayne reached inside her shirt collar and pulled out her locket. Straining the chain, she bent her chin against her neck so that she could read the inscription again and enjoyed once more the warm rush of pride that came when she read the words.

But these pleasurable reflections were interrupted by thoughts more unsettling. What if she couldn't live up to Mum and Dad's expectations? She knew she wasn't as bright as everyone thought. Passing the Eleven-Plus had been a fluke, she was sure of it. A lucky break. Perhaps even a mistake; her papers must have got mixed up with those of someone much brighter than she was. Jayne gnawed anxiously at the ragnail on her left thumb.

In her other hand the locket felt like a dead weight. She swiftly returned it inside her shirt collar and it fell against her skin, cold and heavy.

A girl with long, brown hair held back in a band sat down beside Jayne. 'Hello, my name's Jayne Alexander,' she said, glad of the distraction.

'I'm Catherine Meehan,' replied the girl, allowing herself a brief smile and lowering her gaze under sweeping black eyelashes.

Jayne stole a sideways glance at the girl beside her, who sat bolt upright in her chair with a grave expression on her face. Jayne could tell by the flush in her pale cheeks and the way she glanced nervously around that she was overwhelmed by it all.

She decided that it was only right and Christian to put her at her ease. The girl obviously didn't know anyone; maybe they could be friends.

'What Primary School did you come from?' she asked as an opener.

'St. Mary's,' said the pretty rosebud mouth, her lips very pink against flawless white skin.

'Oh,' said Jayne stupidly, for she didn't know what to say next. The girl was a Catholic; she should have known. The name was a give away. Taig. Fenian. Nationalist. Republican. IRA. Sinn Fein. Traitor. Popery. Everything Jayne knew, thought she knew, or had ever heard about Catholics ran through her head in a matter of seconds. She'd no idea what half of these terms meant, but they flooded unbidden out of a memory she didn't even know she had. She found herself checking Catherine's eyes. Were they close together? Not so you'd notice. Her nose was a little large and her brow a little narrow but all in all she was very striking.

'What about you?' she heard the girl ask, relaxing.

'Riverdale.'

Jayne could tell by the flicker in the dark brown eyes that the information had been

140

registered and processed: Jayne was a Protestant. At least that was out of the way and they both knew where they stood. Anxious to move on from the awkward silence, Jayne thought she'd better say something.

'What class are you in?' she asked brightly.

'IB.'

'Me too.'

There was no reason why they couldn't be friendly. Then Jayne remembered Dad saying that only Catholics who passed the Eleven-Plus came to the Grammar.

'What did you get for passing your Eleven-Plus?' she asked eagerly.

Catherine thought for a moment.

'What do you mean?'

'Presents? Money?' asked Jayne hopefully.

Catherine shook her head slowly, appearing not to understand.

'Everybody gets things for passing their Eleven-Plus. Here,' said Jayne fishing for the chain around her neck. She pulled out the locket and thrust it under Catherine's nose. 'I got this from Mum and Dad and a watch from my Nana as well as forty pounds. Oh, and I nearly forgot, a box of Milk Tray from my brother, Eddie. So, what did you get?' she gushed, conscious that she was babbling on whilst Catherine listened wide-eyed.

There was a pause and Catherine bit her lip. She seemed undecided what to say. For a second Jayne was sure she was going to speak and then she closed her mouth without saying a word. Then, at length, Catherine spoke.

'Nothing,' she said quietly, and looked down into her lap, the faint flush in her cheeks deepening to a crimson red.

'Surely you must have gotten something?' said Jayne, incredulous.

No answer. Jayne frowned and thought what a strange secretive girl. Of course she probably wouldn't have gotten as much as Jayne, no-one at Riverdale had, but Jayne didn't look down on people for that. She was the bank manager's daughter and that meant, naturally, she got bigger and better presents than her friends. It was just the way things were.

Jayne was about to interrogate Catherine again when another, awful, thought struck her. What if Catherine really didn't get anything? Generally speaking, Catholics weren't as well off as Protestants. She often heard Dad say how they couldn't stick at anything and, of all the shopowners and publicans and businessmen Dad knew, none of them were Catholics. And Dad knew everybody who was anybody in Ballyfergus.

Jayne suddenly realised the truth; when Catherine said nothing, she really meant it. A sense of deep shame swept over her. How could she have been so thoughtless? She was trying desperately to think of something to say to rescue the situation when Catherine spoke again.

'That's just bribery. If you're smart you don't need presents to make you do well. You do it for yourself and no-one else,' she said defiantly, looking Jayne straight in the eye. Her cheeks were still flushed red, but her dark pupils glinted cool and hard as steel.

Jayne opened her mouth to argue. People gave you things because they loved you and when she sat the Eleven-Plus exam she hadn't known that she would be rewarded for passing. But if she tried to explain it would sound like Catherine's Mum and Dad didn't love her. So she said nothing.

Catherine almost sighed with relief when, all of a sudden, everyone rose to their feet and a hush fell upon the assembly. The Headmaster and Headmistress, like great owls in their billowing black robes, walked onto the stage. Behind them came a minister all in black and a big girl and boy, both in school uniform. The Headmaster went over to a lectern and the others on the stage sat down on red plastic chairs. At the same time there was a rustle as pupils in the rows behind took their seats and Catherine quickly copied them.

The headmaster surveyed the room slowly.

'Welcome, boys and girls to another year at Ballyfergus Grammar,' he said. 'I hope you have all enjoyed your long holidays and that at least some of your leisure time was devoted to improving and productive activities. I would especially like to welcome those of you who are joining us for the first time this morning.'

He paused and peered purposefully over the top of his half-moon shaped reading glasses at the front rows.

'You have come here not just to excel in your schoolwork but to make new friends and, I hope, leave with happy memories of your schooldays.

We aim to send you out, older and wiser than you are now, with a valuable contribution to make to the world at large. We expect you, whatever your ability, to do your very best at all times and in all areas, whether academically or on the sports field.

'Now,' he continued, addressing the wider assembly, 'it is time to turn our minds to the business of learning and to concentrate on what we have to do this year. Some of you will be taking examinations in June and, whether you are studying for O- or A-levels, my message to you is the same. Your future depends on how well you do in these exams and I would encourage you to work hard and do your very best. The pass rate this year was excellent and I want to see those results exceeded next year.'

He went on to talk about changes that had taken place, teachers moved on and new ones come in their place. The two pupils were introduced as the new Head Boy and Head Girl and a ripple of clapping filled the hall. Catherine thought that she would, one day, like to be up there on the receiving end of that applause.

Then the headmaster paused as he turned the pages of a book that lay on the lectern. 'Please turn to Hymn 319 on page sixty-four.'

Catherine fumbled through the hymn book handed to her on arrival and found the page, but she didn't recognise the hymn. She mouthed the words but it was hard to keep in time with everyone and she hoped nobody noticed. The singing went on for some minutes which gave Catherine a chance to try and quell the emotions

144

raging in her breast.

Trust her to sit down beside a snotty cow like Jayne Alexander. All she could talk about was money and the things she got for passing her Eleven-Plus. Catherine possessed no real jewellery, only childish earrings and necklaces made from plastic beads, and it took all her self-control not to rip the locket from Jayne's throat. Waving it under her nose like that. Rubbing it in.

It hadn't occurred to her that people got presents for passing exams and so she had been caught out unprepared. Normally she would have had a well-rehearsed list all ready. She felt the heat return to her cheeks as the embarrassment welled up again and she fought hard to clear the mist that threatened to condense in her eyes. Why couldn't she get the same things as everyone else? Jayne Alexander would tell everybody and they would all be talking about her, laughing behind her back.

The singing ground slowly to a halt and the minister approached the lectern.

'We are gathered here today to give thanks to the Lord our God for the bountiful blessings he has bestowed upon us; our families and friends, our teachers, good health and this magnificent school with all the facilities available to each and every one of you to excel in your chosen field. Let us pray.'

Catherine inched forward to the edge of the plastic seat in preparation for kneeling when she noticed that no-one else had moved. Instead, they sat where they were, heads bowed and eyes closed. From the end of the row the housemaster gave Catherine a sharp glance. She quickly sat back in her seat and copied the others. Everything was so strange yet everyone else seemed, instinctively, to know what to do. A mumbled chorus went up from the crowd.

'Our Father, who art in heaven, Hallowed be thy name . . .'

'At last,' thought Catherine, 'something I know,' and she joined in enthusiastically.

When the prayer came to the end, ' . . . but deliver us from evil. Amen,' she stopped.

But everyone else kept praying, something about the kingdom, the power and the glory. Opening her eyes, Catherine looked round, confused. Jayne was watching her with a questioning look on her face. Then they were on their feet again and in the commotion Jayne asked, 'What's the matter?'

Catherine didn't want her to see that she was ruffled.

'That bit at the end of the Our Father,' she said casually, 'What's that all about?'

Jayne looked puzzled and then her face brightened.

'Oh, you mean The Lord's Prayer? What about it?'

The singing started, another hymn Catherine had never heard before. All of a sudden, Jayne covered her hand with her mouth and bent her head. Her whole frame shook as she tried to suppress a fit of giggles. She was laughing at her, Catherine was sure of it. She clenched the hymn book so tightly she felt sure she would break the spine. At the same time, a pain, like a mortal wound, began to ache in her chest and filled her heart with misery.

The hymn finished, the entourage filed off the stage and Catherine headed immediately for the exit at the front of the hall.

'Catherine. Wait. Catherine!' she heard Jayne call, but she pretended not to hear. She wove her way through pupils who greeted each other as though the summer had been years long instead of months. She stood on her tiptoes and searched anxiously for Moira amongst the crowd, but she was nowhere to be seen. Catherine felt very alone.

Only two at a time could pass through the exit and soon the stream of pupils ground to a halt. Catherine stood impatiently, waiting her turn.

She thought she heard someone whisper, 'Fenian', but shook her head in disbelief. Catherine had no idea what Fenian meant but she knew it wasn't nice; it was an insult. Sometimes Protestant schoolboys shouted it across the street at you on your way home from school.

Then it came again, louder this time and close enough for Catherine to be sure it was meant for her. She spun round. Two boys looked down, innocently, at their toecaps, hands in pockets. She couldn't be sure it was them. Could she have imagined it? She faced the exit again and inched forward a few feet.

'Fenian. Fenian.'

The word was sung more than spoken, a hiss more than a whisper, just loud enough for Catherine to hear and no-one else. She passed close by a female teacher and thought of reporting them. But what would she say? These two boys are calling me names? They would deny it and the teacher would think she was making it up.

Even if she believed her, she might think she was making a fuss about nothing. She might even side with the boys against her. Moira was always saying she took things too much to heart. And so she filed out quietly, her misery complete.

She'd been right to have doubts. She'd allowed herself to indulge in fantasies that she might find friends here, that she would be accepted because she was clever and bright. But she'd been shunned and humiliated because of who and what she was. The name-calling didn't bother Catherine so much as Jayne Alexander with her airs and graces making it obvious that she didn't belong, wasn't wanted. And Jayne had laughed at her, an insult so grievous, Catherine's face flushed hot with indignation at the thought.

She reminded herself why she was here — to get the best exam results possible. To expect more was only to invite disappointment and rejection.

By the time she'd found her way to the history class for the first lesson of the day, Catherine had worked out a strategy. It was best, she decided, to keep her distance; the less people knew about her, the better. That way she would be protected from scorn and ridicule. She was, therefore, careful to ignore Jayne Alexander when she walked into the classroom.

Catherine sat as far away from her as possible and maintained a dignified calm. She managed to avoid her during the next class, but at breaktime, as they filed out of the temporary mobile that housed the Geography class, Jayne caught up with her.

'Catherine, why did you rush off like that after assembly? I only wanted to tell you that Mr Spencer, the housemaster saw us . . . '

But Catherine cut her short.

'I just wanted to get to class that's all,' she said coolly. 'I'd better go now.'

She noticed with satisfaction the smile fade from Jayne's pretty face and, as Catherine ran across the playground and round the side of the biology labs, she wondered briefly what Jayne had been going to say. It doesn't matter anyway, she thought, for they would never be friends.

★ ★ ★

Daddy was sitting at the kitchen table 'doing the books' when Catherine arrived home. Mammy was sandwiched between the ironing board and the kitchen counter, a big mound of crumpled clothes, fresh off the line, beside her. She smiled distractedly at Catherine and returned to the laundry, her expression a familiar mix of concentration and irritation.

Catherine hated coming home in the middle of chores; invariably she got roped in to help but, even if she didn't, the disruption unsettled her and made it impossible to relax. She longed to come through the door after school and find

Mammy serene and happy and the house all clean and tidy. They would sit down and have a cup of tea and a fresh-baked scone and chat about the day's events. Then Mammy would say, 'Well, off you go and play. I'll get the dinner on.'

But it never happened like that. Mammy was always busy and she had a way of making Catherine feel guilty about the things she did for her and the others. If there were ever any scones made Mammy never seemed to take pleasure in the making, or the eating, and every mouthful tasted of her sacrifice.

Daddy looked up and said, 'How was your first day at school, love?'

'Okay,' replied Catherine, dropping her schoolbag by the door and wondering if there was something to eat.

'Just okay?' said Daddy, raising his eyebrows.

'Yeah.'

'Why don't you come over here and tell me all about it,' he persisted, pulling out a chair and indicating for Catherine to sit down.

'There, that's better. Now, did you make any new friends?'

Catherine relented and let it all spill out.

'No. I sat down beside this girl called Jayne in assembly and she was a snotty so-and-so. All she could talk about was how much money she got for passing the Eleven-Plus. And I didn't know any of the hymns or anything and she laughed at me.'

'Did she now. And why do you think she laughed at you?'

'I don't know.'

'How do you know she was laughing at you, then?'

'I just do. And these two boys called me names on the way out of assembly.'

'What sort of names?'

Catherine hesitated. The word sounded crude and vile. Dirty.

'Fenian.'

Daddy threw an accusing glance at Mammy.

'Is this what she's got to put up with at that Grammar of yours?' he snapped.

'What do you mean 'my Grammar'?' said Mammy.

'You know fine well what I mean. It was you who insisted she go to that bloody school.'

'I don't remember you objecting at the time.'

'What I think doesn't seem to count for anything in this house. You got your way as usual.'

'Now just a minute,' said Mammy slamming the iron end up into the metal rest. 'Where would you have had her go? St Pat's? Where she'd come out like the rest of them with no exams behind her and no future?'

'I don't like the Grammar,' interrupted Catherine close to tears. 'I don't want to go back.'

Daddy sighed and put his big hand on her shoulder.

'Now, now, pet. You don't want to take any notice of people like that. I'm sure there's lots of nice girls and boys there too; you just have to give them a chance. By the end of the week you won't want to be anywhere else. You'll see.'

Catherine nodded uncertainly, feeling a little better.

'I'll never be friends with that Jayne Alexander, though,' she said bitterly.

She thought Daddy flinched ever so slightly at the mention of the name 'Alexander' and he glanced furtively at Mammy. But she was absorbed, grim-faced, in her task and for some reason Catherine sensed not to say any more on the subject. Daddy returned to his papers.

'Can I have something to eat, please?' she said.

'You can have an apple,' replied Mammy. 'And while you're at it,' she continued, as Catherine got up from the table, 'can you please put that schoolbag away and get changed? And when you've done that you can give me a hand putting away this ironing.'

8

Wednesday afternoon was sports day; hockey for the girls, rugby for the boys. They assembled on the wet tarmac outside the school and there was lots of laughing and squealing. Everyone was very excited, including Catherine. When the teachers appeared, the boys and girls were separated and led off, crocodile fashion, out the school gates, across the road and up to the newly-built pavilion overlooking the sports pitch.

Inside, Mrs Watt, the PE teacher, blew the whistle that hung round her neck on a red cord.

'I want you changed and on the pitch in exactly one minute,' she said, looking at her watch. 'Now get a move on. Chop. Chop,' and she clapped her hands together.

A frenzy of activity followed, arms and legs flailing, as the first years struggled to get into the unfamiliar white airtex blouses, and pleated, wrap-around, navy skirts. Catherine noticed that most of the girls had old hockey sticks, battered and bruised, some with bandages of grubby tape wrapped round the handles. Surely, she thought, as they trooped out onto the hockey pitch, they weren't second-hand? Amanda, one of the girls in Catherine's class, ran alongside her.

'What position do you play?' she asked.

'What do you mean?' said Catherine.

'On the hockey pitch. What position do you play?'

'I don't,' said Catherine, 'I've never played before.'

'Oh, right. You'll have a lot to learn, then.'

She must have noticed Catherine's stunned expression for she added cheerfully, 'Don't worry. It's good fun!'

And then it dawned on Catherine. All the other girls, apart from her and Moira, played hockey at primary school. They weren't second-hand hockey sticks; they were well-used symbols of their proficiency on the hockey field, of battles won and lost. Catherine's heart sank as she looked down at the brand new stick in her right hand of which she'd been so proud. She'd been looking forward to this for, generally speaking, she was good at sport. Netball anyway.

She'd been Goal Shooter on the P7 team at St Mary's and they'd won the East Antrim cup. And after school, up on the pitch behind St Mary's, she'd played camogie, a traditional Irish field game for girls played with flat wooden sticks, and very few rules.

Well, it can't be that much different than camogie, thought Catherine, perking up. Both were played on a pitch, with a goal at each end, two teams chasing a ball with the objective of scoring goals. Just different rules, that's all, and, putting a skip into her step, she ran to catch up with Amanda.

Mrs Watt started by sending the girls round the pitch four times, at jogging pace, to warm up. Then they assembled for instruction. Mrs Watt demonstrated some techniques, which they all copied; pushing the stick along the ground to propel an imaginary ball and striking it, being careful that your stick didn't rise above shoulder level. This was different to camogie where you could swing the *camán* anyway you liked. 'Best achieved,' said Mrs Watt, 'by keeping your elbow crooked like this so that it's impossible to get the stick above your shoulder.'

It felt very unnatural and awkward to Catherine as she tried hard to mimic exactly the manoeuvre demonstrated by Mrs Watt. Then the PE teacher called them round in a semi-circle.

'For those of you who haven't played before,' she said, looking at Catherine and Moira who stood together, 'and those of you who have forgotten' she said, looking at the rest, 'here are the rules.'

She spoke loudly and slowly, enunciating her words carefully.

'I don't want to see anyone off-side. That means that I don't want to see anyone up the field ahead of the ball and ahead of fewer than three members of the opposing team. Raising the stick above the shoulder is illegal. You can stop the ball dead with your hand, like this,' she said, showing them the flat of her raised palm, 'but not advance it. Otherwise you can only touch the ball with this side of the stick.'

Mrs Watt rapped her knuckles on the flat side of the striking end of her own, well-worn stick.

'Except of course for the goalkeeper, who can kick the ball or stop it with her body but only while inside the striking circle.'

She waved her hand in the direction of the goalposts which reminded Catherine of football ones, long and low. The goals in camogie were more like rugby ones; one point was scored for hitting the *sliotar* over the crossbar, three points for driving it under. There seemed to be an awful lot of rules in hockey, far more than camogie, and Catherine was struggling to take it all in. She tuned in again to what Mrs Watt was saying.

' . . . must be scored from within the striking circle; otherwise they are disqualified. And own-goals don't count either. Raising the ball by undercutting it, as well as hooking an opponents stick, are also fouls. Finally, there is the obstruction rule: you're not allowed to obstruct an opponent by putting your stick or any part of your body between her and the ball. Or, for that matter, by running between the opponent and the ball. Any questions?'

Catherine had plenty of questions but everyone else just nodded so she said nothing. She glanced at Moira who raised her left eyebrow in a comical expression and shrugged her shoulders. It was obvious that she didn't have a clue either.

'Miss Tweedie will umpire this half of the field,' said Mrs Watt indicating the right side, 'and I'll umpire this half. And remember,' she concluded, 'hockey is a ladies' game so I want to see you all behaving properly.'

'Now, we'll need two teams of eleven. Ruth, you come here to my right, and you,' she said, pointing at a willowy girl with long mousey hair, 'sorry, what's your name?'

'Alison.'

'Right, Alison, you come here to my left. You

two can be captains. Now pick ten girls each, one at a time.'

Catherine was chosen very near the end by Alison and joined the small band gathered round her. The rest of the girls were sent to stand on the sidelines to watch, Moira amongst them. Miss Tweedie appeared with two sets of bibs, one blue, one red. Each bib had big white letters on the back which were meaningless to Catherine. They were dished out randomly and she found herself with a red FB bib.

'That means you're a full-back,' said Amanda helpfully. 'You're supposed to stay at the back of the pitch and help defend the goal and you're not allowed any further forward than the centre line there.'

She pointed to a white chalk line that divided the gravel pitch in half.

Miss Tweedie emerged from the pavilion weighed down with shin pads and two masks with grilles at the front and these were handed out to the goal-keepers. Once everyone was ready, Mrs Watt shepherded them onto the pitch.

Everyone seemed to know where to stand, most of them close to the white centre line.

'Stand back a bit, Catherine,' instructed Amanda. 'That's right. Keep going. Keep going. Okay. Stop. That's far enough.'

'Ready for bully-off?' bellowed Mrs Watt.

The two captains bent over facing each other in the middle of the field, their sticks on the ground, either side of a small white ball. The whistle blew, the two sticks flew off the ground,

157

cracked together, up and down rapidly, a total of three times. Then Alison gave the ball a mighty whack and it rolled along the ground, fast, in the direction of the goal, away from Catherine. Another girl in a red bib intercepted the ball and dribbled it until she was inside the circle marked out with white chalk. Catherine felt a surge of adrenaline and strained to see; her team was about to score!

The girl managed to find a clear space and pushed the ball, hard, towards the goal. But the goalkeeper just managed to jump in front of it, legs together and the ball bounced off and rolled behind the goal-line. Then it was in play again and, suddenly, it was hurtling towards Catherine.

She felt the familiar surge of freedom and exhilaration she recognised from playing camogie as she prepared to meet the ball. But a blue bib stepped in front and claimed it. The girl turned and was preparing to strike the ball, elbow raised, when Catherine slipped in and stole the ball. It was much harder than she had expected, made of plastic, not like the *sliotar* which was covered in leather.

Instinct took over and she belted up the field in the direction of the goal, dribbling the ball and outstripping her opponents. Her hair fell free of its elastic band. She felt it flying untamed behind her and the wind raw in her face. She was past the centre line; the goal came into view. She was close enough to strike.

'Now, Catherine, Now!' a voice inside her head screamed, and she swung the stick as high as she could and, bringing it down, gave the ball a tremendous crack. It flew up in a long semi-circle and, as it started to descend, shot straight and true into the goal, just under the post. The goalkeeper made no attempt to stop it and, instead, crossed her arms in front of her face.

'Wimp,' thought Catherine, delighted. She'd scored!

She noticed that everyone else had stopped already and she came to a halt, panting but elated, her dishevelled hair falling around her face.

'Didn't you hear the whistle? You silly girl,' screamed Mrs Watt, running across the field towards her.

'You broke every rule in the book!' she shouted crossly, as she came to a standstill in front of Catherine. Slightly out of breath, she began to list Catherine's offences, using her fingers as an abacus.

'You obstructed an opponent, you were off-side, you raised your stick above your shoulder, you undercutt the ball and you attempted a goal while outside the striking circle.'

She'd used up all the fingers on one hand.

'I've never seen a display of ill-discipline like it!'

Catherine had to stop herself from laughing. If you think that was wild, she thought, you should come and watch a game of camogie! This was tame in comparison. In truth, Catherine knew of no other way to play.

How could anybody follow all those complicated rules? They just took the fun out of it. You knew you had played a good game of camogie when you came off the field with your ankles sore and bruised. It was rough and ready all right, but nothing lifted your spirits like it and set your heart free.

'What did you think you were doing? You could have seriously hurt someone with that ball. The rules are there for a reason, you know. What's your name?' demanded Mrs Watt.

'Catherine. Catherine Meehan. I'm sorry, Miss. I forgot the rules. I'm used to playing camogie,' she replied simply, realising that Mrs Watt was angry. Really angry.

'Camogie!'

Mrs Watt spat the word out distastefully, like it was the name of an unpleasant disease.

'We don't want any of that nonsense here. That's nothing but an excuse for a bunch of raving savages running wild,' she said, the words tumbling out rapidly.

She appeared to stop herself from saying more and then, lowering her voice, she said, more calmly, 'Get off this pitch until you learn to conduct yourself in a civilised manner.'

Catherine was stunned. She knew she was out of order, but it hadn't been intentional and she'd said she was sorry. She turned to walk off the field, holding her head high, trying to keep her dignity intact.

'Jayne,' shouted Mrs Watt, 'Jayne Alexander. Yes, you. Come over here and show everybody how it's done properly.'

160

Catherine watched Jayne approach, her blonde hair pulled back neatly in a tight ponytail, her slim brown legs elegant and graceful as she strode towards her.

Jayne's expression was grave, her eyes full of pity and concern. Catherine couldn't bear her sympathy and, as they brushed past each other, averted her eyes. How she despised Jayne Alexander with her money and her pretty face and her bloody hockey. Naturally, she would be brilliant at that as well.

Moira was smiling broadly when Catherine reached the sidelines and greeted her with a playful punch in the arm.

'I don't think Mrs Watt appreciates your skills, Catherine. But I thought you were magic!'

'It's not funny, Moira. Didn't you hear the way she spoke to me? And she brought that Jayne Alexander onto the field just to show me up.'

'You can't blame her, Catherine. I thought you were going to kill the goalkeeper!' she laughed, and then, seeing the tears well up in Catherine's eyes, added gently, 'She was cross, that's all. I'm sure she didn't mean the things she said.'

Catherine turned her back to Moira whose attention was diverted by a shrill whistle signifying the start of play. Anger and humiliation welled up inside Catherine and crystallised into one image: Jayne Alexander.

How she hated her guts.

★　★　★

161

The next few weeks weren't as bad as Catherine feared. After her humiliation on the hockey field they couldn't have gotten much worse anyway. There were no more repeats of the name-calling from the first day.

Mrs Watt was nice to her at hockey the next week and even showed her personally how to push the ball along the ground. But Catherine knew Mrs Watt was wasting her time; she would never be able to play in that strange, constrained fashion and she hadn't the heart to learn.

In time she got used to the strange hymns and prayers and learnt to say the add-on to the Lord's Prayer, 'for thine is the kingdom, the power and the glory for ever and ever. Amen' almost, but not quite, by rote. Sometimes, in mass on Sundays, she had to stop herself from trotting it out as the drone of the congregation died away, but it always ran on inside her head. It never felt completely natural to say it, yet it felt strange not to.

As the weeks settled into a predicable routine and fear of the new and unknown gave way to familiarity, Catherine found her confidence growing. She was good at all her subjects, especially Domestic Science. It was like child's play to her, so used was she to helping Mammy with the chores. She found it hard to believe that some of the girls couldn't even boil an egg and their first 'cookery' lesson, when they tackled this challenge along with making toast, was hilarious. Catherine never realised that there were so many ways to get something, so simple, so completely wrong! She, on the other hand, was perfectly capable of turning out a three-course meal for six people.

And yet no matter how good she was at her subjects, or how many times she got top marks for a homework assignment, it was never quite enough. Never enough to give her the self-assurance she imagined all the other children possessed.

She sought academic success with a ferocity and determination that would have surprised her teachers and her classmates had she ever been careless enough to drop her protective shield of modesty and nonchalance. Soon she had a reputation for being very clever, but Catherine knew that it wasn't so much that she was especially talented but rather she squeezed every available drop of performance out of what gifts she possessed. And having two free periods a week when everyone else was taking Religious Education was an added bonus.

The issue of Religious Education, or RE, had come up at the Open Day. Tables were arranged around the perimeter of the assembly hall and parents with prospective pupils in tow moved from table to table chatting to the teachers and introducing their offspring. Behind one of the desks sat two ministers in black clerical dress. There was no priest in sight. Mammy and Daddy went round the room systematically, moving from table to table. When they got to this one they walked on by, nodding civilly at the ministers with a clipped 'evening', and the ministers dipped their heads courteously in return. As Catherine followed her parents she felt the ministers' eyes boring into her back.

'Why aren't we speaking to them?' she asked Daddy.

'Because you won't be going to RE classes so there's no point.'

'Why not?'

'They don't teach Catholicism.'

'Why isn't there a priest? If there was a priest I could go too.'

'Father Molloy won't come,' said Daddy, letting out a long sigh. 'To tell you the truth, Catherine, I don't really know why. The Church prefers children to go to Catholic schools, that's all, and anyway Father Molloy says he doesn't have the time to do the Grammar as well as all the other schools.'

'You'll get your religious education at home,' interrupted Mammy. 'Look on the bright side, Catherine. It means you get two free classes every week. Now come on and stop asking questions.'

If the Grammar didn't cater for Catholics, wondered Catherine, why was she being sent there? But she knew better than to ask.

And so, every Tuesday afternoon, while their classmates went to RE, Moira and Catherine went their separate way to the library. There they sat under the watchful eye of Miss Kingshill, the school librarian, who would tolerate no talking, whispering or gadding about whatsoever.

'You're here to work,' she said, and work they did.

It was great to have an extra hour-and-a-half for homework and, to start with, Catherine

164

believed it a tremendous advantage.

But sometimes, sitting in the solemn old library, which hadn't changed at all since the school was built, she thought about her classmates. She fancied they studied ancient cultures and exotic beliefs like Hinduism and Judaism. She wondered if they ever studied Catholicism, not to learn it of course, just to understand. Catherine wouldn't have minded learning about Protestantism because she had never really grasped what made the religions so different and why it bothered people so much.

One day in the library Moira caught Catherine staring, unfocused, out the rain-streaked window.

'What are you day-dreaming about?' whispered Moira.

'Nothing much,' answered Catherine, turning away from the window to look at Moira who sat expectantly, eyebrows raised, waiting for an explanation.

'If there's one thing I know about you, Catherine Meehan, it's that you very rarely think nothing.'

Catherine relented.

'I was thinking about RE and wondering what they study.'

'God, of course,' said Moira.

Miss Kingshill looked at them over the rims of her large silver-framed glasses and, after some moments of scowling, returned to the papers on her desk.

Catherine lowered her voice.

'What I mean is, I'd be quite interested in

learning about other religions, too. I sometimes think it's not such a good idea, us missing RE, I mean.'

'But we're Catholics,' said Moira, 'what would we want to be going to RE for?'

'It's not just the fact that we're Catholics. I think not going to RE sets us apart from everyone else, makes us different.'

'But we are different, Catherine, and it's nothing to be ashamed of. You wouldn't really want to go and miss out on two free periods every week, would you? Sure it's great.'

'No, I suppose not. I'm just being silly. I just can't help feeling a bit left out, that's all.'

Catherine regarded Moira thoughtfully.

'Are you okay Moira?'

'Yes, I'm fine. Why?'

'It's just you don't seem as . . . well . . . as happy as normal.'

'Why shouldn't I be? It's just this Maths homework. It's really hard.'

'Is everything all right at home?'

Moira put her pencil down and returned Catherine's gaze.

'No it's not,' she sighed. 'It looks like Daddy's going to lose his job. The factory where he works is closing down.'

'When?'

'Next month.'

'I'm sorry, Moira. Do you think he'll get another one?'

'He hasn't yet and Mammy says there's so many people without jobs he hasn't much chance. She's been trying herself in all the shops

166

and supermarkets but she can't get one either. Anyway Daddy says he doesn't want her working and they fight about it all the time.'

'What'll you do?'

'I don't know. Daddy'll have to go on the dole, I suppose.'

'It'll be all right, you'll see,' said Catherine encouragingly. 'Here, let me have a look at that Maths assignment and I'll check your answers.'

'Would you? Oh, thanks Catherine, I don't know what I'd do without you. The work's much harder than St Mary's.'

'Now that's enough from you two,' said Miss Kingshill severely. 'You've done nothing but talk all afternoon.'

Just then the bell went and they were spared a lecture.

'I was thinking of asking two girls from my class if they wanted to have their lunch with us. What do you think?' said Moira on the way out of the library.

'Who are they?'

'Lorraine Graham and Michelle White.'

'They're Protestants, aren't they?'

'And so is everyone else in the class, Catherine! You don't hold that against them?'

'No, I suppose not. They're not snobby are they?'

'No, they're not. Honest. Lorraine's Daddy works in the paper mill and they live in an ordinary house just off Main Street. And Michelle lives in Redcliff.'

Redcliff was a new council housing estate.

'Okay then,' said Catherine.

167

'You'll like them,' said Moira. 'Soon they'll be just as good friends with you as they are with me!'

But Catherine knew that would never happen; she could never drop her guard completely with anyone except Moira.

She thought of Jayne Alexander and her cronies, envy gnawing at her insides. They were an elite group set apart by their privilege and wealth, or so it seemed to Catherine. Ruth Clarke, of Clarke's the furniture shop; Heather Williams, daughter of a well-off haulier; Pamela Black, whose Daddy was a doctor.

They were all somebody and she was a nobody.

9

Autumn 1982

Catherine went to Confession on Saturday, the first time in weeks, and endured the usual rigmarole about going to the Grammar.

'What school do you go to, my child?' said the priest.

'The Grammar.'

A pause, then a soft sigh, barely audible. Behind the yellow metal grille she could see the black shadow of a hand coming up to rub a chin.

'Now what do your parents want to be sending you there for, when there's perfectly good Catholic schools you could be going to?'

The tone was conspiratorial and, intentionally, saturated with disappointment.

'I don't know, Father.' The standard reply.

Father Molloy's question — for despite the anonymity of the confessional Catherine knew perfectly well who was behind the grille, as did he, she suspected — was primarily rhetorical and he continued on as though she hadn't spoken.

'What year are you in, my child?'

'I'll be going into Lower Sixth, Father. I'm going back to do A-levels.'

'Ah, well that's good to hear.'

The tone lifted a little.

'Well, for your penance, I want you to say five Hail Mary's and four Our Fathers,' he continued

169

briskly. 'And try to curb the green-headed monster, my child. It will only lead to misery and unhappiness. I absolve you from your sins,' he chanted, and Catherine could see the shadow of his hand fluttering bird-like behind the grille, 'in the name of the Father, and of the Son and of the Holy Spirit. Amen.'

The door behind the screen was slammed shut with an abrupt thud, so that the privacy of the next confessor on the other side would be protected. Disturbed by the movement, the air smelt of incense and furniture polish. Catherine sat for some moments collecting, and simultaneously analysing, her thoughts.

She always felt guilty after confession even after so long and when it was all so predictable. But today, for the first time, she felt angry. It wasn't her bloody fault she'd been sent to the Grammar! And so what anyway? Was that a sin? No, Father Molloy would never come right out and say that.

So, if it wasn't a sin, why all the insinuation, the snide remarks, the subtle pressure? What was she supposed to do about it? Why was she being punished for a decision that hadn't been hers to make?

Catherine got up and left the confession box, lest the next person wonder what she was doing in there. She dipped her knee cursorily in the direction of the alter and marched out of the chapel, not bothering to bless herself with holy water on the way out.

'He was right about one thing,' she said to Moira as they walked home.

'Who?'

'Father Molloy. Years ago when I told him that I was going to the Grammar he asked me who would take care of my religious education.'

'So?'

'Well, no-one has. Not really. I mean we all go to mass on Sunday and Daddy says grace before dinner. And every now and then, especially during lent, Mammy has us all saying the rosary. But it doesn't mean anything to me.'

'What, not at all? Catherine you can't mean that.' Moira sounded shocked.

'I do though.'

There was a silence and then Catherine went on. 'It wasn't always like that. I remember when I was seven or eight there was this film on TV about Christ. It showed you him dying on the cross and everything and how he'd done it for us. And do you know what?'

'No. What?'

'I went into the bedroom and bawled my eyes out on the pillow.'

'Why?'

' 'Cos I felt unworthy. I vowed to devote my life to Christ.'

Catherine looked at Moira and laughed wryly. 'It seems daft now doesn't it?'

'No, not really.'

'Don't get me wrong; it's not that I don't believe. Okay there's this chauvinistic stuff about the role of women. But that aside, I still believe in the basic idea of it all. But it just doesn't seem important. Or relevant. Like believing in the earth being round. You know it's true but so

171

what? It doesn't change the way you live your life.'

'I think that's really sad,' said Moira.

'You still believe then?'

'Yes.'

'Even after . . . well . . . you know, your Dad and all.'

Moira nodded.

Catherine said, 'I wonder if things would have been different if we'd gone to a Catholic school.'

'Well, it wouldn't have made any difference to me,' said Moira. 'It was my Daddy losing his job that changed things.'

He'd been on the dole for five years and Moira's Mammy now had a job in a launderette.

'Is he still doing it?' asked Catherine.

Moira shrugged.

'Not much now. Only the odd time when he's drink taken.'

'I still think your Mammy should've reported him or something.'

'He's my Dad, Catherine. No matter what he does, he's still my Dad.'

'It just makes me mad the way you accept it. Like it's not his fault. You should do something.'

'What do you suggest? I'll leave home when I'm old enough, but just now there's nothing I can do. And don't forget you promised me, Catherine. Not a word to anyone.'

'I remember,' sighed Catherine. 'I've kept it secret all this time, I'm not going to run round blabbing about it now. Am I?'

There was no-one in when Moira got home and she relaxed a little. Mammy had gone down

172

the town shopping and he was out. At the pub spending the little money Mammy earned from that awful job in the launderette. At least she had a few hours to herself before he came home. Saturday's were always bad, especially round teatime, and then he would fall asleep in the chair in front of the TV.

It had been impossible to hide the truth from Catherine. She was too sharp and it didn't take her long to work out why Moira was always missing PE — so that no-one would see the bruises. And though Catherine was a great friend Moira couldn't tell her everything. Like the fact that he hit her more than she let on and that it had been going on for years. Then there was the other stuff as well.

'I can't leave him,' said Mammy once, nursing a black eye. 'The Church won't give me an annulment and we can't get divorced. Anyway, Father Molloy says that any father is better than no father.'

'Leave him anyway,' said Moira. 'What does Father Molloy know?'

'You don't understand,' said Mammy.

But Moira understood all right; Mammy was afraid of him and what he would do if she told him she was leaving.

Moira heard the back door open and a heavy tread on the vinyl floor. She froze in terror and glanced anxiously at the clock in the hall. It was only half past two! What was he doing home early?

Her breath came in shallow gasps and she glanced round for an escape route. If she could

173

just make it to her room and sit there quietly he wouldn't even realise she was in. He would watch the horse-racing on the TV and then, if she was lucky, fall asleep. She made it to the bottom of the stairs but a creaking floorboard gave her away.

'Who's that?' said a slurred voice.

Moira willed herself to stay calm. Be nice, she told herself.

'It's only me, Daddy,' she said, trying to sound chirpy, but she could not hide the fear in her voice.

He came through to the hallway bumping noisily against the door-frame.

'What're you doing here?'

'Just back from Confession. Why don't you go into the lounge, Daddy, and I'll make you a nice cup of tea.'

'Cup of tea, my arse. Been at confession, have you? Did you tell the priest all your filthy sins, then?' he said, advancing on her.

'No, Daddy, no,' said Moira quietly, covering her ears.

'Did you tell him what a dirty little whore you are? Did you?' He was shouting now.

'Mammy'll be in soon,' said Moira, suppressing the desperation in her voice.

'Your Mammy's gone to see her Ma,' he replied and made a lunge at Moira.

She squealed and tried to run up the stairs, but he caught her by the ankle and pulled. She slid down until she came to a halt on her back on the bottom steps.

'Now are you going to be a good girl and do

what I tell you,' he said into her face, his breath acrid, 'or am I going to have to teach you a lesson?'

* * *

Dressed in her school uniform Catherine considered her reflection critically in the mirror. Instead of white socks she now wore tan-coloured tights and the jerkin was replaced with a navy V-necked jumper. These changes aside, the uniform had changed little since her first day at the Grammar.

But the girl staring out of the mirror had changed. The dark straight hair, brown eyes, and pale skin were just the same, but here and there, to Catherine's annoyance, the odd pimple erupted and she had to wash her face three times a day to keep it grease-free. The slight little figure that once poked, all elbows and knees, out of the school uniform had transformed into a woman-sized silhouette.

She stood, shoulders back and chest out. So far, so good. She took a deep breath and her breasts strained against the buttons on her blouse. Were her boobs ever going to stop growing? Them and her hips. She pulled up her jacket and viewed her bottom critically.

'I wish you girls would put things away when you've ironed them and not leave them lying all over the house,' said Mammy, coming into the bedroom with a pile of clothes in her arms. 'Well, what are you looking at?'

'I'm fat. Look at this!' exclaimed Catherine,

175

thrusting her chest out so that Mammy could appreciate her problem.

'New shirts aren't going to solve that, you'll just have to get used to them,' said Mammy, nodding at Catherine's bust. 'They're not going to go away. And don't be so silly, Catherine, you're not fat. You're curvy. A perfectly normal, healthy young woman. There's plenty of girls would die for a figure like yours. Look, there's not a pick round your waist or under your chin. See! If you were fat I'd be able to pinch an inch.'

'But everyone wants to be straight and thin like a stick,' wailed Catherine, 'and look at me. I'm all lumps and bumps.'

'Men find a curvy figure attractive. Sexy. Just you wait and see.' Then, changing the subject, she added, 'You look nice in your uniform. All set for Monday, then?'

'As ready as I'll ever be,' replied Catherine, unconvinced.

She watched Mammy fold clothes and put them in the chest of drawers. Despite Catherine's attempts to disregard the priest's words from the previous week their memory still rankled.

'Mammy?'

Mammy put away the last item of clothing in the bottom drawer and stood up.

'Yes.'

'Has Father Molloy ever said anything to you about sending me to the Grammar?'

'What do you mean?'

'Well, has he ever said it was wrong or that we should be going to a Catholic school?'

176

'Oh, he mentioned it once or twice at the outset, but not lately. Why?' said Mammy, for once appearing to pay full attention.

'Every time I go to Confession he asks me what school I go to and says that I shouldn't be going to the Grammar.'

Mammy scowled, irritated.

'Well, that's his opinion, Catherine. I know he's a priest and I respect him for that, but there's nothing wrong with you going to the Grammar. Look at your O-levels results; five As and four Bs! You would never have done so well at St Pat's. Your father and I were thinking of your best interests. And anyway don't you think it's healthy for you to mix with other sorts of people?'

From the inflection in Mammy's voice and from experience, Catherine knew 'other sorts of people' meant Protestants.

'Yes, I suppose so. It's just . . . '

'Just what?'

'Well, the Grammar's not a mixed school you know, Mammy. It's a Protestant school and they don't really want us Catholics there.'

'What makes you say that?'

Catherine thought of the school traditions like singing 'God Save the Queen' at the end of prize-giving ceremonies and school plays. They were Protestant rituals, with no attempt to take into account the feelings of the Catholic minority.

'It's hard to explain. Like the focus is always on being part of Great Britain — I don't do any Irish history at all. They always refer to Northern

177

Ireland as Ulster as though they'd choke on the very word Ireland. And no-one seems much interested in understanding Catholicism either. No-one's ever asked me about it. Everyone pretends that the Catholics don't exist and you feel like you're just tolerated so long as you keep your mouth shut.'

'I'm sorry that's the way you feel, Catherine. Is this a recent thing?'

'Oh, no it's always been like that. I've always been aware of it anyway. I suppose I just didn't know the words to describe it before. Insidious. That's what it is.'

'You're sure you're not imagining it, Catherine? Reading too much into things, perhaps?'

She could tell Mammy had lost interest. It was hard to explain because nothing about it was blatant. The discrimination, if that's what it was, was so well done. So subtle.

'No. No, I'm sure I'm not. You'd have to be there yourself. To see how things are.'

With a few exceptions, teachers and pupils were careful not to give offence and, on the face of it, everyone pretended there wasn't an issue. And because the subject was taboo — avoided, skirted around, side-stepped — a latent sense of inferiority took root in Catherine. On one hand she felt that being a Catholic was something to be ashamed of; on the other, she felt pride and indignation.

'I just wish, with hindsight, that I'd gone to St Margaret's, that's all,' said Catherine quietly.

'Would you look at the time,' said Mammy, 'I'm supposed to be away.' It was Wednesday, market day, and the best bargains were to be had early on.

'Will that boy ever get out of his bed?' she asked no-one in particular, raising her eyes to the ceiling and bustling out of the room. She was referring to Michael.

Catherine followed her. 'Don't be so hard on him, Mammy. It's not his fault he can't get a job.'

'I'm not saying it is, Catherine, but it doesn't mean he has to lie around in bed all day. He could make himself useful round here for one thing. Or get himself down to the Job Centre and look for work.'

Mammy banged her fist on the door of the room Sean and Michael shared. Sean was up and out hours ago.

'Michael, will you please get up! It's half-past nine.'

She listened. No response.

'See what I mean about St Pat's?' she said turning to Catherine. 'If Michael had done better in his O-levels he wouldn't be unemployed now. He might have got an apprenticeship or something.'

She opened the door and shouted at the figure lying under the tousled bedclothes. 'Are you getting up, Michael?'

'Yeah, Ma,' came the groggy reply and the bedclothes turned over.

'I want to see you out of that bed in two minutes. Do you hear me? Two minutes,' and she disappeared down the stairs.

Catherine looked in at Michael, his unruly

mop of nearly-black hair just visible at the top of the bed, and sighed. Even though he was older than her, Catherine felt intensely protective towards him. He hadn't had a proper job since he left school last June, apart from a few months working on Harper's lorries, delivering bags of coal around the town. It was dirty work, but Michael didn't seem to mind and then, without warning, he was laid off. He helped Daddy out now and again with the decorating, but Sean was already doing that full-time and there wasn't enough work for the three of them.

Catherine returned to the bedroom, took off her uniform and hung it back in the wardrobe. She pulled on a pair of stretchy blue jeans, a baggy cotton jumper and a pair of trainers.

Downstairs in the small kitchen it was bright and warm, the early autumn sun streaming through the window. Catherine filled the kettle and found a clean mug.

'Geraldine! Are you coming?' Mammy called up the stairs.

'Down in a minute,' came the muffled reply.

'I don't know what she does in that bathroom all day,' said Mammy under her breath and, placing her purse in the bottom of the wicker shopping basket, she pulled on her brown coat.

'Has Michael said anything to you about what he gets up to with those Mulholland boys,' she asked, doing up her buttons without looking, her fingers working in their familiar quick, unhurried fashion.

'No. Why?'

'I don't like him running around with them.

You know Brendan, their Da, was in prison in the 70s.'

Catherine inserted two slices of bread in the toaster and looked up.

'Really? What for?'

'I don't know exactly, it was a long time ago. Something to do with explosives.'

She paused and then continued. 'Your father and him used to be great mates. He was best man at our wedding.'

'I didn't know that! Aren't they friends any more?'

Mammy shrugged her shoulders.

'They just drifted apart. Brendan got married soon after us and moved down the coast to Cushendall. Then we all had children. You get caught up in your own life. That's what happens.

'Anyway,' she went on, more briskly, 'they're not the sort of family I want you children involved with. I think those boys are a bad influence on Michael.'

'I know what you mean,' said Catherine, lifting the butter and jam out of the cupboard. 'I don't like them much, either. Do you know Malachy passed me in the street the other day without so much as a 'hello' and he knows rightly that I'm Michael's sister? Him and his brother, Connor, are very close.'

'Dangerous, more like.'

Geraldine appeared at the kitchen door, her pretty features rather heavily accentuated with make-up. She looked a lot older than fifteen, not only because of the make-up. There was something very mature about Geraldine and although Catherine felt protective towards her, sometimes she wondered who the older sister really was.

'You're not going out like that!' said Mammy.

'Why not?' asked Geraldine innocently.

'Because I say so. Look at her, Catherine.'

'She looks all right to me, Mammy. Don't make such a fuss. All the girls are wearing make-up nowadays.'

Geraldine winked at her mischievously.

'Hmm, well just don't let your father see you like that. Come on, let's get a move on,' grumbled Mammy, moving to the bottom of the stairs.

'Are you up yet?' she yelled.

'Uh-huh,' said a sleepy voice from the top of the stairs.

Satisfied, Mammy returned to the kitchen.

'Right, let's go, Geraldine,' she commanded, opening the kitchen door. She was half-way through the door when she shouted over her shoulder.

'Oh, could you clean up those breakfast things, Catherine, and bring in the washing when it's dry? I don't think it's going to rain,' she said, peering up at the sky, 'but you never know.'

'Yes, Mammy,' replied Catherine, rolling her eyes at Geraldine who, laughing, pulled the kitchen door shut behind them.

Catherine smiled to herself and sat down at the kitchen table with a mug of tea and two slices of buttered toast. Michael came in, bare-footed, wearing a white T-shirt and crumpled blue jeans and sat down opposite Catherine.

'Ma gone then?'

'Yep.'

'Thank God. A bit of piece and quiet,' he said smiling, and stretched luxuriously like a cat just awakened from an afternoon nap.

Catherine grinned.

'Want a cup of tea?' she asked and, without waiting for a reply, got up, poured another mug of tea, stirred two sugars into it and set the mug down in front of Michael.

'Ta.'

They sat for some minutes in companionable silence. Catherine finished eating, put her cup on top of the plate and pushed it into the middle of the table.

'Mammy says that Mr Mulholland was in prison years ago on some sort of explosives charge,' she said.

'So?'

'What do you know about it?'

'That was internment, Catherine. The Brits were lifting everybody, whether you had done anything or not. And even if he was involved in something, so what?'

'Mammy doesn't like you running around with Malachy and Connor. She says they're not a nice family.'

'There's nothing wrong with them and who I run around with is my business. They're sound Republicans and that's good enough for me.'

Catherine laughed.

'You can't be serious, Michael. Since when

have you become a Republican? Sure, you don't even know what it means.'

Michael stared back at her, unsmiling, and took a sip of tea. Seeing he was annoyed, Catherine changed the subject.

'Are you going out tonight?' she asked cheerfully.

'Yeah, thought I'd go down to Riley's for a game of snooker and a pint.'

'Can I come?' asked Catherine, knowing what the answer would be.

'Course not, silly!' said Michael playfully. 'I can't have my wee sister tagging along. The boys would think I was a right cissy now, wouldn't they?' and he reached over and tousled her hair.

That was more like the old Michael she knew, thought Catherine. Mammy was right. There had been a change in him over the last few months, ever since he had started spending most of his time with the Mulholland brothers. They were so different from Michael — sullen, testy, dour — and these qualities were starting to rub off on him. 'Hard men from the Glens' Mammy called them and it wasn't meant as a compliment.

'Well, smarty pants, so you're planning to go to university then?' teased Michael.

'That's the plan, if I can get in.'

'Oh, you'll get in all right. You've got brains, Catherine,' he said, serious now, 'and you should make the most of it. You don't want to end up like me.'

'Oh, Michael,' said Catherine, reaching out and resting her hand on his forearm, 'I'm sure something will come up soon.'

184

'Not for the likes of me it won't.'

'Don't say that. You have to think positively.'

'Yeah, I suppose,' he replied.

Catherine squeezed his arm and withdrew her hand. After a short silence she remembered there was something she had to tell Michael.

'Hey, did you know Geraldine's been seeing a fella?'

'No!' said Michael, astonished, and he lent forward, arms on the table. 'Tell me more. Do Ma and Da know?'

'They found out last night and they're not too happy about it. Apparently, when Daddy turned up to do her living-room Mrs Watson asked him who the fella was she'd seen walking out with Geraldine.'

'Bloody hell,' said Michael. 'Did you know?'

'Of course.'

'And you didn't tell me?'

'Geraldine asked me to keep it a secret. Anyway I knew it was only a matter of time before you'd find out. She's been seeing him for ages.'

'Who is he?'

'Eddie Alexander. His sister Jayne's in the same year as me at the Grammar.'

'A Protestant!'

'Well, yeah, he is. So what?' asked Catherine.

'I don't like the idea of my sister going out with a Proddie-dog.'

'Michael!' protested Catherine. 'Don't speak like that. It's horrible. What's wrong with her seeing a Protestant. There isn't a law against it, is there?'

185

'There should be,' he replied angrily. 'What does he do anyway?'

'He's in the police.'

Michael banged his fist on the table.

'We'll have to put a stop to this nonsense,' he growled.

'Don't be such a bigot, Michael. I expected that from Mammy and Daddy, but not from you. Listen to yourself,' she cried.

'Listen to me?' said Michael, sarcastically. 'Why don't you listen to yourself, Catherine Meehan?'

Michael was standing now, his lovely face twisted with outrage.

'Sometimes I think going to the Grammar has made you forget who and what you are,' he said and stormed out of the room.

★   ★   ★

There was no doubt about it, the tan tights were hideous, even on Jayne's shapely legs. She looked down at them in despair, but it was either them or white socks and there was no way she was going into sixth year wearing knee socks. That aside her slim, athletic figure looked pretty good in the drab uniform. If only she wasn't so flat-chested. Size 34AA was ridiculously small for a girl her age and there was no sign of them getting any bigger.

Still, she thought, fluffing up her bob of blonde hair, what she lacked in the boob department was more than made up for by other assets. Her natural blonde hair for one thing.

And her clear, bronzed complexion. She pouted her lips and then smiled at herself in the mirror revealing small even white teeth.

Suddenly realising the time Jayne grabbed her satchel and hurried downstairs. She heard raised voices coming from the kitchen and stopped. She couldn't make out what they were saying, but she recognised Dad and Eddie's voices. She descended more slowly with a heavy tread. She took a deep breath and went into the kitchen which was square-shaped and spacious.

Mum looked up from the cooker where she was scrambling eggs in the big black frying pan and smiled thinly. She was already fully dressed in a neat black skirt and cream blouse trimmed with red and green at the collar and cuffs. Jayne went over to her, said 'Good Morning,' and gave her a kiss.

Her cheek smelt peachy and was dusted with a light application of face-powder.

'You look smart, Jayne,' said Mum.

'Thanks, Mum. Look at the tights though, aren't they awful?'

'Hmm. I see what you mean, but they're better than knee socks. Want some bacon and eggs?' she asked returning to her pan.

'Yes please, they smell delicious. And some toast. Morning Dad,' said Jayne, planting a kiss on top of her father's bald head.

'Morning, Jayne,' he replied without looking up.

Dad usually had plenty of time for her, but this morning his reply was gruff and he glowered over his teacup at Eddie. He must be really mad, thought Jayne.

She sat down opposite Eddie in one of the antique pine chairs that surrounded the big rectangular table covered in a blue and white gingham cloth. Fresh off the night shift, Eddie was still wearing his jacket over jeans and a pullover. He'd been on night shift all week and his face was pale and drawn. Jayne winked at him but elicited nothing more than a weak smile. Everybody was miserable this morning.

Dad laid his knife and fork across his empty plate very deliberately. He dabbed his mouth with a napkin and then continued where he had obviously left off, this time in a more conciliatory tone.

'I'm not saying I've anything against the girl. Have we Helen?' he said, looking round at Mum for support.

She shook her head soundlessly as she set a plate of bacon, eggs and toast in front of Jayne.

They were talking about Geraldine Meehan, Eddie's girlfriend, again. It was getting tiresome and Jayne couldn't see what all the fuss was about. Lots of Catholics and Protestants went out together these days.

'I'm sure she's a very nice girl,' continued Dad.

'How would you know? You've never met her,' cut in Eddie.

'Well, that's as may be, but I'm trying to explain to you where your mother and me are coming from. And I'm sure Geraldine's parents feel exactly the same way about this as we do. She's far too young to be getting serious about any fella. And you're only eighteen, Eddie. You should be out playing the field at your age, having a laugh. Not getting all involved with a wee girl.'

'I'm not all involved. What's that supposed to mean anyway? I see her a couple of times a week and I still see all my other friends.'

'You know what I'm getting at.'

'No I don't, Dad, and I'm sick of you going on about it all the time.'

Eddie was shouting now.

'Calm down, son and listen to me a minute. There's other things to be considered as well,' he said, glancing across the table at Jayne, as though unsure if he should continue in front of her.

Jayne looked down at her plate and piled a little mound of yellow egg on top of one corner of her toast. Mum leant against the kitchen counter her left arm folded across her stomach, the other arm propped up on it at a right angle. She rested her nose on her knuckles, her hand clenched over her mouth, tense.

'Think of the attention you're drawing to yourself,' Dad continued quietly. 'It's dangerous enough these days being in the RUC without running about with a Catholic as well.'

'Oh, for God's sake!' cried Eddie.

Then he let his head roll back, took a deep breath and swallowed hard before going on.

'Nothing like that ever happens round here. Look Dad, I'm not stupid. If she was Harry Black's or Ian Clarke's daughter you wouldn't be getting on like this. And don't give me all that crap about her being too young either.'

He stood up and looked down at his father.

'You don't like her because she's a Catholic, plain and simple. Why don't you just come right out and say it?'

Eddie's eyes glistened and though he tried hard to control them, the corners of his mouth twitched.

'You're just a prejudiced bigot!'

Dad's eyelids flickered just a fraction, but his steely grey-blue eyes held Eddie's gaze, steady and firm. Then Eddie turned and walked out of the room.

'Eddie, son, don't!' cried Mum and she made as if to go after him.

But Eddie was already half-way up the stairs, his breakfast left congealing on the untouched plate.

'Let him go,' commanded Dad, and Mum stopped in the middle of the kitchen, her arms hanging uselessly by her side.

Dad took a sip of tea, sat back and shook his head slowly.

'Dearie me,' he said, 'harsh words spoken in anger.' Then he added, more confidently, 'Don't worry, he'll come round in time, Helen.'

'I don't know about that,' said Mum sharply. 'He's very attached to that girl and you haven't exactly helped matters.'

'What do you mean? I was just stating the facts, that's all.'

'You've made him angry and, if anything, more determined. It's written all over his face,' said Mum, vigorously scraping Eddie's breakfast into the pedal-bin and letting the lid slam shut with a loud clang.

'But we agreed I should try and talk to him again. Surely you don't want him seeing her?'

'I don't know. All right then, I would prefer if he didn't. But there's worse things he could be doing, you know, than going out with a Catholic. It might all blow over in the end anyway.'

'I think Mum's right,' said Jayne. 'So what if she's a Catholic? It doesn't make her a bad person, does it?'

'No, pet, it doesn't,' replied Dad patiently. 'And as I've said before I've nothing against Catholics. I work with them every day and, for the most part, they're a decent enough lot. But you have to understand that your mother and me are only concerned for your and Eddie's happiness. We know from experience that it's better to stick to your own kind, don't we Helen?'

Mum was energetically scrubbing the frying pan in the sink, but this time she didn't nod her head in agreement.

Undaunted, Dad continued: 'What your brother doesn't understand is that we have his and that wee girl's best interests at heart. For both their sakes it would be best if they didn't get involved. You see Catholics are different from us, Jayne, and at the end of the day, they want different things.

'Catholics want to force us into a United Ireland and subject us to a papist state. Do you think we'd have the freedom to worship and preserve our traditions in a country run by the Church of Rome? No way. Sure look at the priests here. They won't even let the kids go to ordinary schools; no they have to go to Catholic schools so they can indoctrinate them. If there's one single cause of the problems in this country it's the Catholic Church refusing to allow integration.'

'That's not true, Dad. Sure Catherine Meehan goes to the Grammar.'

'Aye, and what do the Catholics do when they get there? Refuse to attend Religious Education in case they learn something. If they're going to go to state schools then they should be prepared to join in like everybody else. Truth is, Jayne, they don't want to be part of Ulster or Britain. Their sights are firmly set on the South and they think they can get what they want by bombing and shooting us into submission, but they'll never prevail.'

He paused and reflected for a moment.

'No, all that idolatry and popery has no place in a Christian home and, if Eddie takes up with that girl, he'll be going against everything this family and country is built on.'

Jayne said no more and looked down at her half-eaten breakfast. Dad was so confident, so absolutely convinced of the validity of his argument, but her silence didn't mean that Jayne acquiesced. She just wasn't able to express with any eloquence views that were only half-formed and which, she knew, would be obliterated by her father's verbal mastery.

She too felt strongly that the Protestant way of life must be preserved and that Ulster should remain within the UK. She felt pride in her heritage and traditions, but failed to appreciate, with the intensity of her father, the threat to their very existence.

As far as Catholicism was concerned, she didn't share her father's intolerance and found instead that she was mildly curious. If she had ever gotten friendly with Catherine Meehan she would have liked to have found out more, but that was not to be. In short, while to a large extent she sympathised with her father's beliefs, her adherence was altogether more open-minded and lacking in zeal. She realised that Dad would be sorely disappointed in her if he knew.

'Don't look so glum, Jayne. Eddie will come round. You'll see.'

Dad reached over and patted her on the arm like he used to do when she was a little girl.

'John,' said Mum, 'you're going to be late for the Bank. It's half-past eight.'

'So it is,' he said, sucking air in through his teeth.

He rose from the table, slipped a dark grey jacket off the back of the chair and put it on. He went to the hall mirror and spent some moments adjusting his tie and smoothing down what was left of his hair. Then he picked up the black briefcase waiting by the door, shouted good-bye, and was gone.

Jayne turned to her mother who, having cleared the breakfast things away, was now wiping the table-mats with a damp dishcloth.

'What do you think about Eddie and Geraldine Meehan?' asked Jayne.

'You heard your father.'

193

'Yes, but what do you think?'

Mum rarely voiced an opinion on controversial matters; ever since Jayne could remember, any important decisions were made by Dad. As she got older she became increasingly aware of her mother's reticence and it was beginning to irritate her.

'Does it matter?' said Mum, drying the table mats with a clean tea-towel.

'Of course it matters. Why won't you say what you think?'

'I think the same as your father. It would be best for both of them if they broke off the relationship before they get any more involved. It would never work. There's too many problems to overcome,' she said briskly, squaring the table mats. She put them in the drawer nearest the table and returned to the sink.

'How can you be so sure?'

'I just know, Jayne. Believe me,' she said slowly, as she rinsed and squeezed out the dishcloth, staring unseeing out of the window. 'It will only lead to heartbreak and misery.'

For a moment she looked very small and fragile, her pretty face contorted with what looked like pain.

'Mum?' said Jayne uneasily, wishing Mum would stop acting weird.

'You'd better get a move on or you'll be late for school,' said Mum briskly, returning to normal. 'And it's your first day back!'

'I'll be ready in a minute,' said Jayne, dashing out of the kitchen and up the stairs. For some reason she felt a terrible urge to tell Eddie that

194

she didn't think like Mum and Dad. That she would never turn her back on him.

He was lying fully clothed on the bed, his forearm bent over his eyes as if to shade them from the light even though the curtains were drawn and the room was dark and gloomy.

'Eddie, it's me,' said Jayne, sitting down on the edge of the bed. The mattress creaked, but Eddie didn't respond.

'I just came to tell you,' she continued, 'that I don't agree with Mum and Dad.'

Eddie moved his arm up slightly to rest on his forehead and regarded Jayne.

'You don't?'

Even in the dim light she could see his eyes were bloodshot.

'No, not entirely. I mean I understand why they're concerned and all with you being in the police, but I don't see what all the fuss is about. It's up to you who you go out with.'

'Dad makes me so mad sometimes, Jayne. He comes off with all this stuff about why it's not a good idea for me to be going out with Geraldine when underneath it all he's scared shitless just because she's a Catholic. He puts on this show of being so broad-minded and tolerant. But he's just a narrow-minded bigot! And Mum's just as bad. She doesn't say anything outright but she's behind him all the way.'

'Oh, Eddie, you're awful hard on them. I know they're only thinking of your best interests.'

'And what are my best interests, Jayne?' he said sarcastically.

'Well, they want both of us to be happy, get

195

decent jobs, settle down and have nice homes.'

'You mean live the sort of safe, middle-class life they've led running to the Church on Sundays and socialising with their small-minded Protestant friends. Pretending they're so liberal and then they nearly have kittens when their son goes out with a Catholic a few times.'

'That's the only way they know how to live, Eddie, and I don't see what's wrong with it.'

Sensing the discord between them, Jayne changed tack.

'Don't you think you're taking this all too seriously, Eddie? Why don't you just ignore Dad? I mean, you're only going out with Geraldine. It's not like you're planning to get married or anything!' she added light-heartedly.

'But what if we were? I mean what if I did love her and wanted to marry her? What would you think then?'

Eddie had rolled over on his side and, propping his head up on his arm, watched Jayne keenly for a response.

Jayne hadn't thought of that possibility. Going out with a Catholic was one thing; marrying one quite another.

'You're not serious; Geraldine's not even sixteen!' exclaimed Jayne imagining the rumpus it would cause.

Eddie looked at her in deadly earnest.

'But what if I was serious?' he asked.

Jayne bit her bottom lip. Granny and Uncle Robert and Aunt Irene would definitely not come to the wedding. Dad might not either. It would cause a rift in the family that might never be healed. And what about Eddie? Would he and Geraldine have to go and live somewhere else and she would never see him again?

'Eddie, do you think that would be a good idea . . . ' she began, but Eddie seized on her hesitancy as evidence of treachery.

'See! You're no better than them. I thought if I could count on anyone it would be you. They've got you well and truly conditioned, haven't they?'

'No, Eddie!' protested Jayne. 'I'm only thinking how much it would hurt Mum and Dad. How I'd be forced to choose between you and them. And how difficult it would be for you and Geraldine.'

'I don't want to hear it, Jayne. Just leave me alone. I have to get some sleep,' and he threw himself back on the bed.

Jayne left the room quietly, collected her satchel and left for school. It was a breezy early-autumn day and the first fallen leaves played chase round her feet. She walked mechanically, staring sightlessly at the pavement, replaying the conversation with Eddie again and again inside her head.

She and Eddie hadn't quarrelled since they were children and then it had always been over stupid things like sweets and toys. This rift marked the first adult disagreement between them. Eddie no longer confided in her the way he used to and, when it came to Geraldine, he would listen to no-one. He was moving out of her influence and into that of another. Eddie had fallen in love.

10

At breakfast David McDowell was wondering what his first day at the Grammar held in store when the music on the radio was interrupted by a news flash. Instinctively, the three of them hushed to listen.

'The Catholic taxi driver kidnapped yesterday in Belfast was found early this morning in the Short Strand area of the city by an RUC patrol. His hands were tied behind his back and he had been shot through the head three times. The victim, a twenty-nine-year-old father of three . . . '

David stopped listening and relaxed; he would not know a Catholic taxi-driver. The people he knew in Belfast were the sons of doctors and lawyers and businessmen and they were exclusively Protestant. Anyway, since they'd moved to Ballyfergus, David felt somehow more remote from it all. He took another bite of toast spread with thick creamy butter and homemade strawberry jam.

Mum stood motionless by the kitchen sink, listening, with a stainless-steel teapot in her right hand. The announcement over, she turned to the table and shook her head.

'Dear God, that poor fella. Sure he's only a boy. Twenty-nine and his whole life ahead of him,' she said, topping up the three mugs on the table.

Dad looked up, a deep furrow in his brow. He wore a grey shirt and a dog-collar with a crumpled old cardigan for warmth.

'Yes, love, it's terrible. God rest his soul,' he said solemnly, before returning to the *Ballyfergus Times*. The headline read 'Fifty Jobs To Go At Power Station'.

'And his poor wife left with three kids to bring up on her own.'

David felt the tension building in his jaw and gripped the mug with both hands.

They'd moved away from Belfast to somewhere more peaceful and quiet, partly for Mum's sake. Why couldn't she just forget about the 'Troubles' and focus on all the good things instead?

'Well it happens nearly every day, Mum. You'd think we'd be used to it by now,' he said, trying to sound light-hearted.

'How can you say that?' wailed Mum, banging the teapot down on the top of the cooker. 'That could be you, son! Lying trussed up somewhere with a bullet through your head.'

'It's not very likely, now is it?'

'Now, David, your mother's upset. Don't be cheeky.'

David blushed.

'I'm sorry, Mum. I didn't mean to be rude.'

'I know, son. It's all right,' she sighed, tucking her hands inside her apron pocket.

He regarded Mum, her face twisted with anxiety, for some moments. Why did she get so het up about total strangers? It was tragic for the people involved, but you couldn't survive getting on like that. Not when there were shootings and bombings nearly every day.

'I know it's not nice to say it,' he said gently, 'but you have to learn to shut it out, Mum.'

'David's right, love. You mustn't let yourself get so upset about people we don't even know,' said Dad, folding his paper and setting it down on the table. 'I know it's terrible, Betty, but it's God's will so it is and there's nothing we can do about it. We'll pray for the family. That'll make you feel better, won't it, love?'

Mum stood facing the window with her arms folded and didn't answer. Dad turned to David.

'Are you looking forward to your first day, then?' he asked cheerfully. David shrugged his shoulders, his mouth full.

'You've been very good about all this, David. Leaving Methody and all your friends. It can't be easy for you.'

He would miss his friends and, given a choice, he would rather have stayed in Belfast. But David was determined to make the best of it. For Mum's sake most of all.

'I don't mind, Dad, really,' said David swallowing. 'I'm quite looking forward to it in fact. They've got a good rugby squad. We played against them last year. And anyway, it's not the first time I've had to move school.'

'No. All part and parcel of being a minister's son. A nomadic lifestyle.'

'Yeah, you could put it like that.'

'So, do you think you'll get on the First Eleven then?'

'I hope so.'

'You're a great lad. At least I don't have to worry about you son,' said Dad, patting David roughly on the shoulder and David knew he was thinking about Mum.

★ ★ ★

The interview brought to a close, David backed out of the headmaster's office and pulled the door closed gently behind him. He swung his rucksack over his shoulder and walked down the corridor in the direction of the school office. He had reached the end of the corridor, where it turned at a sharp right angle, when a figure came sliding round the corner and crashed into him. Books flew everywhere.

'Oh God! I'm sorry. I didn't see you,' a breathless voice cried from somewhere down about his ankles.

David looked down at the girl who was already on her knees picking up the books. He could not see her face, only a river of dark hair coursing down her back.

'It's okay,' said David. 'Here, let me help you.'

His fingers closed on a book at the same time as the girl's and their hands collided, fingers touching.

Simultaneously, they withdrew their hands and looked at each other. They were so close David could smell the faint aroma of shampoo and soap. She held his gaze, her dark brown eyes framed by long lashes that curled up at the ends and arched eyebrows, thick and untamed. Her face was motionless, but her eyes flashed mixed messages of alternate strength and vulnerability. David's usual confidence left him and, although he opened his mouth to speak, for the first time in his life he didn't know what to say.

The girl dropped her gaze and added the book to the growing bundle cradled under her arm. She pushed back onto her knees, stood up and straightened her skirt with her free hand. She was nearly a full head smaller than him.

'I'm sorry,' she repeated, this time to his chest. 'I'd better go, I'm late for class again.'

'No, wait!' said David, regaining his composure. 'I'm David McDowell.'

The girl smiled shyly up at him.

'I'm Catherine Meehan,' she said.

She had a beautiful mouth, her full, deep-pink lips, a seductive contrast to her ivory cheeks. He had to stop himself staring.

'I've not seen you before,' said Catherine, stealing a glance up at his face.

David smiled broadly.

'No, I'm new. This is my first day. I'm in Lower Sixth,' he offered.

'Me too.'

'I've just been in having my interview with Mr Wilson.'

'Oh, Wee Willie. That's what everybody calls him. His first name's William, you see.'

She smiled at him, hugging the books close to her chest. Then she looked at the floor.

After a short silence she continued. 'You're not from round here though?'

He shook his head.

'So where are you from?'

'Belfast. My Dad's the new minister at Greenwood. Do you know it?'

'Yes.'

For some reason he thought he detected the faintest hint of coolness in her voice.

'Look, I'd really better go,' she said, looking along the corridor, 'I'm sorry about, well, you know, nearly knocking you off your feet on your first day.'

'Don't apologise — I couldn't have had a nicer welcome,' he said, surprised at his boldness.

Catherine's face flushed pink and she averted her eyes.

'Bye, then,' she said quickly and disappeared down the corridor.

'Nice to meet you!' David shouted after her, but she did not respond except to raise her free arm in a salute.

David could not get Catherine out of his mind all morning. At breaktime he made his way to the Common Room, a redundant classroom that was set aside for the older pupils — the Lower and Upper Sixth forms. There were about twenty people scattered about, the boys lounging over desks and tables, the girls gossiping in small groups. Catherine was nowhere to be seen.

'Hey, big man,' came a shout from across the room and a burly, ginger-haired bloke came lumbering over. 'Didn't we play against you last year?'

'If I remember correctly we thrashed you,' said David good-humouredly and he put out his hand in greeting.

'David McDowell.'

'Gavin Marshall,' replied the ginger-top taking David's palm in his big ham of a hand and grinning.

'Don't forget who's side you're on now,' he continued. 'And, if I remember correctly, you're one hell of a wing forward! Come on, David, there's some guys I want you to meet.'

He threw his heavy arm across David's broad shoulder and steered him into the middle of a group of rugby players.

'So, aren't you going to introduce us to the new boy?' said a playful female voice.

David hadn't noticed the two girls come up and he turned now to look. The blonde one who'd spoken was slim and pretty. Her eyes twinkled mischievously, a piercing bright blue.

'Ach, Jayne, leave us alone, would you,' retorted Gavin, suppressing a smile. 'This is man's talk.'

'Oh, is it now? Well in that case, we're definitely staying,' said Jayne cheekily, and elbowed her way into the circle. The other girl, not so pretty or so slim, followed suit.

'I'm Jayne,' said the slim one with a dazzling smile, all even white teeth like an advert for toothpaste on TV.

'So I gathered,' he laughed. 'I'm David, David McDowell,' and shook her hand warmly.

The sleeves of her white shirt were rolled up to the elbows. The skin on her arms, like that on her face and neck, was a golden colour speckled with small dark brown moles. She was, David had to admit, a stunner.

The bell went and after a suitably nonchalant

204

pause, everyone made for the door.

'I think Jayne Alexander has the hots for you,' said Gavin and he slapped David on the back.

'Don't be daft,' said David. 'She's only just met me.'

'Must be love at first sight then,' said Gavin, grinning, and he disappeared down the corridor singing, 'It must be love. Love. Love. Nothing more, nothing less. Love is the best . . . ' David shook his head, smiling, and wondered where Catherine was.

At lunch-time he decided to ask Gavin about her. Lunch was served in the hall which had been transformed from that morning's assembly. Dozens of tables filled the room each one surrounded by eight red plastic chairs, quickly filling up with hungry students. Cutlery and crockery banged and clattered, chairs-legs scraped on floorboards and human voices reached a crescendo, died away, and rose again. The noise was tremendous.

Gavin studied the menu; chicken pie or fish, mashed potatoes, peas and carrots followed by treacle pudding and custard. He smacked his lips.

'Think I'll have the pie,' said Gavin. 'You should try the treacle pudding. It's one of the best.'

'I bumped into a girl in the corridor this morning. On my way out of Wilson's office,' said David, as casually as he could.

'And what did the old bastard have to say for himself?' said Gavin, inching up the queue and straining to see inside the aluminium containers

205

from which two sturdy-armed women were dispensing dinners. A powerful smell of fish and overcooked vegetables wafted down the queue.

'Bet he asked you all about the rugby, eh? Between you and me David, the team needs a bit of new blood.'

Gavin took two white plates from a stack and handed one to David.

'Yeah, he asked me about the rugby. About this girl. Her name was Catherine something.'

'How are you today, Mrs C! You're looking lovely as ever. Yes, fine thanks. Chicken, please,' said Gavin addressing one of the dinner ladies, 'and the same for my friend David here?' he asked, raising his eyebrows at David.

David nodded. Mrs C gave them a toothy grin and served two plates piled high with extra pie and spuds.

'Meehan, that was it. Catherine Meehan,' continued David. 'Said she was in Lower Sixth. What do you know about her?'

'Thank you, Mrs C. You're an angel. I swear to God, I'd waste away without you!' declared Gavin, patting his ample stomach. 'Treacle pudding? Do you need to ask, Mrs C? What did you say, David? Catherine Meehan? Well, if you ever get talking to her, she's a nice girl. Real sexy, know what I mean?' he whispered, pushing his breasts up and sticking his tongue out the left hand corner of his mouth in a grotesque fashion like a horny Quasimodo.

David smiled and waited for him to continue.

'Mind you, she keeps pretty much to herself. Doesn't hang round with many of the girls.

Come to think of it, you never see her at lunch-times but she sometimes comes into the Common Room at breaktime. She must go home for lunch.'

He lifted the pudding, a mound of brown sponge smothered in a glutinous yellow substance, onto his tray.

'That looks great! Thank you, Mrs C. See you tomorrow!'

David shook his head at the offer of pudding and followed Gavin to the cutlery trays.

'Keep 'em sweet, that's the secret,' said Gavin, out of the corner of his mouth, and he nodded at his heavily-laden tray. 'Anyway, there's another Catholic, Moira Campbell, in the year and the two of them are close. That's about it really. Now that you're asking I suppose I don't know much about her.'

All of a sudden Gavin paused, his fistful of cutlery suspended in mid-air. 'You don't fancy her do you?' he asked, astonished. 'No,' said David hastily. 'I was just wondering who she was, that was all.'

And he turned quickly and began to search for two free seats so that Gavin couldn't see the disappointment in his face.

* * *

Catherine was deep in thought when she heard Moira's shout. She looked up, but remained seated on the secluded steps that led round the back of the biology labs.

'Catherine! I should have known I'd find you

207

here,' cried Moira, coming up.

'What is it?' asked Catherine irritably. She came here when she wanted to be alone and resented the interruption.

'That's a nice way to greet your best friend. I've been looking for you all over.' She sat down beside Catherine panting slightly.

'Have you heard the news?' said Moira when she'd regained her breath.

'What about?'

'A new guy in Lower Sixth. David McDowell. His Dad's a minister at some Church in the town and they've just moved to Ballyfergus. Everybody's talking about him. He's gorgeous!'

'Oh, I've met him already,' said Catherine casually, her heartbeat quickening.

'What? And you didn't come and tell me? You sneaky devil!' said Moira, digging Catherine in the ribs with her elbow.

'I forgot. It didn't seem important,' said Catherine, pulling away and avoiding eye contact with Moira.

She felt once again the shock of electricity when her hand met David's, the pounding of her heart as she stared into those clear blue eyes. She remembered the blonde curls tumbling into his eyes, and the butterflies in her stomach when he smiled, the corners of his mouth disappearing into dimples.

How she had struggled to act normally when she felt extraordinary. She was still struggling to master those feelings now.

'Not important?' echoed Moira, her voice full of suspicion. 'Imagine keeping that to yourself.

You're a funny one, you are, Catherine Meehan! So, when did you meet him? He's not doing the same subjects as you, is he?'

'I can't tell you if you keep asking me questions, now can I?' said Catherine, laughing.

Looking suitably chastised, Moira was silent and waited for Catherine to continue.

'I ran into him this morning when I was late for French,' said Catherine, matter-of-factly. 'I dropped my books and he helped me pick them up.'

She didn't trust herself to say any more. For some reason she couldn't bring herself to tell Moira the truth. That she thought she was in love with him. That she couldn't get David McDowell out of her mind. His name ran round inside her head like a litany, over and over again. And interspersed was her name. David McDowell, Catherine McDowell, David McDowell, Mrs McDowell. She wasn't normally given to fanciful daydreaming — this was so unlike her. Catherine told herself to get a grip.

'Well, what did he say to you?' asked Moira impatient for information.

'Nothing really. I said I was sorry and he said 'It's all right' and that, and then he introduced himself.'

'Uh huh,' said Moira, waiting for more.

'He'd just been in to see Wee Willie. I told him my name and he said he'd just moved to Ballyfergus from Belfast and that his Dad was minister at Greenwood. And that's it really,' she concluded nonchalantly.

'And what did you think of him?'

209

'Oh, he was all right. Seemed nice enough,' replied Catherine.

Moira nodded her head thoughtfully.

'So you don't think he's the best-looking, most drop-dead gorgeous guy you've ever seen then?'

'Well, he's not bad looking, I suppose.'

As soon as she said it Catherine realised it was a mistake. In trying so hard to appear disinterested, she had revealed far more of her true feelings than she cared to. Moira knew her too well and, besides, a blind man could have seen that David McDowell was the best-looking guy in the whole school.

'I see,' said Moira and she regarded Catherine thoughtfully for a few moments.

'He said quite a lot, then,' she continued, adding playfully. 'He must like you or he wouldn't have taken the time to ask who you were and all. Blokes aren't usually that nice unless, of course, they fancy you.'

'Don't be ridiculous,' said Catherine crossly, jumping up and taking both steps to the path below in one stride.

She felt her cheeks burning, the cool air in the shade of the building failing to fan them.

'You fancy him, don't you!' said Moira, triumphant.

'No, you've got it all wrong . . . ' began Catherine and then the bell went, shrill and long. Catherine could have cried with relief.

'Must go. See you later,' she called out over her shoulder and ran inside, out of Moira's sight.

Catherine found her way to the toilets and hid inside a cubicle with her back to the door. She couldn't possibly go into class until she'd stopped blushing. She put her hands up to her face — they felt ice cold against her cheeks. She held them there, letting the coldness seep into the hot flesh.

Why couldn't she just tell Moira that she fancied David? What was the big deal? But she knew she couldn't tell Moira the truth. David might not fancy her and she couldn't take that risk of rejection. If she let her feelings known she'd have to live with the embarrassment of everyone talking about her.

If David really did fancy her, she concluded, then it was up to him to do the chasing. And then there was the fact that he was a Protestant which made a relationship highly unlikely. He'd probably much rather go out with one of his own sort. There was no point getting her hopes up only to be dashed. She'd try to avoid him as much as possible.

Minutes later Catherine emerged from the toilets, much calmer, and made her way to the classroom. But even though she tried hard to suppress it, hope was still alive.

★　★　★

Moira was waiting for Catherine outside school at a quarter to four and smiled when she saw her. Both girls were heavily laden down with textbooks, too many for their satchels, so they had to carry a bundle under their left arms which were already beginning to ache.

'These books weigh a ton!' complained Moira

as they walked up the hill. 'I don't know why they have to give them all out on the first day.'

'I know,' said Catherine, aware of an uneasiness between them. She would have to clear the air.

'Look, Moira, I'm sorry about running off like that earlier. I just don't like being teased.'

'I know. Let's just forget about it.'

'I don't fancy him and he doesn't fancy me. You do understand, don't you?'

'Yes, perfectly,' replied Moira and, without another word being spoken on the subject, Catherine knew that Moira could see everything.

'Moira,' said Catherine anxious to change the subject, 'did you know our Geraldine's been seeing Jayne Alexander's brother?'

'Eddie Alexander? You're joking! Isn't he in the police?'

'Yes he is,' replied Catherine, casting a worried glance at Moira. 'It started in the summer. Mammy and Daddy are raging. They keep trying to talk her into finishing with him, but she won't listen.'

'Are they serious?'

'You mean Geraldine and Eddie?'

Moira nodded.

'Well she told me she was in love with him.'

'But she's only fifteen, Catherine! I'm not surprised your Mum and Dad are doing their nut.'

'She'll be sixteen soon and anyway it's not about her age. Geraldine's very mature and Dad doesn't object to her going out with boys full stop. It's only because he's a Protestant.'

'I know,' said Moira thoughtfully. 'My Dad would go mental if I brought a Protestant home.'

'Well, what do they expect?' said Catherine angrily, 'They send us to the Grammar where all the fellas are Protestants and then we're not supposed to go out with any of them?'

'Dad says I've plenty of time for that when I'm over eighteen and until then he doesn't want me going out with anybody.'

Catherine thought of Moira's Dad and shivered involuntarily. He gave her the creeps. There was something . . . something not quite right about him. Maybe it was because he drank too much.

'Doesn't that bother you?'

'Not really. I'm not interested in boys.'

'He doesn't like you wearing make-up either, does he?' said Catherine.

'He says it makes me look like a tart.'

'It's like he doesn't want you to grow up.'

Moira said nothing in response and Catherine looked at her closely. She couldn't help but get the feeling that Moira was hiding something from her.

'I don't want to talk about it,' said Moira. 'All right?'

'Sure. Whatever you want.'

'I'm going to go to University,' said Moira suddenly, 'in England. And I won't be coming back here. Ever.'

'What's brought this on?' said Catherine. 'You've never mentioned it before.'

'I've just decided, that's all. Don't look so surprised. It's what you've always talked about.

213

Why shouldn't I go too?'

'There's no reason why not. It's just . . . well, I never imagined you leaving Northern Ireland, that's all. I always thought you were happy here. Not like me.'

'There's a lot of things you don't know about me,' said Moira quietly.

They parted company at the top of the hill and Catherine trudged the rest of the way home, her arms and back aching from the weight of the heavy books. When she got in the kitchen was empty. There was a note from Mammy saying she'd gone to the shops and giving instructions for Catherine and Geraldine to prepare the dinner. Catherine took her books upstairs to the bedroom. Geraldine was already home, sitting on the side of the bed in her school uniform.

'Where's Michael?' asked Catherine, dumping her bag and books on the bed and sinking down for a rest.

When Geraldine did not reply Catherine looked at her face. She had been crying. There were no tears now but her face was blotchy and she held a scrunched up tissue in her fist.

'What's wrong?' said Catherine, immediately going down on her knees and taking Geraldine's hands in hers.

'It's Michael,' replied Geraldine, raising her watery eyes to meet Catherine's. 'He said the most awful things about me and Eddie. Told me to finish with him or he'd sort him out.'

'Oh, Geraldine, don't you pay any attention to Michael. Sometimes he talks a lot of old rubbish.

I know he doesn't mean half of what he says anyway.'

'You think so?' said Geraldine hopefully.

'I'm sure of it. Sure he's a big softy at heart. Okay, so he doesn't like the idea of you going out with a Protestant, but I'm sure he'd like Eddie if he met him. We all would. Just you leave it to me, I'll have a word with him. Now, let's get changed for Mammy'll be home soon and we need to get the dinner started.'

11

David followed Catherine and her red-haired friend out of assembly pushing his way through the crowd. They walked quickly and were already at the bottom of the tarmac drive when he emerged on the steps outside the assembly hall.

'Catherine,' he shouted, running down the steps, but she walked on.

'Catherine! Wait!' he called again and this time the friend stopped and turned. She said something to Catherine and she too came to a halt and waited.

'Hi, there,' he said, panting as he came up to them.

'Hello,' said Catherine, her face flushed, he supposed, from the brisk pace.

'I wondered where you got to yesterday,' he said. 'You just disappeared!'

Catherine did not answer, but shrugged her shoulders and looked at the ground. Then, avoiding eye contact with him, she spoke.

'Oh, this is my friend Moira Campbell. And this is David. David McDowell.'

'Pleased to meet you,' said Moira, grinning inanely.

David turned his attention to Catherine who looked anxiously up the drive as though on the lookout for someone. She did not seem like the same girl who had connected with him only yesterday morning.

'Well,' said David, 'I thought I'd just say hello, that's all.'

There was an uncomfortable pause and then Moira spoke.

'When did you move to Ballyfergus then?'

'Three weeks ago.'

'Right.'

Another pause.

'Hmm. Do you have any brothers and sisters?' asked Moira.

'No, there's just me.'

Catherine looked up at him through her long lashes and held his gaze uncertainly for a moment before she looked away.

'Well, I just thought I'd say hello,' said David, 'that's all. See you around.'

The girls said goodbye and David felt very foolish.

Later that day, between classes, his path crossed with Catherine's. Their eyes met. David felt his heartbeat quicken and the roof of his mouth went dry and pasty. Catherine stared back, her eyes dark and searching, as though she was trying to tell him something. But all she said was, 'Hello', and made no further attempt to speak to him. Confused, David eventually came to the conclusion that she did not like him and her proud, distant bearing was her way of trying to tell him. And perhaps it was for the best, he thought, reminding himself that she was a Catholic.

★ ★ ★

217

The first Sunday after the start of school term, Jayne came to Church. She looked sophisticated and mature in a suit, high heels and cream blouse, not the schoolgirl of the previous week.

'I don't remember seeing you here before,' said David outside after the service was over. 'I didn't even know you were a member.'

'It's a sort of new term resolution. To come every week,' she replied, squinting in the low autumn sun, her pupils contracting to small black dots. He noticed how blue her eyes were, an intense aquamarine, the colour of Mediterranean seas.

'That's my Mum and Dad. Over there,' she went on pointing at Mr Alexander and his wife.

The congregation had filed out through the ancient arch-shaped door of the church and assembled in little groups at the bottom of the short flight of steps.

'Yes, I've met them,' said David.

From where they stood they could overhear the conversation amongst the group the Alexanders had joined.

'I think the new minister delivers a fine sermon,' said Mr Alexander, 'and it's good to have some fresh blood don't you think?'

'Yes, John. Now more importantly,' said Mrs Alexander addressing the wider group 'are all the arrangements made for the Sunday School outing?'

'Yes, only Gail's not well and won't be able to do any catering,' said one of the women.

'Oh, dear, what's the matter?'

'She says it's the 'flu but apparently,' the

218

women went on, lowering her voice conspiratorially, 'there's been a fallout between her and Mrs Steel.'

'What about?'

'Mrs Steel said she'd be better making the pavlovas because Gail's were always soggy. Mrs Steel denies she ever said it, but that's the real reason Gail's not coming.'

'I sometimes wonder,' said Jayne in a low voice, 'if the socialising is the sole reason they come to church.'

'What do you mean?'

'Well, they seem more interested in the gossip and chat than the business of praying. It's more like a social club than a church for some of them. Do you think I'm being uncharitable?'

'I don't know,' said David. 'I hadn't thought about it like that before.'

'I don't know about yours,' said Jayne, 'but my parents hardly socialise with anyone outside the church. It just seems so . . . so insular to me. Anyway, Dad likes me to put in an appearance every now and then. Keeps him happy. I don't suppose you have a choice, being the minister's son, I mean?'

'I suppose not, though I've never really thought about not coming. It seems natural to be here every week. Part of family tradition.'

'Hello, David,' said Mr Alexander who'd come up to them unnoticed.

His crisp white shirt was dazzling against his neat dark suit. The tight collar of his shirt squeezed the little fold of loose skin on his neck into a 'V' just above the top button. He smelt

219

strongly of aftershave.

'How are you settling in at the Grammar then? I hope they're making you feel at home?' he said, winking at Jayne.

'It's great, Mr Alexander. I really like it.'

'Good, good. That's just marvellous, so it is. Listen David, I've been speaking to your Mum and Dad and they're coming over to our house next Saturday for dinner. Why don't you come too? It'll give you a chance to get to know the family better,' he said, glancing at Jayne. 'And you haven't met Eddie yet, have you?'

David shook his head.

'He's a couple of years older than you. Likes a game of rugby himself so you'll have plenty to talk about.'

★   ★   ★

The evening at the Alexanders' was a great success and Mr Alexander had been right about Eddie. He played for Ballyfergus Rugby Club and they had lots in common — it seemed David's reputation had preceded him.

'Why don't you come down on Wednesday night and join the lads for a training session,' asked Eddie, 'followed by touch rugby. See what you think. No reason why you can't play for both the Grammar and Ballyfergus. Playing with men instead of boys might even improve your game!'

David took Eddie up on his offer and soon he was a regular visitor at the Alexanders'.

One night he was sitting at the kitchen table with Jayne and Eddie drinking coffee. Eddie yawned and looked at his watch.

'I've got to go to bed,' he said, 'I'm on early shift tomorrow. I'll see you on Saturday at the club. Don't forget it's a two o'clock kick-off.'

'Night, Eddie, I won't forget,' said David.

'Did you ever see much of the Troubles in Belfast?' asked Jayne when Eddie had left the room.

'No, not really, why?'

'It's just that nothing much ever happens in Ballyfergus. I wondered what it was like and if that was the reason you left Belfast.'

'Well, where we lived nothing much happened either. I got caught in bomb scares in town a few times. You had to go and stand behind a barrier until the army gave the all-clear. And once there was this burnt out bus on the way to school that stopped us getting through. But that was it really. Most of the trouble is confined to certain areas.'

'You mean working-class areas?'

'Well, yes. To be truthful, we weren't affected by it at all. Apart from Mum that is.'

'What do you mean?'

'Oh, it's just she gets all worked up when she hears about bombings and shootings. Dad and I have tried to talk to her, but she takes it all too much to heart.'

'Anyway,' he went on, keen to change the subject, 'your Mum and Dad seem very nice.'

Jayne shrugged her shoulders. 'They are. I just wish this business about Eddie would blow over and then things could get back to normal.'

'What business?'

'You don't know? Hasn't he told you?'

221

'Told me what?'

'Eddie's been seeing this girl. A Catholic. You know Catherine Meehan?'

David nodded.

'Well, it's her younger sister, Geraldine. It's been awful,' said Jayne. 'Dad wants Eddie to stop seeing her and they argue about it all the time.'

Jayne sniffed and rubbed her nose with the back of her hand.

'It's great to have someone to talk to. Outside the family I mean.'

She composed herself and went on.

'I've tried hard to see it from both Dad's and Eddie's point of view, but I can't sympathise with one without antagonising the other. Eddie's hardly been speaking to me this week. And I've really nothing against him going out with Geraldine at all. It's so unfair.'

'I never noticed anything amiss,' said David, wondering if Geraldine was anything like her older sister.

'No, you wouldn't. Everybody's being civil to each other, but the tension's there, under the surface. The thing is Eddie doesn't appreciate how much all this is hurting Dad. And I can understand why Dad gets so upset. I know it's an awful thing to say, but why did Eddie have to take up with a Catholic? If she was anybody else . . .'

Her voice trailed off and she shrugged her slim shoulders hopelessly.

'What does your Mum have to say about all this?' asked David.

'Oh, she agrees with Dad but she won't say

anything in front of Eddie because she doesn't want to fall out with him. Anyway, my efforts to get the two of them talking have failed miserably. I don't know what's going to happen now,' she said flatly. 'I just hope Dad doesn't do anything stupid like throw Eddie out. You don't think he would do that, do you?' she asked, her eyes widening in horror.

'No, it'll not come to that Jayne,' replied David. 'Things have a way of working out in the end, you'll see.'

'I'm surprised he didn't say anything to you,' said Jayne, taking a sip of coffee. 'I thought you two were friends.'

'We're not that close and anyway it's not the sort of thing guys talk about,' said David glad that Eddie had not confided in him.

Perhaps Eddie thought he would disapprove. Obviously the thing to do was finish with the girl, but then again, if she was anything like her older sister, he could understand Eddie's dilemma.

'Jayne, I've been meaning to ask you something,' he said, cradling the chunky hand-thrown mug in his broad hands.

She looked up expectantly.

'Yes?'

'Would you like to go out with me? To the school dance.'

Even though he was confident of her answer he still had butterflies in his stomach. He tilted the mug slightly towards him, little bits of white froth floating on top of the brown liquid, and waited for her answer.

'Yes, David, I'd love to,' she replied quickly and the momentary awkwardness between them disappeared.

★ ★ ★

At the dance they spent most of the evening mixing with other people, but everyone knew they were on a date.

David leant against the wall and watched Jayne dancing. The assembly hall had been converted to a disco for the occasion, strobe lights and all. She wore tight blue jeans and a pale pink shirt with the sleeves rolled up. Tossing a lick of blonde hair out of her eyes she threw him one of her dazzling smiles.

'She's a good catch, David. The best looking girl in the school,' said Gavin who'd come up alongside him.

'You sound jealous.'

'I am. Sure a girl like Jayne would never look at me,' he said, sounding depressed.

Aware Catherine was in the hall, David satisfied himself with furtive glances, but for most of the evening he studiously avoided looking directly at her. However, using his peripheral vision, he was aware where she was in the room and what she was doing at any given time. At the end of the evening she left with Moira.

By the time they'd paid the DJ and finished clearing up the hall it was nearly midnight. David gave Jayne a lift home in his father's car which he'd been allowed to borrow for the night.

'So how much money did we clear?' asked David, changing gear carefully.

'Nearly two hundred pounds after paying the DJ.'

'Not bad for a night's work.'

'Hmm,' said Jayne thoughtfully. Then, 'Did you see the way Catherine Meehan was dressed?'

'No. Why?'

'She looked really unusual, like something out of the 1950s, with that flared red skirt and her hair tied up in a pony-tail. Reminded me of *Grease*. I thought she looked very pretty.' Jayne waited for some response, but got none.

David gripped the steering wheel tighter and fixed his eyes rigidly on the road ahead.

'Didn't you?' said Jayne.

'Didn't I what?'

'Think she looked very pretty.'

'Did she?'

'You didn't notice?'

'No.'

Jayne looked out the passenger window and continued. 'You know there's plenty of blokes in the school fancy her like mad but they're all too afraid to ask her out in case she'll bite the head off them!'

'Is that right?' said David, feigning indifference.

'Do you know we've hardly spoken to each other in all the years we've been at the Grammar together. I remember our first day in assembly. She sat down beside me and I tried to be nice to her and do you know what? She ate the face off me! It's a real shame because she's really very stunning looking, don't you think?'

'I don't know,' said David, by now wishing Jayne would change the subject. He didn't trust himself to talk dispassionately about Catherine.

'Let's talk about something else,' he said.

'Okay,' said Jayne, scrutinising his face.

He concentrated on the driving and tried hard to look indifferent.

'Everyone was talking about us, you know,' she continued, as the car came to a stop outside Jayne's house. 'Saying we're made for each other. We even have the same hair colour and we both have blue eyes. Except your hair's curly.'

David switched off the engine.

'You know, some of the girls think you're quite a catch, David McDowell,' laughed Jayne, her lips parted over perfect teeth.

'And what do you think?'

'Oh, I don't know,' teased Jayne. 'I suppose you'll do for a one-night stand.'

She turned her head in the direction of the house, the windows plunged in inky darkness and said, serious now, 'Well, thanks very much for the lift home David. It's a bit late to ask you in for coffee.'

'I'd better be getting home anyway,' replied David. 'Mum'll be worried about me. She'll not go to sleep, you know, until I'm in.'

'Well, thanks again,' said Jayne. 'I had a really nice time.'

'So did I. 'You'll not be wanting to go out with

me again then?' asked David.

'I could be persuaded,' she replied and swallowed.

David could see her lips, shiny with gloss, in the dim light and her chest heaved gently up and down under a jumper she'd slipped on to keep out the chill.

He leant over and, hesitantly, pressed his mouth to hers. She squirmed closer to him, encircling his neck with her arms. She smelt of vanilla, and he ran his fingers tentatively through the soft silky strands of her hair. David's head began to swim and he was aware only of their lips melded together, his body pressed against hers.

Eventually, Jayne pulled back and glanced over her shoulder at the house.

'I'd better go in,' she said and added, 'and yes I will go out with you again. If you want to, that is.'

★ ★ ★

Soon after the school dance Catherine spoke to Michael. It was Friday night and Dad and Sean were out doing a 'homer'. Mum was up at chapel helping with the flowers for Sunday and Geraldine was round at her friend Paula's. At least that was what she'd told Mammy and Daddy, but Catherine knew she was out with Eddie.

Michael was in the sitting room watching television. Catherine came in and sat down beside him on the sofa.

'What did you say to Geraldine, Michael?'

He laughed at something on the television and then said, 'What do you mean?'

He didn't take his eyes of the screen.

'About her seeing Eddie Alexander. I came home from school the other day and she was in tears. She said you said horrible things about him.'

'All I said was that she shouldn't be going out with him. Nothing more than the truth.'

'But Michael, she's in love with him. It's not her fault he's a Protestant.'

'No, but he should know better,' snapped Michael. 'What does he want running round with a Catholic for anyway?'

'But suppose he loves Geraldine? What are they supposed to do? You can't choose who you fall in love with,' reasoned Catherine.

'Maybe not. Look Catherine,' he said, turning the volume down on the remote control, 'sometimes you have to put duty before personal feelings.'

'Duty? What duty? What on earth are you talking about Michael?'

'I'm talking about keeping the faith,' he said patiently, as though talking to a child, 'being true to your roots. Look what our ancestors fought and died for. People are still dying for the same vision of a United Ireland. The problem with us living here in Ballyfergus is that we're divorced from the reality of what's going on in this country.'

He was excited now, his eyes alive with passion.

'And we've no pride. You know what they say about us?'

'No. What?'

'They say there's no-one keeps their head so low as a Ballyfergus Catholic. We're a laughing stock amongst our own people. Just because we're the minority in this town doesn't mean we have to kowtow to the Protestants.'

Michael's face was flushed red and Catherine too blushed with shame for there was some truth in what he said.

'I know,' she agreed. 'Do you remember being afraid to go out on the Eleventh night? I mean really afraid?'

Michael nodded and Catherine went on.

'I used to lie in bed absolutely terrified that they were going to come and get me and throw me on the bonfire along with the effigy of the Pope. And their bloody Lambeg drums and drunken screams and shouts would keep you awake half the night.'

'They still do,' said Michael. 'But you know what pisses me off? A lot of the bonfires are illegal, but the Council won't do anything to stop them. One of the councillors even had the gall to suggest that the Twelfth is a non-sectarian celebration that Catholics could join in as well.'

'And so we sit at home and wait obediently for the nonsense to end so that we can get on with life,' said Catherine bitterly.

'Exactly.'

Catherine sighed.

'But getting back to Geraldine,' she said. 'I

really don't see what that's got to do with her and Eddie.'

'It's everything to do with them,' replied Michael, raising his voice. 'Can't you see that Catherine? She should stick to her own kind.'

'But Michael isn't that what half the problems in this country are about? If people got on with each other and integrated better then there wouldn't be so much trouble.'

'The Protestants don't want to integrate, Catherine. They want to dominate and that's quite a different thing altogether. The Catholics in this town have done enough grovelling and going out with a Protestant is just the same as being a traitor.'

'Oh, Michael, that's an awful thing to say!'

'Look, I don't mean to hurt Geraldine,' said Michael, softening, 'and you know I love both my sisters. I only say what I do because it's right and I know what's best for Geraldine. And that Eddie Alexander. It'll only lead to unhappiness for there's no future in it. Can't you see that?'

His expression was earnest, his dark eyes gentle and kind, the old Michael come back.

'I know what you're saying makes sense, in a way, Michael. It just seems . . . well . . . so unfair,' said Catherine, biting her bottom lip.

'No-one ever said life was fair, Catherine.' Michael looked at her for a few seconds, his deep red lips pulled into a thin smile. Catherine felt herself entranced by the smouldering intensity of his gaze. His words came softer now, more a form of prayer, an intonation.

'There are some things bigger than us worth

fighting for. Worth dying for. And when the ultimate sacrifice is asked of the sons of Ireland, we must be ready.'

What was he saying? Catherine had heard him talk some pro-nationalist nonsense before, but this was the worst yet. She jumped up, the spell broken.

'Michael, I don't like to hear you talking like this! What's worth dying for? What do you mean by the ultimate sacrifice?'

He leaned back, allowing his head to rest on the sofa and held her gaze, but he did not answer. He shook his head slowly and suppressed what looked like a smirk as though he was the possessor of a great truth that she could not comprehend.

'Are you involved in something? Tell me Michael, please,' pleaded Catherine.

But he was a stranger to her again. He picked up the remote control, turned up the TV volume, crossed his arms and stared hard at the screen.

12

It was funny how you could get things completely wrong, reflected David. He was thinking of Catherine who sat alone on the other side of the library, scribbling furiously on a writing pad. She ripped off a completed page and set to filling up a fresh one straightaway, without looking once in his direction. It was odd that she should make such a point of not looking at him for if he hadn't known better, he would have supposed, from her actions, that she fancied him. But Catherine had made her feelings towards him very clear.

Suddenly he was aware of someone behind him and he felt a warm breath on the back of his neck. For a moment he imagined . . . but Catherine was still on the other side of the library, a model of industry.

'Hi, David,' whispered the voice, and Jayne sat down beside him.

'What are you doing here?' he asked.

'Don't sound so pleased to see me,' said Jayne, frowning. 'I thought I'd surprise you. Mitchell's off with the 'flu or something so I've got two free periods. Thought I'd come and keep you company.'

David glanced over to the other side of the room. There! He'd caught Catherine looking at them.

'Aren't you pleased to see me?' said Jayne, her

eyes following his, her pretty features serious and concerned.

'Of course I am,' said David, 'you just gave me a bit of a fright.'

'Shush!' hissed Miss Kingshill.

Jayne smiled sweetly at the librarian and arched an eyebrow at David. She lifted her satchel onto the desk and rummaged around inside it eventually producing a dog-eared textbook, writing pad, pencil, yellow highlighter and a pen. She laid them out regimentally on the desk and began to work.

Resting his head in his hand David pretended to read the book opened in front of him. He looked across at Jayne. Her hair was tucked behind her small, pink earlobe adorned with a discreet gold stud, the only earring permitted by school rules. She sucked hard on the end of a blue biro, unconsciously pushing it in and out of her mouth, her lips pursed. David shifted uncomfortably in his chair as he felt an erection between his legs. He reminded himself how lucky he was to have her as his girlfriend.

And yet there was something missing from the relationship. Something that David, with his inexperience in these matters, could not quite pin down. It was nothing more than an uneasy sense that there should be more in depth or intensity or closeness. Even though they did a fair amount of fooling about, though going no further than heavy petting, they were more like best pals than lovers. At least that was how he felt.

This vague sense of dissatisfaction seemed to

have grown stronger of late and, to add to his confusion, he was haunted daily by thoughts of Catherine. Even now, right this minute, her very presence on the other side of the room excited him. The more he tried to block her from his mind, the more her image played on his mind. He couldn't help himself; he was obsessed by her smooth round hips and her sumptuous breasts.

'David,' someone whispered and he re-focused on Jayne.

'The bell's going to go in a minute. What are you doing after school?' she asked.

'Nothing. Why?'

'Do you fancy going down to Morelli's before going home? There's a crowd of us going.'

'I don't think so, Jayne. I've got a big essay to do for English tomorrow and I've hardly written a word,' he said.

He did have an essay to do but it wouldn't take him more than an hour and a half which he could easily do after tea. The truth was that he wanted to be alone. To work through the confusion in his head.

'I'm not surprised,' scolded Jayne, 'you've spent half the afternoon staring into space. You'll never get it written at that rate. Look at this.'

She proudly showed him the top three pages of her writing pad, each one filled up with neat blue handwriting.

'That's my essay for Mitchell nearly finished and I did that while you were day-dreaming.'

David couldn't help but smile.

'David McDowell, I do believe you're laughing at me,' she said, trying to sound indignant.

David walked her to the school gates and down The Brae, both of them fighting against a biting wind. The night was closing in and black, heavy clouds threatened rain.

At the bottom of the road, Jayne gave David a quick peck on the cheek.

'I promise I'll think of you working away on that essay while I'm enjoying a nice cup of coffee!' she laughed and they went their separate ways.

David watched Jayne run to catch up with the others and, when she'd disappeared from sight, he turned and walked briskly in the direction of the river.

★ ★ ★

Every time she saw them together Catherine was gripped by a jealousy so violent that it made her feel physically sick. Like just now in the library watching Jayne whisper into David's ear.

Whilst she wrestled with this emotion her rational brain told her there was no logic and no basis for her jealousy. Hadn't she more or less indicated to David, by her behaviour, that she wasn't interested? He'd tried to chat her up, Moira said, that day outside assembly, but she'd mucked it up.

Her embarrassment had been so excruciating, so acute, that she didn't know what to say to him. And he'd seemed so confident, so sure of himself that she'd felt foolish and childish in comparison. He must have thought her a right idiot. If Moira hadn't been there maybe things

235

would have turned out differently. But it wasn't Moira's fault. The fault lay with Catherine, fair and square.

And then he'd taken up with Jayne Alexander, confirming Catherine's opinion that he didn't really fancy her after all. And it seemed to Catherine that Jayne had everything she wanted. Jayne had David and she was a prefect.

The bell went and Catherine started. The seats where Jayne and David had been were empty. Her stomach did a little somersault. Did he look at her, she wondered, when he walked past as he must have done to exit the library? Or was he too busy talking to Jayne?

Jayne. Jayne Alexander. If only she wasn't in the same year, or at the same school, or didn't exist at all, how different things might have been. For Catherine was sure that if Jayne hadn't been on the scene, David would never have given up on her so easily.

She closed her books roughly and shoved them into her green satchel, now faded and worn, a testament to her years of study. She made her way to the locker room, little boys and girls swirling round her feet. Had she once been that small?

She collected her coat, scarf and gloves and considered whether she should go straight home. No-one would miss her if she went for a little walk. She didn't much relish going home anyway. Tension in the house was palpable. Only last night Daddy told Geraldine she wasn't to see Eddie any more and she'd run out of the house in tears.

Down by the riverbank the wind whipped round her legs and the cold soon seeped through her thin woollen gloves. Catherine dug her hands deeper into her duffel coat pockets and watched the river for some minutes.

Calmed by the swirling water and deafening roar, she turned her mind once more to the intractable problem of Geraldine and Eddie. So what if Geraldine was seeing a Protestant and so what if they ended up together? It wasn't the end of the world. There were plenty of mixed marriages nowadays, or so people said.

Catherine shivered and looked up at the sky; it was dark now and she thought she felt the first drops of rain. It was time to go. She bent her head against the weather and started back along the riverbank. She hadn't realised she'd come so far and she picked her pace up to a brisk march.

And then it happened again. She walked head first into David MacDowell. This time there was no fumbling for books and embarrassed apologies. They stood awkwardly regarding each other cautiously. Neither spoke for some moments until Catherine broke the silence.

'We make a right pair don't we? The two of us in this miserable place,' she said, glancing round, 'with faces like Lurgan spades.'

But David did not laugh at the joke.

'What are you doing here, Catherine?'

'I could ask you the same thing,' she replied.

'I came for a walk to clear my head. I had things to think about.'

He seemed troubled, his usual cheerfulness absent.

'You too?' he asked.

'You could say that,' said Catherine, colouring, and looking up at the black clouds she added, 'I'd better be getting home. It looks like rain.'

'No!' said David, making a move forward as if to stop her.

'What I mean,' he said, more softly, 'is that I'd like to talk to you.'

'What about?' said Catherine warily.

'There's things I need to ask you. About you and me.'

David was standing close, his eyes searching hers for a response, any indication of her thoughts.

Catherine was suddenly warm, the duffel coat heavy and stifling. The tiny flame of hope that had stayed alive all these months began to flicker and burn more brightly. Wait, Catherine, she told herself, wait until you're sure.

'What about us?' she asked guardedly.

'Do you have to make this so hard, Catherine?'

David seemed angry. He swallowed and went on.

'I liked you from the first day we met. I don't know what went wrong after that, but I can't help myself. I still have feelings for you. I can't get you out of my mind no matter how hard I try. And I think you feel the same about me.' He stopped and waited for her to reply.

His words were like music to her ears. And yet she couldn't let go and tell him how she really felt for fear of rejection.

'You do?' she ventured.

238

David threw his head back and let out a long frustrated sigh. He clenched his fists by his sides and let them go again.

Abruptly, he stepped forward and Catherine stood her ground. He took her head in his hands and, cradling it, he kissed her for a long time, gently and softly, on the lips.

When they parted, Catherine smiled.

'See,' he said, 'I was right. You do love me, don't you?'

'Yes, I do,' said Catherine.

The first heavy raindrops splattered noisily on the foliage surrounding them.

'Quick,' said David, 'let's hide under here.'

He grabbed Catherine by the hand and led her under a bridge. He put his arm over her shoulder and pulled her close, her head nestled on his chest. They stood there in silence watching the rain. Catherine felt warm and safe.

'What are you going to do? About Jayne, I mean?' asked Catherine eventually.

David frowned as though he had been reminded of an unpleasant chore still to be done.

'I'll have to talk to her, tell her were finished.'

'Yes,' said Catherine.

When they finally left the river, it was well after five o'clock.

'We'd better go up the road separately,' said David. 'In case Jayne sees us.'

'Right,' said Catherine. 'It wouldn't be fair for her to hear about us from someone else. You'll tell her in the morning then?'

'Yes, first thing. I might even phone her tonight.'

He held Catherine's hand until they reached the main road, then he kissed her one last time and they parted.

★   ★   ★

She wouldn't have known anything about it if it hadn't been for Eileen Richardson. She came into the shop, late, when everyone was already onto their second cup of coffee.

'I just saw David, Jayne. Why's he not joining us?' she asked, taking off her damp coat and draping it over the back of a chair.

'He's got an essay to do for tomorrow,' said Jayne. 'He said he was going straight home.'

'He was going in the direction of the river when I saw him. I called after him, but he didn't hear me. Why would he be going down there at this time of night?'

'I've no idea. Are you sure it was him, Eileen?'

'Positive.'

Jayne sat quietly, thinking, for the next few minutes. Something must be wrong though she couldn't imagine what it might be. Whatever it is, she thought, he'll need me.

She left her coffee unfinished, excused herself and went out into the rain and wind. She pulled her hood over her face as she walked briskly towards the river where she stopped on the bridge. She was about to follow the path down to the river when she saw two figures on the riverbank below.

Immediately, she recognised one of them as David. She was about to call out when she noticed, amazed, that he was holding the hand of the other smaller, female figure. And she knew, instinctively, that it was Catherine Meehan. All the times when David acted self-consciously in the presence of Catherine, like today in the library, came to mind. The evidence had been there, right under her nose, all along.

The figures embraced, Catherine raised her face to David's and they kissed. Jayne stood on the bridge, transfixed and repulsed at the same time, until she could bear it no more and ran away.

★ ★ ★

'What's wrong with you?' said Mum, fussing.

'I just don't feel well. I think my period's due,' lied Jayne, willing Mum to leave her alone.

Instead, Mum sat down on the edge of the bed and pressed the flat of her hand on Jayne's brow.

'Well, you don't have a temperature, so maybe that's all it is. Are you sure you don't want any tea? I could bring it up on a tray.'

'No thanks, Mum. Really. I just need some sleep. I'll be all right,' Jayne assured her, forcing a thin smile.

Mum leaned forward and kissed her on the forehead, a gesture so gentle and loving that Jayne burst into tears.

'What is it, darling, what's the matter?'

Jayne sobbed into the pillow, her weeping punctuated only by muffled gasps for air. The back of her throat was tight as though someone had their hands around her neck, strangling her.

'Jayne! What on earth's the matter? Look, I'll phone your father and get him to come home,' cried Mum getting up.

'No, no,' said Jayne, 'don't do that. It's all right.'

Jayne grasped Mum by the sleeve and pulled her down onto the bed again.

She allowed Jayne some minutes to compose herself then said, 'Jayne, dear, please tell me what's wrong. Has something happened?'

'Y . . . Yes. It . . . it's David.'

'Has something happened to David?' said Mum, sounding alarmed.

'No. Yes,' said Jayne, in between sobs.

She took several deep breaths before going on.

'I . . . I saw him. Tonight. With this girl. Kissing her.'

'And you're sure it was him?'

Jayne nodded.

'And you're sure he was kissing her. It wasn't just a friendly peck on the cheek?'

'Of course I'm sure,' said Jayne angrily. 'I know the difference between a snog and a peck on the cheek!'

'Oh, Jayne, love. I'm so sorry. So very sorry. Come here pet.' Jayne sat up and Mum encircled her with her arms. It felt warm and comforting like she was a little girl again.

'I'm not ugly or stupid or nasty, am I, Mum?'

'Of course not,' said Mum soothingly.

'So why did David do this to me? There must be something wrong with me.'

'There's nothing wrong with you. Sometimes things just aren't meant to be, that's all.

242

You'll get over him.'

Didn't Mum know she adored David, that he was the light of her life, the only thing that mattered to her? She'd been so proud being his girlfriend and he'd betrayed her.

'I was so happy, Mum. I'll never get over him,' said Jayne, breaking down again.

'Yes you will, love. In time. Time heals all things.'

'How could I have been so stupid, believing his story about having an essay to write when all along he'd planned to meet her.'

She raised her head from Mum's shoulder and let out a strange cry, a cross between a guffaw and a sob. 'If it wasn't so tragic, it would almost be laughable. There I was, worrying about him, and he was busy snogging Catherine Meehan!'

'Catherine Meehan,' repeated Mum vaguely.

'I wonder how long it's been going on for? Weeks? Months?'

'Don't torture yourself, love. He's not worth it.'

After a little while Mum asked, 'Are you okay now?' and Jayne nodded. 'Look, why don't you come downstairs and have something to eat? It'll make you feel better.'

'I just want to stay here.'

'Okay love, but you let me know if you want anything.'

After Mum left the room, Jayne lay for a long time staring blankly at the wall, the pink-patterned wallpaper becoming blurred from time to time, as her eyes filled with tears.

No matter how hard she tried she couldn't

bring herself to hate David. She still loved him, but he wasn't the person she thought he was.

He'd lied and there was only one thing left for her to do if she was to salvage any dignity from this whole mess. She'd finish with him before he dumped her. Or had he intended to keep this a secret and string her along? Like a fool.

13

'Where've you been, love?' asked David's Mum when he got in. 'I was expecting you home ages ago. Oh, you got caught in the rain.'

She was in the kitchen, a floral apron tied round her thick waist and the room smelt deliciously of bacon and cabbage and cheese sauce. She was tending the pots, a wooden spoon in her right hand and a tea-towel, for lifting the lids, in the other.

'Sorry, Mum,' said David. 'A crowd of us went to Morelli's after school. I didn't realise the time.'

'Jayne there?'

'Yes. Yes, she was,' said David uneasily, pulling off his wet coat and hanging it on the back of the kitchen door.

'That's nice. Well, son, would you get yourself washed please? Dinner will be on the table in five minutes. And could you give your father a shout?' she called after him. 'He's in the front room.'

Dad was asleep in a chair by the fire, a book open on his lap. David went over and looked at the title: *Saved By Jesus Christ: A Personal Testament*. David thought of Catherine and a wave of panic swept over him. Catholics didn't believe in being saved.

'Ah, David! There you are son,' said Dad, blinking.

'I was just going to wake you. Mum says tea's on the table in five minutes.'

'And you know what she's like if we're late,' said Dad, levering himself out of the chair.

They sat round the small kitchen table and ate their tea.

'John Alexander's coming round to see me tonight,' said Dad, chewing on a piece of bacon.

'It'll be nice to see him,' replied Mum, but Dad raised his knife slightly to indicate he had something more to say, swallowed, and then continued.

'He wants to discuss something with me. Something of a delicate nature so it might be best if you and David stayed out of the way when he comes. If you don't mind.'

'No, of course not, love,' said Mum, well used to parishioners calling at all hours for confidential chats.

'Is it about Eddie and Geraldine Meehan?' asked David.

Dad stopped eating and looked up, surprised. 'What do you know about that?'

'Just that he's been seeing her and his Mum and Dad aren't very happy about it.'

'You'll have heard that from Jayne, of course,' said Dad, mashing butter into the floury potatoes on his plate. 'Well, I suppose it's no secret. You probably know as much about it as I do. Has Eddie ever mentioned this girl to you?'

'No, never.'

'Hmm . . . ' said Dad, his mouth full of creamy potatoes.

'I could go and see Mrs Spencer. She's not

246

been very well lately,' said Mum, looking at the wall clock above the window.

'I really should go,' she said to herself and then, turning to Dad, asked, 'What time's John coming round?'

'Seven-thirty.'

'That's it settled then,' said Mum, bristling into action. 'If I get on with these now I should just about make it.'

She carried the dishes over to the sink.

'What about you, son?'

'Oh, I've an essay to do. I can go up to my room.'

★　★　★

When the doorbell went an hour later, Dad answered it and ushered Mr Alexander into the living room. His face was grave, but he brightened up a little when he saw David.

'Oh, David, Jayne's not well. She went straight to bed when she got home.'

'That's strange,' said David, feeling guilty at the mention of her name, 'she seemed okay at school. Maybe I'll give her a ring.'

He got up off the sofa and made for the door.

'No point, David, she's asleep. I'm sure it's nothing anyway, you know what girls are like. She'll be fine in the morning.'

'Right.'

The two men remained standing and, sensing it was time to make himself scarce, David made his excuses and went up to his room on the first floor of the big, old house.

247

A single lampshade hung from the middle of the high ceiling, the bulb making a feeble attempt at lighting the room. David switched on the black anglepoise lamp that sat on the desk and settled down to work.

He re-read the notes he'd made earlier and planned what he wanted to say. But every time he tried to write he found he could not concentrate.

He hadn't really thought through the consequences of taking up with Catherine. The realisation of what they might be was the cause now of his increasing anxiety.

For a start he'd been a right bastard as far as Jayne was concerned. He sat back in the chair, hung his head and sighed. He was ashamed of himself. Jayne deserved better than the way he'd treated her. He realised that he didn't want their late night chats to end, for Jayne to stop confiding in him, for her to be someone else's girlfriend. But how could he do without Catherine either? He'd held her in his arms once, after months of longing. Was he to throw that away and risk never experiencing feelings like those again?

Then there were his parents to consider. What would they think? And the Alexanders and everybody from Church?

David got up from the desk and threw himself on his back on the bed. He lay staring at the ceiling, hands behind his head. He feared losing Eddie's friendship; he dreaded no longer being able, and welcome, to drop by the Alexanders' anytime he wanted. He wasn't certain he could bear the disapproval that would surely come from every quarter.

But, he reminded himself, times had moved on and everybody talked about how they wished Protestants and Catholics could live together in peace. Didn't they pray for it every week at Church?

Maybe him seeing a Catholic wouldn't be so bad after all. A step towards integration of the two communities. Mum and Dad talked about it often enough. Perhaps they would come round to the idea and, in time, they might even see it as a positive thing.

Anxious voices drifted up from downstairs.

David sat up on the edge of the bed, held his breath and listened, remembering why John Alexander had come to see Dad. He heard only the low murmur of conversation. Curious, he got up, moved silently across the room and opened the door carefully.

He stole down the staircase gingerly, avoiding the steps that creaked. The living-room door was slightly ajar and, by standing with his back to the wall, David could hear quite clearly what was being said within.

'How do you know Eddie's serious about this girl? It could be nothing more than a passing fancy,' said Dad.

'I wish it was,' replied Mr Alexander sourly, 'but there's been talk of an engagement. He didn't say anything about it to me, of course, but he told Helen.'

'Hmm . . . ' said Dad, 'it sounds serious all right.'

'I just don't understand it. You spend all your life working hard to bring them up in a Christian home and set a good example. I took them to Church from the beginning, sent them to a good school; there was nothing lacking in their upbringing. And now look at Eddie. He doesn't seem to care about the heartbreak he's causing his mother and me. He's thrown everything we brought him up to believe back in our faces. How could he, Richard? A Catholic?'

'Now, now, John, don't distress yourself. There's always a way to work through these things. You must trust in Our Lord to guide you through this difficult time. The important thing is that you and Helen stay supportive and loving. It's vital that Eddie knows you're both there for him and that he can talk to you at any time. The last thing you want to do is alienate him.'

David was impressed by Dad's wise advice. No wonder people came to share their problems with him.

'What if he runs off and marries her, or worse . . . ' Mr Alexander's voice trailed off and then rallied again. 'Well, imagine if he did marry her. She'd probably have a baby straight away and, God knows, another six or seven after that. What kind of a life would that be for Eddie, supporting her and her bairns, without so much as a two farthings to rub together?'

'The wee girl has obviously got some sort of hold over Eddie and I agree that the sooner he stops seeing her the better. But you and Helen are going to have to be patient. By all means talk to him about it and explain where you're coming

250

from, but do so in a calm, rational manner. I've always found that reasoned logic and gentle persuasion is the best way. And he can't argue with the facts.'

'What facts?' said Mr Alexander.

'I presume she'd want to get married in a chapel and any children would have to be brought up Catholics. Ask him if he's considered that. How would he feel if his child was being indoctrinated by the Church of Rome? He wouldn't have any say in the matter either; Catholics are very funny about that sort of thing. And, from what you're saying, I'm not sure he fully understands the betrayal that such a union would represent to his family, friends and country. He couldn't expect you and Helen, and all his Christian friends and family to condone the marriage, let alone set a foot inside a Catholic church. Idolatry and popery has no place in a true Christian heart.'

'That's exactly how I feel.'

'Well, I wish I could be of more help to you, John.'

'Oh, but you've been great, Richard, really. It's been a weight on my mind and I needed to talk to someone. You've given me plenty to think over.'

'My words may provide some comfort, but the real help comes only from the Lord Himself. I'll be praying that Eddie sees the light and comes back into the fold of the Church. We've missed him on Sundays.'

'You're so lucky with your David, Richard. I could never see him doing what Eddie's done.

He's too much respect for you and Betty.'

'Yes, we are blessed, John. David's a good lad, but we can all stray from the path of righteousness. It's not the first time a decent fella has been bewitched by a Catholic. Rest assured, you and Helen will be in my prayers.'

'Thanks, Richard. At least I don't have to worry about Jayne,' said Mr Alexander. 'I know her and David are only kids, but Helen and I would be over the moon if, you know, it developed into anything more serious.'

David didn't wait to hear his father's reply. He crept back upstairs to his room and closed the door silently. He sat down on the bed and held his head in his hands.

What nonsense he'd been talking to himself only minutes before. Any relationship with Catherine Meehan was totally and completely out of the question. Who had he been trying to kid? Of course Mum and Dad could never accept Catherine.

She represented everything his father stood against: idolatry, popery, the cult of the Church of Rome. It was, according to Dad, a hotbed for demonic beliefs and practices, never mind traitors and Republicans.

Perhaps Dad's views were a bit extreme, paranoid even. But he was a good man, intelligent and wise. There must be some truth in what he said about the Catholic Church.

No, he could not, would not, be responsible for hurting his parents the way Eddie Alexander had done. It was best to break free before he was well and truly hooked. Besides, no real harm had been done; all they'd done was kiss. David touched his lips as though checking if the stain of sin was still on them. He would have to tell Catherine that it had all been a mistake.

The decision made, David experienced a great sense of relief as though he had just thrown off a terrible burden.

★   ★   ★

Catherine never felt a drop of rain on the way home even though her satchel was soaked right through and her hair was plastered to her face when she walked through the door.

'Where on earth have you been?' said Mammy. 'Look at you, Catherine. You're soaked through to the skin.'

'Am I?' said Catherine, looking down. Steam was already beginning to rise from her duffle coat in the heat of the kitchen.

'Why didn't you put your hood up?'

'I didn't realise it was raining so hard,' said Catherine.

And it was true. She hadn't been aware of anything on the way home but the burning sensation in her lips from David's kiss and the warmth of her palm where he had held her hand.

Later on, after tea was over, she and Geraldine washed, dried and put away the dishes while Mammy prepared stew for tomorrow night's dinner. Soon the whole house smelt of sweet, caramelised onions. The men of the family were in the sitting-room, the blare of the TV audible even with the door firmly shut.

To find some privacy, Catherine went upstairs to the bedroom she shared with Geraldine. She laid books open on the bed, ready to be picked up if footsteps creaked on the landing. Then she hugged her knees and laughed out loud and buried her face in her arms.

She'd known what it was to love from a distance, but to have that love returned was incredible. She felt like she could do anything, achieve anything, soar to the sky and fly high above the town. This was the feeling Geraldine had tried to describe. Catherine had not understood then, but she did now.

The next morning she awoke long before the alarm went off. She knelt up on the bed and looked out the window. The sky was leaden grey and warned of further rain, but Catherine bounced out of bed as though it was a sunny summer's morning. A shiver of excitement ran through her when she thought what the day ahead would bring.

'What's up with you?' said Moira as soon as they met at the bottom of Catherine's street. 'You look like the cat that's got the cream.'

For once Catherine put aside the excessive caution that had ruled her life for so long.

'Oh, Moira, I wasn't going to tell you until I was quite sure! But you'll never guess what.'

'What?'

'Me and David McDowell. We're going out together.'

'I don't believe it! I told you he fancied you, didn't I? When did this happen?'

Catherine told her what had happened the night before.

'But what about Jayne?' asked Moira. 'I thought he was going out with her.'

'He was. Well, he still is technically. At least until he tells her they're finished.'

'You mean he hasn't finished with her yet?'

'No, but he will do. This morning. He might even have done it last night on the phone.'

'I see,' said Moira sounding unconvinced.

'He will. He told me he would. Anyway,' said Catherine, noticing Moira seemed preoccupied, 'you don't seem all that pleased for me.'

'I am, Catherine. I have things on my mind, that's all.'

'Is it your Dad again? Has he hit you?'

'No, not me. Mum. She had to go up to the hospital last night.'

'God almighty! What did he do? Is she all right?'

'Yeah. She's fine. Just a black eye. But she thought he'd broken her nose.'

'What did the doctors say? Did she tell them how it happened?'

'No, of course not. She said she'd fallen down the stairs.'

'I'm sorry,' said Catherine and held back the urge to say more.

For years she had berated Moira's Dad and begged her to do something. But nothing had changed and her ranting on about it didn't help Moira. They walked the rest of the way to school in silence.

Catherine watched Jayne slide quietly into her

255

seat at assembly, her expression grim and immobile. Her face was sallow and the dark shadows under her eyes were visible even through the discreet layer of well-applied make-up. David must have finished with her and, from the state she was in, it was obvious that she cared for him a great deal.

Catherine felt a faint flush come into her cheeks and looked away. She'd been eagerly awaiting this, her moment of triumph, but now it was here she could not take the delight in it that she'd anticipated. But, she reminded herself, it was David's free choice; she wasn't responsible for Jayne's misery. She had nothing to be ashamed of.

All the same, Catherine avoided Jayne on the way out of assembly and searched anxiously for David, but he was nowhere to be seen. The bell for first class went and she filed to the classroom, on the lookout for him along the corridors and passageways. By breaktime she was so anxious to see him that she ventured into the Sixth Form Common Room. David was standing on the periphery of the rugby crowd. He saw Catherine as soon as she walked in. He did not smile as he moved towards her.

'I need to speak to you,' he said, his voice little more than a whisper, and walked past her towards the door.

Alarmed, Catherine followed him into the disused kitchen in the Old House, now a repository for lost property. David shut the door behind them. An assortment of clothes, books, and ancient hockey sticks, the accumulation of decades, lay in dusty piles on the huge square table that stood in the middle of the room.

'Why all the secrecy? Have you spoken to Jayne yet?' asked Catherine uneasily.

'There's no easy way to say this, Catherine.' His voice was cold and distant, like a stranger.

He paused and walked over to the window, unwashed for many years. He had the same look on his face the doctor had when he broke the news that Grandad Meehan wasn't going to get better. Concerned but stoical.

'Last night was a mistake. I'm sorry.'

He continued to stare at the grimy window-pane and Catherine's newly-formed world crumbled around her. She found it hard to breathe in the dusty atmosphere.

'Are you saying you . . . you don't love me?' she managed to say after some moments had passed.

He hesitated for a second and then nodded glumly.

'I care for you Catherine,' he mumbled looking down, 'but nothing more.' His voice sounded croaky, but then he lifted his head and continued more assuredly.

'As I say it was a mistake. I don't know what I was thinking of last night. I shouldn't have . . . involved you. I really am sorry.'

'And Jayne . . . ' began Catherine, her voice dying away.

'We belong together, Jayne and me. We're the same sort, you see, Catherine, and you and me . . . well, it just wouldn't work. There's too many . . . too many difficulties to overcome. I couldn't

257

hurt my family that way. You must understand. I'm sure yours would feel the same. I didn't mean to . . . '

Catherine never heard the rest of the sentence for she slipped out of the room. She thought she was going to be sick and stumbled to the bicycle shed where she hid out of sight. When the shock finally sank in, the pain and disappointment took over — and, very soon after that, anger. It was a good forty minutes before she emerged able to face the world again.

'But I don't understand,' said Moira when she told her at lunchtime.

'It's as clear as day, Moira. Can't you see? David's only staying with Jayne because she's a Protestant. Because she goes to the same church, because his parents like her and hers like him.'

What in the name of God had possessed her to think that she could have him? The difference between her and David was that she would have gone against everyone to be with him. But he was spineless, weak, pathetic.

'What a stupid idiot I've been. A bloody, silly, little bitch. I should have known. I should have trusted my instincts. I knew, I just knew it was too good to be true.'

'You don't know for sure that's the reason, though,' said Moira quietly.

'Of course it is. What other explanation could there be? It's because I'm a Catholic.'

The cross they both bore.

'And,' went on Catherine, still fuelled by anger, 'that's the reason I wasn't made a prefect

258

and you for that matter. I can see it now, plain as day.'

'Do you really think so?' asked Moira, but Catherine railed on as though she hadn't spoken.

'Well do you know what Moira? I'm going to show them. The whole bloody damn lot of them. I'm going to get the best grades in the school and make something of my life. Away from this shithole of a town and the ignorant, prejudiced, small-minded people in it. And let them try and take that away from me!'

★   ★   ★

Finishing with David was the hardest thing Jayne had ever done. She avoided the Common Room at breaktime and, by lunch-time, she'd summoned up enough courage to speak to him.

She sought him out after class and, steeling herself, walked straight up to him in the corridor.

'I need to speak to you,' she said, purposefully and waited. Sensing something amiss, David's classmates melted away.

'Not here. Outside,' she instructed, keeping her voice as steady as possible, and David followed her out into the deserted playground.

'I want to finish with you. I know about you and Catherine Meehan,' said Jayne.

'But there's nothing between us, I swear to you, Jayne.'

Jayne wanted to believe him so much, but she'd seen the way he kissed Catherine. She remembered how he held her head between his palms like a precious jewel, shoulders hunched, and pressed his mouth hungrily on hers, his body bending towards her like a reed. It didn't matter what David said, that image spoke a thousand words.

'I saw you David. I saw you with my own eyes.'

'But it didn't mean anything. I'm telling you the truth,' he pleaded.

'You lied to me, telling me you had an essay to do when all along you'd arranged to meet her.'

'I never arranged to meet her. We just bumped into each other . . . I don't know what I was thinking of . . . I told her this morning I don't want to see her again.'

'I'm sorry David. It's over.'

And she resolved to get over him.

14

The last school term before the summer holidays seemed to drag on forever. At least David never went out with Catherine again, not to Jayne's knowledge anyway. But that was little consolation for losing him. Dad arranged a summer job for her in Graham's, the china shop, and she was grateful for the distraction.

The bell above the shop door pinged and Jayne looked up. She recognised the customer who'd been in three times this week already and it wasn't china he was after.

Jayne watched him as he browsed amongst the glass display cabinets full of fine china and crystal. He was only an inch or two taller than she but strong and well-built. She could tell from his steel-capped boots and broad shoulders that he was a working man of some sort. Not the type Jayne would normally go for, but there was something attractive about him. A walk on the wild side.

'So have you decided what you're going to buy your mother yet?' she asked, arching her eyebrows.

'Still looking,' he replied, regarding her with greeny-grey eyes beneath a thatch of sandy coloured hair.

'I want to make sure it's perfect. I might need some help.'

He stroked his square chin as he peered at a

horrible china clock with two fat gold cherubs balanced on top.

'I think you do need help if you're thinking of going for that clock!' said Jayne. 'But I've showed you everything else in the shop. What else can I tell you about?'

'I'd like to hear it all over again,' he said with a big broad grin.

★　★　★

Jayne saw David as soon as she arrived at the Candlelight, a disco held every Saturday night in the Ballygally Castle Hotel on the Coast Road five miles outside Ballyfergus. He leant against the bar, in dark trousers and a short-sleeved shirt, a bottle of beer in his hand. She hadn't seen him in over a month. He must be spending a lot of time outdoors for his arms and face were tanned and his blonde curls several shades lighter from the sun.

Her friends formed a protective cordon around her as they made their way to a table in the corner.

'Are you all right, Jayne?' said Ruth, glancing anxiously towards the bar.

'Yes, I'm fine,' said Jayne. 'Honestly. I'm going to have a great time,' she added cheerfully, perking up and scanning the low-ceilinged room.

'That's the spirit,' said Ruth pleased. 'I know you maybe didn't feel like coming out tonight. But honestly, Jayne, it'll do you good. It's high time you got over David and found someone else.'

Although no-one was dancing yet — it was still too early for that — strobe lights cast a throbbing kaleidoscope of colour onto the small wooden dance-floor, pulsating in time to the music.

On the other side of the room Jayne caught sight of the guy from the shop, watching her. She looked at David for a few moments. Then she made up her mind, got up and, without saying a word to the girls, crossed the dance-floor.

He smiled when she approached and he looked handsome out of his work clothes.

'Hi,' she said, 'we meet again. I suppose we should do proper introductions. I'm Jayne Alexander.'

He raised his eyebrows in surprise.

'You're not Eddie Alexander's sister, are you?'

She nodded.

'I'm Sean Meehan. I think my wee sister's been seeing your brother. And,' he added, squinting one eye as if trying to remember something, 'you must be in the same year at the Grammar as Catherine?'

Afterwards Jayne wondered why she didn't just turn and walk away, right there and then. There'd been enough bother over Geraldine Meehan and Eddie and, by rights, Catherine Meehan should have been her sworn enemy.

'What does Catherine say about me then?' she heard herself asking, passing the question off as small talk, but she hung on every word of his reply.

'I've never heard her say anything. Just that you were in the same year. That's all.'

263

Clearly Sean didn't know anything about David. Jayne wasn't surprised. If she'd tried to steal someone else's boyfriend she wouldn't go round shouting about it either.

She was curious about the Meehans. Why had David chosen Catherine over her? Why was Eddie captivated by Geraldine? They were all attractive certainly but there must be more to the Meehans than just good looks. Perhaps she could find out more about Catherine from Sean.

'So you're working then?' she asked.

'Yeah. I'm a painter and decorator with my Dad. It's a family business he started twenty years ago. He built it up from nothing you know. It's only the two of us at the moment like, but one day I'll take over from him and I'm going to expand.'

'That's interesting,' said Jayne while she thought what delicious irony it would be to go out with Catherine's brother. It would give David a taste of his own medicine. If he was still interested in her enough to care.

'So what sort of plans do you have in mind?' she asked, and listened attentively to his answer.

'What I'd really like is a shop on the Main Street. I can see it now,' he said excitedly. 'And we'd have the shop as well as the painting and decorating business. That way people could buy their paint and wallpaper from us and then we'd do the decorating for them. A one-stop service. What do you think?'

'It could catch on.'

'We'd have to employ more people of course once things got going. Just now there's not enough work to take Michael on as well.'

'Michael?'

'Sorry, my brother.'

'So how many Meehans are there?'

'Four. I'm the eldest, then Michael, Catherine and Geraldine. Michael's on the dole just now. It's a real shame he can't get work. It's no life for a lad. Stuck in the house all day.'

'So where do you live exactly?'

'Slane Drive.'

Jayne knew this was a street in the council housing estate. Six of them crammed into a three-bedroomed house! Catherine must share a room with her sister.

'Do you get on with Catherine, then?'

Sean shrugged his shoulders.

'What can I say? She's my sister. She studies a lot in her room.'

'Does she have a boyfriend?'

'Not one I know about. Hey, what's this anyway? The Spanish inquisition?'

By the time the evening came to an end Jayne was slightly drunk. And angry. David hadn't looked in her direction all evening and she saw him talking to Catherine at the bar.

So when Sean asked if she wanted to step outside, she agreed. She let him snog her, roughly, in the front seat of the white Ford van with a caricature of a little man in overalls holding a paintbrush emblazoned on the side. She let him put his calloused hand down her scoop-necked T-shirt and under her bra. The sensation wasn't unpleasant. She felt a remote tingling between her legs although the eight

Pernod and blackcurrants she'd drunk made her feel a bit nauseous.

'I'd like to see you again,' said Sean.

'Okay,' replied Jayne.

'Maybe it's best if we keep this between ourselves for the time being,' said Sean. 'You know, don't tell our families. I don't know about yours, but mine are all up to high dough about Geraldine seeing your brother. Mind you she's only sixteen.'

'Yes, I think that would be best,' agreed Jayne.

'And . . . I feel really bad about this . . . ' said Sean, 'I'd love to offer you a lift back to Ballyfergus, but I promised to take Catherine and her friend home tonight.'

'That's okay. I have a lift arranged with Ruth already.'

'Are you sure?'

Jayne nodded.

'Well how about next Saturday night then?' asked Sean.

Jayne nodded again.

'Okay, I'll call into the shop one day this week and we'll make the arrangements.'

'Fine,' said Jayne. 'I'll be seeing you, then.'

She got out of the van before he could kiss her again and ran back inside.

★ ★ ★

Catherine fought her way to the bar through a crowd three deep. She was hot and sweaty and the cigarette smoke made her eyes smart. She

266

clutched a black velvet evening bag to her chest and two pound notes in her fist.

'Hello, Catherine,' said a slurred voice at her elbow and Catherine turned round.

It was David. He leaned against the bar with an empty beer bottle in his hand and he looked drunk.

Catherine ignored him and tried to attract the barman's attention to no avail.

'Aren't you speaking to me, then?' asked David with an amused smile.

'I have nothing to say to you,' said Catherine calmly and then, more aggressively, 'and from what I remember you said more than enough to me the last time we spoke.'

'I said I was sorry,' said David. He sounded like a peeved child.

The crowd pushed them together and his breath smelt of stale cigarette smoke. The electricity that had once existed between them was gone. Catherine pulled away and wondered how she had ever fancied him.

'I wanted to ask you,' he went on, 'if you and I could be . . . friends.'

'I don't think so,' said Catherine crisply and she turned her attention once again to the business of getting served.

'Excuse me,' she shouted above the loud music and waived the bank notes in the air.

'You're next, love,' said the barman and he winked at her. 'With you in a minute.'

Across the bar, on the other side of the room Catherine saw Sean. He was talking to Jayne Alexander! She seemed to sense Catherine's eyes on her and looked in her direction. Catherine turned to David.

'So she's finished with you then,' she said thoughtfully.

'Who?'

'Jayne, of course, who else?'

'Yes, I guess everyone knows by now.'

'Right, love, what'll it be?' said the barman.

'Two cokes, please,' said Catherine, wishing she'd been able to get a summer job. She'd applied everywhere she could think of and every one of her applications had been turned down.

'You're not drinking then?' asked David.

Catherine ignored the comment. The two cokes would have to last her and Moira all night unless someone bought them a drink. Sean would buy them a round of course, but it wasn't fair to expect him to keep them in booze all night.

'So,' said Catherine, returning to the subject of Jayne. 'She's finished with you?'

'Yes,' said David sadly.

'Because of me?'

'Yep.'

The barman placed two small glasses of coke in front of Catherine and handed her the change. She put it in the evening bag, slung it over her shoulder and lifted a glass in each hand.

'You know David,' she said, leaning so close to his ear that her lips brushed his hair, 'you got exactly what you deserved.'

And not giving him a chance to respond she disappeared into the crowd.

By twelve o'clock only a few couples remained

268

on the dance-floor, clinging to each other and swaying in time to the slow dance music. Catherine scanned the room once more for Sean and spotted him at last near the exit swinging the van keys in his hand.

'Where have you been, Sean?' said Catherine crossly as she and Moira approached him.

'Here and there,' he replied vaguely.

'We've been looking for you all over,' said Catherine. 'It's time to go.'

'What's the rush?' said Sean.

'It's me,' said Moira anxiously. She had her coat on and her arms folded across her chest. 'I have to go.'

'Sure we've time for another drink.'

'No!' blurted Moira and she put her hand over her mouth.

'I'm sorry, I didn't mean to shout,' she said. 'I . . . you don't understand. I have to be home by twelve-thirty.'

Sean looked at her for a moment and then touched her lightly on the arm.

'It's all right, Moira,' he said softly. 'I'll get you home in time. Come on. We'll go now.'

'Thanks, Sean,' she said and blushed.

In the van on the way home the three of them were squeezed into the front, Moira and Catherine sharing the passenger seat. Catherine remembered what she'd seen at the bar.

'Sean, did I see you talking to Jayne Alexander?'

Sean glanced at her sideways.

'Yeah,' he replied, 'I said a few words to her.'

'How do you know her?' asked Catherine.

269

He looked at the road ahead.

'She works in that shop Graham's on Main Street. I got talking to her one day I was in looking for something for Ma's birthday.'

'Were you with her tonight? When me and Moira were looking for you.'

'Don't you think one member of the family going out with an Alexander is enough?' he said.

'More than enough,' said Catherine and the three of them were silent the rest of the way home.

* * *

Helen and John were in the kitchen having breakfast before Jayne came down.

'Just leave her alone,' said Helen. 'The sooner left the sooner mended.'

She had first hand experience, after all, and she knew how long it took to get over a heartbreak. That was if you ever did, completely.

'But Jayne's still not herself,' said John, concerned.

'I know, but she's back at school now. She's exams coming up and her future to think of. That'll keep her mind occupied. Now, you'd better get a move on or you'll be late for work.'

'But I worry about her.'

'I know you do, John,' said Helen more softly. 'But trust me on this one.'

Later, Helen inspected herself in the hall mirror and scowled when she noticed that the laughter lines and crow's feet were becoming more pronounced. She resolved to buy some of that anti-ageing cream she'd seen advertised on the TV.

She put on her camel coat, slung her green Harrods shopping bag over her shoulder and went out the front door. She left the Volkswagen Golf in the drive and decided to walk for it was such a nice day and it helped to keep the weight off.

There'd definitely been a change in Jayne, she thought, as she walked briskly towards the town centre. She was still a loving beautiful girl, but some of her sparkle had gone. Her laughter wasn't as frequent as it had once been and, when she thought you weren't looking, her face was long and sad. Helen felt a pang in her chest and let out a long sigh.

She wanted so much for Jayne to be happy, to make up somehow for the sorrow that lived deep in her own heart. It was Jayne's happiness that Helen lived for; at times it was only that which kept her going. She thought of Eddie and at once felt guilty. She loved him of course, he was her son, but not with the intensity and absolute concern she felt for Jayne. He was too much like his father. All through their childhood and into their teenage years Helen struggled to be fair and impartial, to hide her preoccupation with Jayne, and so far she'd succeeded. Even her husband had not noticed.

'Hello, Helen,' said a voice with the power, still, to startle her.

Frank stood in the doorway to the bakery, a paper bag in his hand.

'Hello, Frank.'

271

He was still as handsome as ever and Helen concentrated on appearing indifferent.

'Can I have a word?'

Helen nodded.

'Not in here,' he whispered, glancing over his shoulder. 'There's too many folk with nothing better to do than listen into other people's conversations.'

'Walk with me then?' said Helen and Frank accompanied her a short distance along the Main Street where they stopped on a quiet corner.

'It's about my Geraldine and your son,' said Frank, 'We're ... me and Theresa that is ... we're not very happy about it.'

'My John's not exactly over the moon about it either, you know.'

'Could you maybe have a word with Eddie and see if you can't persuade him to finish with her? I don't see that there's a future in it.'

'Like you and me?' said Helen unable to keep the bitterness out of her voice.

'Look, will you speak to him or not?'

'I will not. It's up to Eddie to decide what he wants. I honestly couldn't care less one way or the other. And I suggest you leave it up Geraldine to decide what she wants to do with her life.'

'I suppose you've got a point,' said Frank, thoughtfully, and sighed. 'I haven't exactly made the best choices myself, have I?'

'Don't, Frank. It's too late for what might have been. Much too late.' And with that Helen left him standing on the corner. When she got home she'd forgotten half her shopping including the face cream she'd promised herself.

* * *

At teatime Helen observed Jayne toying with her food again and thought she might be anorexic. She dismissed the idea straightaway. Jayne was a perfectly normal healthy young woman although obviously still deeply troubled by David MacDowell.

But what use was it, thought Helen, her grinding through the years, through the grim routine of coffee mornings and meals on the table and Sunday worship, if Jayne wasn't to be happy? Over the years Helen had devised a measuring system whereby her pain became a barometer of Jayne's happiness. When the emptiness of her life seemed about to engulf her and she could bear it no more, she thought of Jayne. How she was saving her from the trauma of a broken marriage and separation from the father she adored. Perversely, the greater Helen's misery, the more she thought she was protecting Jayne. And so she found the strength to go on.

She had dreamed for so much more for her beautiful daughter. But Jayne was still young and that gave Helen hope. Who knows, perhaps David and she would get back together? Perhaps they weren't right for each other and she would soon come to realise that she was better off without him. One day she would find someone else. Her one true love.

'What are you doing tonight, Jayne?' she asked.

'I thought I'd go over to Heather's for a bit. We might go to the pictures if there's anything good on.'

'Are you okay for money?'

'Fine, thanks. I've still got a good bit saved from my summer job.'

'You know you should be out meeting people,' said Helen, watching Jayne carefully. 'I'm sure there's plenty of fellas queuing up to take you out.'

'Well, I hear Jayne's already taken one of them up on the offer,' said John.

Helen whipped her head round, shocked. John dabbed the corners of his mouth with the napkin, unsmiling, and set it on top of his scraped-clean plate. What on earth was he talking about?

'Isn't that right?' he probed, looking straight at Jayne, his voice laden with meaning. Helen felt her blood rise. How dare he keep something like this from her and then bring it up in front of the whole family.

'What if I am?' replied Jayne defiantly.

'You know I don't approve of you seeing Catholic boys. I've nothing against them, but it would be best if you stuck to your own kind,' said John, evenly.

'Catholic! Did you say Catholic?' said Mrs Alexander, her head shaking with fury.

John's mother had been living with them for nearly a year now. Helen ignored her and turned to Jayne.

'Who are you seeing, Jayne?' she asked, calmly.

'I'm not seeing anyone — we just go out together from time to time.'

'Who is it, Jayne?' Helen said calmly, suppressing the irrational sense of urgency that was taking hold.

Inside her head a voice screamed, 'Answer me. ANSWER ME.'

'Oh, you wouldn't know him.'

'Who is he Jayne?' she repeated, more irritably.

Helen spoke quickly, intent only on ferreting out the crucial information.

'What does his father do?'

'Oh he's quite respectable, runs his own decorating business.'

Helen felt the colour drain from her cheeks and she struggled to maintain an expression of mild interest. Take it easy, Helen, she told herself, there's more than one painter and decorator in Ballyfergus.

'His name's Sean Meehan,' continued Jayne.

Helen sat back, horrified, and was utterly silent. She was sure she could feel Mrs Alexander's eyes boring into her, reading her tainted soul.

'Well, Jayne, you know how your mother and me feel about this subject. So I'm not going to waste time arguing over the table. I expect you to finish with him. Until you're eighteen,' said John, glancing at Eddie, 'you'll do as I say. Do you understand?'

Jayne didn't answer and Eddie was speechless.

'I don't know,' said Mrs Alexander crossly. 'In my day you'd have the strap taken to you,

275

my girl. That would put an end to your nonsense!'

★ ★ ★

When John and Mrs Alexander were in the lounge watching the TV and Eddie had gone out, Helen went upstairs to the bedroom she shared with John. She sat on the end of the cream embroidered bedspread and leaned her head on her right hand and thought. Absent-mindedly, she turned her head slowly, back and forth, dragging her lips over her knuckles and plucking at her mouth with the fingers of her right hand. The touch was comforting, soothing. After a few minutes she felt better. Then she got up, crossed the landing and knocked gently on Jayne's bedroom door.

'It's me,' she said.

'Come in.'

A small lamp perched precariously on the glass surface of the dressing-table, creating a brilliant reflection in the mirror. Jayne squinted her eyes and thrust her face forward into the bright light whilst she applied mascara. Nowadays Helen used a magnifying mirror to put her make-up on.

'Yeah?' said Jayne, without looking round.

'How long has this been going on Jayne?'

'What?'

Jayne pretended to concentrate on applying an extra coat of mascara to her upper lashes. She sometimes forgot how well her mother knew her.

'You know perfectly well what, Jayne. I'm

talking about that boy Meehan.'

Jayne inserted the wand in the tube of mascara and set it on the dressing table.

'A couple of months that's all. We meet up sometimes at discos and he takes me out for the odd meal. It's nothing serious. Anyway I haven't time to sit here chatting about it, I'm late.'

Jayne grabbed her coat and handbag which were lying ready on the bed.

'Bye, Mum,' she said, planted a kiss on her mother's cheek and disappeared.

★   ★   ★

At seven-thirty John went out. 'It's a business do at the Golf Club,' he said. 'I shouldn't be too late.'

Helen was just glad he was gone and listened with relief to the sound of the car tyres on the gravel drive. That left her alone in the lounge with Mrs Alexander.

'There's nothing but rubbish on the TV,' said Mrs Alexander. 'Do you want to watch it?'

Helen shook her head.

'I'll read my book,' she said, picking up a dog-eared copy of Gone with the Wind, a yellow post-it note sticking out of the middle.

Helen read a lot, one of her many strategies for coping. Reading was a good excuse not to have to talk.

Mrs Alexander held the remote control up high in front of her, under the glare of the standard lamp and, after some minutes, found the on/off button. She pointed it in the direction of the TV and pressed the button purposefully; the TV died.

'There, that's better. I think I'll join you, Helen,' she said, looking round for her book.

'I'll get it,' said Helen and, going over to the writing bureau, she picked up a large-print copy of an Agatha Christie thriller.

Helen returned to her seat, opened her book and stared at the page. Scarlett was writing a letter to her Aunt Pitty-Pat, but Helen got no further than the first paragraph. She tried to maintain her outward calm so that Mrs Alexander wouldn't notice anything amiss and after a while she began turning the pages at regular intervals to keep the old lady's suspicion at bay. Mrs Alexander was eighty-eight years old and her sight might be failing her, but there was nothing wrong with her other faculties.

Helen continued with her little charade, aware of Mrs Alexander's beady eyes on her from time to time. Nothing wrong with her eyesight now, she thought. But though she felt her cheeks colouring a little, Helen didn't look up.

Her head buzzed. She tried to take each possibility and deal with it rationally, but before she could get her mind round it others crowded in, demanding attention. She wished she could take a big piece of paper and write it all down so she could make some sense of it. But that was far too risky. She would have to deal with this internally, on her own, as she had always done.

She hadn't anticipated this. It had always been a possibility of course, but it seemed so unlikely, so remote, that she'd never seriously considered it. Things like this happened to people in books and on TV, not in real life. Not to her. Not to Jayne. Perhaps that was why it had thrown her so much; she'd been caught unprepared. After a little while, Helen sensed a comparative calm descend on her and she found she was able to think a little more clearly.

Maybe she should just let things blow over in their own time. They were both young after all, kids really, and most likely nothing would come of it. But what if they were serious? As serious as she'd once been about Frank Meehan. Jayne's nonchalance reminded her of the way she used to talk to her parents about Frank. The past came rushing back, memories jostling for attention, pressing themselves on Helen, unwanted and unbidden. Helen fought them, but they would not go away for the past lived on in the present and would not be denied.

15

It was the 5th December. Helen remembered clearly because she and John had a row about getting the house decorated so close to Christmas. He mentioned it casually one night while Helen was getting undressed and he was already in bed, reading a book.

'I don't want decorators in before Christmas,' said Helen, doing up the buttons on her nightdress. 'The house'll be a mess. I won't be able to get anything done.'

'I don't understand what you're making a fuss about, Helen. The lads will be in and out in a couple of days. No problem.'

Helen pulled back the covers and got into bed.

'But I've still to buy all the Christmas presents and wrap them. The cards haven't been sent yet and I won't be able to put the tree up until they're finished.'

'Is that all?' said John and Helen felt like screaming.

'The house needs a really good clean, but I won't be able to get that done until the workmen are finished. And I'll have to clean up after them as well. If that isn't enough I've a four-course Christmas dinner to organise for your family. You don't understand what it's like, John, stuck at home with a baby all day trying to get things done.'

Edward Alexander, or Eddie, was nearly two and a demanding toddler. He was named after his grandfather and in memory of that loyal son of Ulster, Edward Carson. A good, solid Ulster family name, timeless and enduring, not that Helen had much say in the matter. John and his mother had the name decided before Helen even got a chance to voice her ideas on that front.

In the end John got his way about the decorating too for Helen couldn't be bothered arguing with him anymore. Sometimes it was easier just to give in and get on with it. What difference did it make anyway?

After 'lights out' that night he whispered, 'Are you asleep Helen?'

She tensed in response to the rustling of the sheets as he edged closer. She knew by the husky tone in his voice what he wanted and pretended to be asleep. He rolled over on his back and soon she could hear him breathing deeply, sound asleep.

Helen relaxed. It was a long time since she and John had been intimate. She'd had a difficult birth with Eddie and ended up with stitches and, after she was healed, she was exhausted looking after the new baby. At first, she tolerated John's advances to keep him happy and then, lately, she'd resorted to phantom headaches. John didn't seem to mind; he never had much of a sex drive to begin with.

At breakfast a week later, John dipped white toast soldiers, dripping with butter, into the soft sticky yolk of an egg and gave her instructions on how to deal with the workmen.

'The lounge, dining-room, hall and stairs are to be stripped and papered and the woodwork's getting painted as well. It should take a week. Now, you'll have to watch them like a hawk, Helen.'

'That means I'll be stuck in the house the whole time,' said Helen sullenly.

'Well, if I'm paying for a week's work, it's a week's work I expect to get. I don't want them sneaking off and doing other jobs when they're supposed to be here.'

'Why would they do that, John?' she asked, examining the top of his head.

She noticed that his scalp was now clearly visible through his thinning hair. Sometimes the twelve years between them felt like a generation.

'If someone offers them cash-in-hand for a quick job they'll not say no and then at the end of the week, they'll turn round and say they're not finished. They do it all the time.'

Eddie stumbled noisily into the door and let out a wail. Helen scooped him up in her arms and nursed him until he stopped.

'And don't be giving them tea and sand-wiches,' John continued, in between big gulps of hot tea. 'They're here to do a job so let them get on with it. They'll only end up taking advantage of you. And you've enough to do.'

'Yes, John,' said Helen, topping up his teacup and wishing he would go to work and leave her alone.

She had a terrible urge to throw the water

she'd cooked his egg in, still boiling hot, in his face. He was so irritating, issuing directions and instructions all the time so that everything was just so, according to the John Alexander world view. Sometimes she felt like opening her mouth and screaming at him. No words just one great big, long, loud scream.

But he hadn't an inkling how she felt and would have been completely shocked. He was the way he was and he couldn't help it. The same way she couldn't help the way she was.

'If there's any problems you can phone me at work, love,' he said, then he paused to look at her. 'You know I'm doing this for you Helen, so that you have a home you can be proud of. And I know it's hard work looking after Eddie. But it'll be worth the bother in the end, you'll see.'

Helen smiled weakly and, for the umpteenth time in her short marriage, felt guilty. John was a decent man, only trying to do his best for her and Eddie.

'Is my big boy going to give me a kiss good-bye then?' said John, turning to the baby.

He gave him a kiss on each of his fat cheeks and Eddie giggled delightedly in response.

'Daddy loves, you, Eddie, yes he does,' he cooed.

Helen watched them together and noted with sadness how Eddie had become the focus for much of the affection which should have been expended on each other.

The doorbell went and John looked at his watch.

'Eight-thirty. That'll be them. I'll have a word

before I go. Now you'll be all right with this, Helen, won't you?' he said, giving her a peck on the cheek.

'Yes. Fine John.'

'That's my girl,' he said happily.

Helen forced a thin smile, but John had already left the kitchen. She heard him open the door and let the men in. It sounded like there were two of them. John was doing his usual, issuing instructions.

'There's a toilet here you can use. The sink's a bit small though so you'll probably need to get water from the kitchen. Mrs Alexander will be here all week so just give her a shout if you need anything. Will you put sheets down on the hall carpet? It's only new. And make sure you leave the place nice and tidy.'

'Don't you worry about a thing, Mr Alexander. Me and Ciaran'll leave the place spotless, every night. I promise you. By the end of the week, you won't even know we've been here. Except for your new wallpaper and paintwork, of course!'

The voice was reassuring, vaguely familiar, but Helen shook her head. She must be imagining it.

She heard the engine of John's car, a shiny black Rover P4, grind into action and chug off down the drive. A cold draft came down the hall and she glanced, concerned, at Eddie who was playing happily with the contents of the laundry basket. If they didn't shut the door soon she'd have to take him upstairs to make sure he didn't get a chill. She heard the men talking briefly in low voices and then the clattering of ladders and

284

the thud of a tool bag hitting the carpet. The door was slammed shut, loudly. More talking.

Helen sat down at the kitchen table and fixed her eyes on the dull view out the window. She could see only the tops of some trees at the end of their garden, all but one conifer denuded of leaves, and a vast expanse of endless, monotonous, grey sky. She imagined this was what prisoners saw looking out their little cell windows.

Helen sensed someone standing behind her and waited for them to speak.

'Excuse me, Mrs Alexander, sorry to bother you, but could I get a wee drop of water?'

'Yes, of course,' replied Helen pleasantly, not getting up.

The man crossed the kitchen, put the bucket in the sink and turned one of the taps. It made a squeaking noise, the sound of metal and rubber against each other. She heard the water gush out, hit the bottom of the bucket and splash on the floor.

'Shit,' he shouted, and jumped back.

'I'm sorry. The pressure in that tap's very strong. I should have warned you,' she said, swivelling round in the chair.

The man was tall, dressed in the painters' uniform of peaked cap, white dungarees and steel-capped work boots, everything covered in a fine spray of white paint. He stood there, dripping, strangely motionless. Helen looked at his face. It was Frank Meehan.

'What are you doing . . . ' she began.

'Jesus! Helen, I'm sorry. I'd no idea.'

He shook his head as if annoyed with himself and then continued. 'It was Ciaran who fixed up the job. Alexander. Of course, but it never clicked . . . if I'd known I wouldn't have come. I'd have got Ciaran to do it on his own.'

She mustn't let him see she was upset.

'It's all right, Frank. There's nothing to be sorry about,' she said, getting up and offering him a towel from the chrome rail on the back of the kitchen door.

She glanced in the direction of the hall and lowered her voice.

'It was a long time ago. We're both married to different people now. You've a job to do and there's no reason why you shouldn't do it.'

Helen was amazed at her composure.

'I suppose not,' he answered slowly, dabbing at his face and chest.

'Well, that's settled then,' she replied, picking shirts up off the floor and putting them back in the laundry basket.

Eddie was now standing, back to the fridge door, staring at the tall stranger in white. His bottom lip quivered and he looked anxiously at Helen. She went over, knelt down beside him, and patted his well-padded bottom, comfortingly.

'It's all right, darling, Mummy's here.'

Frank finished filling the bucket and lifted it out of the sink. His sleeves were rolled up and the muscles in his right forearm stood out with the weight of the water.

'You've a grand wee lad there,' he said.

Helen looked away from him and didn't

answer. She couldn't trust herself to speak civilly. She could hear Ciaran whistling in the other room. Here he was in her kitchen, when they hadn't so much as passed the time of day in over four years, and he wanted to make small talk?

Frank went out of the room and shut the door quietly behind him. Helen leant on the work surface, facing the wall, and took a deep breath. Eddie was playing happily again, this time with her tea towels, which he pulled, one by one, off the rail and onto the floor.

Who would have thought, after all this time, that she would still feel this way about Frank? When he was standing in front of her, she'd felt a strong pulling sensation in her stomach, like she was being drawn towards him. She shouldn't be thinking of him like that; she was a married woman with a husband and a child.

His presence made her angry. And bitter. Her life had become what it was because of Frank. Because he didn't love her enough to stand by her. She'd rushed into marriage with John, but that wasn't the cause of her unhappiness. Being without Frank was the reason every day was a trial, a series of chores to get through, demands to be met. A routine of drudgery and boredom.

And now here he was, in her house, a constant reminder of former times Helen would rather forget. Her past was a crusted sore, best left undisturbed, for underneath it was weeping and full of pain. How was she going to get through the next week? The same way she got through each and every day, of course!

With the back of her hand Helen wiped away

the single tear that had slid down her left cheek and clung to her chin. Eddie stared up at her, eyes wide, and she smiled at him, reassuringly.

'I've a lot to be grateful for, yes I have, haven't I?' she said to the baby in a singsong voice. 'A husband who thinks the world of me, a beautiful home, and a healthy, happy baby boy. It's only a week after all.'

She would be polite and civil to Frank and for once she would be happy to follow John's instructions to the letter. No tea, no sandwiches, no fussing. The most important thing, however, was to make sure John saw no change in her and suspected nothing.

The first day wasn't too bad. Helen managed to hide away upstairs for most of the day. She set about sorting out the contents of drawers, but didn't make much progress. Most of the time she sat on the edge of the bed, listening to the sounds of activity downstairs, while Eddie rummaged through the clothes strewn across the room.

When John came home, Helen made sure she was bright and cheerful and sat attentively while he told her about his day at the office. She hardly heard a word of what he said. She was thinking Frank looked well but thinner. She wondered what his wife was like and if he was happy.

'They weren't any bother then?' asked John.

'Who?'

'The workmen, Helen,' said John, looking at her like she was a little stupid. 'They weren't any bother?'

288

'No, not at all. I hardly knew they were here,' she lied.

On the second day, getting dressed, Helen took unusual care in selecting her outfit; a ribbed jumper and a nice pair of brown slacks to show off her still-slim figure. She told herself, as she applied a little mascara, that she was doing it for John. She was sure she saw Frank stare when she opened the door to him and Ciaran.

By Friday, Helen was inexplicably anxious. Although they'd hardly spoken to each other all week Frank's proximity excited her and she didn't want it to end. She also wanted to speak to him. There were things she wanted to know.

Just before eleven o'clock, Ciaran, a tiny man with a wiry body and a face like a ferret, came into the lounge where Helen was playing with Eddie. The room smelt strongly of fresh gloss.

'That's me off, missus,' he said, shifting his weight nervously, from one foot to the other, like an athlete limbering up for a 100 yard sprint.

'Oh,' said Helen surprised, 'are you finished already?'

He shook his head.

'Nearly there though. Frank's going to stay and finish off the last wee bit of paper on the stairs and tidy up. I've a doctor's appointment you see so I was going to go away now.'

He seemed to be waiting for her approval.

'Oh, well, then. Thank you very much Ciaran. You've done a grand job so you have.'

'You're pleased then?'

'Yes, it's very nice.'

After he'd left Helen put a rug over Eddie

who'd fallen asleep on the sofa, the thumb of his right hand lodged deep in his mouth. His long eyelashes lay on his rosy cheeks, fluttering like the wings of a delicate butterfly. Helen stood for a few moments, watching him, then left the room and went upstairs.

Frank was on the top landing, wiping his hands on a rag. The carpet was covered with white sheets and a pair of wooden step ladders leaned against the wall where he'd finished putting up the last piece of paper. His cap lay on the floor, upside down.

'That's it finished,' he said, not looking up.

The landing was long and broad, as landings go, and Helen leaned against the turned wooden banister, resting her palms on the hand-rail.

'Why Frank?' she asked. 'Why did you do it?'

He raised his head sharply.

'What?' he said cautiously, his dark eyes meeting hers.

'Leave me, Frank. Why did you leave me?'

'There's no point going over all that again Helen. It'll just lead to pain. For both of us,' he said dropping his gaze. He kept on wiping his hands.

The anger welled up inside Helen. She wanted to hurt him so that he would feel the pain that had become her life sentence. And she knew his soft spot.

'How's your mother?' she said sarcastically, changing the subject.

Frank stopped wiping his hands.

'She's dead, Helen. She died last year.' His voice was flat and unemotional.

For a moment Helen was pleased. She'd never even met the woman, but she knew that it was Mrs Meehan's influence, and that alone, that had taken Frank away from her. But then she noticed Frank's head bent, his face contorted with anguish. She could see his pain; raw, deep, unhealed.

'I'm sorry,' she said and meant it.

And then she realised it wasn't the death of his mother that grieved him so. There was something else.

'What is it? Are you happy, Frank?' she asked. He didn't answer.

'Are you happily married, Frank?' she demanded. 'I think I've a right to know.' The answer was in his eyes when he looked up at her; two deep, dark wells of sorrow.

'I'm so sorry, Helen. For everything.'

She saw that they were, both of them, trapped in marriages to people they could not love because they loved each other. He'd made tragedies of both their lives!

'You stupid, stupid bastard, Frank!' she shouted, clenching her fists. 'You left me to rot and you went off and married that Theresa Walsh and you didn't even love her! You've ruined both our lives. And all this time I thought you were happy.'

'But you made a good marriage Helen and you have a lovely son,' pleaded Frank.

'A good marriage,' she snorted. 'I married John Alexander to get back at you not because I loved him.'

She had not meant the truth to come out. But

there it was, hanging between them now in the heavy silence, like a bad smell.

Helen buried her face in her hands and tears came, silently. Her slight frame shook all over.

'Oh, Helen. I never meant to hurt you. My darling Helen,' said Frank, taking her in his arms. She didn't resist.

'I could have borne it,' she said, in between sobs, 'if only you were happy. I could have accepted it wasn't meant to be and made the best of my life. But for both of us to be miserable. Oh, Frank.'

'Oh, God. Oh my God, what have I done? What have I done?' he moaned softly into her hair and they rocked gently back and forth, locked in a desperate embrace.

He smelt of sweat and wallpaper paste. His arms held her so tight she could hardly breathe and his chest shuddered violently as he drew breath in short gasps. Helen felt comforted, thinking neither of the past nor the future. Only the now, in his arms, where she belonged.

'I never meant to hurt you, baby,' he said, raising her face by the chin. 'I love you, Helen.'

Helen closed her eyes and felt his lips on hers, a gentle, healing kiss that lasted for a long time. When she felt him pulling away she moaned and kissed him urgently. She did not want the spell broken. He responded to her kisses in kind and ran his hands over her shoulders and back, pressing her to him with his big warm palms.

A rhythm began, their bodies swaying together, pelvises grinding. Simultaneously, they knelt down and lay on the floor, their lips never parting. Helen pulled the straps of his dungarees off his shoulders. Suddenly, Frank stood up and ripped off all his clothes, quickly, urgently, all the time his eyes fixed on hers. His body was magnificent, lithe and taut. She glanced down at his crotch. His fat, shiny dick emerged proudly from a dark nest of a million coiled springs. His balls were just visible beneath the dark public hair, heavy and full. Frank knelt down and pulled open her blouse; she heard two buttons burst. He gave her breasts a savage kiss and, pulling up her skirt, straddled her stockinged thighs quickly. There was no foreplay. She was soaking wet and he went straight inside her, moaning. She writhed against his penis madly, passionately, digging her nails into the flesh of his back until a wave of calm washed over her, followed by another and another until, eventually, she lay still. Sex with John had never felt like this. She knew it never would.

It was over in minutes. Frank lay face upwards on the floor, panting. Helen went into the bathroom, wiped herself dry with toilet roll and came out again, her blouse hanging open. She felt an incredible sense of release. All the anger and hate that had built up over the years was gone and now all she felt was a strange sense of calm.

Frank pulled on his clothes and slipped his feet into his boots at the same time. He looked up guiltily.

'What do we do now?' he asked.

Helen thought of the two small boys she'd seen Frank with on more than one occasion.

'Nothing, Frank. There's nothing to be done. We have to get on with our lives.'

'But Helen . . . ' began Frank.

'What Frank? Are you going to leave your wife and children? Are we going to run off together?'

'No,' he said slowly. 'Theresa wants another baby. A girl this time.'

'It's too late to change things now, Frank,' she said, her voice softening. 'Don't you see? We're both trapped. You'll never leave Theresa, will you?'

In answer he looked down, mournfully, at his feet.

'And I'll never leave John.'

She went over to where Frank now stood, fully dressed, and taking his head in her hands kissed him gently on the lips. Silent tears ran down his cheeks.

'I love you, Helen. I always will,' he said.

'I know. And I'll always love you.'

She let her hands drop to her side. Frank went to speak, but she covered his mouth with her hand.

'Sshh . . . let's leave it like this. There's nothing else to be said or done. You'd better go, Frank. The baby will be awake soon.' And she walked over to the bedroom, went through the door and closed it behind her.

She listened to Frank on the landing outside. He paused for a few moments at her bedroom door and then she heard his heavy tread on the stairs. The front door opened, closed, an engine started and he was gone.

Helen sat for a long time with her blouse

pulled round her until she started to feel cold. She went through to the bathroom, ran a shallow bath, stripped and got into it. She washed her body carefully and quickly, got out, dried herself and put on fresh clothes. She tied her hair up in a neat bun and re-applied her lipstick, mascara and blusher. She got out the sewing basket, retrieved the two buttons from the landing and sewed them back on her blouse before putting it, along with her skirt and stockings, in the laundry basket.

Helen's conscience was completely clear; she felt no guilt. She and Frank had merely acted out the natural order of things, the way they should have been before other people interfered and spoilt everything. She heard a baby's cry from the lounge, left the room and went downstairs.

★   ★   ★

Three weeks later Helen was not surprised when the doctor gave her the news. She knew almost as soon as Frank drove away from the house that she was carrying his child.

It was a cold dry day between Christmas and the New Year and John had gone back to work for the few days in between the holidays. Helen pushed the big blue Silver Cross pram up the hill from the doctor's surgery as, detached and unemotional, she worked out a strategy to protect her and the unborn child.

At the butcher's on the edge of the housing estate, she bought two thick, bloody sirloin steaks. From the shop next door she bought mushrooms, carrots and onions and, from the off-licence, a bottle of expensive red wine, not that there were too many to choose from. Lastly she bought vanilla ice cream and two bars of dark chocolate; she would make her own chocolate sauce with golden syrup and butter, one of John's favourites.

'Why don't we have dinner after Eddie's gone down,' she suggested, when her husband came home. 'That way we can have a glass of wine and relax.'

John seemed taken aback but pleased.

'That's a great idea, Helen,' he said, taking in her high heels and short skirt appreciatively.

Later, when they made love, or rather when John had sex with her, she thought he was never going to come. She responded enthusiastically to help things along and when he did, at last, ejaculate it was accompanied by a series of whimpers, like a strangulated dog. Helen closed her eyes and sighed with relief.

★　★　★

Eight and a half months later, on 20th August 1966, Helen gave birth to a daughter in the maternity wing of Ballyfergus Hospital. She was the most beautiful child Helen had ever seen and when she held Jayne in her arms she knew that her life had, at last, a purpose.

'Thank God you take after me,' she said to the child when they were alone in a private room of the hospital.

It was the middle of the night and all was

quiet and still. She stroked the baby's wisp of white hair and skin, soft as a peach.

'No-one will ever guess and no-one need ever know, my little darling. I'll see to that.'

'She's beautiful,' whispered John, as he held the tiny baby in his arms the next day. 'She's so perfect and so beautiful.'

He stood like that for some minutes at the hospital window and when he turned round there were tears in his eyes.

'Thank you. Thank you,' he said, choked with emotion. 'Thank you for giving me this daughter. And our son.'

He came and sat on the edge of the bed.

'I love you, Helen,' he said, but she could only turn away.

'Can't you say you love me, Helen?' he pleaded.

'Not now, John. Just give me some time,' she said gently.

After a few days they were ready to go home, Helen and her precious daughter. John took the day off work to come and collect them.

'Here I'll take Jayne,' he said eagerly, taking the sleeping baby in his arms, and he accompanied Helen out of the private room and through the general ward. Most of the beds were empty. Except for one.

So preoccupied was John, and bursting with pride, that he did not glance at the occupant in the bed or the visitors beside it. But Helen did.

She saw it was Theresa and in her arms she held a dark-haired little baby. Frank was in the seat beside the bed, two little boys standing shyly either side of him. They all looked up at Helen and John.

Frank started when he saw her and his wife looked at him sharply. Helen smiled thinly, the sort of smile you give to strangers you pass in the street. Momentarily she was consumed with jealousy of Theresa and blinked to hold back the tears. Then she stumbled and would have fallen if John hadn't been there to grab onto.

'Quick,' he shouted to a nurse at the other end of the ward, 'get a wheelchair!' In a second Frank was at her side, holding her up. Helen looked into his eyes and saw the concern and the love in them and she was happy.

The nurse helped her into a wheelchair and Helen sank into it gratefully. 'Thank you,' said John to Frank, 'I've got her now.' Frank returned to Theresa's bedside without saying a word.

'Daddy, Daddy, when can we take the baby home?' said one of the little boys and Frank replied absentmindedly.

'Soon, son, very soon.'

'Could you get the Sister, please?' said John and the nurse went to find her, white shoes squeaking on the linoleum.

'Are you sure you're all right Helen?' asked John.

'Quite sure.'

'Here's the Sister now,' said John. 'Look, I'm not happy about my wife going home in this condition. She nearly fainted just now.'

The sister took Helen's pulse and looked at her closely.

'There's no medical reason why she shouldn't

go home, Mr Alexander. How are you feeling dear?'

'Fine, Sister.'

'I think she just needs to take it easy.'

The nurse wheeled Helen to the front of the hospital.

Outside Helen got in the passenger seat, John placed the baby in her arms and closed the car door. The ward sister waved them off and Helen craned her neck for a last glimpse of the hospital as they drove off.

'Wait 'til Eddie sees his little sister,' said John excitedly. 'He's beside himself. And he's desperate for you to come home, Helen.'

She thought of her little son at home waiting anxiously for her return and his devoted father who adored both her children. And she thought of Frank and his two boys, so vulnerable and small, who must love their Daddy so much.

So many lives would be devastated if she and Frank had followed their hearts. They'd done the right thing. She looked down at the baby in her arms and smiled. She could not have Frank but she had his baby and that was enough. Every day would be tolerable from now on.

16

'Helen?' said Mrs Alexander, awakening Helen from her memories. 'Don't you think it's time we had supper? It's past nine o'clock.'

Helen realised she'd let the book fall into her lap and was staring blindly at the floor. Mrs Alexander peered at her over the top of her reading glasses, the area of wrinkled skin below each eye horribly magnified.

'So it is,' said Helen.

She got up, went into the kitchen and put the kettle on.

Of course after all this time had passed John wouldn't remember that the painter who came to their house nearly twenty years ago was Frank Meehan and the father of Jayne's current boyfriend. Probably just as well.

Helen put four slices of bread in the toaster and set mugs and plates on a tray. She allowed her mind to turn to the problem of Jayne and Sean Meehan.

What if, God help her, they fell in love and had a child. The boy was Jayne's own flesh and blood. Her half-brother for God's sake! She'd read about couples, brothers and sisters, separated at birth, who got married and had children who were hideously deformed. Helen couldn't stand back and allow that to happen, no matter what the consequences. No, she would have to put a stop to it, but somehow she'd have to find a way to do so without revealing Jayne's true identity.

She thought very hard for some minutes while she buttered the toast and poured the tea. Jayne was a good girl and she adored her Dad. She would never hurt him intentionally. All Helen had to do was point out just how much the whole carry-on was upsetting him. That was it! She'd appeal to Jayne's good nature and persuade her that Dad was right.

A sense of urgency seized Helen; there was no time to waste. She would wait up for Jayne tonight and talk to her; put a stop to things before they went too far.

She carried the tea and toast into the lounge.

At ten-thirty Mrs Alexander went to bed. Helen sat on by the fire, relieved that she was no longer under the scrutiny of those small, unforgiving eyes. John came in at eleven o'clock. She made him a cup of tea and he told her all about the committee meeting at the Golf Club.

At length he stood up, looked at the carriage clock which sat on the mantelpiece, and said, 'Are you coming up? It's half past eleven.'

'No, not yet. I think I'll wait up for Jayne.'

'It's not like you to stay up late.'

'Well, I'm not tired and I want to finish this chapter anyway,' replied Helen, raising her book from where it had fallen, forgotten again, into her lap.

After he'd gone, Helen sat and waited for Jayne. She listened for footsteps on the gravel and jumped at every creak the old house made. She got out of her chair at least a dozen times to watch for Jayne's figure at the end of the drive.

At last, when she thought she could bear it no longer, she heard light footsteps coming round the side of the house, the back door opened and slammed shut.

'What are you doing up so late, Mum?' said Jayne, coming into the lounge and collapsing on the sofa.

'Waiting for you. How's Heather?'

'Heather? Oh, she's fine. Sends her love,' replied Jayne, blushing.

'You weren't out at Heather's at all were you? It's all right. I won't be cross.'

Jayne looked sheepish and shook her head.

'Were you out with that fella Sean Meehan?'

Helen found it hard to say the name as though it meant nothing to her and she tried to picture a young boy, not the man she knew. She noticed her palms were wet with perspiration and a giddy nervousness threatened to shatter her composure.

'Yes, I was Mum. The only reason I didn't tell you was that I knew Dad would blow his top. Did you hear the stuff he came out with at dinner?'

'Do you think you should be lying to your Dad?'

'Well I wouldn't have to if he didn't go on like an idiot,' said Jayne defensively, folding her arms across her chest. 'I'm only going out with the guy. It's not like we're engaged or anything.'

Helen counted to five, then said, 'You know your Dad always has your best interests at heart Jayne. The only reason he doesn't want you

302

going out with Sean is that he's afraid you'll get hurt. He loves you very much and this whole thing has upset him terribly. There's no future in a relationship with the likes of Sean Meehan. You do see that, don't you?'

Jayne stared at her, unmoved.

Helen continued. 'It's all very well saying you're just going out with him, but one thing can lead to another and before you know it . . . well . . . you might be in deeper than you want to be. You're getting involved with something you don't understand Jayne. Catholics are different from us.'

'Oh, so the truth comes out at long last,' said Jayne sarcastically. 'I didn't expect much from Dad, but I'm surprised at you, Mum. I didn't realise you were a bigot.'

'I'm not a bigot, Jayne. That's a very hurtful thing to say, but you must understand that you cannot continue to see this boy.'

'You don't even know him. You and Dad are judging someone you don't even know.'

'We know all we need to know, Jayne.'

This wasn't going at all well. Jayne was being far more stubborn than Helen had expected. Very defensive of Sean. Surely Jayne didn't think she was in love with him? Helen needed to know.

'Just how far has this gone, Jayne?' she asked, changing tack. 'Have you kissed him?'

'Of course I've kissed him, Mum, I'm not a child.'

Helen felt a wave of unstoppable panic slowly rise up from her stomach. She fought to maintain an outward calm but her heart was pounding against her chest and she kept her hands clasped together to prevent them from shaking.

'Has it gone further than that, Jayne?'

No answer. Jayne stared at her defiantly.

'Answer me, Jayne. I asked you how far things have gone.'

Still no answer. Helen swallowed hard.

'Have you slept with him?' she asked.

Slowly, a smirk crept across Jayne's face.

Panic took hold of Helen. She's slept with him! Why else won't she answer me? No! Oh my God, dear Lord Jesus Christ save me. What have I done? Helen leapt from her chair, crossed the room in one stride and slapped Jayne full across the face.

'ANSWER ME!' she screamed.

Immediately, she realised that she had never raised a hand to either of her children in her life. She felt like a woman possessed, no longer able to contain her emotions.

'No, I haven't. I haven't,' came a sob from the curled up ball on the sofa. Jayne put a hand up to her burning cheek and stared at Helen like a cowed animal.

Helen straightened up and exhaled in one long rush.

'You must promise me that you will never see him again,' she said, trembling.

'I will not,' said Jayne, jumping up from the sofa and standing square to her mother, her eyes blazing with anger, 'and you can't beat me into submission. I will do what I want, when I want, with who I want. And you can't stop me. Maybe

I'll get pregnant and have to marry Sean and then what will you do?'

A blinding flash made everything pure white and for a moment Helen was aware only of a voice inside her head. 'YOU MUST STOP THIS! NOW!' it screamed.

'You can't marry him,' she cried out. 'He's your brother.'

Helen slapped her hand over her mouth, willing the words back in, but it was too late. The truth was out, sprung to her unwilling lips of it's own accord and there was no going back. Her secret was secret no longer.

Jayne stood motionless and open-mouthed for what seemed like an age. She shook her head slowly to the right and then the left, sorting and sifting the information, struggling to make sense of it.

'I don't believe you,' she whispered at last.

Helen held her gaze, but could not answer her.

'Daddy?' said Jayne. Her voice sounded like a little girl's, hurt and wounded, and her pretty face was pale and drawn.

'No, your Daddy didn't do anything wrong. It was me. Me and . . . and Sean Meehan's father.'

It was heartbreaking to watch Jayne as she tried to take it in. Her eyes were wide in disbelief, her head continued to move slowly from side to side, followed by a flash of comprehension that caused her brow to furrow. The realisation that her Dad was not her Dad at all.

'No, no, it can't be true,' she whimpered, moving backwards, away from Helen. Helen stepped forward with her arms outstretched, desperate to comfort Jayne, to take away the pain, to make things all right again. But Jayne recoiled from her touch, turned, ran out of the room and up the stairs.

Helen followed and knocked gently on the bedroom door, but Jayne would not answer. She tried the door, but it was locked from the inside. Helen rested her forehead on the cool glossed surface and silent tears fell on the carpet. Her poor little baby. Her whole world had been turned upside down in one night. Jayne would never forgive her. And what would happen in the morning? She wouldn't blame Jayne if she told her Dad. It would be too much for him to bear. Their marriage would be over.

Lying quietly on the bed, Jayne tried to take it in. All the previously held certainties about who she was were in turmoil. Her mother had slept with this man, this Mr Meehan and said he was Jayne's father. No it had to be a lie, it couldn't possibly be true. But that expression on her face when she said it. Horror, fear, shame, all rolled into one. And Mum had never, ever hit her before in all her life. Jayne pressed her hand against her still hot cheek and, much as every fibre in her body revolted against it, she knew it was true.

The implications were too awful to contemplate, but they forced their way into her consciousness like unwanted guests at a party. Sean was her half-brother and she'd allowed him to kiss and fondle her! Her attraction to him evaporated immediately and she felt dirty and ashamed. And her father was a man she'd never met. All the Meehan's were her half-brothers or sisters. Including Catherine Meehan. Jayne was nothing like them; she didn't want to be part of them. Catherine Meehan had destroyed her world and now this! It was too much to bear. Why did Mum have to tell her? It would have been better if she'd never known.

And how had it happened? When? Where? Why? Sordid images crowded her mind. Pictures of Mum with some filthy stranger, in a seedy hotel room, allowing him to paw her. Like a tart. She didn't want to speculate anymore; it was too disgusting to think about. Mum, the woman she adored, so pristine and well-groomed and ladylike, was nothing more than a common slut. And poor Dad. Did he know? She recalled the love and affection he showered on her. She thought about the strict moral standards by which he lived and she'd been raised. No, she concluded, obviously he had no idea and he wasn't going to find out from her. It would break his heart.

★   ★   ★

Helen dreamt she was a girl again, free, single, innocent, happy. She was running through the long grass on the edge of the Old Quarry. Frank was up ahead on the promontory where they used to lie in the sun and he was waving at her, calling for her to hurry up. She could see his handsome, smiling face and her heart did little somersaults as she ran along, fast as she could, to get to him. And then, suddenly, she lost her footing and fell, head first, into the quarry. But she didn't hit the bottom, she just kept falling and falling and falling, further and further away from Frank.

And then she woke up. She'd heard people say that when you finally shared a long-held, painful secret, no matter how awful the consequences, you felt a sense of release. Helen lay in the early morning gloom considering if this was true in her case.

She was, strangely, at peace. A kind of still calmness had come over her, whereby she felt removed somehow from the world around her. Not happy, nor sad, just there, existing, waiting for the inevitable. For Jayne would surely tell her Dad and that would be it. Helen's life would change forever. Overnight, just like that. And after all these years when she'd kept her precious secret so closely guarded. In a moment of utter madness, she'd thrown away everything she'd worked for — Jayne's security, Jayne's peace of mind, Jayne's happiness.

Helen turned her head to the left. The digits on the electric alarm clock, made from little matchsticks of red light, told her it was 06:36. She lay and waited, willing the minutes to pass slowly, each one taking her nearer the moment when she would be exposed. The alarm went off precisely at 07:15, John grunted, rolled out of bed and went straight to the bathroom along the hall. Helen slipped quietly out of bed, put on the clothes she'd laid out the night before, twisted her hair into a bun and went downstairs. She forgot to put on make-up. By the time John had washed and shaved and came back into the bedroom to get dressed, Helen was downstairs grilling bacon. She turned the thin slices over with a pair of stainless steel tongs Jayne had bought her for her thirty-seventh birthday. The first 'real' birthday present she had chosen and paid for with her own pocket money. A pang of sorrow jabbed her breast.

Suddenly the minutiae of her daily life seemed very dear to Helen. If this ended today what would she do tomorrow and the day after? Where would she go? How would she live? Who would want her?

Where was this sense of release people talked about? The fear of detection which had haunted Helen for the last eighteen years, was replaced with another kind of fear. The fear of the unknown, of loneliness and rejection.

By the time John came downstairs hot toast was on the table and a plate of bacon and eggs keeping warm under a low grill. The whole operation was honed to military precision over the years.

When Jayne came down for breakfast Helen couldn't bring herself to look her in the face. She managed to say 'good morning' in a shaky voice only by keeping her back turned and concentrating on topping up the teapot. Neither John, Eddie or Mrs Alexander noticed that Jayne did not reply.

'Dad,' said Jayne and Helen waited, tense.

This was it. She broke out in a cold sweat and turned to the window.

'Yes, love?'

'I think I'll walk to school today.'

Helen stopped herself from crying out by biting the knuckle of her right hand.

'Don't you want a lift?'

'No, not today. I'm running a bit late and I'll only keep you back.'

The panic subsided and Helen waited for Jayne to speak again, but when she did it was only to ask for the milk. Mechanically, Helen began to move around the kitchen, finding little jobs to do, putting things in the dishwasher, wiping here, tidying there. Anything to avoid having to sit down. Waiting for the axe to fall. Having psyched herself up for the moment when her adultery would be revealed, oddly Helen felt disappointed when the blow did not come. So what was to happen now?

'Wait, Dad!' shouted Jayne when John was half-way through the front door.

This must be it. Helen gripped the side of the sink.

But Jayne flung her arms round John's neck and said, 'I love you, Dad.'

'What's brought all this on then?' said John, beaming with pride.

'Nothing.'

'Well, I love you too, darling,' said John, planting a kiss on her smooth brow. 'See you later.'

Helen was beginning to feel like a cat with nine lives. Two down, seven to go.

Jayne came back into the kitchen and picked at her breakfast in silence. When Eddie left for work and Mrs Alexander had gone for her morning walk to get the paper, they were alone. Helen was summoning up the courage to speak when Jayne beat her to it, her voice deliberately cold and distant.

'Don't worry,' she said, 'I'm not about to tell Dad your dirty little secret or anyone else for that matter. Much as you disgust me, I will not be responsible for hurting Dad. I know that he couldn't forgive you for what you've done and it's better that he never knows. You don't deserve him and I hope you feel guilty every day of your life. You're nothing more than a dirty whore.'

Jayne stared at her, her blue eyes steel-hard and her face slightly flushed.

Helen closed her eyes momentarily. The words bruised her but it was no worse than she'd expected. No worse than she deserved.

'Jayne, sit down a minute, love. I'm sorry I hit you last night. I shouldn't have done that and I will never, ever raise a hand to you again as long as I live. I swear. I love your father and we're very happy together.'

'Phfff!' said Jayne, exhaling. She remained standing, contemptuous, like she did not want to be within touching distance of Helen.

'Really we are. This all happened a very long time ago and only the once. Your Dad and I were going through a rough patch. Eddie was a toddler and I think I was . . . I was . . . suffering from some sort of depression. Looking back I must have been for I wasn't thinking straight and, I suppose, I was emotionally vulnerable. Since Eddie had been born your Dad and I

311

hadn't been, well, 'close' and I felt lonely and isolated stuck here all day in this big house.'

But Jayne stood her ground, unmoved.

'I don't want to hear your dirty story or your sordid excuses. As far as I'm concerned you're not my mother.'

'Please, Jayne . . . ' cried Helen.

She stood up, put her hand out and touched Jayne on the arm. Both of them were sobbing now, but Jayne refused to be comforted.

'Don't you touch me,' she screamed, shrinking from her mother's touch. 'Don't you ever touch me again. I hate you. Do you understand? I hate you. I hope I never see you again, ever. I hope you die and I never have to speak to you again.'

With that, Jayne ran into the hall and out the front door.

Helen sat down, stunned and shaking. She doesn't mean it, she tried to reassure herself. She's only a child. She's just upset. But what did she expect? Her own daughter couldn't stand the sight of her. She'd made a complete and utter mess of it last night; she'd panicked and over-reacted. She should have slept on it, taken the time to work things through in her own mind before speaking to Jayne. The chances of the relationship with Sean coming to anything were so slim, at Jayne's age, that she should have let things be. She should have been wiser and all this would, most likely, have petered out.

Her relationship with Jayne would never be the same. Jayne would never trust her for her whole life had been exposed as one big lie. Jayne could see clearly that Helen didn't love her father, that they existed in a loveless union bonded together by a combination of children, duty, loyalty and pressure from the community in which they lived. Helen realised then that she could survive John finding out and the end of their marriage and the disapproval that would come with it. But she could not bear to lose the love of her precious daughter. The only thing that mattered.

Helen put her head in her hands and wept for a long time.

* * *

The name Sean Meehan was not mentioned in the house again until one night in bed a couple of weeks later. John put the tasselled marker in his book and set it on the bedside table.

'I haven't heard any more about this fella Sean Meehan, have you Helen?'

Helen tensed, but remained motionless, lying on her back looking up at the ceiling.

'No, John.'

'Do you think Jayne's finished with him then?'

'I'm sure she has.'

'Did she tell you that?'

'No.'

'How can you be sure then?' asked John, doubtfully.

'I just know.'

'A 'feminine intuition' thing?' said John, teasing.

'Something like that,' said Helen, thinking she really didn't want to pursue this line of questioning. But she would have to convince John.

'She hasn't been out, except with her girlfriends, these last few weeks,' said Helen. 'She told me so and I'd know if she was seeing someone. She must've finished with him after what you said to her that Saturday night.'

'Yes, you're probably right,' said John. 'Well, it's good to hear at any rate. She's a great girl, our Jayne, and I'm glad she's the sense to take our advice. We really are blessed, Helen. I just wish that brother of hers would take a leaf out of his little sister's book.'

17

'I'm pregnant.'

Geraldine sat on the side of the bed, feet spread apart on the carpet, kneading her hands between her thighs.

Catherine looked at her sister's stomach. Geraldine still had on the red nylon overall that she wore to work in the supermarket where she was a check-out assistant. What started as a summer job had become Geraldine's full-time employment on leaving school nearly two years ago. She could have done better — maybe got an office job up in Belfast — but Geraldine didn't want to leave Ballyfergus. Because of Eddie.

The overall was of tabard design, edged in blue piping, and joined at both sides of the waist by a strip of fabric that buttoned the front and back pieces together. It reminded Catherine of a maternity smock. A name badge pinned above her left breast said 'Miss G Meehan', blue writing on a white background.

'Are you sure?' began Catherine, but something about Geraldine's worn-out expression told her it was no mistake.

Geraldine nodded as though it took a great deal of effort.

'Does Eddie know?' Another nod, this time more vigorous, as if the inference that he might not know was insulting. 'And Mammy and Daddy?'

Geraldine was shaking her head before Catherine had even finished the sentence. They would go absolutely ballistic.

'Oh, Geraldine,' she moaned.

Catherine sat down on the bed beside Geraldine and put her arm around her shoulder.

'You poor thing. Come here.'

Geraldine collapsed gratefully into her arms and sniffled into the tissue she held scrunched up in her left hand. Catherine's head was racing. How? When? Where?

Then she dismissed these thoughts as irrelevant. The only important thing now was what was to be done. She was not as shocked by the revelation as she should have been; there was something inevitable about it. The situation with Geraldine and Eddie had been going on so long that something had to happen to bring it to a head. And there was only one thing worse than marrying a Protestant: having a bastard. Catherine sensed that, even in her distress, this thought had crossed Geraldine's mind.

'How long have you known?'

'I found out two days ago. I bought one of those kits from the chemists and did the test in the toilets at work. I would have told you straight away, Catherine,' she said, looking up at Catherine's face, 'but I had to tell Eddie first.'

'Of course you had to tell Eddie. You don't have to apologise to me,' she replied soothingly.

She paused and then went on. 'I know you haven't had much time to think about it. But what are you going to do? Do you want to keep the baby?'

316

'Why yes, of course I'll keep the baby,' said Geraldine, looking at Catherine with a surprised expression. 'There's no question of that. Me and Eddie will get married.'

★   ★   ★

Mammy and Daddy reacted as expected.

Catherine sat beside Geraldine on the sofa, holding her hand, while she broke the news. At Catherine's suggestion she had waited until Michael was out with Sean. Based on Michael's recent form Catherine feared he would blow his top and say something awful. At least this way he would hear about it second-hand and was (slightly) less likely to say something hateful to Geraldine.

'I knew it! I knew it! I knew this would happen,' cried Mammy, wringing her hands together like she sometimes did when she was praying very hard in chapel. 'Oh, God, what have I done to deserve this? What are we going to do?'

'The bastard,' shouted Daddy, jumping up and clenching his fists together like a boxer itching for a strike. 'I'll kill the bloody bastard. I will. I'll kill him. And you,' he said, pointing at Geraldine, 'you're nothing more than a little slut.'

Geraldine bowed her head, but proudly, and did not cry.

After a few moments Mammy took charge as Catherine knew she would.

'Frank, calm down. Don't speak to her like that. Sit down,' she ordered.

Daddy obeyed, but sat on the edge of the chair, his hands forcibly idle on his knees.

'Does Eddie know?' said Mammy.

'Yes,' said Geraldine.

'And what does he have to say for himself?'

'We're going to get married.'

'You're not marrying that Protestant pig! Taking advantage of my little girl,' said Daddy.

He thought for a moment then his eyes widened in horror.

'Did he rape you?'

'Don't be silly, Frank,' said Mammy, giving him a withering look and she turned round to continue where she had left off.

'And what do his parents have to say about this?'

'He hasn't told them yet.'

'Hmm,' said Mammy.

'What are you talking about marriage for? She's little more than a child herself, Theresa. She's just out of school for God's sake.'

'I know Frank,' said Mammy patiently, and then softening her tone, she continued, 'Geraldine, you don't have to get married you know. Not if you don't want to. There's no need to rush into anything right now. There are lots of other options you could think about.'

She glanced at Daddy before going on. Catherine sensed Geraldine wasn't going to like what was coming next. She squeezed her sister's hand.

'Like what?' said Catherine.

'Well, you could have the baby adopted.'

Geraldine looked round fearfully at Catherine.

318

'Or,' she added hastily, 'the baby could be brought up here. As your sister rather than your daughter. Lots of families in . . . in this position do just that.'

Daddy looked bewildered.

'No! We're getting married and I'm keeping my baby. I've already told you,' cried Geraldine, looking to Catherine for support. Catherine squeezed her hand tighter and smiled reassuringly.

'Just listen to me for a minute, Geraldine,' said Mammy more forcibly. 'You have to think of your future. You're far too young to be thinking of settling down. A baby brings a lot of responsibility and it's not something to be taken on lightly. And a mixed marriage isn't a good idea in this climate; people don't like it and you would be in for a rough ride. Especially with Eddie being an RUC man. I can't see his family being very happy about this either.'

'Can you see John Alexander standing by and letting his grandchild be brought up a Catholic?' snorted Daddy. 'Not likely.'

Geraldine looked at the floor.

'You have discussed this with Eddie?' asked Mammy, raising her eyebrow.

'No, we haven't got round to that yet,' said Geraldine slowly.

'Well, these are the things you need to be thinking about. Seriously. Your Daddy and I warned you about getting involved with this fella.'

Mammy paused and sighed heavily. 'We just don't want you making a mess of your life,

Geraldine. Have a think about what we've said and don't be making any hasty decisions.'

Daddy said nothing, but nodded his head gravely in agreement.

★ ★ ★

Much later that night Catherine lay awake in bed. It was long past the time when she was normally asleep.

'Catherine,' said Geraldine, her voice little more than a whisper.

'Yes?'

'Are you awake?'

'Yes.'

'If Mammy and Daddy try to stop me marrying Eddie, we'll run away together.'

'Geraldine, don't be saying that.'

Catherine felt a sinking feeling in her stomach.

She leaned up on one elbow and whispered, 'Please don't Geraldine. What would I do without you? I'm sure Mammy and Daddy will come round. They got an awful shock tonight; it's going to take a week or two to sink in. Just give them time.'

★ ★ ★

Jayne was as shocked as Mum and Dad.

'You are joking, Eddie,' said Mum.

'It's not something I would joke about. Geraldine's pregnant,' he repeated flatly, as though they had not heard the first time round.

But they had heard all right. They were in the

lounge where Dad stood on the hearthrug, his face growing more crimson by the second. Jayne cowered on the sofa, opposite Eddie, afraid of her father's wrath. She processed the information, taking into account the recent revelations about her own parentage. What would a child by her half-brother and a half-sister be to her? She glanced resentfully over at Mum and reminded herself why she hated her so much. Why the hell did Eddie have to get mixed up with that family?

'So she's trapped you then? At long last,' spat out Dad. 'And you've gone like a lamb to the slaughter. You stupid fool.'

'It's not like that, Dad. We love each other.'

Jayne looked across the room at her brother. She had never seen him so strong, so sure.

'Love? Don't talk to me about love. Next thing you'll be talking about marrying the little whore!'

'John!' exclaimed Mum.

Eddie leapt out of his seat and stood in front of Dad only inches from his face. Jayne saw the muscles in his neck stand out like taut ropes and a red flush swept over his face.

'Don't you dare talk about Geraldine like that, EVER. Do you hear me?' he screamed.

'Eddie, Eddie,' pleaded Mum, 'calm down. Your father doesn't know what he's saying. Sit down both of you.'

Neither obeyed although Eddie, glancing at Mum, backed off and began to mill about the room like a caged animal.

'Are you really serious about marriage?' asked Mum.

'Yes,' said Eddie firmly, 'I am.'

'And what does her family have to say about it?'

'I don't know. She's telling them tonight.'

'Have you thought about where you'd get married?' asked Mum, looking anxiously at Dad.

Eddie stopped in the middle of the room.

'No. And I don't care.'

'You'd not marry her in a Catholic Church?' demanded Dad fearfully, calmer now. His anger was replaced by an anxiety, which was, to Jayne, even more terrible to watch. His eyes were red-rimmed as though he had gone a few nights without sleep and he suddenly looked very old.

'If needs be,' said Eddie.

Dad visibly buckled, like someone had punched him in the stomach, and he held onto the mantelpiece for support. He shook his head, slowly, in disbelief and turned his watery eyes on Mum who, shocked and speechless, stared blankly back. Jayne wondered with disgust what memories were rushing through her mind.

Eventually, Dad let go of the mantelpiece and directed his gaze at Eddie. His eyes narrowed and hardened until they were just the same as Nana Alexander's and he pulled himself up to his full height. He spoke precisely and evenly so there would be no mistake that he meant every word of what he said next.

'If you marry that wee girl in a Catholic church, it'll be over my dead body.'

And then, with a measured step and his head held high, he left the room.

* ★ *

Some good news wouldn't go amiss thought Catherine walking down the road with Moira. They were on their way to the Grammar where the A-level results were to be posted outside the school office at ten o'clock. It was a sunny June morning, but Catherine's spirits were low.

Moira glanced at her watch.

'It's five to ten — we'll need to hurry up,' she said, grabbing Catherine's arm and urging her along.

'Aren't you excited?' she asked, giving Catherine's arm a squeeze.

'Yeah,' replied Catherine, unenthusiastically.

'Oh, I'm sorry. I forgot about Geraldine. How are things at home?'

Catherine shrugged her shoulders in reply. Two weeks had passed since Geraldine broke the news of her unwanted pregnancy, unwanted that is by everyone it seemed except Geraldine.

'As you'd expect,' she said at last. 'Mammy and Daddy are still trying to talk Geraldine out of marrying Eddie and they don't want her to keep the baby. Geraldine's really upset about it all and I've tried to tell them to leave her alone, but they won't listen.'

'That's terrible so it is. Poor Geraldine,' said Moira.

'Yes, she's under a lot of stress. It's beginning to tell.'

They were nearing the school gates now and, despite her preoccupation, Catherine felt adrenaline pumping through her body. A line of cars

323

were parked outside the gates, more and more arriving as the girls walked, faster now, down the hill. Pupils, unfamiliar out of their school uniform, and some accompanied by their parents, made their way up the slight incline to the office.

When they reached the gates, Catherine could see a crowd already gathered outside the school building. As they approached the throng a loud roar of chatter rose up into the charged atmosphere, punctuated now and then by nervous shrieks and laughter.

Catherine knew she would pass. But her grades were of crucial importance. Not only because she needed to get into university but because she had to get the best grades in the school. That was the reward she had worked so hard for these last two years. It was her revenge, her vindication. Just as they joined the others, the big blue doors opened and everyone pushed forward into the foyer in front of the office.

At first they couldn't get near the sheets of paper sellotaped to the office window. They waited impatiently until those in front read their results, then fought their way past them, out of the crowd. Some pushed past jubilant, grinning from ear to ear and punched a 'Yes!' with their fist in the air. Others kept their heads down, red-faced, and tried to hide their disappointment with brave smiles. Moira looked at Catherine and groaned.

The crowd thinned out and Catherine shuffled closer. The sheets of paper were computer printouts, green-and-white striped with perforations on the vertical edges. She strained to see, another wave of adrenaline coursing through her veins, making her slightly giddy. She elbowed her way to the front and peered at the faint print, searching for the M's. All the Mac's were first, lots of them, then Malcolm, Marshall. There it was: Meehan, Catherine. Three A's.

She let out long sigh of relief and allowed the crowd to surge forward. Next thing she knew she was at the back and Moira ran towards her.

'I passed, I passed,' she yelled. 'Can you believe it?

She flung herself at Catherine and they hugged and laughed.

'What about you?' asked Moira.

'Three A's.'

'That's unbelievable, Catherine! No-one will have got results like that.'

Catherine blushed.

'What about you, Moira? What did you get?'

'Three C's.'

'That's fantastic. I thought you said you'd failed History.'

'I know! Isn't it wonderful? But not as brilliant as you. My best friend's a genius!' she said, ecstatic.

When the crowd had thinned a little, they examined the sheets more leisurely to see how others had done. Catherine looked for only two names. She ran her finger quickly up the lists, backwards.

MacDowell, David; one A and two B's.

Good.

Alexander, Jayne: three B's.

Even better.

Satisfied she turned and walked away.

Everyone was going to Morelli's to celebrate and Catherine and Moira joined them.

'Congratulations!' said Lorraine to Catherine, when they arrived. 'Three A's! You must be over the moon.'

'I know,' agreed Michelle. 'I wish I was half as bright as you.'

Catherine allowed herself to wallow in her victory, savouring every moment of it.

'Have you thought about which university you'll go to?' asked Lorraine.

'I've applied to Edinburgh,' said Catherine, 'to do Business Administration. But that was before the results came out. I might reconsider.'

'And you, Moira,' continued Lorraine, 'what are you going to do?'

'I've applied to do nursing at Loughborough. And Strathclyde. I should get in to either with my grades.'

Catherine sat back and listened to the conversation. She would be welcomed at any university she choose, her achievement impossible to ignore. Like she had been ignored all these years at the Grammar. Overlooked, snubbed, humiliated. Made to feel inferior.

She saw Jayne standing in the corner chatting to her friends and smiled. She was vindicated, at last! Revenge, thought Catherine, is sweet.

At eleven-thirty she turned to Moira.

'I'd better go home; I want to tell Mammy my results.'

'I think I'll just stay on a bit,' said Moira, looking at her watch. 'I'm not in any hurry.'

Mammy was in her bedroom, stripping the double bed, when Catherine came in. She told her, excitedly, about her results, but Mammy was less than enthusiastic.

'I'm sorry Catherine, you've done really well. Really you have and I know Daddy will be proud,' she said, a bundle of dirty bed-linen in her arms.

'But it's Michael,' she went on, eyes filling up with tears.

'What about him? Is he hurt? In trouble?'

'No, no, nothing like that.'

She sighed and sat down heavily on the mattress. 'He says he's decided to go to America. To emigrate.'

'What? Where is he?' said Catherine.

She must talk him out of this madness straight away.

'He's away out,' said Mammy flatly. 'Gone to MacLeans' to sort out a flight.'

'But he can't just go to America, can he? He'll need a visa and he'd never get in, not without a job here to come back to.'

'He's it all worked out, Catherine. He says he'll buy a return ticket but just not come back. That's what all the Irish do, apparently. According to him there's plenty of work to be had, not like here.'

'But where'll he get the money from? He's skint.'

'That's what I thought, but he says he put some by when he worked for Harpers and the bits and pieces he's done for your Dad. Saved it up for an emergency, he said.'

'He never said anything to me about having money put by,' said Catherine, frowning.

'Well, it seems he has and there's nothing can be done about it. He says he's determined to go.'

'When did you find out?'

'Only half an hour ago. Some fella phoned here for him about eleven o'clock, said his name was Gerry Flanagan. I knew straight away something was up by the way Michael got all excited and waited for me to leave the room. He told me as soon as he came off the phone.'

'Who's Gerry Flanagan?' said Catherine.

'He was a few years ahead of Michael at St Pats. He went out there a couple of years ago. He was phoning from Boston. You know who he is; his Dad has the bookies down Pound Street.'

Gerry Flanagan was no friend of Michael's. Not to her knowledge anyway.

'Your Dad doesn't even know yet,' wailed Mammy, 'and he'll be gone in a fortnight!'

'A fortnight!' repeated Catherine.

Time never passed so slowly as Catherine waited for Michael to come home that afternoon. Her euphoria at achieving her goal, of proving herself the best, was completely quashed by a looming sense of depression. The whole family was in crisis; first Geraldine and now Michael.

Her beloved Michael. He'd always been there for her, right from the beginning, a source of comfort and strength. He understood her like no-one else, loved her like no-one else. He was the centre of her world. Why was he going away when she needed him?

But she wasn't being fair, she told herself. Michael had no prospects here; she'd no right to hold him back. She couldn't expect him to sit around Ballyfergus, unemployed, with no future. Especially when she'd plans of her own, plans that involved being a long, long way from Ballyfergus and everybody in it. Catherine sighed and wished life could be simple again, uncomplicated, like it was when they were children.

When Michael came in she followed him upstairs to his room. It was even smaller than the one she shared with Geraldine, so much so that the boys had to sleep in bunk beds. Michael leapt up on the top bunk with one agile movement and lay down, his arm bent behind his head. Catherine stood at the end of the bed, watching him.

'I'm going Catherine and you won't be able to talk me out of it.'

'But why, Michael? Why all of a sudden?'

'I just decided that's all. There's nothing for me here, Catherine, nothing but a life on the dole. The Brits and the Unionists have seen to that. I'm not smart like you Catherine. The best results in the Grammar.'

He paused, let out a long, low whistle and shook his head in amazement. Catherine blushed and looked at the floor.

'That's some achievement, so it is,' he went on. 'You've got prospects ahead of you that I never had: the pick of universities and the choice of the best jobs when you come out. And you go for it Catherine; make the best of it.

'But me, well, the States can offer me a chance to make something of my life. There's work for anybody that wants it and I've plenty of mates out there who'll help me get started. Probably a building site at first and then I'll move onto bar work. There's more money in that.'

'But you don't know anyone in Boston.'

'Yes I do. I know Gerry Flanagan and he has mates out there who'll help me. That's how it works; everybody helps each other out. He says it's great.'

'I didn't know you were friendly with Gerry Flanagan. I never heard you mention him before.'

Michael smiled down at her.

'I don't tell you everything little sis.'

'But I'll miss you,' said Catherine, taking his hand.

'I know. I'll miss you too,' said Michael, sadly. 'But you will come and see me, won't you? When you've got this great, well-paid job you're always on about,' he teased, 'you can have all your holidays in Boston! Sure it'll be great.'

Catherine felt Michael was holding something back, but she said nothing. She smiled and blinked to clear the mist that blurred her vision. They remained like that, holding hands, until Mammy called them down for tea.

Daddy was more pragmatic than Mammy even though it was usually the other way round.

'I'll be sorry to see you go son and I know it'll

330

break your mother's heart,' he said patting Mammy's hand.

The gesture struck Catherine as odd and then she realised that her parents rarely showed physical affection towards each other.

'But,' continued Daddy, taking his hand away, 'I can see where Michael's coming from, Theresa. At least in the States he can get work and make some sort of future for himself. There's nothing here for him.'

'Da's right, Mammy,' said Sean. 'God knows, I don't want to see Michael go any more than you do, but he can't go on like this. I just wish we could get enough business to keep the three of us employed. Maybe in a couple of years things might pick up.'

'I think it's for the best, I really do,' said Daddy. 'You'll be okay for money son? I could . . . '

'No, Daddy. I'll be all right,' said Michael quickly, 'but thanks for the offer anyway.'

18

For the next two weeks everyone put Geraldine and the pregnancy to the back of their minds and worried about Michael instead. As the day of his leaving came ominously closer Catherine felt a sadness descend upon the house as though a loved one had just died.

It was the night before Michael's departure. Geraldine went upstairs to lie down, partly because of her condition, but mainly because things between her and Michael weren't good and she was taking his leaving very bad.

Surprisingly, when he found out Geraldine was pregnant, Michael said very little. He was angry, of course, but his wrath manifested itself by him sending poor Geraldine to Coventry. He disowned her, he said, not because she'd gotten pregnant, but because of who the father was. And Catherine, not wanting to fight with him when he was going away and because she knew it would make no difference anyway, didn't argue with him.

Michael refused to speak to Geraldine, or sit at the same table with her, preferring to take his meals off his lap in front of the TV. Normally, Mammy would never have tolerated this, for mealtimes were a civilised family affair, taken together, squeezed round the kitchen table. But under the present circumstances, normal rules didn't apply and, to keep the peace, Mammy let him be.

'I'm going out for a couple of pints,' he said after his meal, bringing his tray in from the sitting-room. 'To say good-bye to the boys. I won't be late.'

'Don't be having too much to drink now,' warned Mammy, 'for you've an early start in the morning.'

'A couple of pints and I'll be home by eleven o'clock,' said Michael. 'I promise.'

'Now your Da's going to take you to the airport so you'll need to leave at, what?' Mammy asked the kitchen clock as though it would tell her the answer, 'eight-thirty to be on the safe side. According to someone Sean was talking to you have to check-in an hour beforehand.'

Michael's flight was leaving from Aldergrove airport, this side of Belfast, for London at 10.30 a.m. There he would have a four-hour wait before catching an afternoon flight to Boston.

'I'll make you a few sandwiches to keep you going while you're waiting in London,' continued Mammy with an unsteady voice. 'You don't know what sort of muck you'll get on those planes.'

Then she added, as though she'd experience of it, which she hadn't, 'And the price of food in these airports is horrendous.'

'Honestly, Ma, stop fussing,' said Michael light-heartedly. 'Everything will be all right. You'll see.'

He went upstairs and Catherine watched Mammy carefully prepare four rounds of ham sandwiches, Michael's favourite, and wrap them tightly in cling film. Then she buttered four homemade scones and wrapped each one in metal foil. She put them in the fridge, along with the sandwiches, for the morning.

It was just a case of waiting now, trying to say the things you said to a brother who you might not see again for years.

Catherine went up to her room and watched Michael across the landing get ready to go out. This was the biggest thing to have happened in his life so far and it must be frightening. Going to a strange city, a strange country, far away from your family and the people who loved you. His small suitcase, which used to belong to Grandad, sat at the top of the stairs already packed. The remains of faded stickers, from long-ago seaside holidays spent at Ballycastle and Portrush, clung to the sides like the imprint left by limpets when you knocked them off a rock. The plastic handle was broken so that you had to carry the suitcase, awkwardly, under your arm.

All of a sudden, Catherine felt very protective towards Michael. What if something happened to him? He could get mugged. Murdered. America was terrible for that sort of thing: you heard it on the TV all the time. She looked anxiously across the hall and saw him take what looked like a black woolly hat out of the chest of drawers and slip it into the pocket of the army surplus jacket he always wore. Curious, she got up off the bed, walked across the landing and leaned against the door-jamb of his room.

'What are you taking that for?' she said. 'It's summer!'

334

Michael jumped and turned round.

'What are you doing there?' he snapped. 'I didn't know I was being spied on.'

Catherine flinched.

'Sorry,' she said, 'I was only asking.'

'No, I'm sorry,' said Michael, and the anger leached from his eyes. 'I didn't see you there. You gave me a fright, that's all.'

He closed the drawer with his knee, straightened up, and looked around the cramped room. Apart from the bunk beds there was room only for a tall chest of drawers which partially obscured the window.

'I'm going to miss this place,' said Michael, 'even though it is a dump!'

'You can always come back if things don't work out,' said Catherine, hopefully.

'I won't be coming back,' he said so firmly that, for some reason, it sent shivers down Catherine's spine.

'So what's it for then?' she asked, anxious to move the conversation onto safer territory.

'What?'

'That hat or whatever it was,' she said looking at the bottom, left-hand pocket of his jacket.

'Oh, that. It's for Eamonn. I said he could have it.'

'An old woolly hat?'

'Yeah, he wanted it. Something to remember me by, I suppose,' he said and grinned broadly.

'Well, sis,' he went on, and patted down the four pockets on the front of his jacket, as if checking all was in order, 'I'd better be going.

Now don't be getting all weepy on me. I'm not away yet!'

His laughter was hollow and his smile faded quickly. He scanned her face closely, as though trying to memorise the details. But his eyes were not sad. They burnt with a vital intensity that frightened Catherine. He seemed excited, on edge, and while he had a big day ahead of him tomorrow, she wasn't convinced that alone accounted for his strange behaviour. He was definitely holding something back. What was he keeping from her?

'You won't be doing anything stupid now, will you?' she said thoughtfully.

'Like get drunk, you mean? No, not tonight. Mammy would kill me!' he said mistaking her meaning, deliberately Catherine thought.

She backed onto the landing as Michael came out of the bedroom. Then, stepping forward she embraced him wordlessly. He put his arms around her and kissed her gently on the top of her head. Catherine closed her eyes and when she opened them he was gone, the spot on her head still warm from his kiss.

★ ★ ★

They were coming for her. The flames from the bonfire were a hundred feet high; great licks of red and orange leapt into the night sky like huge, obscene, tongues. The banging got louder and louder. The angry crowd battered the front door, trying to break it down. To get at her and take her away. To throw her on the bonfire where she would burn alongside the Pope.

MAMMY! DADDY!

Catherine mouthed the words, every syllable an effort, but no sound came out. She must get out of bed, down the stairs and out the back door. That was her only chance of escaping the mob. But her limbs wouldn't respond. She fought with all her strength, but she couldn't move. The banging on the door intensified.

Catherine woke up suddenly and sat up, panting. Her nightdress was damp. Strands of hair stuck to her face. She looked around frantically and listened. The night was still and quiet apart from an intermittent, and loud, thumping noise. Someone, a very persistent someone, was at the front door.

Catherine slipped out of bed and groped for the alarm clock. She felt her way to the end of the bed and peeled back the corner of the curtain. Down on the street below, something caught her eye. An armoured police vehicle, more commonly known as an APV, dark and menacing with it's metal skirts designed to stop people rolling petrol bombs underneath it, was parked outside their house. She could see the end of a cigarette glimmer in the dark as someone in the driver's seat took a drag, then it disappeared. In the orange glow of the streetlamp outside the window she could see the hands of the clock. They said twenty minutes past two.

She looked over at Geraldine, went to call out to her, thought better of it, and slipped out onto the landing. The light was on and Daddy was

337

already half-way down the stairs fumbling with the ties of his dressing gown. Mammy followed him out of their bedroom, her long hair loose over her shoulders and a wild, fearful expression in her eyes. No-one spoke.

Daddy opened the door and Catherine saw, over his head, the familiar peaked caps of the RUC. Her stomach churned and she held on to Mammy's arm. The men exchanged a few words with Daddy and he stood back, flat against the door, and let them into the hall. The door was left open and Catherine shivered in the chilly night air. She'd never been this close to policemen before.

They both wore dark green, bullet-proof vests over their jackets which made them seem chubby, oddly comical. They carried worn pistols in the holsters on their hips. Their caps were pulled down low over their foreheads obscuring their eyes. But you could see that their faces were grim, their angular jaws set in tight-lipped expressions.

They all stood there in the hall and stared and waited for one of the policemen to speak.

'I'm afraid I have some bad news for you. Some very bad news,' said the taller one.

His voice was toneless, the sound of a man who delivered this sort of news regularly.

Mammy made a little squeaking noise and Catherine felt her sag. She gripped her arm tighter.

'There was an incident earlier on tonight out the back road to Glenarm. We think one of the men involved was your son.'

'Michael?' said Daddy, incredulous.

The policeman nodded.

'Is he all right? Is he hurt?' shrieked Mammy.

There was no warmth in the policeman's voice when he spoke.

'The bodies have to be formally identified before we can say, Mrs Meehan.'

The bodies.

Mammy sank to the floor and Catherine guided her onto the bottom stair. Sean and Geraldine appeared and stood behind Mammy.

'Is Michael in his room?' asked Catherine looking at Sean.

He shook his head, confused.

'What is it?' said Geraldine.

The policeman spoke again and everyone turned towards him.

'We need you to come down to the station with us, Mr Meehan, to see if you can identify either of the bodies.'

'What makes you think it's Michael?' said Catherine.

They were mistaken. Obviously, it was someone else.

'One of the policemen involved, a local man, thought he knew him. But we have to be sure,' he added quickly, inclining his head towards Daddy, 'that's why it has to be next of kin.'

'What policeman?' asked Geraldine, but the constable did not answer.

'If you'll get your things . . . ' he began, addressing Daddy.

'Yes, yes,' said Daddy absentmindedly, and he turned to go up the stairs.

At the bottom step he stopped and looked down at Mammy where she sat huddled against the wall. He laid his hand on her shoulder for a brief moment.

'Don't worry, Theresa. It'll not be him. I'm sure of it.'

Then he climbed the stairs gripping the banister like an old man.

The policemen shuffled their feet and looked at the floor.

'We'll wait in the van,' they said eventually and disappeared from the doorway.

'I'm going too,' said Catherine, pushing past Sean and Geraldine on the stairs.

She ripped open the wardrobe and, over her nightdress, pulled on jeans, T-shirt, jumper and trainers. She was downstairs before Daddy. She squeezed past Sean who sat on the bottom step with his arm round Mammy rocking her gently like a baby.

They rode to the station in the back of the APV, sitting on hard metal benches. Daddy was all dishevelled with dark bristle on his chin and he wore an old red sweatshirt and brown trousers he'd grabbed in the dark. He was still wearing his slippers.

The policeman who had done the talking sat up front; the other one sat in the back of the van on the bench opposite Catherine and Daddy.

'So what happened?' said Daddy after some minutes had passed.

'Look, the full details aren't clear yet,' said the policeman coolly, 'but I understand that a car containing three men failed to stop at a routine security checkpoint. Shots were discharged from the car as it drove past the APV and two officers were hit.'

Daddy looked up.

'Shot?' he asked.

Just then a shaft of yellow light came through the small grill of a window and fell across the policeman's face. Catherine could see that his lips were set firm and the muscles in his jaw tightened. He paused, seemed to compose himself, and continued without looking in their direction. 'They've both been rushed to the Royal. One's on the critical list, shot through the neck. We don't know if he's going to survive.'

His voice was bitter, angry.

'At least we got the bastards that did it,' he added.

'What about the men in the car?' ventured Catherine.

'The remaining officer returned fire forcing the car off the road. One of them seems to have died in the car crash; the other was badly injured. Should be dead, the bastard. The third one escaped from the crash and threatened the remaining officer who shot him dead in self-defence. He deserves a medal for it,' he added, turning his face to them for the first time.

'Who were they?' asked Catherine.

'We think two of them are brothers. Mulholland, Eamonn and Malachy. Names mean anything?' he asked icily, watching them closely.

Catherine did not reply, but looked at Daddy.

341

He shook his head violently.

'My son's not a terrorist,' he said, almost shouting. 'This is a mistake.'

'Well, if it's not your son then that's all right, isn't it?' said the policeman sarcastically and they all fell silent.

Afterwards Catherine would not be able to remember everything that happened at the station. Some things would be embedded in her memory, vivid and clear; others she would struggle hard to recollect. Daddy had to answer lots of questions at the desk. Then they were seated on two hard plastic chairs in a grey corridor lit by fluorescent strip lights. After a short delay a man came up, dressed in a dark suit and he held a clipboard in his hand.

'We're ready now Mr Meehan.'

Daddy nodded and stood up. Then he followed the man down the corridor.

Catherine sat there for what seemed like a long time looking down the corridor in the direction Daddy had gone. The station was alive with activity and new officers, men and women, came into the station every few minutes. They walked along the corridor in twos or threes, whispering, and fell silent when they passed her, studiously averting their eyes. No-one spoke to her. Before she heard the names of the Mulholland brothers, Catherine was absolutely convinced, certain, that this was all some crazy mix-up. That Michael would turn up in the early hours, full of drink and apologies.

'The celebrations just got out of hand, Mammy,' he would say and she would scowl at him crossly, secretly pleased that he'd had a good time.

But now, sitting under the harsh fluorescent light inside the barricaded police station, a place she never thought she would ever set foot, a treacherous uncertainty began to creep into Catherine's thoughts.

She remembered Michael's uncharacteristic reaction when he found out Geraldine was pregnant. As though he had much more important things on his mind than a silly little sister who'd got herself pregnant by a Prod. Then there was the sudden decision to go to the States and the money for the trip appearing out of thin air. The feeling that he was holding something back from her. The black hat stuffed into his pocket and lied about.

And, most chilling of all, she recalled Michael's zealous talk about a United Ireland and kicking the Brits out and how he hated Protestants. Come to think about it, lately that had been the only thing he talked about with any fervour. She thought back to the time she'd tried to talk to him about Geraldine and Eddie. His eyes had been vibrant and alive when he spoke.

'There are some things bigger than us worth fighting for, worth dying for,' he had said.

She heard his voice in her head as though he was right beside her, saw the glint of pride and passion in those dark eyes. Had he done something to further his idealistic dream of a United Ireland? Was this the sacrifice he had talked about? What the hell was he doing in that car anyway? Why didn't it stop at the checkpoint? Where were they going? Surely nothing was worth dying for? Surely Michael couldn't have been so stupid? Catherine closed her eyes.

The clues were all there, but she'd failed to piece them together. Not wanted to see what was right in front of her eyes.

By the time Daddy reappeared at the other end of the corridor, she knew Michael was dead. Daddy stumbled up the passage, one hand gripping the other just above the wrist, bouncing off the wall, repeatedly, like a wonky bumper-car. He looked like a drunk they'd picked up to keep in a cell overnight. Two men followed him; one of them she recognised as the man who had led Daddy away.

At first Catherine felt nothing at all. 'Michael is dead', she said to herself, but the words wouldn't compute, didn't mean anything. Just words. Her mind couldn't process the information and tell her what it meant. What it should feel like. Catherine realised she had no experience of death, she had never lost a loved one. Apart from Grandad, but that was when she was a little girl and she hadn't really known him.

Daddy hadn't cried then, not to Catherine's knowledge anyway. He'd been quiet and thoughtful for weeks after the funeral and Mammy told them to leave him alone. It soon passed though and life went on as normal. Mammy said that Grandad's death was a blessing really for he was so far gone.

And still a little part of her believed it wasn't true. Michael couldn't be dead. He was young

344

and handsome and warm and alive. When they horse-played, even now, and he caught her in his arms they were thick and strong. He played Gaelic football and hurling and he ate like a horse. Grandad had been ready to die; Michael wasn't. There was too much life in him.

The pain only started when Daddy got close. It was as though his grief made it real. The rubber soles of his slippers made a squeaking noise on the linoleum and Catherine looked up. His swarthy face was unnaturally white and he moved his lips, but Catherine could hear no sound. She felt the back of her throat tighten and she found it hard to breathe.

She stood up and took a few steps forward, towards Daddy. He looked at her, but did not appear to see her. She flung her arms around his neck. She ached to sob, to cry out but no sound would come. She felt like she was being strangled, the pain inside her boiled up until she felt it would eclipse her totally. Her eyes burned dry with it. She could feel the weight of Daddy as he leaned heavily on her and she felt his cold, wet tears on the side of her face.

'It's him. It's Michael. They shot him in the face,' he gasped into her neck.

And then his whole body shuddered and he said no more.

Hot tears coursed down Catherine's cheeks, but they brought no relief, only an intense physical pain that twisted her gut and stabbed at her chest. The tightening in her throat got worse and worse and she opened her mouth to cry out, to lessen the pain. But only a strangulated howl came out, a high-pitched wail that carried up the corridor and made people at the other end turn their heads before looking away.

They stood there together for a long time until Catherine thought she would collapse with Daddy's weight. She manoeuvred him over to the plastic chairs and they sat down. Daddy put his head in his hands and wept. Catherine rocked back and forth in her seat, her arms wrapped around her body, comforting herself.

When the tears had stopped and Daddy sat motionless, staring straight ahead at the grey wall opposite, the same two men that had escorted him out of the mortuary came up. The one with the clipboard glanced uncomfortably at his colleague before he spoke.

'I know it's been a terrible shock for you, Mr Meehan, but there are some things we need to ask you. Do you think you're up to answering a few questions?'

Daddy nodded, leant his hands heavily on his knees and dragged himself to his feet. He moved painfully like Grandad used to with his arthritis.

'Are you all right, love?' one of them said to Catherine.

The voice was softer than before, but she could still detect the note of reservation in it.

She nodded.

'Maybe you would be more comfortable in one of the interview rooms. Away from here,' he continued.

She shook her head.

'A cup of tea?'

'No.'

'Do you want me to get someone to come and sit with you?' he persisted, looking concerned. 'One of the girls?'

'No, I'm okay,' she said and hugged her arms tighter around her body.

She didn't want any of them near her. She knew what they were all thinking. That Michael was a terrorist, an IRA man. Scum. And she was ashamed.

'I'm fine here.'

'GO AWAY' she wanted to scream, but turned instead sideways and pressed her forehead against the wall. She heard them move away and she was glad to be alone.

Catherine thought of Mammy and Sean and Geraldine. Someone should tell them. And then she realised that the fear and the anxiety of not knowing was nothing compared to the torture of knowing the truth. No, leave them as long as possible she thought. Spare them even a few minutes of this unbearable pain. For once they knew, their lives, like hers, would never be the same again.

She watched three men emerge from a door at the end of the corridor. A man in civilian clothes came out first followed by a tall sandy-haired policeman in uniform, minus the peaked cap. He was followed by another man in civilian clothes. Although they wore plain clothes, the two men had short cropped hair and the look of policemen about them.

She watched the little group approach. The one in uniform had his head bent down as though he was searching for something on the floor. He seemed to falter and his feet scraped the linoleum. They stopped. One of the other men touched his arm in a gesture of solidarity, patted him on the back and said something. The policeman nodded and raised his head. It was Eddie Alexander.

Catherine, who had been lying slumped, her head resting on the back of the chair, sat up. Her eyes locked with Eddie's and he stared back pale and fearful, before dropping his gaze to the floor. Catherine went to get up to tell Eddie the terrible news and then checked herself. Something was wrong. Eddie knew very well who she was and would always nod and say 'Hello' if they passed each other in the street. But, as the little procession came up, walked by and continued on down the corridor, he showed no sign of recognition. It was then that Catherine knew who had killed her brother.

★   ★   ★

'Everything's going to be all right son,' said Dad, patting Eddie on the back. 'I've just spoken to the Chief Constable, Archie Fairweather. We went to the Grammar together you know. He's keeping an eye on things for us.'

Dad looked strained and his attempt to smile reassuringly wasn't altogether successful.

Eddie didn't look all right to Jayne. He was nervous and on edge and he hadn't slept for two days. He sat in the chair rubbing his hands together, obsessively, round and round and round like they were very cold, even though it was summertime.

It was three days since the shooting and he hadn't been back on duty since. The papers were full of it, not that the police were giving much away, and the phone hadn't stopped ringing.

'What did he say?' said Mum, referring to the Chief Constable.

She was white as a sheet and looked like she hadn't slept in weeks.

'It seems pretty clear-cut according to Archie, mainly because of the four AK49s found in the car. The terrorist that survived, that Mulholland fella, is still unconscious so they haven't been able to question him, not that he'll give much away I dare say.

'Archie reckons they were moving the guns to a safe house in the country outside Glenarm. The pistol found beside Meehan had his fingerprints on it so it's a straightforward case of self-defence. Naturally, there'll be a full internal inquiry and Eddie will be temporarily suspended, but he's not anticipating any problems. They're going to throw the book at the Mulholland fella.'

Eddie didn't seem to hear anything his father said.

'Eddie,' said Dad, 'you did what you had to do and I'm proud of you. At least now you know what type of family the Meehans are. The scum of the earth.'

Jayne flinched. The nightmare was never-ending. She was related to a family of terrorists. Gunmen! The shame of it bore down on her.

349

It was awful. She looked across at Mum and narrowed her eyes. She'd brought all this on Jayne. The dirty bitch. She'd betrayed Dad and made her a bastard. Sometimes Jayne just felt like blurting it all out, the burden was too much for anyone to bear.

The only thing that stopped her was Dad — she knew it would kill him — so she bit her lip and kept her silence. And now that a Meehan had brought all this trouble on the family, if Dad knew who she really was, maybe he would hate her.

'And as for that Meehan girl, well at least you know what to do now,' Dad went on.

'What do you mean?' said Eddie, waking up from his reverie.

Dad looked surprised, as though the answer to the question was obvious.

'Well, you can't have anything to do with her now. What she does with that baby is no concern of yours Eddie. Not after this.'

'But it's my baby and I love her.'

'Dear God, Eddie. Listen to yourself. She's the sister of a bloody IRA bastard who tried to kill you. Wake up, son!'

As he spoke, Dad dropped to his knees and shook Eddie violently by both arms, the lick of hair that normally covered his bald patch, fallen forward into his eyes. But Eddie just sat there and stared at Dad, his eyes watery and vacant.

'You know there was nothing left of his face,' he said matter-of-factly. 'You could have put your fist right through and out the other side.'

He closed his fist and stared at it, remembering.

'Eddie, love. Eddie,' wailed Mum, fingers clawing at her face.

Jayne put her hands over her ears, but she could still hear him.

'He was this close to me, you know, and the blood on the road. You should have seen it Dad!' said Eddie excitedly, letting out a loud guffaw that sent chills running through Jayne.

'It was like a river! A river of black blood. And all this stuff flowing out of his head . . . onto the tarmac . . . all grey and soggy . . . '

And then he stopped, put his hands over his face and wept loud, anguished sobs.

'Pull yourself together, son!' said Dad sharply. 'Helen, take Jayne out of the room. NOW.'

But Jayne was already on her feet. She brushed past Mum, eyes streaming, and ran to her room. She made sure the door was locked behind her for, sure enough, Mum came after her and knocked on it, repeatedly, for a long time.

'Jayne, let me in please,' she cried. 'I just want to talk to you.'

Jayne could hear the tears in her voice, but she covered her ears with a pillow and would not answer.

She couldn't live with this anymore. It was too much to bear. Eddie was losing his mind. And much as she loved him, she couldn't help him. He was in a place beyond her reach and part of her didn't want to reach him. For the fact that she was related to Michael Meehan made her

351

feel like a fraud, a traitor. She longed for the past before she found out her identity and this awful thing happened to Eddie. She could never go back to being the girl she'd once been. Her life was a mess; no-one could understand, comfort her, help her. No-one except David.

Jayne sat up. She remembered their late night talks, the way he listened, how he always made her feel better. She wouldn't tell him everything of course — the shame of being a Meehan in all but name was too hideous even to share with David — but he would listen to everything else and he would make things better. She would go to him now.

★ ★ ★

It was David who opened the door. He stepped back with surprise when he saw her. She looked down at herself to see what she was wearing; an old tracksuit and trainers. She hadn't stopped to check her hair or wipe the tear-stains from her face. She looked up and struggled hard to stop her voice wavering as she spoke.

'I came to see you,' she said simply. 'To talk.'

And then she covered her face with her hands and burst into tears.

David took Jayne by the hand, closed the door gently behind him and led her round the side of the house and down to the bottom of the garden. They sat on an old wooden bench, stained with bird droppings and lichen, and they stayed there, talking, until dusk was long past and it was dark.

19

When he died, Grandad's body sat for three days in the front room, his head propped up on a silky cream cushion so that you could see his face side-on if you stood on your tiptoes at the door.

Nowadays it was customary for the corpse to stay at the funeral parlour before going straight to the chapel and then onto the Catholic section of the graveyard. But Mammy insisted that Michael's body came home. Everybody agreed it was a bad idea.

'Especially under the circumstances,' said Aunt Bridie, in hushed tones when she thought Catherine couldn't hear. 'It's too badly disfigured for anyone to see, so what's the point? Frank identified Michael more by the poor boy's clothes and the St Christopher round his neck than what was left of his face. They had to check his dental records to be sure it was him.'

But Mammy was adamant and no-one dared challenge her. Daddy made sure the coffin lid was screwed down firmly and that's the way it stayed until it was lowered into the musty wet earth, alongside Granny and Grandad Meehan.

It lay in the sitting room on a makeshift trestle table that didn't look strong enough to take the weight, the head of the coffin up against the window. A large bronze crucifix sat in the middle of the window-sill and, on either side, two tall yellow candles in brass candlesticks burned in front of the closed venetian blinds.

Catherine remembered Mammy buying the crucifix and the candlesticks years ago at a sale of work at the convent. 'You never know when you might need them,' she'd said then. She could never have foreseen using them to send her son into the next world.

For the three days the body was in the house Catherine hardly slept at night. She listened to Geraldine sobbing quietly into her pillow, before her sister finally fell asleep, exhausted, only to wake up in the early hours tossing and turning, fitfully, in her bed. And then Geraldine would remember and start to cry again and Catherine could offer her no comfort.

Sometimes she felt a flash of terrible hatred towards the child growing inside Geraldine and then it would pass and she would feel ashamed. The child was an innocent and so was Geraldine. No matter how awful it was for Mammy and Daddy and her and Sean, it must be ten times worse for Geraldine. No-one but Moira outside the immediate family knew about Geraldine's condition which was just as well, for things were bad enough as it was.

The Mulhollands came round to offer their sympathy the day the body came home and Daddy went berserk.

'You killed my son!' he screamed at them as they stood on the doorstep, their faces worn and grey.

'If it hadn't been for you, you bastard,' he shouted at Brendan Mulholland, 'filling those boys' heads with republican propaganda, our

Michael would still be alive today.'

'Ah, Frank, now, now,' he replied sadly, 'haven't we both lost a son? Dear God, do you think I don't feel it the same as you?'

'Don't you speak to me, Brendan,' hissed Daddy and he was shaking with rage. 'Don't you dare stand there and lecture me. I should've seen this coming. Letting my Michael run around with your two. Filling him with poison. Get out of my sight!'

Daddy looked at that moment like he was truly capable of murder. Aunt Rose came up behind him and dragged him back inside.

'Come on, love,' said Brendan Mulholland, leading his wife away. 'We're not wanted here,' and Catherine sensed that along with their grief they felt a certain sense of pride.

Malachy was buried the day before Michael. She found out afterwards that men in combat jackets, black balaclavas and black leather gloves had fired a gun salute over his coffin.

And the police wanted to talk to Daddy about Michael and his friends and his habits. Uncle Pat had to go down to the station with Daddy four times before they were satisfied and left him alone.

Aunt Bernie and Aunt Netta took charge of the arrangements. The funeral was to be at three in the afternoon on Tuesday and only close friends and family were invited back to the house. They went up to see Father O'Neill, choose the readings and the hymns for the funeral mass, saw to the flowers, food and drink, the funeral cars, went and got Mammy a black dress, and checked to see that Daddy, Sean and the girls had something decent to wear.

Mammy and Daddy, in their different ways, were incapable of doing anything. Mammy stayed upstairs in bed with her sisters taking her up cups of tea and talking in hushed whispers in the kitchen. Daddy sat in the shed at the bottom of the back yard, only coming inside after dark smelling of whisky and stale cigarettes.

The house was full to overflowing with aunts and uncles and Catherine had to give up her bed to Aunt Mary and sleep on the floor.

When she arrived, Aunt Mary disappeared out the back and stayed with Daddy in the shed for a long time. When they eventually emerged she led him by the hand into the house as though he were a child. He went upstairs and had a bath and a shave for the first time in three days. Aunt Mary sat down heavily at the kitchen table and asked Uncle Bobbie for a glass of gin. Even though it was only half past two in the afternoon, she drank it in one gulp.

★　★　★

Catherine did not cry at the funeral. She felt as though she was watching the burial of a stranger, from a distance. Like watching a film on TV. And she was amazed by her aunts' efficiency.

Back at the house the sitting room had been transformed. Gone was the trestle table, that had held the coffin, the crucifix and the candlesticks. The sofa had been pulled back into the middle of the room. The only giveaway that things were not quite normal was the way the cushions were fluffed up and sat on their corners in a neat row on the sofa. Steaming cups of tea were dispensed from two great big teapots her aunts had borrowed from somewhere.

They took it in turns to go round the house offering sandwiches and biscuits and cake to the mourners, a kind of culinary relay.

The atmosphere was totally different from how Catherine remembered Grandad's funeral, which had been almost jolly. There was no laughter and joke-making. The men maintained a dignified sobriety and the women cried into lace handkerchiefs or handfuls of Kleenex tissues. Even the younger children seemed to sense the solemnity of the occasion and were uncharacteristically subdued.

Aunts and uncles and cousins she hadn't seen in years kept coming up to Catherine, kissing her and hugging her, saying they understood and how brave she was. But Catherine stared blankly back and, aware of the concerned glances cast in her direction, went and sat in her room.

She listened dry-eyed to the hushed noise down below. Aunt Mary came up with a plate of sandwiches and a mug of tea.

'Thank you,' said Catherine as she watched her set them on the small bedside table. The crusts of the sandwiches had started to curl up at the edges.

Aunt Mary sat on the edge of Geraldine's bed and thought for a moment before she spoke.

'You know, sometimes it's better just to let it all out, Catherine. Have a good old cry,' she said,

357

raising her eyebrow encouragingly.

But Catherine only turned her head and looked out the window through the narrow slats in the blinds. Dusk was falling fast and the low sun lit up the sky with an orange glow, so that it looked much the way it did the night before the Twelfth of July. But this time Catherine didn't feel afraid. The worst had already happened. She remembered how once she confessed her fears about the bonfire to Michael and he promised he would protect her.

'I'll always be there for you, Catherine,' he said.

But he had broken that promise and now she was on her own. If you believed everything the priest said then Michael had gone to a better world where he would never suffer physical pain and he would never grow old. He might have to do some time in purgatory, but who didn't? None of us were perfect. But after that, when he'd paid the price for his sins, including shooting those policemen, Catherine was sure he would go to heaven.

So why did everyone cry? Because they would never see Michael again. Because they didn't want to face life without him. Not because Michael's life was over, for it wasn't; it had just taken on another form. But because their lives would never be the same again.

When Catherine looked round again, she was alone in the room and a milky scum had formed on the top of the cold tea. She went through to the bathroom and was about to close the window when she heard voices from below, in the back

358

garden. It was Sean and Moira. Surprised, she paused and listened.

'I'm so sorry about Michael.'

'I just miss him so much, Moira. I never thought we were particularly close, but now, everywhere I look I see him. Night times are the worst. I keep having these dreams.'

'It must be awful,' said Moira.

'I feel like I should have done something. I should have known what was going on. But I never noticed a thing, I swear to God. I was too wrapped up in my own life.'

The suffering in his voice was laid bare. Catherine put a hand to her mouth to stop herself crying out.

'It's not your fault, Sean. You couldn't have known what would happen.'

There was a muffled sound, like a sob.

'Please don't go away, Moira,' he cried suddenly. 'Don't leave me! I love you so much.'

'There, there baby,' said Moira soothingly. 'It's okay. I'll not go to England. I'll take that place at nursing college here instead.'

'Thank you. Thank you,' he sobbed.

'Come here, love. Sshh, my darling. I'll stay. I promise.'

Then there was silence and, ashamed of herself for eavesdropping, Catherine closed the window very gently.

After the funeral was over, Mammy's sisters stopped coming round every day and Daddy, Sean and Geraldine all went back to work. Her schooldays over, Catherine stayed at home with Mammy and waited for the time when she would leave for university. On the face of it, things more or less went on as normal.

And it was only then that Michael's death really hit home. It was impossible to get through even a couple of hours without breaking down in tears. Catherine would be setting the table for dinner and put out a place for Michael by mistake. Counting out potatoes for dinner she allowed for six and then remembered they were only five now. Sometimes she wondered what Michael would make of this or that when she told him about it. And then she would remember that he was dead. Lying in that cold, damp grave.

It took Mammy a long time to get back into her routine. She became forgetful and distracted and, within a week of Michael's death, her hair started to turn grey. Sometimes she stopped in the middle of doing something and went into a sort of trance or walked into a room and forgot why she had come in. And often tears ran, silent and unchecked, down her pale cheeks into the sink where she was washing dishes or peeling carrots.

Daddy took to going to the pub after work and Sean came home alone. By the time he came in for dinner, Daddy was red-faced and smelt of whisky.

One night Father O'Neill, the parish priest, came to see Mammy and Daddy and sat in the sitting-room nursing a cup of tea. His grey old face was dry and lined and a deep furrow on his brow indicated the depth to which he was troubled.

'It is a terrible thing to lose a child, Theresa,' he said. 'No parent ever expects them to die before they do. Especially under such terrible circumstances.'

Catherine offered a plate of biscuits. He took a chocolate-covered wafer and set it on his plate. He looked into his cup and went on.

'But it is your cross and you must both bear it. You have to be strong for it is God's will.'

Catherine could listen no more and slipped out of the room. Geraldine had just come in from work.

'Who's that?' she said, sinking down into a chair in the kitchen.

'Father O'Neill.'

Geraldine nodded glumly and Catherine noticed that her stomach was starting to look decidedly rotund. The subject of Geraldine's pregnancy and Eddie Alexander had not been mentioned in the house since Michael died. The horror of it was too much for any of them to contemplate. What the hell was Geraldine going to do?

As if she could read her thoughts, Geraldine sighed and looked up at Catherine. The suffering of the last few weeks had left it's mark. There were black circles around Geraldine's eyes and the whites were yellow and crazed like a very old piece of china. But she was calmer than she had been these last few days and, despite her wretched appearance, she conveyed a sense of composure.

'I've decided what I'm going to do Catherine.'

'Yes?' said Catherine attentively.

'Eddie hasn't been the same since . . . well, you know,' began Geraldine.

Catherine winced at the mention of his name, but steeled herself for Geraldine's sake.

'I'm going to go away with him,' Geraldine blurted out. 'To England. The police know about it, but no-one else. He hasn't told his family. And I'm not telling Mammy or Daddy. I think it would be best if . . . if I just went,' she said, looking down at her stomach.

'But Geraldine! How can you? He killed your own brother for God's sake. He killed Michael!'

'I know,' said Geraldine patiently, closing her eyes. 'I know that, Catherine.'

'How can you even consider running away with him, being with him, having his child? He murdered Michael!'

'Catherine!' hissed Geraldine and she opened her red-rimmed eyes.

When she had secured Catherine's attention she lowered her voice again. She spoke in a dead-pan tone, devoid of emotion. Like an old woman.

'I know Catherine, but he didn't mean to. He had no choice. It was either him or Michael. I love — loved — them both, but we can't turn the clock back. I've got to think of the baby and I love Eddie. It's best this way — that we go and never come back.'

She paused for a moment, and seemed to Catherine many years older than her seventeen years.

'And you must go away too, Catherine,' she said. 'Take that place at university and get out of

362

this godforsaken country. Make something of your life for Michael's sake. You can't stay here with Mammy and Daddy. Not the way they are now. It'll ruin your life.'

Catherine simply nodded.

'When are you planning to go?' she asked.

'Tonight.'

'So soon! You can't go just like that.'

'It has to be tonight. It's all arranged. We're getting the night boat. And I . . . we . . . we need you to help us,' she said.

'What will you do? Will you get married?'

'It's a bit late for that,' said Geraldine holding her stomach.

'Okay,' said Catherine. 'Just tell me what you want me to do.'

'Help me pack. Eddie's going to pick us up in his father's car and then we need you to drive it back to his house.'

'But I haven't got my driving licence!' said Catherine.

'No. But you can drive, can't you? Michael showed you.'

Catherine nodded.

'Yes, I'll do it.'

After tea, Geraldine got up from the table and put her plate in the sink.

'I'm having an early night,' she announced.

'Me too,' said Catherine, feigning a yawn. 'Once I've helped Mammy with the dishes.'

'Night everyone,' said Geraldine and she paused at the doorway and looked at each one of them. Catherine hoped that no-one else noticed the tears in her eyes.

When Catherine came upstairs Geraldine's meagre possessions were laid out on her bed.

'You can use this old grip of mine from school,' said Catherine. 'The zip's broken, but it'll have to do. We can't get into the loft for a suitcase.'

They packed the bag in silence and when it was done they both got into bed, fully dressed, and sat in the dark and waited.

It wasn't long after eleven o'clock when they heard the bathroom being used. They listened to the creaking floorboards in both bedrooms and then the house went silent. It was eleven-thirty.

'Let's go,' said Geraldine in a whisper. 'Can you take the bag and I'll carry my coat and handbag?'

They crept out onto the landing and down the stairs. They paused in the darkened kitchen and listened. Catherine's heard the beat of her own heart, pounding in her chest. No-one stirred. Outside it was a clear, still night.

Eddie was waiting at the bottom of the street, with the car engine turned off. He jumped out of the driver's seat when he saw them and ran to Geraldine. He threw his arms round her and kissed her fiercely on the lips. Catherine felt a lump in her throat and looked away.

A light came on in a nearby house and Catherine said, 'We'd better get going.'

'Thanks,' said Eddie as he took the bag from her and put it in the boot.

Catherine said nothing and got in the back of the car. When the car light came on she noticed Eddie was unshaven and he pulled almost desperately on a cigarette. His left hand shook where it rested on the steering wheel and he changed gear jerkily. Geraldine's hand came up and rested on his momentarily. The shaking stopped.

They drove to the dock in silence.

'Just dropping off,' said Eddie at the security checkpoint.

The guard examined the tickets and peered in the car window. Catherine met his inspection with what she hoped was a friendly smile. The last thing they needed right now was an interrogation.

Satisfied, the guard directed them to the dropping off point.

'You'll need to hurry though,' he said. 'The boat leaves in fifteen minutes.'

Catherine accompanied them into the near deserted terminal building which smelt of stale cigarette smoke and fried food.

'Would all remaining foot passengers please board now,' said a voice over the tannoy and Gelaldine turned to Catherine.

'That's us then,' she said bravely. Her expression was grim.

'Come here,' said Catherine and she pulled Geraldine to her and kissed the top of her head.

'I love you, Geraldine,' she said.

'I love you too.'

She released her and Eddie took Geraldine's hand.

'Catherine,' he said and faltered. He looked at Geraldine who nodded encouragingly for him to continue.

'Do you forgive me? For Michael.'

Catherine did not reply. She looked into Geraldine's face and her eyes were beseeching. Begging. She wanted to hate Eddie for killing Michael, but found instead she felt sorry for him. And for Geraldine.

'Please say you do,' said Eddie his voice strangely childlike. His head was bowed so low Catherine could not see his eyes.

Part of her had forgiven him already. Part of her probably never would. But this might be her only chance to give both him and Geraldine the peace of mind they both craved. God knows when she would see either of them again. She knew that if it hadn't been Eddie that night it would have been another policeman. Faced with the same situation anyone would have done the same as Eddie. It was him or Michael. And she couldn't really blame him for choosing to live.

'I . . . ' began Catherine, but her voice failed her. She swallowed and tried again.

'I forgive you,' she said in a quiet voice.

Eddie looked up and there were tears in his eyes.

'Thank you, Catherine. Tell your Mum and Dad I'm sorry too.'

Catherine nodded.

'If you're travelling on this sailing you have to go now,' interrupted a dark-suited official, shepherding Geraldine and Eddie towards the door.

'Bye, Catherine,' shouted Geraldine as they moved off.

'I'll look after her, Catherine. I promise,' shouted Eddie.

'Bye. You will write, won't you?' Catherine called out.

'I will. I promise.'

Catherine went to the window and watched them proceed up the gangplank and disappear into the side of the ship. And then the tears streamed down her face.

The car was big and the dashboard, with all its lights and knobs, daunting. Somehow she managed to get out of the ferry terminal without attracting any attention in spite of the kangaroo jumps and false starts. She took the most straightforward route to the Alexander's house, up the steep Grammar Brae, avoiding traffic lights and junctions. She put the car into first gear and crept as smoothly as she could into the driveway. Halfway up the drive she stopped, not daring to go any further for fear the noise of the gravel would give her away.

She took the key out of the ignition, wrapped it in a clean tissue and stole up to the house. She paused and looked at the upstairs windows and imagined Jayne asleep behind one of them. She felt an extraordinary flash of empathy. She'd lost a brother and a sister and in the morning Jayne would have lost her brother too. Then she opened the brass letter-box, dropped the key inside, turned and ran down the drive.

★　★　★

'She says she's gone to England with Eddie Alexander. Did you know she was going?' asked Sean, holding the note Geraldine had left in his hand.

Catherine leaned against the kitchen doorframe and nodded. She was shattered after last night.

'Why didn't you say anything?' he asked.

'She'd have gone anyway and this avoided a big row. That's the way she wanted it and she asked me to help and I did.'

'How did you help?'

'I saw them off at the boat and drove the car back to the Alexander's house and left it there.'

'I can't believe you helped that bastard, Eddie Alexander,' said Sean, throwing the note down on the table in disgust. 'How could you even speak to him?'

Catherine shrugged her shoulders.

'It seemed the right thing to do. I tried to hate him for what he'd done, but I couldn't. The more I think about it, the more I realise it wasn't his fault.'

'What do you mean it wasn't his fault? If he didn't pull the trigger who did?' said Sean, angrily.

'I know it's hard to do, but try putting yourself in his shoes. I don't see that he had any choice really. Faced with the same situation what would you do, Sean?'

'Why are you defending him?' he demanded.

'I'm not. I'm just trying to make sense of it. And heaping all the blame on Eddie Alexander doesn't solve anything.'

Sean sat down heavily on a kitchen chair, put his arms on the table and leaned his head on them, face down. He stayed like that for a few minutes and then looked up at Catherine.

'I suppose you're right,' he sighed. 'I want to blame someone too, but we're going to have to face the fact that Michael brought it on himself.'

'He asked me to forgive him, you know,' said Catherine.

'Who?'

'Eddie.'

'And did you?'

'Yes.'

'I don't know if I could go that far.'

'He said he was sorry. And I think he meant it. He looked like he was on the verge of a breakdown. And I did it for Geraldine's sake, as well.' Catherine paused and looked at him. 'I'm going to go to university,' she went on. 'I had a letter the other day. The term starts in a couple of weeks.'

'So you're going ahead with that business course?'

'No, I've changed my mind. I'm going to do teaching.'

'What's brought this on?' said Sean, surprised. 'What happened to the well-paid job in the city? You'll make even less money than me as a teacher!'

Catherine looked out the window and was quiet for a moment. 'It's not about money. That doesn't seem . . . well, it doesn't seem important anymore. I want to do something worthwhile in itself. If I could have Michael back. And

369

Geraldine. And things the way they were before, I'd never ask for anything as long as I live.'

'I know,' said Sean softly. 'But why teaching? You never struck me as the teaching sort, Catherine.'

'You know the way they're talking about setting up an integrated school in Ballyfergus?'

Sean nodded.

'Well, apparently it's going to be a real integrated school, not like the Grammar, with a fifty-fifty split Protestants and Catholics. And I thought that by the time I was qualified, there might be more of them. And that's what I'd like to do — teach in an integrated school. Maybe even here in Ballyfergus.'

'But you were always so determined to get out of Northern Ireland and especially Ballyfergus!'

Catherine looked at him and smiled.

'Yes, I know,' she said and then went on, 'I haven't told Mammy and Daddy that I'm definitely going yet. I'm not sure they'll be able to handle it. And if I go that'll leave you on your own.'

'I'll be all right. You take your chance while you can, Catherine. I'll look after them, don't you worry.'

They were silent for some moments and then Catherine said, 'I know you and Moira are an item.'

He looked up surprised.

'She told you then.'

'No, I overheard you speaking the day of Michael's funeral. I'm glad you've got each other. I really am.'

They heard footsteps on the stairs and stopped talking.

'They're going to take this very hard,' whispered Sean, refolding the note and putting it back on the kitchen table where he'd found it. 'Very hard.'

20

Nana Alexander died in her bed the Friday after Eddie disappeared. Of a heart attack. Jayne accompanied her father to the funeral director's to make the arrangements for the burial. They sat in red velvet chairs with cups of tea and waited to be seen.

'You don't think Nana's death was brought on by the strain of the last few weeks?'

'Oh, I don't think so, Jayne,' said Dad. 'Your Nana was very old. And she had a good innings. More than her three score years and ten.'

Jayne fell silent and Dad asked, 'What is it, love?'

'I was just thinking about Nana. I remember every Easter she bought us a new set of clothes and an Easter egg each. And it was the same at Christmas and birthdays and when we went on holiday to England. She was always buying treats — ice cream and rides on the ponies. Do you remember?'

'Yes,' said Dad and he smiled for the first time in weeks. 'She loved you and Eddie. I know she wasn't given to hugging and kissing and telling people she loved them. But she did. More than you know.'

That was the first time Dad had mentioned Eddie's name since he'd run away with Geraldine. Jayne still couldn't believe he'd gone, just like that. And the fact that he hadn't told her hurt more than anything.

Dad was convinced that Geraldine would be the ruin of Eddie, but Jayne didn't agree. Geraldine might be the only thing that could save him from losing his mind. She wished he would get in touch if only to let her know he was all right.

Jayne looked at Dad and wondered if Nana had known about Mum's affair with Frank Meehan. She thought not. Her daughter-in-law's infidelity would have been nothing compared to the crime of consorting with a Catholic.

'What are you smiling about?'

'Oh, I was just thinking about the time a girl at school called me names and Nana went down to the school and demanded to see the headmaster.'

'Your Mum was furious!'

'It worked though. No-one ever called me names after that.'

★　★　★

There was a good turnout for the funeral and Reverend McDowell did a respectful service. Afterwards, the procession made its way to the Protestant section of the council graveyard where Nana was to be buried beside her husband.

Jayne listened absentmindedly to the minister's graveside intonations and thought of the part Nana had played in her life. Even though, in recent years, she could not agree with her bigoted views she believed Nana was, essentially, a good woman. She was a tough old boot and a bit misguided perhaps, but Jayne had loved her and understood her. And so she did not judge her too harshly. Nana was the product of a different time when the enemy was popery, and the greatest threat, the territorial aspirations of the Free State. For most people of Jayne's generation all that had changed. All they wanted was peace and normality.

Jayne looked up at Mum who stood opposite, her face partly obscured by a big black hat. Her eyes were cast downwards and her face betrayed little emotion. Jayne was not surprised for she had always known there was little love lost between Nana and Mum.

The minister said the bit about ashes to ashes, dust to dust and threw a handful of brown earth into the pit. It rattled noisily on the wooden coffin and he wiped his hand on his cassock.

Suddenly Jayne was acutely aware of her own mortality. This would be her own end one day, lying in a hole in the ground somewhere. Fear swept over her as she acknowledged to herself, for the first time, that she did not believe in 'another life'. Nana was dead and that was it — there was nothing else. There would be no judgment day, no passage into heaven, no eternity, no second chance. On earth, here and now, was all we had. And then Jayne realised with a jolt that the next time she stood over a grave like this it could be Dad or Mum down there in the coffin.

Panic seized her. Mum! What if she died and Jayne never had the chance to put things right between them? All this time she'd harboured resentment towards her for what she'd done. She'd cultivated a coolness between them that was perceptible only to the two of them and she'd used it to punish Mum, to deny her the intimacy of their former relationship.

How stupid she'd been. She'd never taken the time, or the blinkers off her eyes, to consider things from Mum's point of view. She'd never asked or attempted to understand. She'd tried, judged and condemned her mother from the limited perspective of a selfish teenager and she'd never questioned that she had the right to do so.

What if Mum had really loved this Frank Meehan? Apart from this one incident Jayne was sure her mother had been faithful to Dad. She wasn't flighty and given to having affairs; it just wasn't in her nature. If she slept with this man and conceived his child she must have really loved him.

Images from childhood flashed through Jayne's mind confirming her suspicions. The lack of physical affection between her parents, Mum's inexplicable sadnesses, the joyless atmosphere. Instantly, it became clear to her.

Mum loved Frank Meehan. Maybe she still did. Maybe it was the only true love Mum had ever known.

And it was only then that Jayne appreciated the enormity of her mother's sacrifice. She'd stayed with Dad for the sake of her and Eddie, to ensure that they had a stable and loving home. Jayne flushed with shame when she recalled how she'd repaid that sacrifice.

How awful it must have been for Mum, living without the one person she truly loved. She wished she could turn the clock back and change things somehow so that Mum could live her life all over again. She couldn't change the past of course, but she could make amends. She must tell Mum she was sorry. That she forgave her. It wasn't too late.

★ ★ ★

The minister finished and Helen watched as John stepped forward and threw a single pink carnation, Nana's favourite flower, into the grave. He looked tired and his face was drawn. She took his arm supportively as the rest of the mourners began to disperse, stopping to offer words of consolation. She saw Jayne a little way off talking to David McDowell and wondered if they might get back together.

'We'd better go, John,' said Helen gently. 'The mourners will be at the hotel soon. The buffet's ordered for four o'clock.'

'Let's stay a moment longer,' said John and she stood silently beside him. The gravediggers waited at a respectful distance. After a few minutes he spoke again.

'You know my mother was never that keen on you. She said you wouldn't make me happy. But she was wrong you know.'

He paused and looked at her. 'I know I wasn't your first choice, Helen. But I hope I've made you happy. I tried to.'

She thought of the life they'd had together and

the love he'd showered on Jayne and Eddie. Suddenly, she was ashamed of herself for yearning after Frank Meehan all these years. Her infatuation seemed almost juvenile and she wondered if their love would have survived the realities of everyday living. But John's love had endured all these years even with little encouragement.

'You have made me happy,' she said. 'You've been very . . . good to me.'

John cocked his head to one side and squinting in the sun, he regarded her thoughtfully.

'I sometimes wonder if you would've been happier married to Frank Meehan,' he said.

Helen started.

'Oh, I knew about him,' he said, seeing her surprise, 'I knew you only took me on the rebound. But I thought you could learn to love me.'

Helen looked into those kind eyes glinting in the late summer sun and they were full of love. She touched John softly on the cheek with the tips of her fingers and he closed his eyes. She would never love him the way she loved Frank. This was different; more gentle and considered, a safer sort of love. And none the lesser for it.

'I do love you, John,' she whispered.

He grasped her hand and held it to his lips and kissed it.

'My darling,' he said and put his arms around her. And she returned the embrace.

★　★　★

'I know my timing's maybe not the best with your Nana and all,' said David. 'But I need to know. We'll both be going to uni soon.' Jayne looked across the graveyard at her parents. She seemed more intrigued by what they were doing than by him.

'Sorry, David. It's just there's something funny going on over there with my Mum and Dad. They're hugging each other.'

'So?'

'Oh, nothing. Anyway, what were you saying?'

'Do you want to get back together or not, Jayne?'

Her answer was immediate and firm.

'No, David, I don't.'

'But I don't understand. You came to see me that night. To talk. I thought . . . '

'Because I needed a friend.'

'Don't you feel anything for me?' pleaded David.

'Of course I do. I suppose I always will,' she said gently. 'But not as a boyfriend.'

'But I love you, Jayne,' he said desperately.

She couldn't be doing this to him. He'd lost her once before through his own stupidity. He couldn't bear to lose her again. He could see pain in her face and his hopes rose.

'Not enough you don't,' she said sharply.

He winced. She was referring to Catherine of course.

'Please don't make this any harder for me than it already is, David. I did love you once, but I couldn't trust you, you see. Not completely.'

An image came to mind of Catherine as he'd

last seen her, that night at the Candlelight, her luscious curves draped in black velvet. The forbidden fruit. The details of their conversation at the bar weren't altogether clear, but he remembered she'd given him the brush-off. He'd only been trying to make amends for the way he'd treated her. And for that he was truly sorry.

'I know I did something very stupid, Jayne, which I'll always regret. I just wish you could forgive me.'

'I do forgive you. But I've realised that you and I aren't meant to be, that's all.'

With that she turned and walked away.

*   *   *

Jayne caught up with Mum and Dad, slipped between them and hooked her arms in theirs. If Mum was surprised she never showed it and they walked that way to the car.

The day dragged. When the mourners finally left the hotel Uncle Robert and Aunt Irene came back to the house. Uncle Robert and Dad reminisced about Nana and Papa and what it was like when they were children. Jayne was restless and at ten-thirty she excused herself and went upstairs.

She changed into her nightwear and sat on the stool in front of the dressing table and listened for sounds from below. At last there were voices in the hall, the front door opened and closed and then silence. Some five or ten minutes later a heavy tread on the stairs, a door closing at the

379

end of the landing. A loud belch confirmed it was Dad.

Jayne went downstairs to the kitchen where she knew Mum would be. She paused outside the door and listened to the familiar sounds emanating from within. The click-click-click of Mum's high-heeled shoes on the lino. The sound of the table being laid for breakfast: the soft thud of tablemats on the table, the clatter of cutlery being selected from the drawer and the clink as each piece was positioned on the table. The scrape of the black frying pan being hauled from it's place under the sink.

Jayne's heartbeat quickened. Up until this moment she had not considered how Mum would react. Jayne might be ready to forgive, but was Mum ready to forgive her? There was only one way to find out. She opened the door.

Mum looked up, surprised.

'Can you not sleep?' she asked as she set the frying pan on top of the cooker and laid a fish slice on the counter beside it.

'No,' said Jayne.

'Never mind,' said Mum. 'I'll make you a nice cup of tea.'

She pressed down the on button on the automatic kettle, already filled for the next day.

Jayne sat at the table and watched Mum take eggs and butter out of the fridge for the morning and two mugs out of the cupboard. The kettle boiled and she made the tea in a china pot, setting it down on the table to brew.

'I suppose you're upset about Nana,' said Mum kindly.

'Yes. Well, no, not really,' said Jayne. 'I mean I'm sad she's gone and everything, but that's not what's bothering me.'

Mum poured the tea, set a mug in front of Jayne and sat down. 'There's something I want to say to you,' began Jayne, a little shakily, but she gained confidence as she went on. 'Something I should have said before now. I'm sorry it's taken me so long.'

Mum sat motionless, her face, from years of practice, unreadable. She did not touch her tea.

'When you told me who my real father was,' said Jayne, pausing momentarily in response to her mother's involuntary wince, 'and I reacted the way I did, well, I was angry. And I've been trying to punish you ever since by being aloof and cold towards you. And I'm sorry. Please forgive me.'

Tears rolled down Jayne's cheeks and she bent her head.

'Oh, Jayne. Jayne. It's me who should be saying sorry. I never should have told you, not the way I did. There was no need for you to know, for me to spoil things for you. Not when you adored your Dad so much. I panicked, you see, when you said you were seeing Frank Meehan's son. I should have kept my mouth shut. It wasn't fair of me. And it broke my heart to see the way I'd hurt you.'

Jayne looked up through the tears and sniffed.

'But I'm glad you told me. Really I am, Mum. I should have been more . . . more understanding. I didn't realise you see, until today that is, what you did for me and Eddie.'

Mum's concerned expression changed to one of puzzlement, her brows knitted together.

'You see, Mum,' said Jayne earnestly, 'I understand the sacrifice you made for us. You stayed with Dad because of me and Eddie, didn't you?'

Jayne did not wait for an answer but continued on. 'It just dawned on me you see, when I was standing at Nana's grave, how awful it must be to love someone and lose them. I know you loved Frank Meehan or you never would have slept with him. You did love him didn't you?'

Mum's lovely features contorted with pain and she covered her face with her hands. Shocked, Jayne waited for her to speak.

'Oh, yes,' she said at last, from between delicate white fingers, her voice little more than a whisper.

'Tell me about him, Mum,' said Jayne gently.

Mum shook her head, hands still covering her face.

'Please Mum. I'd like to know. He is my father after all. Please.'

Mum dragged her hands downwards, leaving trails of dark brown mascara on her cheeks. Her eyes shone bright with tears and memories.

'I loved him more than you can know, Jayne. We went out together for years, long before I met your Dad. We were to get married and everything . . .'

Her voice wavered and she blinked to hold back tears before going on.

'Your Granny and Grandad Simpson weren't happy about it, but that wouldn't have stopped me. I'd have gone against their wishes and married him all the same. But Frank. Ah, that was a different story altogether. He had this strong, overbearing mother you see and he couldn't stand up to her. She made no secret of the fact that she didn't like me because I was a Protestant. I wasn't good enough for her Frank. And do you know she never even met me? Not once in over two years, though I dare say she made it her business to find out all about me. Anyway, that's beside the point. In the end he went and married someone else, a girl called Theresa Walsh. I'll never forget the day I heard that name for the first time. Soon after that I married your father. And that was the end of it, or so I thought, until years later, we met again and well, you know the rest of it.'

'But how did you meet? Where? When?'

'Here, in this house. Frank had a painting and decorating business. Still has. He came to the house to do some work for your Dad just before Christmas. There was him and this other fella. What was his name? I remember, Ciaran something . . .'

Mum paused, reluctant to go on. Jayne was torn between the desire to know the truth, including the intimate details, and the desire to spare Mum any further pain. But she had to know.

'So what happened?' she asked.

Mum cleared her throat, swallowed, and looked at the table as she finished her story.

'They were in the house a week, papering the living room, hall, stairs and landing. I can't even remember what the paper was like now, it's so long ago. On the last day Ciaran had to go early — I can't remember why — and me and Frank were left alone in the house. Your brother Eddie was having his afternoon nap. We started to talk and it turned out that Frank wasn't happily married either. I couldn't believe it. Well one thing led to another and that's where it happened. On the landing. Upstairs.'

Involuntarily Jayne looked upwards. She tried to picture the scene, but couldn't. It seemed incredible that prim middle-aged Mum could have participated in an act of instant sexual gratification.

'So what happened then? Afterwards, I mean?'

Mum shrugged her shoulders despondently.

'Nothing. We knew there was no future for us. He had a couple of kids already and I had Eddie. You have to understand that things were different then, Jayne. It was the sixties and people didn't get divorced and run off together. Not in Ballyfergus anyway. I had no independent means to support myself. And we both had responsibilities.'

'Does he know about me?' asked Jayne.

'No. No-one knows, although I always suspected your Nana had an inkling. But if she did, to her credit, she kept it to herself.'

'I see,' said Jayne.

Her father didn't know she existed. Without hesitation Jayne decided that she would keep it that way. She had no desire to meet Frank Meehan.

'So now you know,' said Mum, glumly. 'What

384

do you think of your mother?'

'Oh, Mum, I'm so sorry. I can't imagine how awful it must have been for you . . . '

Mum interrupted, close to tears.

'Please, Jayne, please don't say any more.'

She stopped and dabbed at the corners of her eyes. She took a hankie from her left hand sleeve and blew her nose.

'I've made my bed and I have to lie in it, as your Nana would have said. Your Dad's a good man, Jayne, and I've no cause for complaint. I never should have married him, but it was my choice. Nobody forced me into it. I am happy with him although it wasn't always that way. Over the years, well, I've learned to love him.'

She leant forward then and grasped Jayne's hand tightly, her voice imbued with passion.

'That's all I ever wanted for you, Jayne. For you to be happy. You and Eddie.'

They sat like that for a little while and then Jayne got up and stood behind Mum. She rested her chin on the blonde curls, thinning now, that smelt of Elnett hairspray. Tears ran silently down her cheeks as she wrapped her arms around Mum and hugged her. Her frame felt small and frail in her arms.

Mum's shoulders shuddered and relaxed, and she sobbed quietly in Jayne's embrace.

* * *

Catherine came round to see Moira shortly after Michael's funeral. She showed her into the front room and made them both a cup of tea. It was early evening and Moira could hear the shouts of children playing in the street outside.

'Sean told me you know about us,' she said when they were both settled on the sofa. 'Are you cross with me for not telling you?' Catherine looked at her and shook her head. 'I would have done,' explained Moira, anxious for Catherine's approval. 'Told you I mean. I was going to, and then Michael got killed and I thought it best to say nothing until the funeral and all was over.'

'It's okay,' said Catherine. 'I really don't mind.'

Moira relaxed.

'There is one thing, though, I wanted to ask you,' said Catherine.

'Yes?'

'I overheard you saying that you were going to do nursing here and not go to college in England. Is it true?'

Moira nodded.

'Do you love Sean?' Catherine asked bluntly and Moira felt her cheeks colour.

'Yes, I do,' she answered. 'He wants to get engaged.'

'Oh, Moira, I'm so pleased for you. For both of you.'

Moira heard the back door slam and her stomach churned. She looked at her watch. It said five-thirty.

'Shit,' she said. 'He's back already.'

She shot a worried look at the door and they listened in silence to footsteps in the hall. Daddy appeared in the doorway and Moira shivered involuntarily.

'Hello, darlin',' he said to Catherine, leering, and Moira could see her friend cringe.

'Hello, Mr Campbell,' said Catherine, respectfully.

He sat down in a chair and began to read the paper.

'Well, I'll be off then,' said Catherine obviously eager to be gone.

She got up and Moira accompanied her to the door.

'When does the course start?' said Catherine.

'In a week or so. The same time you go off to uni.'

'It'll be strange us all going our separate ways, won't it?' said Catherine. 'Kind of sad really.'

'I never thought I'd live to hear you say that.'

'What do you mean?'

'You were the one who couldn't wait to get away from here. You hated the Grammar and everyone in it.'

'Did I say that?'

'More or less.'

'I don't hate anybody. I just wish, well, that things could have been different and I might have enjoyed school more.'

Moira watched Catherine walk down the street, her long hair swinging, and wondered at the changes she'd seen in her over the past few weeks. In spite of Michael's death she seemed calmer, more at peace with herself. She thought of her own life so far and how it had been ruined, ruled by fear. But she had Sean and he loved her. The future would be different.

Inside Daddy was in the hallway, watching her.

'Out of my way,' she said angrily and pushed past him into the kitchen. 'Don't you talk to me like that!' he bellowed and grabbed her arm.

Moira twisted and broke free. A fury took hold of her that transcended the fear. She saw the knife block by the cooker and lunged for it. She pulled out a long carving knife and brandished it. For the first time in her life she fought back.

'Get away from me!' she screamed. 'Get away from me.'

She was hysterical and yet she felt incredibly strong and powerful.

'You bastard. YOU BASTARD!' she yelled. 'I hate you.'

Her father backed away and he looked almost afraid. Mammy appeared in the doorway. Moira was shaking and couldn't stop. The blade of the knife flashed in the evening sun that shone through the small kitchen window.

'And don't you ever, ever lay a finger on me again,' she sobbed, between tears, 'or I swear to God, I'll kill you.'

'Leave the room,' said Mammy sharply and Daddy obeyed.

'It's all right, love. It's all right. He's gone now. Put the knife down.'

Her voice was soothing.

'Here, let me have that,' she said, as she approached with her hand outstretched. 'You don't know what you're doing.'

It was tempting to give in. To be consoled. To keep pretending. But not any more.

'No,' cried Moira. 'Get away from me.'

She thrust the knife in front of her and

Mammy jumped back, surprised.

'What is it?' she asked. 'What now?'

'You knew all along, didn't you? DIDN'T YOU?' she shouted.

'What do you mean?' said Mammy and the horror in her eyes told Moira she understood.

'You knew he did things to me and you never tried to stop him. You never helped me,' she said in between sobs.

Mammy put her hands over her ears.

'You bitch!' screamed Moira. 'Of course, you don't want to hear the truth. Did it make things easier for you? Saved you a few black eyes, did it?'

'You don't understand . . . ' began Mammy.

'Understand? I understand all right. You could have left him. Anytime. But you didn't and you let him use me. How could you? Your own daughter. Get out of my sight.'

When Moira had calmed down she went into the sitting room where her mother was sitting on the sofa. She paused and looked at the snivelling woman in the black leggings and acrylic jumper. Her father had disappeared.

'I'm going away next week to nursing college. I won't be back. I don't want either of you to ever try and contact me. Understand?'

'Moira . . . I did the best I could . . . '

'Don't! Don't you dare try to speak to me. You disgust me.'

Moira put on a coat and went outside. She walked past the kids bouncing a deflated football off the kerbstone and tried to remember what it was like to be that age. But all she could remember was fear.

She saw her father for what he was. A bully. If only her mother had fought back years ago. But it was too late for wishful thinking. She walked to the edge of the housing estate and leaned on a fence and looked out over the shorn field. The sun was an orange ball in the sky and square bales of hay were strewn haphazardly across the field. She wiped the tears from her face and for the first time in her life she was no longer afraid.

'What's the matter? Have you been crying?' asked Sean when he picked her up later.

'It must be a touch of hayfever,' said Moira, sniffing. 'They've just cut the hay in the field next to the estate.'

They drove to the beach at Ballygally, parked and, as night fell, looked out over the Irish Sea. She nuzzled up to him and he put his arm around her.

'I'll always look after you, Moira. You know that?'

'Will you protect me? And keep me safe from harm?'

'Always.'

They sat like that in silence and then Sean spoke.

'I've decided what I'm going to do,' he said.

'About what?'

'The business. My Da hasn't been himself since Michael died. It's time we got back to work, but Da can't face it.'

'What can you do about it?'

'I've been down to the Job Centre to see about taking on a couple of kids for work experience.

That'll tide us over until Da's back on his feet. If any of the lads are any good, I'm sure I could find them a full-time job. It's time we started planning long-term anyway for Da's not far off retirement age. And I've been to see the bank manager about a loan to start the shop. You remember Tweedie's, that old-fashioned shop that used to sell material?'

'Yes, it's been closed for years.'

'Well, it's up for lease at a very reasonable rate and I've had a look inside. It's been lying empty for ten, maybe fifteen years, but all it needs is a lick of paint. It's got a great wooden floor and there's shelving that was used for rolls of material. It'll be perfect for displaying wallpaper.'

'I can't believe you've done all this, Sean. You're fantastic.'

Sean blushed.

'It'll not be much to start with, Moira. The bank manager says to take things slow and see how it goes. If we get our fingers burnt we won't have invested too much in it. And if it takes off, well that'll be our future, kid.

'I think it'll help Ma and Da as well,' he added. 'It'll give them something to focus on instead of . . . well, you know. I might even persuade Ma to do a few stints in the shop. It'll do her good to get out and meet people.'

'I know it'll be a success. I just know it,' said Moira and she leaned over and kissed him on the lips.

21

Frank leaned against the headstone wet with rain and remembered Michael as a little boy with his cheeky grin and his tinkling laugh. It was funny that. How he always saw him as a child and not the young man he'd been when he died. Almost as though he never grew up.

The grave was still fresh, and the few plants he'd put in hadn't yet taken root. He leaned down and wiped some soil off the base of the marble headstone with a tissue.

Where had he gone wrong? Maybe things would have been different if they'd gone to England like so many other people did when the troubles started. Michael might still be alive.

And how different life would have been if he'd married Helen. Michael would never even have been born. Helen. He still loved that name. He looked up and started. There she was, holding a bunch of pink dahlias in her hand, the hood of her fawn jacket pulled up in defence against rain.

'What are you doing here?' he asked.

She indicated over her shoulder.

'My mother-in-law's buried over there. She died last week. I came to put these on her grave.'

She nodded at the gravestone and asked, 'Do you mind?'

He shook his head and she came closer, hunched down and read the inscription on the headstone.

'That's lovely,' she said and then she gently placed the bunch of flowers on the grave. When she looked up at him her eyes were full of pity.

'I'm sorry, Frank. I'm sorry that you lost your son and I'm sorry for the part my son played in it.'

He nodded.

'Have you heard from him and Geraldine?' he asked, hopefully, after a pause.

She stood up.

'Only a message through friends. They've a place to stay and they're all right. They'll let us know where they are in their own time. When some of these wounds have healed,' she added and looked at the grave.

'I keep thinking it's all my fault,' he said. 'I should have done something different. How did a son of mine get mixed up with the IRA, Helen? And Geraldine, getting herself pregnant. What was she thinking of?'

'You did the best you could, Frank, we all did. If this country wasn't so riddled with hatred then things might have been different. For all of us.'

He scanned her face seeking out the girl he'd known. She was carefully made up and wore pale pink lipstick. He noticed fine lines at the corners of her eyes and the first hint of slackness round the jaw. She was still a handsome woman, but older, like he was. And she seemed at peace with herself as though her age fitted her like a comfortable pair of slippers.

'I didn't do right by you though, Helen, did I? All those years ago.'

'It doesn't matter now, Frank. It really doesn't.

We've both got to make the best of the lives we have now. Maybe it was for the best anyway. Who knows how things might have turned out between you and I. It might have been a complete disaster,' she said and smiled wryly.

There was no bitterness in her voice, only a tinge of regret.

'Does that mean you forgive me?'

'I forgave you a long time ago, Frank,' she said softly and then after a pause, 'where's Theresa?'

'At home. She won't visit the grave. Yet.'

'How is she?'

Frank sighed. Theresa was a changed woman. The strength and decisiveness on which he'd come to rely was gone. She'd become vulnerable and almost frail. And Frank felt immensely protective of her. For the first time in their marriage he felt she really relied on him. And in spite of the horrific circumstances it felt good to be needed.

'She's bad, Helen. Very bad. It's going to take her a long time to come to terms with this,' he said, glancing at the grave.

Helen placed a hand lightly on his shoulder. The gesture brought tears to his eyes. He longed to be in her arms, taking comfort, but knew it would never be again.

'You seem very happy,' said Frank. 'Very . . . at peace.'

'I am, Frank.'

He nodded, glad that she had found happiness without him.

They stood silently side by side for some time.

The rain had stopped and the still air smelt of wet earth.

Frank thought of Theresa at home alone and said, 'I'd better be going. I don't like to leave Theresa on her own too much.'

'Yes, go home to her Frank. She needs you. Now more than ever.'

He looked up gratefully into those beautiful eyes. And Helen smiled.

★   ★   ★

'I'll not see you off at the boat tomorrow,' said Moira. 'That's why I've come round tonight.'

They sat facing each other on top of the beds in Catherine's bedroom. Moira was on Geraldine's old bed, now covered with a dust sheet. A suitcase full of clothes lay open on the floor waiting for last minute items to be packed in the morning.

'When are you off to nursing college then?' Catherine asked.

'The day after next. Sean's going to take some time off and take me up to Belfast.'

'Your Mum and Dad aren't taking you then?'

Moira snorted and shook her head vigorously.

'I don't want anything off that bastard. I . . . ' she said and then stared intensely at Catherine for some seconds.

'What?' said Catherine and there was a long pause.

'If I tell you something, promise you'll never tell anyone. Especially Sean.'

'I promise,' said Catherine lightly and waited.

395

'I mean really promise. No-one. Not ever.'

'Yes, yes, I promise,' said Catherine, her curiosity aroused. 'What is it?'

When Moira spoke her bottom lip quivered and her voice was unsteady.

'My father . . . All those times . . . Do you remember I told you he hit me?'

'Yes,' said Catherine, uneasily. Suddenly she didn't want this confidence forced on her.

But it was too late.

'He did other things too,' said Moira flatly and stared at her hands which she held clasped tightly in front of her.

'Like what?' said Catherine slowly, but she knew already. Moira wanted to tell her and she must listen, confirming the suspicions that Catherine had suppressed for so long.

'You know. Sexual things. Things he shouldn't have done.'

Catherine looked away and swallowed. Be strong for Moira's sake she told herself.

'I'm sorry,' she said. 'I really am.'

'I know you are,' said Moira.

'Why didn't you tell me, Moira? All those years. I could have done something to help.'

'But you did help, Catherine. You were there for me. Sometimes I don't know what I'd have done without you.'

Not trusting herself to speak Catherine smiled weakly. Moira was so brave. Catherine felt anger welling up inside and checked it.

'I don't think I could have survived what you have,' she said hoarsely. 'He could still be prosecuted, you know.'

'No, I don't want that. It's too late now.'

'No it's not,' said Catherine evenly. 'What about those priests accused of abusing school-boys years ago? They're taking them to court over it now.'

'I just want to forget about it,' said Moira and then, matter-of-factly, 'anyway, it's dealt with now.'

'What do you mean it's dealt with?'

'I threatened him with a knife and told him that if he ever touched me again I'd kill him.'

'Oh my God,' said Catherine.

Moira went on talking as though she hadn't spoken.

'And it worked. He's avoided me ever since. I told the two of them that I was going away to do nursing and didn't want to have anything to do with them again.'

'Your Mum as well? But why?'

'She knew all along what was going on . . . '

'No!' said Catherine.

' . . . and did nothing to stop it.'

It was inconceivable that Moira's Mammy knew and allowed it to go on.

'But how can you be sure? Surely no mother . . . ' said Catherine.

'I am sure. She more or less admitted it.'

Catherine put her face in her hands and shook her head.

'Oh, God, that's awful. You poor thing.'

'I'm all right, Catherine. Really. It's over,' she said finally.

Catherine wriggled to the edge of the bed and planted her feet on the floor.

'But why did you decide to tell me, Moira? Now, I mean, after all this time.'

'Now that it's over I felt you should know. I couldn't tell you before. You want everything to be perfect, don't you?' said Moira, close to tears. 'And you think that if you pretend it's not happening then it's not real.'

She sighed and looked down at the bedspread.

'And will you tell Sean?' asked Catherine gently.

'No!' said Moira looking up sharply. 'And neither will you. You promised me. I've only told you.'

'Okay. A promise is a promise.'

At the front door, they embraced and said good-bye.

'I'll miss you, Moira.'

'I'll miss you too.'

'I hope you and Sean work out.'

'I know we will,' said Moira confidently and she smiled, 'Now you will keep in touch won't you? And come back and see me?'

'Of course! And you have to come over and see me in Edinburgh.'

Catherine watched her disappear into the balmy night and felt a lump in her throat. Then she went inside and sat on the sofa beside Daddy. They watched the TV in silence while Catherine thought of Moira. She tried to imagine what it must have been like for her. She looked sideways at Daddy and tried to visualise . . . But the idea was so horrific she couldn't entertain it for a second. She shivered involuntarily.

'That you all organised then, love?'

'Yes, Daddy.'

'You know your Mammy and me, we'll miss you.'

'I know,' said Catherine and she looked at him. 'I thought I would be dying to get away. Leaving this place, Ballyfergus I mean, was all I ever dreamed of as a child. But now that the time's here I don't feel as though I want to go. I mean, part of me does and part of me doesn't.'

'It's only natural,' said Daddy.

He looked at her for a moment and rubbed his chin. 'Your Mammy used to think you'd get yourself into trouble, Catherine, because you were such an envious little girl. But it turned out you weren't the one we should have been worrying about . . . '

His voice faded and Catherine looked at the floor.

'Anyway,' he continued more upbeat, 'it's a great opportunity for you and, after all that's happened, it might be a good idea for you to get away for a while.'

'I worry about you and Mammy though,' said Catherine. 'Will you be all right?'

He sighed heavily.

'It's just going to take time, Catherine, especially for your mother. And prayer. A lot of prayer. And we have Sean about the place so it's not as though we're on our own.'

'Did he tell you about his plans for the business?'

'Yes, he did,' said Daddy.

'What do you think?'

399

'We'll see,' he replied, absentmindedly, 'we'll see. It might do your mother some good to get involved in the shop. When she's ready.'

And Catherine felt at peace. For though she still grieved for Michael she knew she didn't have to worry about those she was leaving behind. Mammy, Daddy, Sean or Moira. It would take time, but they would survive.

* * *

From the ticket queue in the terminal building Jayne watched Catherine say good-bye to her parents and brother, Sean. She cowered behind the woman in front anxious to remain unnoticed. But she needn't have worried; they never looked in her direction.

'Can I have a ticket for the two o'clock sailing please?' she said to the man in the ticket office.

'Do you want a return, love?'

'No, just one way.'

She stared at Frank Meehan, searching for a family resemblance, but could find none. He was dark and swarthy, so different from herself. She looked for the handsome youth that had won her mother's heart, but could see only a worn-out middle-aged man in an anorak.

He pulled his daughter to him and hugged her, almost fiercely, while Mrs Meehan stood by dabbing at her face with a tissue. Jayne wondered what it would have been like to have him as a father. And then she realised that her interest stemmed from idle curiosity rather than any real desire to find out.

400

'Just yourself travelling?'

'That's right.'

She paid for the ticket and rejoined Mum and Dad who waited in seats by her luggage piled on the floor. Daddy had on a suit, shirt and tie and Mum wore a smart navy suit. They looked affluent in comparison to the Meehans.

'We didn't want to move in case we lost these seats,' explained Dad. Jayne nodded. The summer season hadn't quite come to an end and the terminal building was busy with holidaymakers as well as the normal freight traffic. They sat for a while mesmerised by the noise and activity. Then Jayne saw David walking purposefully towards them.

'I don't believe it,' she said, horrified.

'What is it, love?' said Mum.

'It's David,' she replied. 'What on earth's he doing here?'

'Hello, Mrs Alexander. Mr Alexander,' said David politely. 'Could I have a word, Jayne?'

Jayne looked at Mum who nodded encouragingly.

'Well, okay then,' said Jayne hesitantly. 'But it'll have to be quick for the boat's leaving soon.'

She followed him outside and they stood in the brisk sea breeze. He held a set of car keys in his hand which he tossed nervously from one palm to the other. Jayne folded her arms.

There was an awkward pause and Jayne felt obliged to break the silence.

'Did you borrow your Dad's car to come down?' she asked.

'Yes,' he replied. 'Look, Jayne, I know we

haven't a lot of time. I wanted to see you before you went. To ask you one last time . . . '

Jayne shifted from one foot to the other.

'David, I've told you already. I don't . . . '

'Let me finish, please,' he said, and waited until he had her attention before he went on. 'I really want to get back with you.'

'Well, I don't. I've told you already, David.'

'You don't mean that.'

His arrogance irritated her and she spoke more harshly than she perhaps intended. But she meant every word.

'All I know is I don't ever want to see you again. I've decided I deserve much better than you. Someone who'll be faithful for a start.'

Jayne heard an announcement from inside asking all foot passengers to board.

'I'd better go,' she said and David turned and walked away without saying another word.

She watched him go and felt proud of herself. And happy.

Inside she found Mum and Dad; there was no sign of the Meehans.

'That's me then,' said Jayne.

'Come here,' said Dad and he enveloped her in his arms.

'I'm going to miss you, love,' he said, his voice breaking up. 'You're just the bestest daughter in all the world. I love you.'

'I love you too, Dad,' said Jayne.

She nuzzled into his chest, so safe and warm. He was her Dad in the only sense that mattered; he loved her as his own. He had earned the right to be her Dad.

'I'm very lucky to have you as my Dad,' she said leaning back and he smiled proudly down at her.

When he released her, Jayne turned to Mum. She threw her arms around her and hugged her tight.

'You will be careful now Jayne, won't you? Let us know if you need anything. And don't ever be stuck. We're always here for you. We love you.'

'I know, Mum,' said Jayne. 'I love you too.'

'And we'll let you know when we hear anything from Eddie,' said Mum, reading Jayne's thoughts.

Jayne looked at Dad warily.

'I thought you weren't going to speak to him ever again?' she said.

Dad looked at her sadly. 'If I don't come to . . . to terms with it, I'll lose a son. That's what your mother says.'

'It'll take your Dad some time to get used to the idea. There's no rush, sure there's not, John?'

Mum looked at Dad and smiled encouragingly.

They said their final good-byes and Jayne followed her fellow passengers out of the terminal building, glancing back just once. She saw her parents holding hands and they waved and smiled.

★ ★ ★

Weighted down by two large holdalls Jayne wandered round the boat looking for a seat. She eschewed free seats in the bar, the restaurant and

403

the cinema and then she realised she was looking for Catherine. She found her in a row of seats by the tall windows that afforded a clear view of the dockside. What impulse had brought Jayne to seek her out? She didn't know, only a vague sense that they should be friends. They were sisters after all.

'Is this seat free?' someone asked and Catherine looked up from her window seat.

She was surprised to see Jayne.

'Yes . . . yes, it's free,' she said hesitantly, glancing at the empty seat beside her.

Jayne stowed one hold-all under the seat, the other under the seat in front, took off her jacket and sat down beside Catherine. The steel hulk of the boat shuddered and creaked as the engines revved and Catherine watched the dockers untie the great ropes that held the boat. The ferry peeled itself away from the quay until it was several hundred yards out, turned and the view of dry land was gone. Flat, blue sea stretched out before Catherine as far as she could see. Turning her attention to the inside of the ferry, Catherine noticed there were plenty of free seats available. Why had Jayne chosen to sit beside her?

'Are you going to Edinburgh?' asked Jayne, pleasantly.

'Yes, that's right. To do teaching.'

'Somebody told me you were going to do Business Administration.'

'I changed my mind,' said Catherine coolly, not wanting to explain herself to Jayne.

She was silent for some moments and then decided it would do no harm to be civil.

'What about you?' she said, and turned round to look properly at Jayne for the first time. 'Where are you going?'

'Manchester. To do medicine.'

'That figures,' said Catherine blandly.

'What do you mean?'

'It's what your parents would want you to do. Safe, secure, good prospects.'

'I'm doing it because I want to help people,' said Jayne, annoyed. 'I don't care what my parents think.'

'Don't you?' said Catherine and watched her keenly for a response.

'No,' said Jayne firmly and then, after a pause. 'You know, we're not so different, you and I.'

'In what way?' asked Catherine, intrigued.

'We're both running away.'

The truth of it made Catherine look away. She stared out the window for a while thinking of Michael and Geraldine and all the things she hated about Ballyfergus. Eventually she turned her gaze on Jayne.

'What are you running away from?' she asked softly.

'The small-mindedness of it all. And you?'

'The same, I suppose. And because of Michael of course. It's all I ever wanted, you know.'

'What?'

'To get out of Northern Ireland.'

'So this is your dream come true.'

'Hardly,' said Catherine, softly. 'With a brother dead and a sister eloped.'

'I know,' said Jayne. 'I'm sorry about Michael.'

'Anyway,' said Catherine, 'I'm not going for

good. I'm thinking about coming back here to teach in an integrated school.'

'You are? That's fantastic!'

'You think so?' said Catherine, cautiously.

'Yes, I do. It's what this country needs.'

Catherine looked at those honest blue eyes and they reminded her of Eddie. She'd forgiven him; now it was time to forgive Jayne for simply being who she was.

'There's something I want to tell you that . . . that I'm not particularly proud of,' said Catherine. She swallowed and forced herself to go on. 'I hated you from the very day we first met.'

Jayne winced, but Catherine smiled reassuringly and went on.

'I used to think that you had everything; money, clothes, toys and you lived in a big house on the hill. I think I made you a focus for my resentment because you appeared to have everything I wanted. Or I thought I wanted — like David.'

'So that's why you tried to steal him,' said Jayne sharply.

Catherine looked at her in surprise.

'Oh, you've got the wrong end of the stick there, Jayne. I never ran after him. It was him who chased me and I only went out with him because he said he was finished with you.'

'Well, whatever,' said Jayne. 'It doesn't matter now anyway. I don't want to have anything to do with him.'

'Me neither.'

'How do you feel about me now then?' asked

Jayne, returning to the original topic.

'Those things don't matter to me any more. All the time I had Michael and Geraldine I hankered after something else. And now they're gone.'

'Geraldine's not gone. Not forever,' said Jayne, earnestly.

'No, but it'll be a long time before I see her and things will never be the same again.'

'No, I suppose not. It'll be the same with me and Eddie,' said Jayne, wistfully.

They were silent and stared companionably out the window together, side by side. At length Jayne spoke again.

'I used to envy you,' she said quietly.

'Me?' asked Catherine, incredulous. 'But why?'

It couldn't be possible that the golden girl who'd plagued Catherine's happiness for so long was actually jealous of her!

'You're so clever and confident. At least that's how you always appeared to me. I used to find schoolwork so hard and you sailed through it.'

'I just worked hard, that's all.'

'No, Catherine, it was more than that. You were always the one that knew the answers in class and nobody gets three A's just by working hard. No, you're a lot smarter than me.'

'There's more important things in life than being clever,' said Catherine.

'I know, but I worried about failing all the time. And letting my parents down. I suppose I still do.'

Catherine looked at Jayne and saw her for the

very first time in a different light. Her insecurity and honesty made her human. And Catherine was humbled.

'Catherine, you don't hate me anymore do you?'

'No,' said Catherine, 'I don't.'

'Do you think, then, that you and I could be friends?'

Catherine looked out the window, but saw nothing for the tears in her eyes. All her life she'd wanted nothing more than to be accepted and now, her greatest enemy wanted to be her friend. She was ashamed of herself for disliking Jayne. A perfectly nice person. She regretted what could have been. Happier schooldays for one thing, if only she hadn't been so sensitive. If only the society they'd been brought up in had been normal. That's what made her so angry and bitter and sad about it all.

'Yes,' she said, gently, 'I'd like that. We're practically family anyway.'

'What do you mean?' said Jayne, a little nervously, Catherine thought.

'Eddie and Geraldine. We'll both share the same niece or nephew.'

'Oh, I see!' said Jayne, sounding relieved.

They talked for a little while and then Catherine excused herself.

'I'd like to go up on deck for a bit of fresh air,' she said and squeezed through the narrow space between the rows of seats.

'You know, I'm glad we're going to be friends,' said Jayne and then she added something, more to herself then to Catherine.

'You can be the sister I never had.'

Outside, Catherine made her way to an observation deck at the stern of the ship. The sun was bright and it was a mild day. There were few people on the deck. Catherine walked to the railing and lent over. Seagulls followed the ferry, swooping and diving in the frothy wake.

Ireland was in the distance now. Catherine watched the green fields and white dots of seaside towns merge into one. Soon the Glens of Antrim were indistinguishable. The landmass became dark green and then greeny-black, softened by mist. And then the island disappeared altogether.

Catherine raised her head to the sky and felt the fresh wind blow through her long hair. It felt good to be alive.

We do hope that you have enjoyed reading this large print book.

Did you know that all of our titles are available for purchase?

We publish a wide range of high quality large print books including:
Romances, Mysteries, Classics
General Fiction
Non Fiction and Westerns

Special interest titles available in large print are:
The Little Oxford Dictionary
Music Book
Song Book
Hymn Book
Service Book

Also available from us courtesy of Oxford University Press:
Young Readers' Dictionary
(large print edition)
Young Readers' Thesaurus
(large print edition)

For further information or a free brochure, please contact us at:
Ulverscroft Large Print Books Ltd.,
The Green, Bradgate Road, Anstey,
Leicester, LE7 7FU, England.
Tel: (00 44) 0116 236 4325
Fax: (00 44) 0116 234 0205

Other titles published by
The House of Ulverscroft:

PROMISES TO KEEP

Alexandra Raife

Ian and Miranda were childhood friends in Glen Maraich, and student sweethearts who married while still at Edinburgh University. But those carefree days come to an end when Miranda becomes pregnant. Alexy is a demanding baby and the marriage collapses under the strain of sleepless nights and domestic responsibilities. Left to bring up her daughter alone, Miranda painstakingly establishes a viable life for them both, but is forced to uproot them when she receives an imperious summons from her father-in-law. She returns to the glen, and to Ian's neglected family home. With the new resolution she has learned, Miranda gradually brings warmth to the house — and thaws the hearts of its occupants.

THE DANCING DAYS

Maggie Craig

The depression is beginning to bite in 1930s Glasgow, but Jean Logan is determined to stay positive and decides to dance her family's troubles away by becoming a paid dancing partner at one of the city's many palais de danse. When she is taken on at the new and sophisticated Luxor, it seems as if all her dreams have come true. Soon, though, her desire to support her loved ones draws her into a sinister world that lurks behind the club's glamorous facade. Trapped, degraded and forced into having an abortion, she reaches rock bottom. It takes all Jean's reserves of physical and moral courage to escape and build a new life for herself. But, fifteen years later, her past returns to haunt her . . .

JOSEPHINE AND HARRIET

Betty Burton

Josephine turns her back on the conventional role for respectable young women in Victorian England. She has an indomitable spirit, but her chosen path is far from easy, as female journalists are practically unheard of — let alone ones who specialise in crime reports. Harriet is content to drift from one opportunity to another, from man to man, living by her singing, resorting to occasional prostitution when times get tough. It's an uncertain life, cut short by tragedy. Josephine is fascinated by the case. If circumstances had been different, could this have been her? The two women are close in age, their families not so very different. What made one life turn out this way?

FAST FLOWS THE STREAM

Connie Monk

When war breaks out in 1939, Sally Kennedy and Tessa Kilbride have already enjoyed several years of close friendship. Although superficially very different — Tessa is married to glamorous film star Sebastian while Sally's husband Nick is his accountant — they feel as close as sisters. Warm-hearted Tessa is content to be a home maker, but Sally yearns for more. With war comes change — by 1940 both Nick and Sebastian have volunteered for the armed forces and Sally has landed a job translating foreign radio broadcasts. None of them imagines how anything other than war could shape their destiny, but nothing prepares them for the unexpected challenges and heartache peacetime will also bring . . .

SECOND CHANCE OF SUNSHINE

Pamela Evans

1950s: No one would blame Molly Hawkins if she envied her best friend Angie Beckett. Blessed with financial security and a loving husband, Angie has everything that Molly lacks. Brian Hawkins is too idle to seek regular employment, and there's never enough money to provide for Molly's six-year-old daughter, Rosa. What's more, Molly is forbidden to go out to work. But when Angie's father dies suddenly and leaves Molly a share in the Beckett pottery, it's on the condition that she takes a job there. Seizing the chance to bring in much-needed income, Molly gains strength from her new-found independence — a strength she will need to take her through the tragedy that lies ahead . . .

A RARE RUBY

Dee Williams

It's 1919, and for fourteen-year-old Ruby Jenkins and her family, life isn't easy. Ever since Ruby's father returned from the war, shell-shocked and incapable of working, Ruby and her mother Mary have had to sacrifice all comforts. Amidst the bleak poverty of their Rotherhithe neighbourhood, Mary earns money doing washing. Ruby spends her days collecting and delivering, scrubbing and ironing. When she gets a paid job at Stone's Laundry, a whole new world opens up to her, and she starts dreaming of one day having a husband and children of her own. Then, sudden tragedy strikes at the heart of the Jenkins family, leaving Ruby distraught and desperate . . .